Simon Raven was born in London in 1927. He was educated at Charterhouse and King's College Cambridge where he read Classics. After university, he joined the army as a regular officer in the King's Shropshire Light Infantry and saw service in Germany and Kenya, where he commanded a Rifle Company. In 1957, he resigned his commission and took up book reviewing. His first novel, *The Feathers of Death*, was published in 1959. Since then he has written many reviews, general essays, plays (which have been performed both on radio and television), plus a host of successful novels including the highly acclaimed *Alms for Oblivion* series.

Also by Simon Raven

Novels
*The Feathers of Death*
*Brother Cain*
*Doctors Wear Scarlet*

'Alms for Oblivion' Sequence
*The Rich Pay Late*
*Friends in Low Places*
*The Sabre Squadron*
*Fielding Gray*
*The Judas Boy*
*Places Where They Sing*
*Sound the Retreat*
*Come Like Shadows*
*Bring Forth the Body*
*The Survivors*

Belles-Lettres
*The English Gentleman*
*Boys Will Be Boys*
*The Fortunes of Fingel*

Plays
*Royal Foundation and other Plays*

*Simon Raven*

# The Roses of Picardie

*A Romance*

A PANTHER BOOK

**GRANADA**
London Toronto Sydney New York

Published by Granada Publishing Limited in 1981

ISBN 0 586 05126 0

First Published in Great Britain by
Blond & Briggs Ltd 1980
Copyright © Simon Raven 1980

Granada Publishing Limited
Frogmore, St Albans, Herts AL2 2NF
and
3 Upper James Street, London W1R 4BP
866 United Nations Plaza, New York, NY 10017, USA
117 York Street, Sydney, NSW 2000, Australia
100 Skyway Avenue, Rexdale, Ontario, M9W 3A6, Canada
PO Box 84165, Greenside, 2034 Johannesburg, South Africa
61 Beach Road, Auckland, New Zealand

Set, printed and bound in Great Britain by
Cox and Wyman Limited, Reading
Set in Linotype Pilgrim

Granada  ®
Granada Publishing  ®

Oh, no man knows
Through what wild centuries
Roves back the rose.
                    Walter de la Mare:

                                        *All That's Past*

# I
# Temporal Princes

Mitte sectari, rosa quo locorum
sera moretur

*Horace:* Odes; *I 38*

'*Le cheval pour m'sieur,*' said the croupier at the bottom of the table, assembling a pile of seventeen *jetons* of the lowest denomination (five francs) which was current in the Casino at Aix-en-Provence.

The man towards whom the croupier now pushed the pile with his rake was shabby, middle-aged, pustular and furtive. And yet he was not wholly wanting either in style or in confidence. He took a *jeton* from the top of the pile and tossed it back to the croupier with the air of one who knew the form – who knew, that is to say, that by tipping on a mere 17 to 1 win (when it was the custom to tip only after a win *en plein*) he was doing something rather unusual and was thereby staking a claim to the croupier's future service and regard. Both his manner and his action implied that he expected to become a person of consequence at the table.

The croupier, apparently unimpressed by his seedy client's generosity, called his thanks with perfunctory politeness, tilted his head backwards, audibly hissed the word *fâcheur* and turned away to place a bet for another and more appetizing player. At this the *fâcheur,* who had shown, only a moment before, a fair degree of dignity and calm in his fashion of bestowing a tip, was seized by panic. His hand twitched and scrabbled along the croupier's arm; as soon as it had won the man's attention, it soared upward and then stabbed down repeatedly with its forefinger at the *roulard* of five-franc counters, sixteen in number after the tip, which sat on the green cloth where the croupier's rake had left them.

'*Le premier,*' mouthed the *fâcheur* violently: 'number one; the lot.'

'*Premier,*' repeated the croupier with no enthusiasm. He counted out the sixteen five-franc pieces. '*Quatre-vingt* francs,' he said, and hurled them through the air in a cluster to his colleague at the top end of the table. 'Quatre-vingt francs,' intoned the colleague, coaxing the *jetons* into a *roulard* again and slotting the *roulard* into a runnel. 'Premier,' prompted the croupier at the far end. 'Premier,' confirmed his colleague by the wheel, making up the sum of eighty francs with three pieces, worth respectively fifty francs, twenty and ten, and slapping these down in the square marked '1' with an air of consigning them to Beelzebub. 'C'est fait.'

This performance had a soothing effect on the *fâcheur*, who was now smiling and rolling an unspeakable cigarette with stubby yellow fingers. He no longer concerned himself with what was passing before him; he merely sat and smoked his filthy cigarette and gazed at the clouds of smoke which rolled from his mouth over the table. He ignored alike the activities of the other players (who were now piling on their final bets for the next coup), the exhortations of the croupiers, the quickened wheel and the white ball . . . which circled the upper rim of the casing, hesitated, hovered, and then idly descended towards the revolving disk of numbers, hovered again, and sidled into a slot with a light clunk.

'Premier,' called the croupier at the top end of the table: 'rouge, impair, manque.'

The head of his rake rapped on the *fâcheur*'s eighty-franc stake, lifted slightly, then rapped again in benison.

'Plein,' the croupier announced, *urbi et orbi*.

The *fâcheur* came out of his daze and nodded complacently, accepting his good fortune as his right. This time, when his winnings were pushed to him, he did not tip, though he had won a reckonable sum, nor did he make fresh bets, with or without panic, with or without the croupiers' assistance. He simply rose from his chair, slipped the plaques he had received into the side pockets of his sagging and frowsy tweed jacket, nodded curtly at, rather than to, the croupier nearest him, and walked away towards a large alcove at the far end of the room.

'Banco,' he called as he approached the alcove.

'Banco is two thousand francs,' said the *chef* at the *Table de Chemin-de-Fer*. 'M'sieur can show that amount?'

The *fâcheur* showed some of his plaques.

'Very well. Banco from the floor.'

The holder of the bank, a stout woman with fierce orange hair and thick orange lips, examined the *fâcheur* with a distaste which changed quickly into visible foreboding, made as if to pass the shoe, stiffened and shrugged, then primly dealt cards from the shoe, two for herself, two for her opponent. A croupier passed his pair to the *fâcheur* on a plywood spade. The *fâcheur* looked at his cards and laughed and went on laughing.

'M'sieur, will you draw or stand?'

'I'll draw. But she may as well pay me now. She can't win.'

'Madame would prefer, I think, to find that out in the normal manner. Madame?'

The orange lady turned over her cards. A nine and an eight; a count of seven; she must stand on that.

'And now a card for m'sieur.'

The orange lady snapped a card from the shoe and placed it face upward on the table: the nine of hearts. The *fâcheur* went on laughing.

'I told you she couldn't win.'

He showed the two cards which he already held: the Queen and Knave of diamonds, which together equalled baccarat but with the third card made a winning nine.

'The twins,' said the *fâcheur*, as a croupier sorted the counters and plaques on the table: 'the twins in diamonds. As soon as they showed me that they were here, I knew I couldn't lose.'

The croupier who was sorting the lost stakes placed them to one side, reached into a bureau behind him, and passed a 2000-franc plaque (white, stripped with cerise and purple) up to the *chef*. The *chef* beckoned to the *fâcheur* and handed him the plaque as he drew near.

'Move on,' whispered the *chef*. 'I won't have that talk here.' He made a quick gesture with the first and fourth fingers of his right hand, turning them towards the ground.

'I've a perfect right—'

'—I know, I know. Just move on. There's a greasy fat Greek with a bald head running a baccarat bank in the private room. Go and see what you and your twins can do to him.'

'Good advice, and thank you for the tip. They may not stay long, my twins, and a baccarat bank will offer maximum returns for as long as they do. I must be careful not to be too greedy though.'

'Just move along,' said the *chef*.

The *fâcheur* moved along: out of the alcove, back across the floor of the main salon, past a fountain of four baby dolphins, through funereal curtains of purple velvet (on the other side of which a footman attempted to bar his passage but bowed himself off when the *fâcheur* slipped him a fifty-franc disk), and over an ankle-deep carpet to the *Table de Banque*, where the greasy bald Greek presided over eighteen persons who were avid to win his money, of which (according to a prominent notice) he was prepared to risk as much as 20,000 francs per person per coup.

The *fâcheur* had not got 20,000 francs: he had the 2000 francs which he had won at the chemmy table plus the 2800 he had won at the roulette table less the fifty he had given the footman: 4750. But now one came running to him to say that his eighty-franc bet on the *premier*, which he had left there after his first win, had won once more. The *fâcheur* was rapidly becoming a man of note in the Casino and was, after his latest good news, worth 7550 francs, less 550 which he grandly bestowed on the messenger from the roulette table: 7000 francs.

'Stay with me, my friends,' said the *fâcheur* out loud. 'I shall not be greedy. See, I am betting only 5000 of the 7000 you have sent me.'

He staked one plaque of 2000 and three of 1000 against the bald Greek's bank, waved away a chair which three footmen were bringing up for him, and began to roll another ghastly cigarette. As he lit it, an old man, who had a rug over his knees and was attended by a starched and stainless nurse, put up the maximum wager and was passed the cards to play for that half of the table which was patronized by the *fâcheur*. Having turned up a natural nine to win, he had a sudden seizure and was whisked out by the three footmen, chair and all, in ten seconds flat. The nurse paused to pick up and pocket his winnings, winked at the *fâcheur*, with whom she apparently found herself in some affinity, and with bust held high followed what was left of her employer throught the velvet curtains. This meant that the *fâcheur*, who had left his winnings on the cloth along with his original stake and was thus putting up 10,000 for the next coup, was now the highest player at his end of the table. He still declined a chair but accepted the next lot of cards ... and threw down a natural eight, the Queen of diamonds and the eight of hearts, to beat the bank's six. Again he let his stake lie, won 20,000 francs with the Knave and six of diamonds against the bank's three-card baccarat, withdrew 20,000 from his pile on the table leaving the maximum of 20,000 still to run, and won and withdrew 20,000 francs off six coups running with combinations of cards which always contained at least one diamond. At the next coup he displayed a natural eight which consisted of the four of spades and the four of clubs, informed everyone round him that he would now be beaten, and was indeed, by the bank's natural nine.

'The diamonds have left me,' he explained to the other players as his stake was raked away, 'and so now I must leave you.'

## MYSTERY OF THE IMPASSE DIANE

Early this afternoon, a patrol of police engaged in enforcement of the summer regulations of urban hygiene was scandalized to encounter the battered body of a middle-aged man lying concealed among the plastic containers of refuse in the Impasse Diane, a mews just off the Rue Cardinale in Aix-en-Provence.

The man, who had been dead for about twelve hours, carried no official identification, but in the inside pocket of his jacket was a card of admission to the Casino of Aix bearing the name of 'Monsieur du Touquet'. In the same pocket was also the sum, in notes of 500 and 100 francs, of 142,000 francs, no less.

Certain of the authorities and personnel of the Casino, invited to view the corpse, have deposed, despite the disfiguring injuries, that it is beyond question that of a man who won this sum in aggregate, variously at roulette, chemin-de-fer and baccarat, on the evening of 25 August. M. le Directeur and others of the establishment have further deposed that this same man, after refusing to take the cheque advisable in the case of so significant an amount and insisting on being paid his 142,000 francs in cash, left the premises shortly after midnight. Nothing is known of his movements between the time he departed from the Casino and 14.17 hours today, when his body was discovered by the police in the Impasse Diane.

The police at once ask themselves why the money was left on the victim's person. Did the assailant not know of his victim's sensational winnings? But surely so huge a pile of notes, even in an inner pocket, could not have escaped the murderer's notice. Was the motive then other than theft? But if so, what?

The answer might be more clear if the police had more

clear a notion who 'Monsieur du Touquet' truly is. But so far there has been no proper identification of the corpse, and nothing can be discovered of the dead man's family or normal place of residence.

## THE CASE OF THE DEAD GAMESTER

It is now nearly a year since the body of a man, brutally battered to death by an unknown assailant, was discovered by the police in the Impasse Diane, a few minutes' walk from the Casino in Aix-en-Provence. Mark carefully this locale; and now attend to what later transpired of the cadaver.

—The man, who was so horribly transformed into a pitiful pulp by blows delivered (it is believed) with a bar of iron, had been none other than Clovis di Cannaregio Baudouin du Bourg de Maubeuge, Vicomte du Touquet, the 53-year-old son and heir apparent of Clovis d'Outremer Baudouin du Bourg de Maubeuge, Comte de la Tour d'Abbéville. (This latter, it so happened, died of sclerotic senescence, in the Infirmary of the Magdalene at Amiens, only a few hours after his son had been butchered in Aix.)

—The body of the Vicomte was identified as such by a friend and distant cousin, an Englishman called Mr Balbo Blakeney, who read of the matter while on holiday in France and came forward to offer his assistance to the police. Although he had met the Vicomte only at irregular intervals during his life and not at all for many years previously, Mr Blakeney was able to make a decisive identification by his description of a certain birth-mark (a mauve stain in the shape of an elongated rhomboid some six inches above the Vicomte's left knee), a description which he rendered with great precision *before* being allowed to inspect the body.

—With the deaths of the Vicomte and his father, there is now extinguished one of the most ancient, noble and, in its heyday, illustrious and powerful families of Northern France, renowned for its territorial aggressions, its illicit venery and its love of high play (a taste, as we shall see, highly relevant to our present discourse). Its history, stretching back to the 11th century, is superb, outrageous and multicoloured, the dominant colour, however, being that of blood. Of this history we shall have something more to say later. Meanwhile, we should note that the fortunes of the family began to decline even so long as 200 years ago, and that for the last 100 before the death of the Vicomte and his father it had been ever more degraded by poverty.

—Although the Vicomte du Touquet was murdered nearly 12 months ago, in the late August of last year, there have since appeared no clues either as to the murderer himself or his motive. Theft is ruled out; for on M. le Vicomte's dead body was found by the police, untouched, the full sum of 142,000 francs which he is known to have won that evening in the Casino. (All of this money was claimed, on news of the Vicomte's death, by his numerous creditors, among whom it is still being apportioned by the courts.)

—There are several points of abundant interest about the Vicomte's visit to the Casino on this, the last evening of his existence. First, there is the astonishing affair of his immense and spectacular win – a win of over 140,000 francs achieved, apparently, from an initial capital of a single five-franc piece. Secondly, we must take note of some very curious speeches which he is reported as having addressed to some among both the croupiers and the other players: speeches which seemed to imply that he believed himself to be under some species of supernatural guidance, which might at any moment be withdrawn. And thirdly, we have to recall the most peculiar matter of the procedure – or rather, the unwarranted omission of the procedure – necessary (at Aix-en-Provence as everywhere else in France) before his admission to gaming rooms of the Casino:

Attend me closely here. On the Vicomte's body was found no official card of identity, only a ticket of admission to the gaming rooms dated '25 Aug. 1973' in the name of 'Monsieur du Touquet'. However, to obtain such a ticket the dead man should first have been required to surrender a piece of identity to the clerk of admissions at the desk in the foyer. The number and provenance of this piece of identity and other basic information should then have been recorded by the clerk on a card for later inclusion in the files of the establishment. Only after this procedure had been observed and the prescribed fee paid and recorded, should the clerk have given to M. du Touquet his newly stamped ticket of ingress.

But behold, what do we find? We find, charming readers, that application to the files and records of the Casino at Aix-en-Provence (made by the police soon after discovering the murder) reveals no information of M. du Touquet, no entry of a fee paid by him, no details of his identity card, in short nothing whatever to do with him.

In sum, then, and to avoid the proliferation of wearisome technicalities, it would strongly appear that the ticket of admission found on the Vicomte du Touquet's corpse, *while incontestably genuine in its kind*, signifies the total violation of the Casino's most rigid and supposedly inescapable formalities.

We now find ourselves confronted, sage reader, with the following question:

WHAT RATIONAL (OR OTHER) EXPLICATION CAN THERE BE OF SO FANTASTIC A CONCATENATION OF MYSTERIES?

For see before us:

1) A gambling win against almost infinite odds, whereby one minute *jeton* was converted into a fortune;

2) The sincere profession, by the gamester, that he was receiving supranatural aid;

3) The bestial and seemingly motiveless murder of the gamester a little while later;

4) The extinction, into nothing and nobody whatever, of a family once most noble and almost sovereign – an extinction so utter that the Vicomte's corpse had needs be identified by an English 'cousin' in the fifth or sixth degree.

And 5) a final titillation – the possession, by M. le Vicomte du Touquet, of a perfectly genuine ticket to the gaming rooms in the Casino of Aix-en-Provence – but a ticket that was never applied for, never paid for, never even issued.

It is this last item, at first sight so trivial, yet (as all frequenters of Casinos will confirm) in truth so unthinkable, that may give us the clue to the entire aggregation of bizarrerie.

*To be continued*

So they're raking up all that old tale again, thought Jacquiz Helmut.

He put down the *Paris Fiche* and went to the window. Marigold should be back at any moment, and she would be coming, since she was walking back from Cambridge, along the path which ran beside the river. Jacquiz was eager to see Marigold, for a number of reasons, and now looked hotly for her over the meadow, but saw, to his purpose, nothing; only three cows, the willows beyond the path, the reeds beyond the willows, and the brown streak of water under the far bank of the Cam. I hate this meadow, thought Jacquiz, and I hate those bloody cows and I hate being out here at Grantchester. After all those contented years in the best rooms which Lancaster had to offer, the Lauderdale Set in Sitwell's Building, no less, why did I have to move out here to bloody Grantchester? Because I got married, that's why, married to bloody Marigold. I wish she'd come quickly, I've thought of something new, this time, perhaps, it will work.

But still no Marigold – though she was already forty minutes late. Back in time for tea, she'd said: they always had tea at 4.15 and now it was almost five. Why was she so late – so late, so inconsiderate, so unreliable, such a bloody selfish horrible bitch? Jacquiz fidgeted across the room and found himself looking down at *Paris Fiche*. He had originally picked it up, some twenty-five minutes ago when he had first started to fuss, simply in order to hold it and thus to associate himself, in some remotely vicarious fashion, with the delinquent Marigold, who had bought it in the Transit Lounge of Orly Airport on the way back from their holiday in Siam. But having once picked it up, he had out of long scholarly habit investigated its contents and had come on the article about that wretched fellow, du Touquet. Why, Jacquiz wondered as he began to read the article a second time, had Marigold not mentioned this piece to him? She must have spotted it: it was heavily advertised on the cover, which was probably why Marigold had bought the rag in the first place. Yes, she had bought the *Paris Fiche* to read about du Touquet, had presumably long since read about him, and had not told Jacquiz. Why not? Bloody, deceitful bitch.

Marigold bounced into the room, ginger hair disordered (oh, adorable), freckles prominent (which meant mischief) in round, snubby face.

'I never saw you cross the meadow.'

'I got a lift by road.'

'You said you were going to walk.'

'But instead I got a lift.'

'Who from?'

'That spotty research student who helps you curate the College manuscripts. Or whatever you do with them.'

'*Collate* them. As you very well know, I am *Collator* of the Manuscripts of Lancaster College. That young man is my Temporary Under-Collator. He does not live in Grantchester, he is unmarried and lives in Lancaster. So how can he have given you a lift here? Why would he be coming here at all?'

'*In order* to give me a lift. Then he was going to drive back.'

'Why on earth should he trouble himself to do that?'

Both of them knew how and where the conversation was going to end, thought Jacquiz, but one must play by the established rules and carry on the rally stroke by stroke.

'Because I asked him to,' said Marigold.

'Why?'

'Because I was tired.'

'Why?'

'Because he'd just been sucking me off and I'd had three

20

colossal orgasms. Bang on the table where you curate your manuscripts.'

'Collate them. Did you suck him off?'

'No. I gave him a hand job and let him finish off between my tits. Which reminds me. I left my bra behind in your manuscript room—'

'—Chamber of the Manuscripts—'

'—So bring it back with you next time you go in.'

'Do you tell me all this to torture me?'

'I thought it excited you.'

'It does. It also tortures me. To think of you ... with just anybody. All the time. On the slightest whim.'

'But oh my God, you're excited, aren't you? You're revolting.'

'And *you* are sly!'

'No, I'm not that. I've told you it all straight out.'

'But you didn't tell me about that article in the *Paris Fiche*.'

There was a long silence.

'Bugger,' said Marigold a last. 'I should never have left the fucking thing about.'

'You call that a response? Answer my question. Why didn't you show me that article?'

'Because I didn't want you poking your snooty Jewish snout in.'

'Why shouldn't I be interested?'

'Because you're interested in the wrong way and for the wrong reasons.'

'How do you know?'

'Because I was there when my father told you the story of the Roses. It was that time, just before our wedding, when we went down to see him at Sandwich. Even though we weren't yet married, I was beginning to run out of illusions about you—'

'—Then why did you marry me?'

'You made a change. Like your Under-Collator's spots. I've a weakness for feeble men. And then at my age a girl begins to need some security, and the one thing about you that isn't feeble is your bank account. And in a funny sort of way I loved you, then as now.'

'Ah, Marigold.'

'But then as now my eyes were open. I watched you, while my father told you the story down at Sandwich, and I saw your eyes cross and your schnozzle twitch, and I knew what you were thinking. This is what I need to make me big, you were thinking: if I could sniff out the Roses of Picardie, they'd all have to take me seriously at last. The Provost and the dons and the students and the porters, instead of saying, "There goes that long yellow streak of Jewish piss who's so pompous about his joke job with the mouldy manuscripts", they'd all have to bow down in adoration in front of great big Jacquiz Helmut who'd brought off the antiquarian coup of the century.'

'There's nothing wrong with ambition of that kind. At least I shouldn't just be treasure-hunting.'

'Because you have treasure already. You're rich, Jacquiz, but you're also second rate as a scholar and unloved ... except perhaps by me ... for yourself. So you think that what you'll do to make up is to buy yourself a great big load of esteem. You'll buy your way to the Roses, and then you'll use *them* to buy reputation and regard.'

'Nothing of the kind. I simply wish to solve a mystery.'

'By spending money which other people wouldn't have to spend.'

'By *risking* money which other people are too cowardly to risk.'

'But lessening your risk by using the special knowledge which comes from my family.'

'Why waste it?'

'Because my family, Jacquiz, wants the whole thing forgotten.'

'And yet it was your father who told me about it in the first place.'

'He thought he was telling you a curious after-dinner tale – a tale now so old and so remote that no one would even consider following it up.'

'But if I choose to follow it up, why not?'

'Because, Jacquiz, if there *is* anything to find at the end of the trail, it will be something exceedingly nasty.'

'If all scholars were deterred by the prospect of nastiness, Marigold, very few trails would be followed at all.'

'Nasty for you, Jacquiz, not just in the past or in the abstract, but nasty, injurious, dangerous, perhaps lethal, to you in person.'

'Why this sudden solicitude for my welfare? For all this "love" you talk of, you have never shown me any *care*. Take this afternoon—'

'—Jacquiz. Whatever it is . . . this nastiness that goes with the Roses . . . it's very old-fashioned. It goes back to a period when husband and wife were deemed to be one flesh. Some of it would probably rub off on me.'

'So now we have it at last. You're scared.'

'Yes. I'm fascinated, as you are, as my father is, but like him I'm also scared, and since I share only your fascination and not your pitiful ambition, I want the thing left entirely alone as it has been left by my family for three centuries.'

'Then why did you buy the magazine with that article?'

'I've just told you: like anyone else who hears it, I'm hooked on the story. I wanted to read . . . about IT; but to read is all I wanted.'

'Well, now that we've both read this piece, we can put our heads together and see what it tells us . . . about IT.'

'Nothing. It's about the death of du Touquet. IT has been out of his family for three hundred years.'

'Ever since it came into yours.'

'A distant branch of mine, lost and forgotten.'

'So you say. But they're still around somewhere, for all we know, and therefore still possible to find again. And IT with them.'

'Perhaps. If that branch of the family survives, and if they still have IT. Two big "ifs", Jacquiz. And in any case that article can't help you. As I've already said—'

'—That article is about the death of du Touquet, and du

Touquet had nothing to do with your family or with IT. But don't you see where that article is leading?'

'No.'

'Oh yes you do. I shall be very careful, Marigold, to buy the issue which carries the next instalment.'

## THE CASE OF THE DEAD GAMESTER Part II

*Today we continue our special correspondent's enthralling study of the circumstances in which M. le Vicomte du Touquet (son of the last of the line of Comtes de la Tour d'Abbéville) met his terrible death almost exactly one year ago.*

At this stage in our investigation, I must unroll a little of history – the history of the ancestors of our unhappy Vicomte.

The tale begins with a certain Baudouin du Bourg, who was a cadet of a cadet branch of the family of the Counts of Boulogne. In 1096 Baudouin accompanied his cousin, Eustace III, Count of Boulogne, on the first crusade to the Holy Land. In due course of time Baudouin du Bourg became the trusted factor and deputy of Bohemond, Prince of Antioch, while Eustace perished and was succeeded by his younger brother, another Baudouin, who now became Count of Boulogne and Count of Edessa (the latter feoff having been achieved during the march on Jerusalem).

Not long afterwards, Count Baudouin was chosen to become King of Jerusalem. Compelled to leave his county of Edessa in order to implant himself on his new throne in the capital, he summoned his cousin Baudouin du Bourg, on grounds of *res et fides familiaris*, to leave the service of Prince Bohemond and take over the governance and guardianship of Edessa on his senior kinsman's behalf.

Baudouin du Bourg, obeying the summons, celebrated his departure from Antioch by appropriating a casket of jewels from the treasury of Bohemond. The jewels in question had been looted by Bohemond shortly after the capture of the city; or rather, they had been looted by a party of his serjeants, from whom they were subsequently confiscated by him. The serjeants yielded their booty quite willingly to

Bohemond, as the aged Hebrew of Antioch who rightfully owned the jewels and was butchered while defending them had cast a curse, while he lay bleeding to death, on the serjeants who stole them and on all into whose hands the jewels might subsequently come. Or so the legend has always stated. Certain is this at least: that one of the serjeants died of a hideous crimson flux within hours of the theft, thus encouraging his comrades' belief in the Jew's curse and persuading them to pass on the jewels, without objection, to Bohemond. Bohemond, knowing of the curse, boasted that he was too big a man to heed it; but one may remark that when the jewels were pilfered, as related above, by the departing Baudouin du Bourg, Bohemond made no effort to repossess himself of them, being glad, we may hazard, to be quit of them.

So du Bourg went rejoicing on his way to take over his High Stewardship of Edessa – where, very soon, he was afflicted with what the chronicler (an English monk called Godart who wrote in Latin under the name of Salopius) describes as '*totius corporis ruina et exesio, quae gesta est maculis per membra rodentibus ac squalentibus* – the collapse and decay of his whole body, which was brought about by scaly patches that crept over his limbs'. Whereupon du Bourg, being so pointedly reminded of the curse which the jewels purported to carry, swiftly disembarrassed himself by giving them, as a bounty, to his young cousin and esquire, Clovis du Bourg. This latter was about to return to the North of France, where the rich and eminent Marquis de Maubeuge, impressed by rumours of the du Bourgs' flourishing fortunes in Outremer, had promised him one of his daughters in wedlock.

The moment Baudouin du Bourg handed over the jewels to his cousin Clovis, the disease left him ('*velut gelu de gramine dissolutum* – like a frost thawing from a lawn', as Salopius remarked). Although this Baudouin was in time to succeed Baudouin of Boulogne as King of Jerusalem, it is not to our purpose to say more of him; for it is the fortunes of Clovis, founder (though not, as will be seen, progenitor) of the dynasty in which we interest ourselves, that must now concern us.

The said Clovis, then, having set sail for France and his promised bride, at first enjoyed fair winds and refined entertainment at the ports which lay on his route; but before long he too was subjected to cruel misfortunes, 'considered by his crew', wrote Salopius, 'to be caused by the Jew's curse which attended the jewels, from which, however, Clovis would in no wise be parted, saying that he had mighty use for them whensoever he should come into France'. Whatever this purpose might be, it began to seem improbable that he should ever reach France to pursue it: for storms, contamination of stores, plague, shipwreck and imprisonment by the Moors of Tunis all impeded Clovis du Bourg so disastrously that he eventually reached Mentone only through the good offices of his contracted father-in-law to be, who paid a stiff ransom to the Moors to redeem him.

On reaching Mentone, Clovis sold most of the jewels in the Jew's casket, 'reserving only twelve fine and glistering rubies of which he was much enamoured', to a travelling Venetian merchant, journeyed to Rouen, and there used the proceeds of the sale to hire 'a goodly band' of knights, mounted serjeants and well armed footmen. The first expedition he made with this company was to the Château des Larmes, near Reims, where the Marquis de Maubeuge was then in residence. Clovis, having apparently arrived in amity, asked for his bride and her dowry, 'which the noble Marquis Carlus would there and then have fain delivered to him (less the sum paid for his ransom), had it not been discovered to his ears by a treacherous servitor of the Lord Clovis that his master the Lord Clovis had been shorn of his manhood by the knife of a Moorish chirurgeon. On being so apprised, the Marquis Carlus deposed that the law both secular and ecclesiastical forbade him to marry his daughter to an eunuch; upon which the Lord Clovis caused his company to massacre the noble Marquis, his wife, his sons, his daughter that was betrothed to the Lord Clovis, and all retainers and servitors whatever down to the puling babes of the meanest serf of the cloaca. This extermination being completed, the noble Clovis did proclaim himself Lord of the castle and of all the lands of the Marquisate, upon surety whereof he raised gold from the Jews of Strasbourg to augment his chivalry and puissance.'

So formidable a warlord did Clovis now prove himself that before long he prevailed upon the King to recognize him in the title, as won by conquest, of Marquis de Maubeuge, and in the possession, as royal feudatory immediate, of several castles, counties, baronies, feoffs and lordships in the North of France, which had been overrun by him at the head of his growing private army. At this stage a majority of the chief magnates in the area, who had hitherto merely despised Clovis, decided that it would be more discreet, at least for the time being, to appease him; and after a labyrinthine process of bargains and concessions (few if any of the latter being made by Clovis) an accommodation was reached which confirmed the new Marquis de Maubeuge as holder of his dignities and territories, not only by assignment of the King who reigned in Paris but (rather more to the practical point) by consent of the Peers who ruled in Picardie.

Such a record of conquest and attainment might have seemed to discount the legend of the Jew's curse – had not Clovis, within two years of becoming, so to say, respectable, been impaled by the portcullis of the Château des Larmes while waving off a guest, none other than the Duc de Picardie, at the castle gate. How this hideous accident occurred has never been explained, though there were those, according to the chronicler, who affirmed at the time 'that a youth of fair, smooth face and lustrous hair of gold, a stranger to all, was observed mingling with the company of the Duke's esquires just before His Highness departed from the castle; and that this youth was taken by the Lord Marquis' his men to be one of the Most Noble Duke's but afterward denied by His Grace and all his attendants, who vouchsafed they knew him not but had taken him for a squire or page of my Lord Marquis; and that this youth was seen to walk into the guard house by the gate-tower, wherein was the hinged stanchion of iron that released the portcullis at need, and wherein was no man else as all were gathered in the castle yard to do honour to His Highness; and that it was but a moment after the youth had gone thither that the portcullis fell on my Lord Marquis; wherefore search high and low was afterwards made for this youth, who was seemingly gone into the air ...'

But whatever the cause of Clovis's death, dead he was and without an heir. His recently acquired lordships and estates lay open for any man to grab, and might well have been seized by claimants true or false within days; but it so happened that the Duc de Picardie, during his visit to the Château des Larmes, had been much diverted by the attentions of Clovis's widowed sister, the Lady Philippa, 'who had come to his chamber nightly and there lewdly disported herself on the person of the Duke's Highness, though ever afterward she swore herself pure, and said that the wench who went ramping to His Grace, though young and tender almost to childery as was herself and dark withal of her own raven blackness was another (yet who she could not say) and that as for herself, it was for her songs and wit and company that His Highness did her favour ...' Howbeit, whatever the reason for the Duke's partiality for the widow Philippa, whether it was her social arts or her sexual graces, His Highness proved a good and strong friend in time of need: he took Philippa and her son under his protection, and negotiated a royal deed of inheritance, whereby the baby boy, though he was not allowed to succeed to the Marquisate of Maubeuge, was declared perpetual castellan of the Château des Larmes within that Marquisate and true heir to all other lands and titles whatever of which the late Lord Clovis had been seised, the chief of these honours being the Countship of La Tour d'Abbéville.

Philip, the infant child, was now renamed Clovis Philip du Bourg de Maubeuge – the latter being retained as a Christian name, no doubt to compensate for loss of the title. In course of time he grew, under the tutelage of his mother and the

Duc de Picardie, to be a fine young man, commanding yet courteous, noted not only for his martial skills but for his intellectual tastes, unusual attributes in a nobleman of the period. However, just as he had reached his prime and married a bride of almost royal rank, a most gruesome stroke of fate obtruded itself. A learned alchemist, whom the young Count was lodging at the Château des Larmes while they conducted certain experiments together, administered to his noble patron a potion which would in supposition induce celestial visions but in fact afflicted him with a profound and unassailable melancholy, after some weeks of which he slit his throat with a hunting knife. The alchemist later swore that none of the ingredients in the potion, as he mixed it, could have brought about this unhappy result, and accused his apprentice of adding dangerous substances while his own back was turned. But the apprentice, a youth who had been seldom seen by the inmates of the castle and always appeared in a cowl so deep as virtually to mask him, had fled shortly after the potion was administered and was never found that he might be put to the question; and the alchemist himself answered at the stake for the young nobleman's misfortune.

Meanwhile, the Comtesse de la Tour d'Abbéville was swollen with her dead husband's child, which issued as twin boys, the second of whom died at birth. Once more the fortunes of the house rested upon an infant in arms whom grotesque disaster had rendered fatherless; once more the mother of the infant found a protector (her cousin, the Cardinal Archbishop of Chartres) to ensure to her offspring the dignities and domains due to him.

The succession of an infant heir was to become a common event in the turbulent history of this family, in whose affairs during the next 150 years a pretty consistent pattern was seen to establish itself. The Comtes de la Tour d'Abbéville (whose family name was finally defined, in 1174, as du Bourg de Maubeuge) usually came very young to the title, were well protected during their childhood, prospered mightily in their early maturity and were then struck down, at their zenith, by obscene accidents or illnesses which in the long run or more commonly the short proved lethal. Their untimely and painful deaths were attributed to the Curse of the Jew of Antioch, which attached itself, in the public belief, to those jewels of Baudouin du Bourg's original gift that had been retained by Clovis du Bourg on his return from Outremer. These had continued in the family and were, as we have already learned from the chronicler, 'twelve fine and glistering rubies' – which became known, around 1300, as 'The Twelve Roses of Picardie', while the curse associated with them was henceforth called 'The Curse of the Roses'.

At this stage, one might well inquire why the family did not sell or otherwise rid themselves of the fatal Roses. The answer appears to be that they had come to regard the rubies, not only as carrying a curse, but also as at the same time promoting, in some mysterious way, the undoubted wealth and worldly power of their line. If pressed in the matter, the du Bourgs de Maubeuge would have argued that during the time the rubies had been theirs the family, though previously of mediocre fortune, had won and kept, in addition to the fine countship of La Tour d'Abbéville, the almost equally rich countships of Douai and Valenciennes, the Viscountcy of Le Touquet (in those days just a square tower on an island in a salt-marsh but nevertheless a thing of esteem), the Honour of Vouziers, the Baronies of Montreuil, Péronne and Gournay, and, among numerous seigneuries, those of Bapaume, Clermont, Montvidier and Forges-les-Eaux (Forculus Aquarum). Now, if it were the rubies that had conferred all the family's afflictions since their acquisition, why should it not be they that had also conferred the concomitant and palpable distinctions? With the rubies had come the glories as well as the calamities; if the gems had bestowed the latter, why not the former? If one had then urged that there was no legend of a Blessing, only of a Curse, the du Bourgs de Maubeuge would have retorted that legends of benevolence are less readily transmitted, that many men must have possessed the rubies before the Jews of

Antioch, and that there was no reason why the power of the gems for good or ill should not owe as much to the unreported charity of a previous owner as it did to the much publicized spleen of the Hebrew. Which being the case, the intransigent du Bourgs de Maubeuge would have continued, they reckoned they had a fair bargain, provided the riches and prestige brought by the rubies were always theirs to enjoy during the really quite generous intervals which separated the catastrophes.

So the rubies continued in the family and the family continued in general prosperity and occasional bane. We might take 1497 as a year typical of their fortunes. Three things of note occurred: the Roses were sent to Venice to be set in a necklace by Lorenzo di Torcello; the Count of the day, Clovis Raymond, visiting Venice to collect the finished necklace, won a handsome palace on the Canale di Cannaregio in a game of dice; and his eldest son, back in France, had the top of his head taken off in a friendly jousting match with his younger brother.

This last was one of the few instances in which the curse attacked a child of the family rather than the head of it. After such instances the reigning Count was sometimes allowed to attain an unusual length of years – as indeed happened here, for Count Clovis Raymond was over 70 before he died of a fit while fornicating with a whore called La Lubella in his Venetian palace. One should add that his successor survived him by barely two years; he fell through rotten boards into a castle cesspit, leaving an heir of five years old and thus reverting to the family pattern.

The affairs of the family marched on in much the same way, (usually prosperous, intermittently and briefly marred by savage calamity) for another 150 odd years, until 1652. Behold now the young and widowed Countess of that time (her husband just dead in a duel over a game of backgammon) fretting herself with boredom in a family mansion near Montreuil. Her two-year-old baby, the new Count, is an ugly and noisy child whom she puts largely in the care of nurses. Since the rule of law is more efficacious than it was in the days of the early Counts, she has no fear for her own or her son's property, and she can therefore safely leave the administration of money and estates to the type of dilatory but more or less honest lawyers and factors who have had such matters in charge for some generations and have never robbed the family of more than a tolerable three livres in twenty.

Thus the lady has no solid occupation and indeed has only two interests of any kind: the Necklace of the Roses, which as we saw, had been made up on Count Clovis Raymond's instructions in Venice, and a young Dutch painter, Richard Van Hoek, who lodges in nearby Montreuil.

The Necklace should be in hands other than hers, in secure keeping as an heirloom, but the lawyers like things to go on easily and do not wish to cause fuss and offence by insisting that she should part with it. Almost hourly she takes it from the box of alabaster in which she keeps it, and meditates, not on the curses or the blessings with which it may be informed, but on the rich, deep glow of the splendid stones and on the intricate work of gold in which Lorenzo di Torcello set and linked them. As for the painter, Van Hoek, she dotes on his youth, strength and purity, and is further pricked to desire by his manifest disdain of herself. Daily he comes to the mansion to finish the portrait of her husband on which he was engaged when the Count was killed; daily she presents herself to him while he works, gazes at him in supplication, flutters her hands in vain caresses of the air, indicating that such caresses would be for him if he wished them; and daily her worship, her caresses, the bare throat which she displays – all are ignored or when not ignored despised by the proud young man at his easel. For he loves another, a young girl in Montreuil, Constance Fauvrelle. Her he would marry, save that her family is protestant and to marry a protestant in France is to draw invidious attention to oneself. Marriage must wait till both of them can leave France; they cannot leave France until he has money; he will not have money until he has finished the portrait of the late Count to the widow's satisfaction; the widow will not be satisfied until she has sampled his flesh; and this the young painter will not permit, as he wishes to remain chaste for his Constance and is in any case disgusted by the perfumed and fluttering Countess Jezabel and her proffered harlotries.

But one day the Countess shows him the Necklace of the Roses of Picardie. He has, of course, heard of it, but has never seen it until now. Dazzled by its magnificence, mesmerized by the fathomless pools of crimson, he exclaims that he will meet all her desires if only she will give him the Necklace. Now, though the lust is hot in her young and pampered veins, the Necklace is very dear to her; she knows, too, that it is very valuable, indeed invaluable; she knows that she is forbidden by law to give it away from the family; she knows that the du Bourgs de Maubeuge have had it for over 500 years and that their fate, for good or ill, is joined with it. She therefore makes a plan and then a bargain: she will give the Necklace to the painter, she says, if he will come twenty times to her couch and each time give her pleasure after a different fashion. The painter accepts the challenge; the lady laughs within her bosom, knowing that even if he succeeds in providing the almost impossible variety promised and takes away the Necklace after the twentieth coup of love, she has only to denounce him as a thief and the Necklace will be brought back to her.

Richard Van Hoek, overcoming his physical and moral disgust in his eagerness to possess the matchless Roses, informing himself from rare books of devices wherewith to meet the demand of the Countess, comes to her nineteen times and each time pleasures her limbs and loins in a new manner. On the twentieth he pleasures her as never before (for despite himself he has begun to take pride and joy in his office); when he has done with her she swoons away from extremity of rapture, and (though he does not know it) her heart, which was but feeble, now ruptures itself from her excess. Leaving her in her chamber, taking the Necklace which he has worthily won, he returns to Montreuil – where he hears at once the cry of 'Plague' throughout the streets.

For many days all is fear and confusion in the land. The

34

trusted servants in the mansion of the Countess assume that their mistress, whose face is black with suffusion of blood, is dead of a sudden stroke of the plague. They bury her hugger-mugger and fly with the child to the distant Château des Larmes, not concerning themselves, in this hour of dread, with such trifles as jewels or necklaces.

Meanwhile Van Hoek falls sick of the plague. He hands the Necklace to his beloved Constance, in reparation of his faithlessness to her, and dies. Constance, desperate to escape from Montreuil, which is guarded and ringed about by the King's men that no bearer of death may leave it, bribes into marrying her an Official Purveyor of Meats to the Army, by offering the Necklace as her *dôt*, and is smuggled away by him in one of his conveyances out of the stricken town.

Time passes; the plague abates; order is restored. The young Comte de la Tour d'Abbéville returns from the Château des Larmes to the mansion near Montreuil, under the wardship of an uncle and aunt. The family lawyers at length discover the disappearance of the Necklace, at first assume that it has been looted during the plague, are then put on a more accurate trail by one of the servants, who makes report of his mistress' liaison with Van Hoek. No doubt of it, Van Hoek will have the necklace. But Van Hoek is dead; where is his betrothed, Constance Fauvrelle? Fauvrelle no longer, her scandalized parents tell the lawyers: she has married an Army Contractor, one Louis Comminges, a Catholic for shame, in order to escape from Montreuil and desert her own kind and kindred. But where is he? Where has she taken the Necklace? No one knows or wishes to know. Her family now looks on Constance as dead. Shortly afterwards, fearing renewed persecutions as protestants, they leave Montreuil for Sandwich, in England over the Channel. They will never again hear of Constance or be of any help to the lawyers who wish to trace her. Very well, say the lawyers: this Louis Comminges who married her, him we can surely trace, a Contractor who provides the military Commissariat cannot vanish into the air.

But Louis Comminges has done exactly that. He has sold

his office as Purveyor to another contractor – and he has taken his wife, and she has taken the Roses of Picardie, and they have gone. Where? Into the vastness of France.

From that time on the Necklace of the Roses disappeared completely. What became of Louis and Constance Comminges, who were their descendants, whether or not the Necklace was retained by them – all this is unknown to us. What is known, however, is that once the Comtes de la Tour d'Abbéville lost the Necklace their fortunes steadily declined. True, they no longer suffered the occasional and devastating visitations of the Curse; true also that after the events just recounted most of the family have died of old age in their beds. But the beds in which they died have been ever more hard and more narrow – and even, towards the end, verminous. For mark this, sage readers: since the 17th century the family of Du Bourg de Maubeuge has descended slowly but inexorably from riches to comfort to bare competence to selling heirlooms to cadging meals to performing menial tasks to the outright poverty in which the last Count died in Amiens. This sad deterioration invites first a comment and then a question. The comment: it is known that the family continued, right up to the last, to attribute its pauperization to the absence of the Roses, which had been the guardians of its fortunes as well as the scourge of its members. And the question: how did the lately dead Vicomte du Touquet, who a few days before his death was expelled in total destitution (so it was said in the court of inquest) from a lodging house in the slums of Lille, contrive to pay his way hundreds of miles down to Aix-en-Provence and into an expensive Casino?

Ah yes, but we now recall, from our inquiries of last week, that there is considerable doubt as to whether Monsieur du Touquet *did* indeed pay his way into the Casino and as to the manner in which he achieved entry. This recollection brings us back to the whole mystery of the Vicomte's death. It is in order to cast light upon this that we have opened up for you the above panorama of history. For given that history, and given the circumstances of the Vicomte's

so sanguinary death, we believe that there is but one explanation of the whole *guignol* ... an explanation both fascinating and shocking ... with which we shall enlighten our
charming readers next week.

*To be continued*

Oh, poor Clovis, Balbo Blakeney thought: will they never
let him rest? He put down the *Paris Fiche* on the ante-room
table, wondered how long the Madame would keep him
waiting and which girl she would allot him (Electra, the
Greek with the moustache? Or Ton-ton, who was rather
good at pretending to come?), and then thought again of
Clovis, last Vicomte du Touquet.

Balbo Blakeney belonged to a cadet branch of a substantial Norfolk family, being second cousin to the 19th
Baron Blakeney of the Marsh. In 1861 (or was it '62? Balbo
asked himself) the youngest sister of the 15th Baron had
been married to the 33rd Comte de la Tour d'Abbéville
(Clovis Maximillian di Cannaregio Baudouin du Bourg de
Maubeuge). Since the girl was plain, ill-tempered, thirty-one
years old and given to the bottle, the Blakeneys were very
eager to be shot of her; but although marriage to the Count
was clearly her last chance, the Blakeneys would never have
allowed it had they known quite what manner of man was
His Excellency. The marriage, in short, was based on recip-
rocated misunderstanding: the Count thought that the Hon-
ble Caroline Blakeney's little trust fund could be broken into
by her husband (it couldn't); and Lord Blakeney, though
aware that the du Bourgs de Maubeuge had been going down
hill for some time, thought that they had not yet reached a
state of actual disrepute (they had). Although they still had
*some* money and one respectable house, the house had been
mortgaged from cellar to chimney top, largely to provide the
somewhat curious entertainments that alone gratified the
33rd Count.

But questionable as the Count's affairs had been when he

wedded Caroline Blakeney, they were positively radiant (Balbo reflected) by comparison with what was to come later. Not, of course, that he, Balbo, had yet been on the scene to witness these things, but Great Aunt Hetta's celebrated narratives had rendered them vividly enough.

'Foreign muck,' said Great Aunt Hetta on one occasion to the pop-eyed and velvet-knickered Balbo, 'that's all that lot ever was. The only distinguey thing about them was some jewels, which blessed them with wealth and cursed them with early death, some potty tale of that kind, but they'd even gone and lost those – ever so long before. As for this 33rd Count of Arsyville, Clovis Minimax Fartwin de Malbugger or whatever he called himself, he started by decking Caroline out as a schoolgirl at her first communion and shagging her from behind at the altar in the family chapel, and then got her up as an orphan in boots and black stockings and beat her rump until it went purple. And when he found out that he couldn't get at her money, he really let rip and rigged up a sort of Edgar Allan Poe machine out of *The Pit and the Pendulum* – though of course you're much too young to have read *that*.'

Great Aunt Hetta's notions about what was suitable fare for young children had been eccentric, comprehending as they did her own unrefined exegesis ('It's the truth, ain't it?'), but also firm in their way, excluding all fiction whatever as 'trumped-up fibbing done for money – you need to be grown up before you read it to see what rubbish it is'.

'Now, Caroline was a nasty little vixen enough,' Great Aunt Hetta had gone on to Balbo, 'and don't sit there looking so mealy, boy, I tell you she was a sneaking little rat and I mean it, even if she was my own auntie. But even Caroline didn't deserve what this Count Mauve-Hairs dished her out with, and small wonder she came running home to Norfolk. I wasn't more than a gel of six then, but I wasn't no fool neither and what I didn't work out for myself what my old nanny filled in. First off, Caroline was preggers – "though how he got her swelling if he shoved it where she says he did beats me rotten," said nanny, "everywhere but where he ought to do Missy Caro say." For seconds, the Count was demanding her back and threatening to exert his legal rights: he wanted his heir to be born in France, he said, so would they send Caro over at once – or else a nice little chunk of money to make up. Well, dear' (Great Aunt Hetta chortled) 'Caroline was no picture at the best of times, and when she was preggers she was like something out of the zoo; and what with that, and what with her filthy tongue and her sucking down brandy half the day, my poor Pa would have been glad enough to be rid of her. A chivalrous man he was, but, chivalrous or no, he'd not have been above packing her back to the Count – who, when all was said, *was* her husband – but Mama spoke up and said, "She's blood of your blood, and you can't send her back to that Frenchy sod, so pay up and look big and make up your mind she's going to drop her brat here."

'So Pa paid up and looked sick and paid up again and looked sicker, but he stood to Caroline as a brother should, and six months later, despite all that brandy, she whelped an eight-pound boy with a face like a cowpat and a prick as long as a donkey's, and that was the grandfather of this Clovis du Touquet who's about your age and coming to stay next week – though Gawd knows why he's been asked and you watch out for any filthy foreign habits he tries to teach you' – this accompanied by a sharp tweak at Balbo's private parts.

About what happened between the birth of Clovis du Touquet's grandfather in 1864 and the introduction of little Clovis (aged nine) to Balbo (aged eight) in 1929 Great Aunt Hetta had been even more scathing.

'Caroline and the boy scrounged off my Pa for nearly twenty years,' she told Balbo on the day before little Clovis was due at Blakeney Staithe, 'but then Caro's husband died of a fit of something foreign, and she took the boy to France to see what was left for them. About 1884 that would have been. And precious little she found – except a lot of good cognac in the cellar, so she decided to stay there and drink it. No one to stop her – my Pa had always reined her in a bit here, but no one was going to bother there, least of all her crappy son – and in four years she was dead of the stuff and good riddance. The son – Rupert she called him, not Clovis, to spite her husband – sold the house and the rest of the cognac for what he could get and set up as a high-class pimp, only he wasn't any good at it, and got lower and lower, till he married one of his own doxies and spawned little Clovis's father – *if* he was got by Rupert and not by one of the clients, which is just as likely. Clovis they called him, going back to the family custom, Clovis d'Outremerde or some such rubbish. Born in 1896, and now thirty-three years old, and all he's good for is picking up the banana skins in a park in Nancy' – Great Aunt Hetta contemptuously pronounced it like the English Christian name – 'whatever sort of place *that* can be. Anyway, ten years ago he got under a bush in his park with a skivvy from one of the local tradesmen's houses and forgot to use one of his banana skins, because before you could say "ooh la la" there was this little Clovis on the way, the one you're going to meet tomorrow. The family kept the skivvy on condition she got married, and they let Clovis d'Outremerde sleep in the house in return for doing odd jobs like mending the loos. And they've made rather a pet of little Clovis. It was their idea to send him over here to see his English relatives this summer, and that fool Blakeney couldn't think of a way of refusing. So he's been asked over from France, and you've been asked over from Sheringham to play with him, and as I've told you before, watch out for any rude Frenchy tricks he tries to teach yer.' She aimed a heavy flick in the region of Balbo's testicles. 'His full name – and I'm not joking, Balbo, because he's going to be our guest and we must get it right – is Clovis di Cannaregio (that's an Italian bit, as if it wasn't bad enough being French already). . . Baudouin which is French for Bald-win . . . du Bourg . . . de Maubeuge, Vicomte du Touquet, or Viscount of Le Touquet, as we should say, which is where the rich froggies go to sun themselves and lose their money at roulette. Quite a grand name for a little boy whose mother is a skivvy in a grocer's house and whose father picks up banana peel . . .'

Balbo had loved Clovis at first sight. A spindly-limbed and yellow-skinned boy, two inches shorter than Balbo although one year older, Clovis moved with a vivacity and suppleness which endowed his physical defects with the charm of some improbable creature in an animated cartoon. His snub nose stirred in Balbo a sentimental and protective fondness, his cheeky, knowing eyes incited an aching curiosity. Great Aunt Hetta had been right: Clovis put out the air of being up to any number of 'rude Frenchy tricks', reprehensible, beyond question, but also magical. Oh, that he would teach them to me, Balbo thought, writhing with frustration as Clovis chattered away in French (offering God knew what marvellous secrets) and Balbo failed to comprehend more than one word in twenty.

But quite soon they had managed to converse. Clovis, though well enough able, one would have guessed, to take care of himself in his own world, needed all of Balbo's advice and assistance at Blakeney Staithe. Driven by his need, the little French boy first mimed his desires or doubts, then described them in pidgin French. Balbo would respond by miming or enacting the solution, with a slow commentary in pidgin English. Balbo's intelligence and love of Clovis, Clovis's shrewdness and love of 'face', quickened a process of elementary instruction into one of sophisticated mutual understanding. Within five or six days the two boys could discuss everything around them, including Great Aunt Hetta, whom they nicknamed by the hybrid phrase Tantie la Finger, a reference to her habit of seating both boys in her enormous lap and fiddling in their crutches while at the same time explaining that this was just what they must not do to each other since it constituted 'filthy foreign habits'.

In fact, although they often climbed into each other's beds to play games which combined violence with endearment, Clovis and Balbo did not indulge in 'filthy foreign habits' together, largely because 'Tantie la Finger's' cumbrous caresses, though not particularly disagreeable, had failed to rouse either of them to a point where they wished to investigate such techniques any further. It was more fun to hit, squeeze and gouge, and then to go under the bedclothes together and see who farted the fouler smell. In any case, Blakeney Staithe had more interesting things than beds to offer. Whereas Clovis was a town child, Balbo was a country boy and Norfolk at that; he knew the creatures of the dunes and salt marshes, how to watch them, follow them, catch them, cook and eat them, or (if inedible) preserve them. He also, even at the age of eight, had a considerable didactic gift. Clovis was happy to come with him, listen to him, imitate him, learn from him; and Balbo, as he realized by the time their three weeks were up, had been so busy teaching his own 'tricks' that he had left himself no time to be instructed in Clovis's – fascinating as he had thought, on Clovis's arrival, that these must surely be.

'What can you show me?' said Balbo bluntly on their last day. "This afternoon I have shown you what lives in this pool. What can you show me?'

'I can show you what lives in the streets,' said Clovis without recommendation or apology. 'I will show you this, if you wish, when you come to me in Nancy.'

For between the boys it was now agreed that Balbo should visit Clovis as soon as possible in France. But it was not, of course, agreed by anyone else. How long had it been (Balbo wondered as he sat in the ante-room awaiting his turn to fornicate) before he had seen Clovis again?

Eight or nine years, he thought: 1938, that was it. In Amiens ... whither Clovis's parents had moved in the mid-thirties, when the grocer from Nancy decided to shift his family and his business there. Clovis's mother was now a senior maid in the grocer's domestic establishment, while a job had been found for his father in the abattoirs. Balbo's visit, long blocked by Balbo's parents, had eventually been arranged by the grocer's wife, who had learned from Clovis of the friendship begun in Norfolk and had wished to sustain it. However, what with one thing and another nearly a decade had been allowed to pass before she managed to bring the two boys together again, and by the time she did they were strangers, having grown apart into widely diverging modes of adolescence and being further separated by the now all too evident disparity in their social positions. Clovis, Vicomte as he might be, was the son of a maidservant and a porter in the shambles, and depended on the patronage of his mother's employers, with whose sparing aid he hoped to complete several joyless and statutory years of grind at a provincial university before becoming, with luck, a lawyer. Balbo was the child of a country gentleman in ample circumstances and was about to begin a year's tour of Europe, at the end of which a place was waiting for him at Lancaster College, Cambridge, where he would have the spending of a large allowance and be under no obligation to do a stroke of work if he did not choose to.

The encounter, then, was at first an utter failure, and Balbo's sojourn in the grocer's house (nominally as the guest of Clovis but in fact as that of the family, who had both boys to meals at which they were waited on by Clovis's mother), was hideously embarrassing for all. The grocer's wife, a kindly if economically minded woman, realized that something was painfully wrong but could not conceive what to do about it. In the end it was Balbo who divined the answer. Although reminiscences of Blakeney Staithe, of Tantie la Finger or the fauna of the seamarsh, now made Clovis snarl like a pi-dog, one such recollection, calculated by Balbo to operate on Clovis's regard for 'face', saved the entire situation: 'Do you remember,' Balbo had said, 'that time at Blakeney when you promised to show me "what lives in the streets"? I know you meant Nancy then, but the streets of Amiens must be just as exciting. So come on, Clovis – show me.'

Clovis, challenged, had shown him. Amid the cheap bars and cook-shops, the cafés and cathouses of down-town Amiens, their friendship had revived. Madame the grocer's wife and Madame the Countess her servant accepted with relief the boys' repeated absence from meals, almost total absence from the suburban household. Meanwhile Clovis and Balbo cruised, mingled, investigated. Balbo lost his virtue and caught crabs; Clovis laughed when shown them, shaved off Balbo's bush for him, applied an ointment he knew of, and then, suddenly baring his own thighs (and showing a mauve rhomboid birthmark on the left one), casually commanded Balbo to toss him off and himself served Balbo likewise. This did not happen again (*'Alors, mon vieux, on n'est pas Tantie la Finger'*), but the incident was remembered from time to time, with affectionate and mildly deprecating giggles, as being *'une mode moins chère et moins dangereuse que les filles'*. An autumn fair provided a shabby yet oddly enchanting scene (painted pleasure-domes of paste-board under September trees) for their last week of innocent depravity, at the end of which they parted with warm tears, Balbo to meet his bear-leader in Paris and proceed on his tour of Europe, Clovis to a chilly precinct of blue brick and legal learning. They would meet again in the summer of 1939, they promised, as soon as Balbo was back from Italy and Clovis released from his studies.

But before that summer could come Balbo had been called home by anxious parents and Clovis called for a *poilu*. By September of 1939 Balbo would have been similarly conscripted in England, had not the subject which he was to read at Lancaster been on record as Natural Philosophy (*i.e.* Science). Scientists, even suckling ones, were privileged and Balbo gratefully accepted his privilege. Ignoring a plume of white feathers which Great Aunt Hetta sent him as a present for Christmas, Balbo buried himself quietly in snug wartime Cambridge, did his work conscientiously, discovered a talent for certain branches of bio-chemistry, was encouraged to research, was appointed a Fellow of Lancaster, and was sent, late in 1944 and with the rank of Major, to an 'Army Special Treatment Centre' (so called) on Salisbury Plain. Here he was required to investigate possible methods of infecting the enemy with bubonic plague by dropping plague rats by parachute, an ingenious scheme which came to nothing (rather to Balbo's relief) since the rats, intelligent as they were, could not be got to understand that it was their duty to infest German soldiers only and to stay clear of allied troops advancing. However, Balbo was deemed to have passed the war usefully and with honour (forgiven even by Great Aunt Hetta once he had been gazetted in a military rank), was made a Member of the Most Excellent Order of the British Empire, accepted the distinction but did not write himself M.B.E., and returned to Cambridge early in 1946 to pursue a more congenial line of experiment which had to do with the efficacy of alcohol as an haematic disinfectant.

He was relieved to be out of the Army; yet however unpleasant and demanding his war work might have been, it was noticeable that he came back looking younger than when he went: he had always had a smooth, youthful complexion; now it was more so than ever, his forehead, in particular, being totally without mark, crease or line.

When he arrived back in Cambridge, he started to inquire after Clovis. Before the fall of France he had recieved two or three letters in which Clovis wryly congratulated him on his good fortune in remaining at Cambridge and deplored the boredom and discomfort entailed by his own duties as a common infantryman of the Line – though he was at least lucky enough to be stationed some hundreds of miles behind it. The last of these letters, written some time in April 1940, had stated that Clovis, already promoted Corporal, was being considered for a Commission in some ancillary corps, even the approximate nature of which the censorship forbade him to reveal. All correspondence between Balbo and Clovis had then ceased, and Balbo, having verified with some difficulty that Clovis had not come to England among the Free French either as officer or private man, had resigned himself to hearing nothing more until the war ended. Well, now it had ended, there had been ample time for Clovis to send word, and no word had come.

The first step which Balbo took was to write to an old school friend, a Captain Christopher d'Arçy Carr, who was on the staff of the Military Attaché in Paris. Balbo gave the designation of the unit with which Clovis had been serving when last heard of and expressed the hope that somehow or other the name of du Bourg de Maubeuge, Vicomte du Touquet, might perhaps be traced even in the chaotic aftermath of two invasions of France. Some weeks later Captain d'Arcy Carr wrote back to say that Clovis had apparently been granted an Emergency Commission in the rank of full Lieutenant in May 1940, his duties, which sounded dubious to say the least, being connected with the 'constraint and reassurance of civilians in the event' (by then the reality) 'of a German breakthrough'; or in other words, as Captain d'Arcy Carr opined, Clovis had been one of the many chosen at that time to exert the prestige of a uniformed French Officer in persuading the French population to accept, and even collaborate with, the victorious Germans. Whether or not Clovis had undertaken this invidious task willingly remained obscure; but it was quite clear, from the records left by the collaborating Police, that a certain 'Chief Inspector Le Vicomte du Touquet, former Lieutenant of the Provost Corps', had been very active in Amiens, from October 1940 to the summer of 1944, in controlling and disciplining such elements of the citizenry (particularly the lower elements) as were dissident from the Vichy régime or otherwise embarrassing to Marshal Pétain's Administration. Chief Inspector du Touquet, it appeared, had been particularly adroit in extracting information from whores, petty criminals and keepers of estaminets, and in using it to seek out, destroy or delate to the Gestapo urban cells of the predominantly left-wing resistance. Not surprisingly, the Chief Inspector had disappeared during the time when the spearhead of the Allied advance was thrusting towards Paris (though whether by his own agency or that of the hostile maquis was not known) and had not been heard of since.

So he found a use for his knowledge of the streets, Balbo had thought bitterly, and for the friends we made together that summer: well aware of their needs, vices and vulnerabilities, he had bullied, lulled, blackmailed or cajoled them into betraying their countrymen. Then Balbo inquired no more of Clovis and would perhaps in time have forgotten – had not Clovis turned up one evening, grinning rattily, behind the bar of the Hotel Terminus-Gruber in Strasbourg, whither Balbo had gone to attend an international conference of bio-chemists in September 1948. Appearances had been against him, Clovis declared next day, when he was off duty and they had a chance to talk privately. True, he was still using an *alias* (Baudouin Boule), and admittedly the reason why he worked in Strasbourg was that he liked to have a frontier handy (not that crossing into French-occupied Germany would change anything much); but in fact he was in little danger, having been in real trouble only with the fanatical left and being now forgotten (he thought) even by them, as they'd had plenty of fatter fish to fry during the last three years. In a year or two at most he would be able to resume his own name and identity . . . though for a while he might be prudent to stay away from Amiens. All of which was all very well, Balbo replied; but if he was to believe what he was told, Clovis had in fact double-crossed and betrayed his own people and the patriotic army of the Resistance. Even if, as Clovis claimed, he was in trouble only with the extreme left, that must be because others had shorter memories or (now the war was over and things were looking up) had assumed easier attitudes; but lapse of time and the apathy of the self-indulgent could not disguise or excuse Clovis's wartime treachery.

'You do not, *mon vieux*, understand.'

'Understand what?'

'How it was in those days of the occupation. The Resistance – the maquis – some of it consisted of brave and good men who wished only to free France from the Boche. But much of it, *mon vieux*, was made up of bad men, men of the left, who wished to remove the Boche only in order to impose their own brand of piggery. And indeed, when the British and Americans and de Gaulle came and freed us, such men for a time succeeded in all the confusion – until the British and the Americans and de Gaulle saw what was up and stopped it. Now, it was these bad men of the left – and only them – whom I myself had striven to be rid of.'

'I don't follow you at all, Clovis.'

'Then listen, my dear, it is very easy to explain. You remember the people who were our friends in Amiens years ago? The tarts and the guttersnipes and the hucksters and the people of the fair ground? The keepers of estaminets and the like?'

'Indeed I remember them.'

'Now, what *these* people wanted was to live as discreetly and quietly as they could under the Germans until the Allies came to free them and restore France to what she was in 1939. What they did *not* want was for the so-called Resistance to make trouble by annoying the Germans and then later to claim the right, as fighters against the Germans, to impose their filthy politics when once the Germans were gone. So they came to me, these people who had been your friends and mine, and they said: "M'sieur du Touquet, you at least understand us. There is this man here and that woman there who are upsetting the Germans by hostile acts and making life more difficult for all. This man and that woman say they are fighting for our freedom, but we shall have that all in good time when the Allies come. Meanwhile we want peace – and we do not want this man and that woman, who are spoiling what little we have left to enjoy now and will assuredly spoil our freedom when the Allies bring it later. *Alors*, M'sieur du Touquet," our old friends would conclude, "you are a police officer of the French Government: please rid us of this man and that woman." '

'And so they informed, and you . . . you turned "this man here and that woman there" over to the Gestapo?'

'A neat way of being rid of the nuisance.'

'A betrayal of patriots. Collaboration with your country's enemies. Treachery.'

'But the Germans were no longer our enemies. We were officially at peace with them. I was employed by the Government of France to help bring to the French people the good order which they wanted. *Our* enemies were those who destroyed good order – "this man and that woman" of the Resistance.'

'These people who wanted good order under the Germans – so far you have only instanced the rabble of Amiens.'

'Our friends once.'

48

'Yes. But rabble. Who *else* wanted good order under the occupying Germans? No one, we were told in England.'

'Then you were told wrong in England. *Mon vieux*, nearly *everyone* wanted good order under the occupying Germans. Nearly everyone was ready, as you call it, to collaborate. Only, when the Allies came, it was considered advisable to pretend otherwise – and to turn against people like me, who were conspicuous by their position and because of that position could not pretend to have been other than they were. I myself anticipated being turned against in this manner by disappearing just in time.'

'And now you've popped up here as a barman in Strasbourg. Well, Clovis: convince me that, as you say, nearly everyone in France wanted good order under the Germans, and I will exonerate you of having betrayed your country.'

'But how to convince you? If only you had been here at the time. It is no good now. No one much bothers to speak against those like me any more, but no one comes either to speak *for* us, to admit that everybody, *then*, thought and behaved much as we did . . . But I think I see a way to convince you. *Mon Vieux*, think carefully and honestly, and then tell me: what would have happened if the Germans had occupied England? Some men would have got away to be the Free English Army and to return with the Americans, but what of those who were left behind?'

For some minutes Balbo thought carefully and honestly as he had been invited to think. Then he said:

'Most of us, I believe, would have wanted good order under the Germans. The English would have been ready . . . even anxious . . . to collaborate. I pray to God that this is not true of me, but I suspect that it may well be. It is, in any case, true of a huge majority. Clovis, I acquit you. You gave the people of your country only what they wanted.'

And so relations had been (albeit a bit cautiously on Balbo's part) renewed. In 1949 Clovis, who had resumed his proper name and was now manager of a small hotel in Nancy, came over to England to the May Week Ball at

Lancaster, bringing with him a soft and haughty red-haired girl of six feet and six inches whom he had previously billed as 'Mlle de Stermaria, my fiancée – pots of cash'.

The evening was gay and drunken; it revived the fondness that had been between the two men as boys, it removed any mistrust that still lingered in Balbo after the meeting in Strasbourg, and it marked, though neither of course could know it, the high point in the personal and professional fortunes of both.

For after 1949 their respective affairs had begun to go down hill. In Balbo's case the decline was gradual and at first hardly perceptible; in Clovis's case much sharper. The trouble with both men had been dissatisfaction with what they were doing. Balbo, quite simply, had become bored with bio-chemistry as he came to realize that his line of research would reveal nothing new, would upset nothing old; was, in a word, at an impasse, leaving him with nothing to do but teach elementary formulae to first-year undergraduates. Clovis, for his part, had found it impossible to tolerate the airs and total lack of graces of the petty bourgeois salesmen and tourists who frequented his hotel; he was sacked, and deserved to be, a few months after the May Ball; and on top of this he was jilted by Mlle de Stermaria, whose parents had lost their money and who must now look out for fatter birds than Clovis (though sadly admitting to him that nowhere would she find her game so well hung). Whereas Balbo took refuge from his disappointments in a discerning (if never more than amateur) taste for the visual arts, and in a fastidious (if ever more copious) taste for the wines of Burgundy, Clovis's retreat was into melodramatic rows and neat absinthe. Reared and nearly crushed in a horribly hard school, having fought every inch of his dirty and difficult way, Clovis had not the stamina left to cope with serious set-backs; and any chance he had of surviving on the managerial level which he had attained was destroyed by a sudden spate of denunciations (skilfully delayed till he had thought all danger was passed) from wartime partisans who were now bustling in regional politics. Once more Clovis disappeared into hiding ... whence he emerged, nearly five years later, sodden with Pernod and self-pity.

Fortunately or otherwise Balbo, whose father's death had left him with a considerable private fortune and whose own deterioration was still vinous rather than spirituous, had been on hand to pick up the remnants. He had fed and clothed Clovis, indulged him with a long holiday in England, employed an expensive French lawyer to ascertain that his friend was no longer subject to public prosecution or private vendetta, returned with him to France when, in 1956, amnesty was guaranteed, and settled him in lodgings at Le Crotoy, where Clovis obtained employment as a waiter. Reform lasted only a matter of months. Rejected both as a lodger (too aristocratic in his habits) and as a waiter (too degraded in his habits) Clovis disappeared again, on this occasion with £2000 which he had coaxed as a loan from Balbo 'to buy a little shop'.

By the time Clovis turned up once more in rags and repentance two years later, Balbo himself was ruined. Or at least comparatively so. The family bank, in which most of his fortune was involved, had suddenly broken one summer's morning, and when the fragments were counted and the few reckonable ones reassembled, Balbo was told that his private income, once £6000 per annum, would now be a bare £600. He was no longer in a position seriously to subsidize Clovis, and Clovis, when he heard the news, displayed admirable phlegm and understanding.

'Never mind, *mon vieux*. I will just go away.'

'Sorry.'

'You will give me my fare back to France, I think.'

'Yes.'

'And some money for food on the way.'

'Yes.'

'And a little to have when I am home ... wherever "home" may be.'

'A *little*.'

'And then no more.'

'No more. Let me know how you go on ...'

But Balbo had heard nothing from Clovis of how he went on ... until, years later in 1973, he read of 'Monsieur du Touquet's' death in a French newspaper which he had bought while on a cheap and brief holiday in Nîmes. The paper said that there was difficulty in identifying the corpse; so Balbo had gone to Aix (at grievous expense and inconvenience) to perform the last duty to the friend whom he had not seen for fifteen years by attesting the well re-membered birth mark on the left thigh. A few months afterwards, he himself had finally forfeited his lectureship in bio-chemistry and with it his Fellowship at Lancaster, having for the fifth or sixth time fallen flat on his face from brandy in the middle of a chemical demonstration and employed violently obscene language while failing to get to his feet. And now, here he was, a year after Clovis's death, reading all about the poor sod in this nosy French paper ... while he sat in the ante-room of a Cretan brothel, waiting to shag some overblown whore. With only £600 a year and the little he earned by teaching English, he couldn't afford to be too fancy; cheap it might be living in Crete (provided he stuck to the sleazier restaurants and to Greek cognac at 6p a tot), but a fellow had to watch his treats. Where was that bloody Madame anyhow? And what, thought Balbo, scrunching up the *Paris Fiche* in his irritation and im-patience, is the 'explanation both fascinating and shocking' of Clovis's being hacked up which this filthy mag is going to publish next week?

Well, if Balbo was right (thought Balbo) and if all this history was anything to go by, it was pretty obvious what was coming next. Yet surely not; after all this time it surely couldn't be *that* – even in a silly season series in the *Paris Fiche*. Well (Balbo thought) wait and see.

'My gracious, you are tearing this French book.'

The indignant Madame eased the *Paris Fiche* from Balbo's grip.

'Ton-ton will be furious. She 'as it special from Parigi every week.'

'I'd like to see next week's copy when I come.'

'But you 'ave torn this one.'

'It's next week's I want to see. Are you letting me have Ton-ton now?'

'No. Ton-ton is with another client. You can 'ave Cleo for three hundred drachs or Electra for two.'

'What's Cleo got that Electra hasn't?'

'One big clitoris. It stands up stiff if you rub it.'

Just for a moment Balbo was tempted. But 100 drachmai was a lot of money in Heracleion; lots of lodging and lots of Greek cognac.

'Make it Electra. Perhaps she'd like to shave first?'

'What dat?'

'Nothing.' Balbo rose. 'Bring me to Electra forthwith. And please ask Ton-ton to keep me next week's edition of that mag.'

## THE CASE OF THE DEAD GAMESTER Part III

*Today our special correspondent continues and concludes his sensational investigation of the strange death of the Vicomte du Touquet in Aix-en-Provence a year ago.*

With what, then, are we presented in this weird affair?

First, as readers of my initial article will recollect, we are presented with the Vicomte's miraculous gambling win in the Casino of Aix-en-Provence on the evening of 25 August of last year – a win, be it noted, which was accompanied by curious utterances from the Vicomte ... utterances which implied to those who heard them that the Vicomte was in some fashion supernaturally protected or guided – and also, perhaps, threatened. Nor should we neglect to remind ourselves that there was irregularity, indeed mystery, in the Vicomte's manner of entering the gaming rooms; that, while he had a ticket, he had apparently neither purchased it nor been given it, but had simply ... obtained it ... without any knowledge on the part of the vigilant clerks of admission.

Secondly, we are presented with the bloody butchery of the Vicomte a short time after he left the Casino with his enormous roll of notes – notes which the butcher did not attempt to remove from the cadaver.

And thirdly, as the charming readers of last week's *Paris Fiche* will vouch, we are presented with the Curse of the Roses of Picardie; with 12 'glistering' and fateful rubies, first acquired by the Vicomte's ancestors, after a sequence of murders and treacheries, early in the 12th century, later assembled into a necklace by a Master Jeweller of Venice in the 15th century – 12 rubies, I say, which bestowed down the generations both pre-eminence of power and prematurity of death upon the Counts of La Tour d'Abbéville. The Rubies continued in the family, a legacy of mingled calamity and prosperity, until the mid-17th century, when they were purloined from a frolicsome Countess by an opportunist painter, who gave them, on his death bed, to a Huguenot maid, one Constance Fauvrelle, who, in her turn, married a suitor called Comminges and then disappeared. Since then the Rubies have been seen neither by the Counts of La Tour d'Abbéville nor by anyone else who is known to us.

. . However, sage reader, my contention now will be that it is the Curse of the Roses of Picardie, wherever these may be, that has undone the Vicomte du Touquet. How can this be? you will cry. For while the alternation of high winning wagers with sudden death is typical of the *bouleversements* once effected by the Curse of the Rubies, neither curse nor rubies, the latter long vanished, ever attached themselves to M. du Touquet.

But wait. We know, from the evidence recorded at the inquest, that a few days before his death M. du Touquet was 'expelled penniless' from a lodging house in the slums of Lille. The present writer, recently proceeding to these lodgings in order to uncover for you what was there remembered of M. du Touquet, was received by a 12-year-old girl, the rest of the family being out on their occasions. As it transpired, this little girl clearly remembered that, on the morning of the day on which the Vicomte was expelled from the house, a letter had arrived which she had carried to him and by which he had been much excited. She remembers nothing of the postmark or the envelope, but her mind was much impressed by the avidity with which the addressee tore open the missive, by the emergence therefrom of what appeared to be a money order, and by the almost hysterical manner in which M. le Vicomte kept repeating:

'The pretties. I must make haste. Oh, the pretties.'

The girl further remembered that she went to inform her father of all this, and that her father, having heard of the money order, went to M. du Touquet to demand considerable arrears of rent. Chancing to overhear the ensuing conversation through an open door, the little one gathered that M. du Touquet had an important journey to make, that he would need all the money he had been sent to make it, but that as a result of it he would be rich for life (so he claimed) or at least well able to pay her father what he owed him and a generous bonus to boot. Not surprisingly the father was sceptical and began to demand what he was owed with vicious menaces . . . until all of a sudden he fell to the floor in a 'foaming fit' of something which sounds from his daughter's description like epilepsy. The child's mother then appeared, so I was told, and threatened to call the police. But the child (who, notwithstanding that she had informed her papa of the money order, had a tenderness for M. du Touquet) then threatened to tell the police that all violence had been initiated by her parent; and an arrangement was reached whereby M. du Touquet was allowed to leave immediately and without paying in return for his own and the little one's silence about the criminal assault on him. M. du Touquet therefore departed 'penniless' only in the sense that all he had was a money order as yet uncashed; and as for the fiction of his 'expulsion', it was later put round the district by the woman in order to save face and prevent further scandal or inquiry. (It was from the same motives, doubtless, that she suppressed the true facts of M. du Touquet's departure when questioned in the Court of Inquest.)

And now, my sage and charming readers, is it idle to propound a theory? Is it vain to speculate that the 'pretties' which so excited the Viscount were the Roses of Picardie, that the letter he had received was from some person who had them (or knew where they were) and wished (from whatever motive) to see them returned at last to their true and former owners, and that the money was sent in good earnest of this intention – to enable the Vicomte to make the necessary expedition?

The thing is wild, you will cry, there is nothing to support it, how ridiculous to suppose that the Rubies should suddenly be offered back (by whom, for God's sake?) after the lapse of three centuries, this writer has culled the whole idiocy from the fickle winds of disordered fancy. Perhaps. But kindly note, censorious reader, that the theory does after all explain, and make in a manner consistent, *everything* that occurred from the moment the Viscount had his letter. For once granted that M. le Vicomte was in a practical way to repossessing himself of the Roses, he could in a fashion be deemed to be their owner; he would therefore be subject to the Curse of the Roses, and also apt to receive the benefits conferred by them. All this he would know for himself. He could therefore expect, as indeed he received, their influence on his behalf in the Casino (hence his strange comments to the croupiers and others), their potential desertion and even hostility (hence his words of foreboding), and his own early destruction . . . though he might have expected, as would we, that he should be allowed to collect the jewels first – which, for all we know, he did, only to have them stolen at his macabre demise. Also explained by my theory would be the nagging matter of the ticket of admission. Once understand that the Vicomte was under some form of supernatural guidance, and it is not difficult to conceive that the forces concerned to provide that guidance might arrange for him the procurement of a ticket and the placing of it in his pocket as an indication to him of whither he should next propel himself.

One posits, in short, that M. le Vicomte, being en route to collect the Rubies, was compelled to pause overnight in Aix before continuing on his mission; that the 'influence' or 'spirit' of the Roses (more than one, perhaps: did not the Vicomte refer at the tables to 'twins'?) guided him through the mechanism of the gratuitous ticket, into the gaming rooms; there allowed him to win a fortune; then, as he foretold, abandoned him; then finally destroyed him. Whether or not, when he left the Casino, he went to collect the Rubies and was then robbed of them – the motive for the murder – we cannot say; it seems more in the spirit of the Roses' past record that death should have been violent and sudden simply for the sake of being violent and sudden. But in either case, if my theory be true, what we can assert is this: that Clovis di Cannaregio Baudouin du Bourg de Maubeuge, last Vicomte du Touquet, having unexpectedly had restored to him the ownership if not the actual physical possession of the Roses of Picardie, came once more under the ancient Curse of his family, by which he was briefly exalted only to be pitilessly destroyed.

*concluded*

# II

# Gentlemen in Attendance

'Yet,' said Miss Wade, looking full upon them, 'you may be sure that there are men and women already on their road who have their business to do with *you*, and who will do it. Of a certainty they will do it. They may be coming hundreds, thousands, of miles over the sea there; they may be close at hand now; they may be coming, for anything you can do to prevent it, from the vilest sweepings of this very town.'

Charles Dickens: *Little Dorrit;*
Chapter 2

And a great load of rubbish it was, thought Jacquiz Helmut as he put down the *Paris Fiche* which contained the final instalment of The Case of the Dead Gamester. All that about the Curse – silly season stuff at its silliest. True, Marigold and her father Johannes would probably go along with it (at any rate to judge from what Marigold had been saying the other day, that she and Johannes believed that there was something very nasty in among the Roses), but then both of them, for all their intelligence, had a very silly streak.

And yet, thought Jacquiz Helmut, as he looked over the meadows, past the cows and the sedge to the Cam, and yet ... If that wretched scribbler in *Paris Fiche* had got his *facts* even half way right, one thing was quite apparent – that Clovis du Touquet believed that something special was running for him, that *something* was going to present him with a fortune or at least a competence. He had had a letter with a money order, and he had come south to Aix-en-Provence to seek whatever the letter promised him; furthermore, if the little girl in Lille had correctly reported what he'd said on receipt of the letter, and if the author of the article had correctly reported the little girl, Clovis had believed that there was urgency ('I must make haste') and he had believed that whatever was promised was beautiful and plural ('Oh the pretties').

And more: not only had Clovis believed that a treasure of 'pretties' was waiting for him in the south, he had also believed, if one might infer from the remarks attributed to him, that this treasure exerted a supernatural influence, part protective and part malign, on his affairs. Now, Jacquiz himself and any other sane man might know that any such belief was nonsense, but the fact that Clovis had held it almost certainly meant that Clovis equated the treasure that was waiting with the Rubies, the Roses of Picardie, which had been alleged for centuries to have exerted just such an influence on the affairs of his family with just such a combination of blessing and bane.

*Ergo*, thought Jacquiz Helmut, if one pared the thing down, if one stripped away all legendary and magical accretion, if one did not allow oneself to be dazed or diverted by the incidental melodramas of baccarat and murder, one was left with this plain deduction: there had been evidence, sufficient at any rate to convince Clovis, that the Rubies still existed. That he had been infatuated by the old myth of their powers did not necessarily mean that he had misjudged the new evidence of their survival; though gullible in the first respect, he could well have been shrewd enough in the second.

In sum: if Clovis had believed that the Rubies still existed, then very possibly they did still exist; and if they did still exist, then they were somewhere, perhaps somewhere near Aix-en-Provence, in any case *somewhere*, to be found. Which being so, why should not somebody start looking for them? And why should not that somebody (Marigold and Johannes notwithstanding) be himself?

But first he would need to know everything that was to be known, far more accurately than it had been purveyed by the French hack in *Paris Fiche*. He must go to his father-in-law, Johannes Faff, direct descendant of the seventeenth-century Fauvrelles of Montreuil (Faff being the inelegant but economic anglicization effected when the family came to Sandwich) and persuade him, reluctant as he might prove in any way to assist this enterprise, to rehearse once more the story of the errant Constance Fauvrelle, of how she had the Rubies of her lover who had them of the young widow Countess's naked corpse.

Balbo Blakeney, having contrived to commandeer Ton-ton's new copy of *Paris Fiche*, read the last instalment of The Case of the Dead Gamester at about the same time as Jacquiz Helmut. His reactions, since he was a Natural Philosopher and not an Historian, were rather different. Like Helmut, he was interested only in fact, but unlike Helmut he was prepared to recognize as such only what had been observed and sworn to by a trustworthy witness, allowing no validity to unconfirmed reports, however plausible. As he walked from Madame's establishment near the docks of Heracleion towards the centre of the city, where he was due to give an English lesson to one Kyrios Pandelios (an estate agent), Balbo listed the few facts in the case which he would regard as absolute and incontestable, and therefore to be accepted as evidence by himself as a scientist. They amounted to these: Clovis had died a year ago of a battering; his body had been found by the police in the Impasse Diane, near the Casino in Aix-en-Provence; and at the time his body was found he had on his person 142,000 francs in banknotes, which had been paid out to him by the cashier in the Casino the previous evening. For the first item he was prepared to accept the testimony of his own eyes, as he himself had identified the body; for the other two items he was prepared to accept the word of the police inspector who had informed him of them (thus officially corroborating what he had read in *Marseille Soir*) while accompanying him to the morgue. Even here, he felt, he was being somewhat less than scientific; and as for any allegations made in *Paris Fiche*, about lodging-keepers or their children, about croupiers or their attitudes, about the manner in which Clovis had wagered or what he had said while wagering, he simply dismissed them entirely. Some of them might well be true, of course, but how was one to tell which? The whole corpus of such allegation was beneath the notice of a scientist, and there was an end of it.

And so, he asked himself as he walked uphill from Madame's-by-the-Harbour, what could he deduce from the three facts which he did allow as proven? Only this: that Clovis had got lucky in the Casino and had later died in a brawl, the other party or parties to which had, for whatever reason, left his loot intact on his body. Certainly, there were questions to be asked, but not the questions which the writer in *Paris Fiche* was asking; and if the latter kind of questions were asked, they could be very curtly answered. 'Is it idle to propound a theory?' the hack inquired. Yes, was the answer to that, totally idle, unless he had facts to support it, which he did not. 'Is it vain to speculate . . .?' the man had continued. In Balbo's view it was always vain to speculate, and he had the ruin of his family's merchant bank to uphold him in that opinion. As for this article, then, it just did not begin to hold together; for even if one believed the hack's second-hand reports about what Clovis had said (*e.g.* about the 'twins' and so forth) one could not be sure that Clovis himself had meant it, and even if he had meant it that did not mean it was true. To conclude from a few alleged utterances, which might as well have been the result of drink or of a disordered sense of humour as of anything else, that Clovis believed he was protected or threatened by supra-natural powers, was merely wilful; so project from his supposed belief a whole revived apparatus of Jewels and Curses was positively dishonest.

Once and once only had Balbo and Clovis discussed the Rubies and the Curse, and that had been during the night of the May Ball at Lancaster which Clovis had attended with his intended in 1949. The subject had come up because Mlle de Stermaria had a ruby hanging from either ear.

'Some say they are unlucky,' Clovis had said at supper. 'Certainly those of my family were supposed to be. Lucky too, of course.'

'Do you believe in any of that?' Balbo had asked.

'In the Rubies, the Roses of Picardie, of course. We know they existed – and are long since gone for ever.'

'What about the Curse?' said Mlle de Stermaria.

'As with all families, there were good times, and bad; as with all great families, there were conquests and catastrophes. And that is all.'

A very sensible remark, Balbo had thought at the time. Of course, it had been made twenty-five years ago, and Clovis, much affected by drink and adversity, might have changed his mind on the subject before he died, might have come to believe that the rubies had, after all, bestowed both bane and boon on his family and that they might, even now, be recoverable. But whatever Clovis had or had not believed – here was the nub – made no difference to reality. Even if Clovis had believed with all his heart and all his brain that he was on his way to collect the Roses, now at last to be restored to his line, this belief in itself, unsupported, that was to say, by proven fact, meant nothing. It mined no Rubies, conjured no Curses, magicked no cards. Clovis had been lucky at the tables, and had then been killed, and that, as he himself had put it twenty-five years ago, was all.

What a pity, thought Balbo, as he walked into the little square in which Kyrios Pandelios lived, that the 142,000 francs had been snapped up by the creditors. What a pity Clovis did not live long enough to stand a few treats; he always liked splashing it round if he had it. He might even have paid me back what he owed me, thought Balbo, looking with pleasure at the carved Venetian well-head (vine and acanthus) in the centre of the square. Some hope, God save his rotten soul, thought Balbo, as he approached the barley-sugar columns and ogee arch of the Kyrios Pandelios' front door.

'Ah, it is you, old trout,' called the Kyrios Pandelios from a window above. 'Push on the portal, my dear one, and it will open sesame – then I will find the bottle of rot-gut and we shall 'ave a bloody great snort.'


'What can I possibly tell you,' said Johannes Faff to Jacquiz Helmut, 'that I haven't told you before?'

They were walking by the narrow canal that ran under the southern rampart of Sandwich. Small boys sat whispering on the shady bank, their fishing rods dipping down to motionless floats. On the far side of the canal some cricketers crept heavily over scurfy yellow grass, while amid languid applause a ginger-haired youth with huge shoulders and calves approached the wicket in dirty pads.

'You *know* the story,' said Johannes Faff. 'I have *told* you the story. You know what happened to the Rubies until the time when they came into the hands of my ten-times-Great Aunt Constance Fauvrelle, and you know what happened then. She married an army contractor, Louis Comminges, who took off her and the jewels both. Since he was a Catholic, her Huguenot family would have no truck with it, and any chance of reconciliation or communication was finally finished with when the Fauvrelles moved over here to Sandwich a few months later. The Fauvrelles, soon to be Faffs, neither knew nor cared what happened to Constance and her pork-broker, or to their descendants, then or ever. What more can I possibly say?'

The ginger-haired boy opened his shoulders and hit the ball up in a huge hyperbola which descended sheer as a rainbow into the canal. The floats swayed briefly in the wash and then once more were still. A reluctant fieldsman fished the ball out with a net. Jacquiz looked over the field, to where the ginger boy lounged on his bat by the stumps listening to the congratulations from the pavilion. The wicket-keeper was saying something to the boy, who smiled awkwardly out of a face that could have been Apollo's had it not been just too heavily jowled. God, to be young and strong and beautiful, thought Jacquiz, oh God, to be applauded on a summer's afternoon.

'What more can I possibly say?' repeated Johannes Faff.

Jacquiz looked for a last second at the big-boned smiling face on the cricket field, turned back to his father-in-law, took three deep breaths, in and out, in order to collect himself, and then said:

'The circumstances of Constance's departure. Did she give her family any warning? Or did they just find an empty bed? Did she leave nothing behind, Johannes, which might have hinted to them where she was going? After all, they knew with whom she had gone.'

'Knowing that, they wanted to know nothing else ... even if she told them. They put her from their minds.'

'Did she correspond, afterwards, with *nobody* in Montreuil?'

'What if she did?' said Johannes Faff, stone-walling.

'Her correspondent . . . the descendants of her correspondent . . . might have some clue as to where she went.'

'After three hundred years? Why should they – or you – be interested in where Constance Fauvrelle absconded to, three hundred years ago?'

'Because she took the Roses of Picardie with her,' said Helmut patiently.

They had turned away from the canal and were walking down a street, little wider than a path, on one side of which were two long, gabled warehouses, on the other a row of neatly kept and warped little cottages. Faff walked a few paces ahead of Helmut, in silence.

'There might be a trail,' continued Helmut. 'Constance and her husand went to such a place, their children moved on somewhere else, and their children . . . You see?'

'The concept is hardly novel,' said Faff. 'And you assume, of course, that where the trail ends you will find the Rubies?'

'I assume that at some stage one might at least find out what has happened to them.'

Faff did not answer this. He struck across a road, went down a passage to the left of what looked like a disused meeting house, and led Helmut out on to a piled wharf, where he stood looking down at a barge which was comfortably decomposing into the River Stour.

'What do you want with these Rubies?' said Faff.

'I want to find something rare and beautiful which has been lost. I want people to know about my discovery and to be grateful to me for it.'

'I see. They say, Jacquiz,' said Faff very gently, 'that those jewels are best left alone.'

'*They say*!' said Helmut. 'They say the first thing that comes into their heads.'

'It is sometimes a true thing, Jacquiz. I wouldn't want you to be . . . made a fool of; or worse.'

'I can't be made a bigger fool than your daughter has already made of me.'

Faff shrugged and looked, for a moment, sad.

'At least she has made no worse of you. Those Rubies . . .'

'What about them?'

'Let me put it like this. They have a very long history and no one knows where it began.'

'It began in the earth,' said Helmut.

'You seem determined to misunderstand me this afternoon.'

'And you to misunderstand me, Johannes. Once and for all, I am not to be put off with silly stories about curses and calamities. Have you never in your life heard the word "co-incidence"? If those jewels appear to have exerted an influence, malignant or otherwise, it is simply due to that. I want to find the necklace, Johannes. If you can help me with any information about Constance Fauvrelle and her husband, Louis Comminges, good. If you can't or won't, so be it. What do you say?'

'I say,' said Faff, walking along the wharf and peering into the pathetic inwards of the barge beneath, 'that if you are so determined, you deserve your own way. You have been warned, and you have refused to listen, and you deserve your own way. So I will do what I can in order to assist you to get it. Now then.' He jerked his head up and stabbed his face into Helmut's. 'I have records of my family which date back to well before our emigration from Montreuil. If my memory is true to me, there are two references, and only two, to the matter of Constance' marriage and departure. The first is a scathing denunciation and an excommunication *in perpetuum*. The second is less melodramatic, it is, one might say, jejune. It is this latter which may interest you, Jacquiz, and if you will be so good as to return with me to my house you may examine it for as long as you please.'


'You looks knackered,' said the Kyrios Pandelios as he ushered Balbo into his sitting-room over the ogee arch. 'You really is creased.'

Pandelios adored slang; indeed it was chiefly to learn new

slang that he had engaged Balbo as his tutor. There was a pretence, kept up before the Kyria Pandelios, that Balbo was teaching her husband the English idiom of estate agency; but since the Kyria (a bulbous little creature everlastingly encased in black weeds on account of uncles and cousins who seemed to die weekly) was very seldom present at the tutorials, these consisted almost entirely of an exchange of dubious anecdotes dressed in a vernacular, part gamey and part puerile, which Balbo had dredged up from memories of school and the Army.

'Thou art really pooped,' said Pandelios, setting a huge drink of neat ouzo in front of Balbo. 'Just suck that juice down.'

'I've walked all the way up from the harbour,' Balbo said.

'You horny old toad, thou. You bin to that cathouse once more.'

Balbo nodded furtively.

'No come to be shy about it. As I've said you before, I was often wont (real stylish, that "wont" and thank you for teaching me), yes, I was often wont to whizz down there for a quick shag myself. I only gives it up when German Momma died.'

'German Momma?'

'So called, my dear one, because she makes a very warm welcome to German troops in the war. Very few whores in Crete then, and those there are won't go with sodding German pig-shit, but German Momma, Hera Andreatos her real name was, getting on in years even then – German Momma, she opens herself up to all the German Army and piles up so much stuff (not cash, old brick, but tinned goods and cigarettes and booze) that when she sell it after the Germans piss off she get rich enough to begin her own great big knocking shop with sluts she import from Athens and Italy and even France.'

'Why didn't they get her for collaboration?'

'Oh, she was cute enough to keep herself in with the resistance. Now and then, old bean, she pass on information or help them catch an officer with his knickers down. Besides, every mans jack of us likes to go to German Momma's, the ephor and the nomarch and every mans else. Then she kick the bucket, poor old sow, four, five years ago now, and leave her bizwhacks to Madame her niece from Lecce, and I give up going for old time's sake, being sad for German Momma and too being buggered up with my fat cow of a wife, who forces me do boom-boom on her three times weekly, which I cannot oblige her, being now older, when I shot my jolly lot up some piece of meat in Madame's.'

'I see.' Balbo took a drink. Pandelios was clearly in a chatty mood today; so much the better for Balbo. All he need do was prompt his pupil with an occasional comment or question and he would be off again for minutes at a time.

But this was not to be that evening, because the door now opened and Kyria Pandelios waddled in. This was unusual but not unprecedented; what was quite definitely unique was that the Kyria was wearing a light blue dress with white spots instead of a black sort of sack, and was looking extremely angry. Her customary mode, when consorting with her husband before Balbo, was submissive, almost grovelling; but now Balbo was getting his first view of the kind of spirit which the Kyria doubtless deployed in private from time to time, possibly (Balbo thought to himself with glee) when compelling her reluctant Kyrios to render his thrice-weekly tribute of 'boom-boom'.

'Dirty swine,' said the Kyria in Greek. 'Barbarous, money-grubbing, blood-sucking, child-starving swine.'

'Please to speak in English in front of our guest, my darling one,' said the Kyrios Pandelios, retaining a commendable ratio of composure.

'You are one turdos,' said the Kyria, more or less complying.

'What 'as come to you, old girl? Calling such names and all got up in that so tarty a dress.'

'It is the name day of Andreas,' screeched the Kyria. 'I 'ave been to the tea party.'

'Andreas is her brother,' interpolated Pandelios for Balbo's benefit.

'Andreas is 'alf cuckoo with worry and sadness, and it is all your fault.'

'How so, my life?'

'Andreas,' said the Kyria to Balbo, 'is the foreman of the workers employed by the American Professore Ezekial Truss on the excavations. So Andreas make good money, he feeds 'is wife and kiddies proper, he repairs 'is roof before the winter's rains.'

'I married a great deal under me,' Pandelios explained blandly to Balbo. 'My wife's family, the Kommingi, must take menial tasks. They are all — what is that word you tell me? — muck. All muck,' he repeated with relish.

'Not muck,' yelled the Kyria, still addressing herself to Balbo. 'Skilled men who know old things. In the excavations, in the museums, in the ruins, in the churches — everywhere you will find the Kommingi. There is one cousin who make guide-talk at Delphi and one more at Tiryns. There is one brother who is caretaker of mosaic church at Nicopolis — and there is here Andreas, who lead the team of workers for the excavation of Professore Truss. And now Professore Truss say that next year he cometh not because' — she turned on Pandelios like a corpulent shrike — 'this piece of pig-crap 'as sold the land to the nomarch who make build one fucking great 'ouse right bang slap on Andreas his excavations. Bleeding sod,' she said, waving a pudgy fist in Pandelios's face.

'Where did you learn such expressive English?' was all that Balbo could think of to say.

'This clever cunt, 'e show 'is off to me,' raged the Kyria, 'and now I show it back.'

'My darling one,' said Pandelios, 'I do not sell that land. It is not mine. It is Petros Vlassos, old sweetie pie, who sell the land to the nomarch.'

' 'E sell it through you. 'E not sell it without you advice. 'E sell it for two millions of drachmas and you take one 'undred tousant. So Professore Ezekiel Truss, 'e cometh not again, and next year Andreas is starving and his wee ones. I shit myself on your rotten head, you greedy ponce,' said the Kyria Pandelios, and flounced vibrantly out of the room, slamming the door so hard that Balbo's ouzo slopped up and down in his glass.

'Cri-*keee*, old scout,' said Pandelios. 'She is hot under the combinations, I think. The Kommingi, they think such great shakes of each other and are eager for the honour of their house.'

'Kommingi,' said Balbo. 'Where have I heard that name?'

'Like she says, they are everywhere with antique things. Museums, castles, everywhere. They are the mans who takes five drachmas and gives you the ticket, or follows you around so you don't nick nothing. Low peoples, for all I married one.'

'No,' said Balbo, 'it wasn't anything to do with museums.'

'What wasn't, my dear one?'

'The connection in which I heard the name. And yet . . . antique things . . . Is the family Cretan?'

'You 'eard 'er. They spread all over, cousins here, brothers there. Low peoples, always getting the boot. She say they have bad luck. I say they 'ave stinking dirty tempers – like you saw 'er just now. She say they 'ave been rich, rich way back in Kerkyra, Sicilia, Italia, way, way back. 'Er brother – the one who sweeps out the church at Nicopolis – 'e fills 'er 'ead with rubbish when he comes here, what he reads in books, that they were long ago rich merchants with great 'ouses and gold and jewels, but something shitty 'appen and they leave their 'ouses and float south. But if you ask me, old fruity, they was always low peoples, the Kommingi, and the nearest they ever 'ad to a merchant was her uncle who sold sausages in Volos and got slapped in the chokey for mincing up dead dog with the pork.'

'Kommingi,' said Balbo, remembering the mingled smell of feet and stale Greek cigarettes in Madame's ante-room and the slippery feel in his hands of *Paris Fiche*. 'How very slow I'm getting. Simply the Greek equivalent of Comminges.'

'And just who are the Comminges when they're at 'ome?' asked the Kyrios Pandelios.

Since there were still twenty minutes of the lesson to run, Balbo told him.

'Montreuil?' said Marigold Helmut. 'Why do you want to go there?'

'Montreuil's just the beginning,' said Jacquiz. 'It could be a very long trip. You like trips, that's one of the few things about you of which I can be certain. Do you want to come or not? I'm going in any case.'

'A long trip? Like how long?'

'Two or three months. Even more, perhaps. I don't know.'

'But the Michaelmas term starts in a month from now.'

'I'm due a Sabbatical Year. No one will mind if I take it at short notice. No one will miss me. As you're so fond of pointing out, I'm only a figure of fun.'

Marigold looked his long angular frame up and then down, and pouted.

'But why Montreuil?' she insisted.

'Because it's a pleasant place, only forty kilometres or so from Calais, which means a nice easy drive for the first afternoon off the boat. Because there's a decent hotel which serves excellent food – the Homard Cancalaise is the best thing to be had this side of Rouen. And because,' said Jacquiz 'there is, or may be, somebody there whom I want to talk to.'

'Who, for Christ's sake?'

'Name of Vibrot.'

'Him or her?'

'I don't know. All I know is what the account book said.'

'The *account book?*'

'Kept by Guillaume Fauvrelle – an ancestor of yours who brought your family over from Montreuil to Sandwich. Johannes showed it to me. On October the fourteenth 1652, Guillaume paid ten louis to a certain Widow Vibrot, "mistress of the lodging house within the castle gate, in consideration of monies owed to her by Richard Van Hoek the painter, now deceased, sometime betrothed of my daughter Constance *cui parcat deus nam non egoment* – whom may God pardon for I will not". Rather a dramatic entry to make in a mere account book, and it doesn't stop there. For half a page or so the accounts turn into a kind of diary – Guillaume taking the chance to get it all off his chest, I suppose.

It turns out that *la veuve* Vibrot had been rather a friend of Constance, whom she often saw when she came to visit her fiancé Van Hoek in the widow's lodging house. Then Van Hoek died of the plague, owing la Vibrot ten louis, for which la Vibrot later applied to Guillaume on account of the family connection. Constance had previously promised that she would make the debt good on the dead Van Hoek's behalf, but apparently she'd gone off with her pork-contractor, Comminges, so quickly that she'd overlooked the matter. What she *had* done, however, was write to la Vibrot, from a posting house in Sens, to apologize for this and also to request la Vibrot to go to her father for the money as her new husband allowed her none. Guillaume, as he records, paid up in order to preserve the family's reputation for honouring its promises, although it was really no affair of his and he was soon to leave Montreuil in any case. He then says one thing more. In her letter about the debt, Constance had said that she would write further to la Vibrot, the widow being her only friend left in Montreuil, in order to let her know where she was and how she was going on with Comminges, of whom she already had grave doubts. She wanted, you see, to think that *someone* in her old life would know what became of her. So, said la Vibrot to Guillaume after he'd paid her the ten louis, would Guillaume like to be kept informed when and if more letters arrived from his daughter? Guillaume searched his heart and then said no: *quocumque vel ipse ibo vel illa ibit, mihi et meis interiit*— whithersoever I shall go or she shall go, for me and mine she is dead and buried. And on that happy note the entry in the account book closes. But you see what I'm getting at?'

'Yes,' said Marigold. 'There may have been more letters to mother Vibrot from Constance, whether Guillaume wanted to know of them or not. If there were, they may still be in the possession of the Vibrot family, because in France people keep things for a long time in case they turn out to be useful later. And if there are any such letters, we may learn where Constance and her husband finally settled.'

'You sound quite interested.'

74

'I am.'

'But you said, only the other day, that I shouldn't follow this business up.'

'I meant it. I also said I was fascinated by the whole thing. If you've made up your mind to go on with this hunt, then I propose to make the best of it. I propose to come with you and enjoy the trip – trips, as you rightly said, being about my best things ever – and put my mind to it and help you all I can.'

'Marigold. I'm so glad you're coming, Marigold.'

'But just remember this,' said Marigold. 'I have warned you against it, and so, unless I'm much mistaken, has my father. So if something nasty comes out of a cupboard and starts gobbling you up, don't blame me – and don't expect me to hang about trying to rescue you. I *am* interested, Jacquiz, and I *am* coming with you, but my priority is me, as that man Amis is always saying, and if anything starts to smell too strongly for my comfort, then I'm off like a fart down a tube.'

Well and why not? thought Balbo. The whole thing was a Chimaera hunt if ever there was one, but if Kyrios Pandelios was prepared to subsidize it, in however modest style, why not?

'There could be something in it, old bean,' Pandelios had said after hearing the story of the Roses and the part played in it by the Comminges, 'so why not go and see? After all, you have nothing better to do, and you need a change. If you find fucknothing, you find only what you expect and are none the worse for it; and if you do rumble the Rubies, you could be stinking rich.'

'I've no money for gadding about,' Balbo had said.

'I was coming to that. I think God 'as made me some signs. First, 'e allows me to make a 'undred thousand drachs out of that fool of a Vlassos, who should only 'ave paid fifty. And secondly a quarrel with my she-camel of a wife has accidentally revealed to me that she, as a Kommingi, may be descended from these Comminges you talk of. Her brother at Nicopolis can put you on the trail, back through time and space, so that you can make the journey of the family in reverse. Sooner or later you must reach a place, and be told of a time, at both of which the Comminges were known still to possess these Roses of Picardie. Then you may find out what has become of them.'

'I'm still no nearer to having the money for the trip.'

'I told you, I was coming to that. Since God 'as made me these signs, I will support you. You shall not go first class in luxury cruisers, but go you shall.'

'I'd never be able to pay you back.'

'Oh, but you might. If you find the jewels, you shall give me half the proceeds.'

'Even if I find them, that doesn't make them mine.'

'That depends on who has them, my dear one. For all we know they are in a hole in the ground. They'd be yours then all right. In any case, if you find them, the story, the fact of the discovery, will be worth money.'

'*If* I find them.'

'Don't just sit there like a dying duck. Get off your botty, my old banana, and go and look.'

All right, thought Balbo, six hours later in the Bar Ariadne; I'll go. As Pandelios says, I haven't got anything else on. It'll be a change from rotting to death in Heracleion, and it is, I suppose, just conceivable that something might come of it. I shall have a purpose, however scatty; for the first time in years I shall have some kind of goal. And then it will be fun travelling round the scattered Kommingi, while looking at their museums or whatever will be very much to my taste. I have never, for example, seen Nicopolis and the 'mosaic church' there, of which Kyria's brother is caretaker, is an obvious and inviting first port of call.

Balbo finished his cognac and called for another – Metaxas Five Star instead of the usual Three Star, to celebrate his decision. There was nothing to delay him, he thought. Pandelios had promised him a sum in drachmai for the Greek part of the expedition and 300 dollars, out of a highly illicit hoard, for use beyond Greek waters. Pandelios, as he had found before, was a man of his word; Balbo could simply collect the money in the morning and go.

But stay, he told himself: might it not be that the offer had been made out of pity, that Pandelios, having been presented with a flimsy excuse by all this waffle about Comminges and Kommingi, was merely socking him a holiday under pretence of making a business deal? Balbo called for another brandy, drank it in one, moved from his table to the bar, and ordered another.

'Get a hold on yourself,' he said aloud; 'you can't pass this up.' As he drank down the brandy he thought of the fetid little room which was waiting for him, of the cracked and crusted basin with its slimy plug-hole and its one narrow, dribbling tap. 'You *must* get out for a time,' he said, 'even if the offer is mere charity, you must accept. You no longer have a choice in such matters.'

'Kyrie?' said the man behind the bar.

'Cognac,' said Balbo.

'I think that . . . the Kyrios is not quite himself. Perhaps he should go away now?'

'Indeed he should go away,' said Balbo. 'One more cognac first.'

'One more, Kyrie: the last.'

Greeks hated drunks, Balbo thought as he swallowed his Metaxas; how right they were. Drunks were dangerous and disgusting, always apt to fall or vomit or fight. What had turned him into that kind of drunk? Boredom? Disappointment? Failure as a serious scientist, a frustrated hankering after the arts? It was too late to worry about that. At least he was now a man with a mission, with *something* to look forward to in the morning; so now he would finish his cognac and pay for it and be a man and go. No one should accuse him of hanging about where he wasn't wanted. Besides, he had important things to do. He had a bag to pack and a journey to make, a journey to the rainbow's end.

'What's your programme when we get to Montreuil?' asked Marigold Helmut.

'Check the bookings at the Hôtel du Château, leave the bags and garage the car, walk round the ramparts, take a nap, then order Homard Cancalaise for dinner.'

With this Jacquiz put the Continental Rolls into gear (he had insisted on gears when he bought it) and drove on to the Dover–Calais car ferry.

'You don't seem exactly ... urgent,' said Marigold, giggling.

'The thing to do, on this kind of expedition, is not to rush round hysterically but to establish a steady speed and stick to it. When I check our bookings, I shall ask Madame the Proprietress, who is a very local lady, to find out for me whether any descendants or connections of the Vibrot family survive, and where they live. By dinner time she will have a list ready, and we can go visiting tomorrow morning. By lunch time tomorrow we shall have heard what the Vibrots have to say and we shall know where we must go next. We can then decide whether to start in the afternoon or to stay another night in Montreuil to try Madame's celebrated Rognons à Trois Moutardes.'

'Couldn't we have them for lunch?'

'Too heavy for lunch. We should have to stay another night for them.'

'Isn't all that rather smug?' said Marigold as she followed Jacquiz up the stairs from the car-deck. 'Aren't you taking rather a lot for granted?'

'You mean Madame may not have any Homards or Rognons?'

'I mean, suppose Madame may not have any Vibrots. Or they may not have anything to tell us.'

'We know that Richard Van Hoek, Constance's betrothed, lodged "within the castle gate". We shall go and look in the castle.'

'And suppose we draw a blank there too?'

'I have several more ideas for getting on to the trail, which I shall explain to you as and when it may be necessary. The thing to remember is that we must neither hasten on the one hand nor despair on the other. If the Rubies are still there, they will wait for us.'

'Are you sure no one else is interested?'

'If someone is, then sooner or later we shall encounter him *en route*. We can deal with him then.'

'Suppose he's finished the *route* and got to the loot before us?'

'Then we shall simply follow him until we see what we should do. Time and chance will tell us. Meanwhile, first things first. Be a good girl and go to the duty free shop. Buy two bottles of the best cognac on offer and two of white whisky.'

'Money?' said Marigold, who was rather impressed by this new Jacquiz, the suave and confident commander of their expedition.

'Here. Keep five hundred francs for yourself. And I think I should also like a large flask of eau de cologne de Monsieur Givenchy.'


Since Balbo's one suitcase, a relic of more prosperous days, was large and leather and therefore exceedingly heavy even if he did not put much into it, he decided to take a taxi down to the harbour. But although he was starting his journey so elegantly, this was not the way, he reminded himself firmly, that he meant to go on. He had 3500 drachmai which Pandelios had given him and 500 more of his own, the aggregate being worth about sixty pounds; and for use when he left Greece he had only Pandelios's 300 dollars. If he was to remain away for more than a very few days, he would have to pig it.

Well, he told himself as he paid off the taxi on the quay, he was used to pigging it by now, and it would be a nice change to pig it somewhere other than in a greasy third-floor room near to leeward, in the wind which normally prevailed, of Heracleion's abattoir. He showed his ticket, heaved his suitcase up the gang plank (cursing his thin feeble arms and the lack of stature which caused him to scuff the beautiful leather against the sharp angles of the steps), shoved it under the bench which ran round the second-class lounge, and sat down above it on the square foot of thin cush that must serve him as sole berth for the twenty-four hours which it would take the boat to reach the Peloponnesian port of Patras. From Patras there would be, he imagined, a bus to Previsa by the mouth of the Gulf of Actium, in Previsa there would be, he supposed, a gamma class hotel to suit his pocket or even with luck a delta, in the delta hotel someone would know, he hoped, the cheapest way of travelling the five miles to the ancient site of Nicopolis, and somewhere on the site, in a shack near a long-abandoned monastery, he would find – or so the Kyrios Pandelios had informed him – the Kyria's brother, Stavros Kommingi, who lived alone, guarding the fine mosaics on the broken floor of the windy basilica, and dreaming of his ancestors, rich men furnished with ability and splendid in their generation.

# III

# A Beast in View

Quis est hic,
Qui pulsat ad ostium,
Noctis rumpens somnium
Me vocat? o
    virginum pulcherrima,
Soror, coniunx,
    gemma splendissima,
Cito surgens
    aperi, dulcissima.
        Peter Damian: *De Beata Maria Virgine*

Who is this
That knockest at the gate,
Breaking the sleep of the night?
That crieth
O of all virgins fairest,
Sister, bride,
Gem that is rarest.
Rise, O rise,
Open, sweetest.
            The above lines of Peter Damian,
                translated by Helen Waddell.

# 1. Cloister with Yewtree

'It's going too well,' said Marigold Helmut, 'it's going much too pat.'

Jacquiz took a large mouthful of his lobster Cancalaise, sniffed at his Montrachet '47, sipped it, gulped it, drank the lot of it, and then remarked:

'There's no reason why things shouldn't go pat. They sometimes do.'

'For a bit. Then they go sour. The patter they went, the sourer they go.'

'Nothing very special has happened. Madame the Proprietress has told us that there *is* a branch of the Vibrot family living here, as we suspected there might be. A man and wife, as was always probable. Caretakers of the Youth Hostel inside the Castle – an office comparable to keeping "lodgings within the Castle Gate", which is what the *veuve* Vibrot did in the seventeenth century. I perceive a decent continuity here, nothing more. Nothing particularly pat, no necessary prospect of anything's turning sour. What's your worry, Marigold?'

'You. You annoy me when you're smug.'

'I'm not smug, simply logical. An informed guess has proved true. So far, so good. For the rest ... we shall see tomorrow morning when we wait on M'sieur and Madame Vibrot at the Youth Hostel within the Castle Gate.'

'I wonder.'

'What do you wonder?'

'How soon things will start turning sour. Like your stomach for instance, if you go on eating and drinking like this. About a pound of fresh foie gras, and now that lobster in a sauce of royal purple. You might give me some more of that wine.'

'With pleasure, if you'll only stop complaining.'

'I never felt happier in my life. That's the trouble. I know that if I enjoy all this too much, it'll go wrong. So I keep pretending not to enjoy it, so that the gods won't grudge it to me and start spoiling it. That's all I really meant. Nice Jacquiz. Can I have *Crêpes Suzettes*?'

'Do you think the gods would approve of that?'

'I didn't think *you* bothered about them.'

'More than you realize. This is my last chance, Marigold, my last chance to . . . to *make it*, as the undergraduates say nowadays. In the circumstances, one must bear oneself with great caution. But I don't think the gods will grudge us food and drink – certainly not a few pancakes. *Crêpes Suzettes pour deux, Madame*,' Jacquiz called to the hovering Proprietress. 'You are sure about the couple Vibrot?'

'*Mais oui, M'sieur*. They are there in our Castle of Montreuil since many years, and others of the family before them. However . . . there is one thing of which M'sieur and Madame should be warned.'

'Indeed, Madame?'

'Indeed, M'sieur. They have an imbecile son.'

'Here we go,' said Marigold. 'Poor child.'

'The "child" is nearly fifty years, Madame, and will probably be visible when you visit the Vibrots, as it is their amiable custom to employ him in trivial tasks about the Castle. Now then, M'sieur, *est-ce que vous voulez commander les Crêpes Suzettes pour deux?*'

'Yes,' said Marigold. 'One clearly needs ample nourishment for what is in store tomorrow morning.'


What was in store tomorrow morning was, in the first place, rain, and in the second place a notice on the Castle Gate announcing that the precinct would be closed for two weeks for works and restorations.

'*That* was something that know-all Proprietress didn't know,' said Marigold, 'though the hotel's not a furlong away. What are we to do, Jacquiz? Sit about for the next fortnight eating fresh foie gras and lobster until they open up?'

'Don't be silly. Of course there's a way of getting in to see the Vibrots.'

'Find it quickly, there's a sweetheart. I'd forgotten how penetrating northern French rain can be – it goes right through you like their voices.'

Jacquiz yanked at a bell handle to the right of the gate. A panel slid back; a ribald face opened its mouth, revealed three widely separated teeth along with most of their roots, cackled, and slid the panel shut.

'The imbecile's doing sentinel,' said Marigold. 'I hope he's getting as wet as I am.'

Jacquiz took a ten-franc note from his pocket and yanked once more at the bell. The panel opened again. Jacquiz waved his note at the ribald face, which cackled with happiness and disappeared. A wicket in the right-hand half of the Great Gate sprang back to welcome them. As soon as they were through it, a torso like a barrel carrying the ribald face on top, supported by two stubby legs beneath and wrapped in a kind of mackintosh hold-all, bowled up to them, shot out an arm through an invisible aperture in the holdall to snatch Jacquiz' bank note, and led the way, at a rapid lurch, up a very muddy path, to the door of a small lodge which was situated some fifty yards beyond the gate and appeared to be a recently built addition to a far older wing that extended from the Gate House.

Inside the lodge was a rack of dirty, crinkled postcards, three glass bottles of green and pink boiled sweets, and a large notice on a stand behind the counter announcing that in no circumstances would anyone be admitted to the Castle less than an hour before its official time of closure. Also behind the counter, standing shoulder to shoulder with the notice as if to reinforce its ordinance, was a woman with no chin and the pointed snout of a swordfish: Madame Vibrot.

'You are the English,' she proclaimed. 'Madame the Proprietress of the hotel has telephoned that you are coming. That is why Auguste here was waiting for you. Otherwise, no one is admitted during the restorations.'

'What is being restored?' asked Jacquiz politely.

'Nothing is being restored. The students who have stayed in the Hostel during the summer have blocked the conveniences with throwing down rubbish. The conveniences are being cleared.'

'Why close the Castle,' said Marigold, 'just for that?'

'Because the law says it must be closed when there are restorations.'

'But you just said that nothing is being restored. It's only that the conveniences—'

'—The workmen insist on the work being called "restorations". Otherwise they would feel foolish, clearing conveniences and perhaps being seen to do so by the public. So not to *épater* the foolish workers we are having "restorations" and the Castle is therefore closed by law from this morning when the workers at last consent to begin. What is it you want, M'sieur?'

Jacquiz started to explain about Constance Fauvrelle and how the last person she was known to have been in touch with was (very probably) a distant ancestor of Madame's husband, M'sieur Vibrot.

'If of 'im, then of me,' said Madame. 'We are cousins.'

Auguste chortled.

'*Tais-toi*,' snarled Madame.

Auguste started to cry. Snot ran from his nose in streams. He bent his head down towards the mackintosh hold-all, in which he was still encased, and tried to wipe his nose on it. Marigold nudged him and found him a handkerchief. Auguste looked at the handkerchief uncertainly, until Marigold applied another to her own nose and blew it, whereupon her pupil imitated her with noisy gusto, examined the contents of the handkerchief immediately afterwards, and whimpered with pleasure. Madame pursed her lips as at an example of wicked waste, and turned to Jacquiz.

'So what do you wish of me?' she inquired.

Was there still by any chance any knowledge within the family of the seventeenth-century Veuve Vibrot's connection with Constance Fauvrelle, or any surviving example of their correspondence?

'Yes ... in a sort, M'sieur,' said Madame Vibrot indifferently. 'You shall hear.'

Auguste looked at her reproachfully. She moved along the counter, opened a door, and called into vacancy:

'Auguste.'

The *père* Auguste appeared instantly, jerking through the doorway like a doll propelled from the interior of some ingenious toy. He looked flimsy and benign, with a thin, silken beard, for all his age like Christ talking to the little children in a cheap coloured picture book.

'The letters of Constance Fauvrelle, Auguste,' Madame stated with malicious aplomb.

Auguste *fils* shifted unhappily. His father cleared his throat and began to explain mournfully and with no immediate relevance that certain exceedingly simple tasks in the administration of the Youth Hostel were assigned to 'that boy there'. (More unhappy fidgeting from Auguste junior.) Among other things, 'that boy there' was entrusted with the care of the lavatories. On an occasion early in September, finding that the stock of newspapers in the lavatories was exhausted, 'that boy there' had been in a quandary about servicing the conveniences and had lost his head.

At this stage in the narrative, Auguste minor began to sniff vibrantly, but desisted when encouraged by a smile of sympathy from Marigold.

'Surely,' she said, 'you could have sent him to the chemist to buy the – er – commodity required?'

'Prudence, *chère Madame*,' grated la Vibrot, 'does not sanction the provision of luxuries for students.'

Marigold crumpled but was somewhat restored by a reciprocal grin from Auguste *fils*.

'In any case,' Monsieur Vibrot pursued, 'that boy there, being in his way exceedingly conscientious, was determined to provide for his clients. He therefore went to the bureau in my office where he found some large sheets of paper which he thought would serve.'

The point of the story was now becoming clearer.

'Large, very thick sheets?' Jacquiz said.

Auguste *fils* nodded repentance.

'Sheets that had been written on?'

Auguste *fils* nodded with infinite sadness, though smiled on once more by Marigold.

'In short, the letters of which you speak,' yapped Madame. 'It is they wherewith the students have blocked the conveniences last month. Auguste has destroyed them,' she intoned, her eyes shining with pleasure and spite. 'So you see, we cannot oblige you.'

'A pity,' said Jacquiz. 'They were valuable.'

'No. There is everywhere in France old letters – two, three hundred years old – family letters. Who cares now?'

'Then why had you kept your family's?'

' '*E* kept 'em,' said Madame pointing at Monsieur, 'because he is a sentimental fool.'

'Then you read them?' said Jacquiz to Vibrot. 'Can you remember what was in them?'

' '*E* never read 'em,' scowled Madame. 'The writing was too difficult. Lines crossing, so.'

She crossed the first two fingers of her left hand with two of her right.

'So you looked at them too?' said Marigold. 'Can't you remember *anything* which you read?'

'She cannot read nothing,' said Monsieur in gentle tones, as if pronouncing a blessing. 'She was a child in the Big War in Arras. Bad place then. Nobody teach her nothing . . . except what the soldiers teach her.'

'Pish,' said la Vibrot poisonously. 'You were glad enough of the money when you come home to marry me.'

'If it had only been money you got from them,' said Vibrot serenely, 'I should not have complained. I do not complain much as it is. It would be interesting to hear what little Auguste would say . . . if he could say it.'

Little Auguste cackled. Marigold winced.

'Perhaps,' said Jacquiz soothingly, 'when the workmen

have cleared the sheets out of the pipes, I could still manage to read them?'

'No,' said Monsieur. 'In the beginning I try to clear the pipes myself. I got out two, three, four sheets – I cannot tell how many because all are one rotten lump that is parting to pieces.'

'Then that's that,' said Marigold. 'I knew things were going too pat.'

As they made their way to the gate, accompanied by M. Vibrot, Auguste *fils* came up behind. He plucked at Marigold's sleeve and made soft mewing noises, as of condolence or love. Then he opened his mouth and agitated his three teeth at her, more and more energetically, while at the same time he gestured with one hand in the air, like a child waving a sparkler.

'He knows something,' said Marigold. 'He wants to tell us something.'

'What can he know?' said Jacquiz. 'The poor brute understands nothing.'

'I think he understood quite a bit just now. He followed the trend of the discussion. He knew he'd done wrong, putting those letters to be used in the bog.'

M. Vibrot opened the wicket in the gate. Marigold lingered, looking at his son, whom M. Vibrot now tried to shoo away. But 'that boy there' continued to wave his hand in circles and zigzags through the air.

'It's no good,' said Marigold. 'I can't get the message.'

She raised her hand in farewell and stepped through the wicket. As Jacquiz followed, she heard Auguste *fils* choke violently with what she knew was disappointment.

'Lunch,' said Jacquiz.

'And then?'

'Time to make another plan.'

She nodded miserably, still hearing the choke of sorrow and frustration that rose from the far side of the wicket.

'Right,' said Marigold, 'lunch is now over, except for that enormous glass of Grand Marnier you seem to be having. Time to make your next brilliant plan.'

'I offered *you* a Grand Marnier.'

'Like M'sieur Vibrot, I'm not complaining . . . much. I'm saying that it's time to make this plan you were going to make. You'd more or less thought of it already, you said: the plan you were going to make if the first idea went wrong.'

For a moment Jacquiz looked simply silly. Then, avoiding Marigold's eyes and directing his own into the space beyond her left shoulder, he looked astonished.

'We have a visitor,' he said.

Down the dining-room of the Hôtel du Château de Montreuil came the vast mackintoshed figure of Auguste (*fils*) Vibrot. Madame the Proprietress fluttered behind him.

'Madame, M'sieur, he insists,' she wailed.

Auguste *fils* stopped at Marigold's side, reached over to Jacquiz' glass of Grand Marnier, lifted it, and placed it firmly beyond Jacquiz' reach, and then waved his clenched fists up and down over the table.

'He wants us to go with him straight away,' Marigold said.

'He might let us finish lunch first.'

'We have, except for your Grand Marnier. And you can see he doesn't approve of that.'

'It's no affair of his to approve or disapprove of my habits.'

August *fils* croaked at Marigold.

'He says we must go *now*,' said Marigold, smiling and nodding at Auguste. Auguste agitated his three teeth at her in response. 'Or there may not be another chance for a long while.'

'Damned cheek. Chance of what?'

'Come on and we'll see.'

Marigold rose and Jacquiz after her. Auguste galloped out of the dining-room followed at a canter by Marigold. Jacquiz turned to retrieve and gulp his Grand Marnier and then ambled after them, cross and sceptical but not proposing to be left out.

When they came to the Castle Gate, Auguste solemnly raised the palm of his right hand to his mouth to adjure all present to silence, unlocked the wicket with one of a bunch of keys, and crept through it with the huge, high step of a stage spy in a joke melodrama. When Marigold and, after some time, Jacquiz had followed him through, he closed the wicket with elaborate care, repeated his mime of silence, and led them away from the Gate House, under the wall of the wing which extended from it, until they came to a low, narrow door some twenty yards short of the entrance into the Vibrots' shop cum ticket office. Auguste pointed to the latter, put his head on one side, and made a snoring noise, then turned to the low, narrow door, unlocked it with another key from his bunch, crammed himself through it with some difficulty, and beckoned to Marigold and Jacquiz to follow. Having closed the door behind them with concentrated caution, he led them up a flight of wooden steps into what looked, at first sight, like an empty hay loft, but turned out, if one was to believe a notice on the wall which proclaimed numerous and draconian sanctions, to be the 'Recreation Room' of the Youth Hostel.

'It makes one glad one is no longer young,' Marigold said after examining the notice.

Auguste breathed in heavily and wagged a finger in front of her lips. Then he shuffled across the bare wooden floor and started to unlock a padlock which hung, apparently securing nothing and merely symbolical of prohibition, from a U-shaped bracket in a side wall, just beneath a sky-light which provided the sole illumination. Auguste had some difficulty with the padlock, which was obviously either jammed or rusty, but eventually the lock gave with a little screech and the flange came out with a sharp crack which caused Auguste to freeze and listen attentively for nearly a minute before he resumed operations.

'He's very afraid of being caught,' said Marigold. 'He's obviously on forbidden ground.'

She craned forward as Auguste pulled out of the wall a small square of wood which had been held in place by the padlock. In the aperture thus revealed was a door knob. This Auguste turned and pulled, causing a broad and previously invisible door to swing back from the rest of the wall. He then stepped rapidly across to conceal the wide gap he had made; turned; looked with adoration at Marigold; moved aside with a swift and surprisingly graceful step; gave Marigold another look as if to say, 'Here is my gift'; and pointed rapturously to the area now uncovered.

After about ten seconds,

'Sweet Jesus Christ,' Marigold said.


'Even the most dispensable of men,' said the Right Honourable the Lord Constable of Reculver Castle and Right Worshipful the Provost of Lancaster College, Cambridge, 'even the most dispensable of men are apt to leave annoying gaps when dispensed with. We shall not miss Doctor Helmut for twelve months but we shall, for approximately ten minutes in each of them, miss his knowledge of the college archives, muniments and manuscripts.'

'As you say, Provost,' said Ivor Winstanley, wondering uneasily what this had to do with him.

'Which being the case, Ivor, I must ask you to frequent the Chamber of Manuscripts from time to time and be prepared to furnish whatever we may want whenever we should happen to want it.'

'Rather a comprehensive request, Provost? I don't understand Helmut's system.'

The Provost rose, walked to a tall window, and looked out from his Lodge over the back lawn of Lancaster. The set of his back indicated that Winstanley would have to find a better excuse than that, if indeed any excuse were acceptable.

'There is an assistant there, Provost, a research student, whom I believe to be familiar with all the documents.'

'A research student is not a Fellow. We must have a Fellow, Ivor, a commissioned officer so to speak, in charge of every department of the College. How far you rely on this research student is your affair. In any case whatever, you will be held responsible.'

The Provost turned from the window with the manner of a Field Marshal condescending to instruct an otiose Major on the keeping of Mess Accounts.

'All you have to do,' said Lord Constable, courteously but implacably, 'is make yourself properly acquainted with Helmut's catalogue.'

'Rather a long order?' said Winstanley peevishly.

'And when you have done so, Ivor,' continued the Provost, totally ignoring the protest, 'I should be very glad to know if you have chanced to find any . . . irregularities or dubieties in that area.'

'I beg your pardon, Provost?' said Winstanley, curiosity now beginning to displace reluctance.

'Doctor Helmut, Ivor,' said the Provost in a new and soothing tone, 'has been heavily preoccupied during these last months because of a change in his private situation. I wish to be sure that this has not blunted his academic efficiency.'

'It would hardly have been likely to sharpen it,' said Winstanley, confident that he now knew where the wind lay.

'Precisely. Radical changes in circumstance when they come in middle age, are liable to unsettle even men of the soundest habit.'

'And the more so if flaws were already apparent.'

'I thought you were a friend of Helmut's,' said the Provost, in sharp and sudden rebuke.

'I was, Provost,' quavered Winstanley. 'But if you remember, there was an incident back in 1967 . . . a case of evasion . . . desertion . . .'

'How good of you to remind me.' His ruse having been successful and Winstanley's hostility to Helmut having been satisfactorily acknowledged by both of them, the Provost resumed his soothing tone. 'You will understand what I mean, then? Helmut, let us say, is not at his best under pressure.'

'And *what* a pressure,' said Winstanley, with a vulgarity induced by the relief at the Provost's apparent relaxation.

'The new cares and distractions . . .'

'. . . And the perennial possibility of cornutation.'

'The what?' said the Provost.

'I thought, Provost, that we were discussing the new Mrs Helmut.'

'*I* was discussing Helmut's lavish inheritance of money nine months ago. It is disgraceful that so large an accession of wealth to a single individual should still be possible. It is also enervating and corrupting to the individual himself.'

'That's as may be, Provost. But whereas he was always pretty comfortable about money he was never before married. So it stands to reason that his wife, being the unfamiliar element, must be the thing that's getting on top of him.'

Winstanley giggled at his own play on words.

'I think,' said the Provost statuesquely, 'that we should concern ourselves with the effects on Helmut's work rather than the niceties of their cause.'

'Just so,' said Winstanley, coming swiftly to heel. 'I am to understand, Provost, that while Helmut is away on his Sabbatical I am to . . . survey . . . the condition of his department?'

'And to report.'

'And to report. Just so. Do we know, by the way, where he has gone or what he is doing? He must have research of some kind.'

'Of some kind, no doubt. I was happy to let him go without pressing him for details. I think that's all we have to say, Ivor.'

Winstanley made for the door.

'Oh, Ivor . . .' said the Provost as he reached it.

'Provost?'

'Your reference to Helmut's work reminds me: how is your edition of Cicero's poetic works coming along?'

'It's coming along, Provost.'

'Good. There are those, you know, who say that these days you Latinists are a luxury. One can only defend you on grounds of substantial achievement. How soon will the College Council be able to congratulate you on the completion of your edition? And, we trust, on its acceptance for publication by the Syndics of the University Press?'

'Well, not this year, Provost, I'm afraid.'

'Next year?'

Winstanley stood silently with his hand on the door-knob.

'I think I understand the position, Ivor. And if I understand rightly, it will soon be very important, as I'm sure you will agree, that I should have something – other than your unfinished Ciceronian endeavours – on the strength of which I can justify your continued maintenance by this College. The matter of your renewal comes up in January, I believe?'

'Provost?' mumbled Winstanley.

'In January,' snapped Constable. 'Always a worrying time for a Fellow, when the date for his renewal draws near. However, Ivor, if you prove . . . conscientious . . . in this new task which I have just allotted to you, I think I can promise that you will be invited to retain your Fellowship without serious opposition on our part or embarrassment on yours.'

'I'll do my best, Provost,' said Winstanley brightly, like a sexagenarian boy scout.

'Go to it then,' said Lord Constable, and gravely nodded dismissal.


'Let us simply consider the facts,' said Jacquiz Helmut to Marigold. 'Never mind our emotional reactions when Auguste first uncovered that picture. Let us simply recall what it was.'

'It was revolting,' Marigold said.

They were back in their hotel, sitting on the balcony of their room in the evening sunshine which had at last broken through the dismal rains of the day. Although it was now clear to them, as a result of the revelations engineered that afternoon by Auguste, exactly where they must go next, there was also much else to discuss, and they had decided not to leave until the next morning. After what they had seen in the Recreation Room, they needed time, as Jacquiz had put it, to take a few deep breaths.

'It was revolting,' repeated Marigold.

'That is precisely the kind of comment that helps least. Facts, sweetheart. What was *happening* in that picture?' Jacquiz took a sheet of paper from his pocket. 'It's a pity Auguste was too nervous to let us stay longer,' he said, 'but I did manage to take quite comprehensive notes about the thing. "Oil-painting, approx. five feet long by three feet high",' he read out, ' "preservation fair, seventeenth-century Dutch in style and feeling, clear signature 'R. Van H.' – surely Richard Van Hoek. Landscape with building and figures. In background the Abbey of Jumièges before it was dismantled, conclusively recognizable from the high twin towers, square at base and octagonal above, which rise over the West Door of the Abbey Church. The buildings are perhaps 250 yards from the point of the artist's vision. In middle ground the Abbey Wall and a track running beneath it where the road runs today. In foreground a field or meadow where cafés, *etc.*, stand today, opposite Abbey Gate. Time: night (three-quarter moon seen between towers) and winter (total barrenness of trees in right foreground)." You agree with all that?'

'I think so. I've only ever been to Jumièges once – with Papa when I was still at school. But I think it fits. So much for the landscape and the buildings, Jacquiz. What about the figures?'

'Ah,' said Jacquiz. 'Auguste was getting very twitchy by the time I got to *them*, but I think I've got 'em right. "On track in middle ground at extreme left of painting two small figures (?? three inches high), a man and a woman, walking side by side. From manner of gait and freshness of faces they are clearly youthful. Dress: seventeenth-century; man in black hose and breeches, short black coat, black cloak with small area of scarlet lining visible, cavilier hat; woman in white cloak and full, plain, white dress, bare-headed." All right, Marigold?'

'Go on.'

' "Artist uses strip cartoon technique to portray successive events against constant background. The same two figures seen a little larger and standing in meadow about a foot (*i.e.* fifty odd yards by the scale and perspective of the picture) to the right of their first appearance on track. They are deep in discussion, huddled towards each other, heads nearly touching, faces visible in profile, showing sadness and reluctance on hers, urgency on his." '

Marigold nodded and shuddered slightly.

' "Same two figures seen yet again, a foot further to right (*i.e.* two feet equals one hundred yards, from left end of painting), with backs to viewer. Man's right hand clasps woman's left wrist. Woman hanging back. Man appears to be leading or even dragging woman across meadow, away from viewer, back towards track under Abbey Wall." '

Jacquiz licked his lips.

' "Man and woman next seen",' he continued, ' "a further six inches to the right, now in middle ground and on far side of wall and track, traversing open space on slight uphill slope between Abbey Gate and Library. (This appears in picture to stand twenty or thirty yards to SW of SW corner of church, though I recall far smaller distance in fact. ??Van Hoek painting from defective memory. ??Van Hoek bad at perspective.)" '

'Van Hoek telling a story,' Marigold said. 'Didn't give a damn about detail.'

'On the contrary, some of the detail is exquisite.'

'Where it matters. Go on, Jacquiz.'

' "Couple approaching entrance to Library. Man now has his arm under woman's. Woman slightly bowed. Man looking back over own shoulder and woman's, with free hand cupped round face, concealing face from woman, as if about to address an 'aside' to viewer. Man's face at first seems to be smiling; on close inspection seen to be grinning with a combination of lust, hatred, intent to pollute, infect and destroy." '

'Exquisite detail,' Marigold said.

' "Couple seen for last time about a foot from right-hand edge of canvas, on sky-line of low ridge (where there is now a stone terrace), well to S and E of minor Church of St Peter, which is itself south of, parallel with, and almost adjacent to the main and much larger Abbey Church of Our Lady. To reach the ridge they must have passed through the library, out of a far door into the Cloister, eastwards across the Cloister (to S of Our Lady), into St Peter's by the West Door, some way up the nave of St Peter's and out of it by the South Door, through a wilderness visible in painting (now a garden) and so on to the N end of ridge and along it to S. Figures are now therefore distant from view and very much smaller." And at that point,' said Jacquiz, 'Auguste hustled us out. But we both, I think, have a pretty vivid recollection of that last scene on the ridge. No need of a written memo about *that*.'

'No,' said Marigold huskily, and shuddered once more.

'*Calma, calma*,' said Jacquiz. 'Before we consider that scene, let us again consider the long route, mostly invisible in the painting, which took them to the ridge from the place where they had previously appeared. This was just in front of the Library. Already we are being warned, from the expression on the man's face, that something is about to go wrong. Where, we ask ourselves, and what? What happened *en route*, Marigold, to account for what we see on the ridge?'

'He married her,' said Marigold flatly.

'I agree. In the Library they gathered up the officiating priests and a congregation of monks – Benedictines they were in this Abbey. In the Cloister ... in the centre of which, Marigold, I remember a fine yew tree ... they picked up ... more guests for their wedding. And in the smaller Church of St Peter, under the tenth-century galleries, they were married.'

'A choir of monks chanting,' said Marigold listlessly.

'Yes. That would be right. The Benedictines have always been proud of their music.'

'The bell, the book, and the ring,' Marigold intoned. 'But something is not right. She shrinks from putting out her finger. The shadows close behind her, and two hands take hers, forcing it forward and spreading five fingers, so that the ring may be duly placed and herself given to . . . to her lord and lover.'

Yes . . . What then, Marigold?'

'A procession out of the Church, out of the South Door and through the wilderness in the painting, which, you say, is now a garden. First the chanting monks, then the priests, then the bride and groom, and then, Jacquiz, then . . .'

'. . . Then the guests who came from the Cloister. The guests from under the yew tree . . .'

'. . . Cowled, like the monks, faces deep in shadow, hands folded, invisible, into sleeves . . .'

'. . . And so they came to the ridge, where we actually see, in the painting, the monks chanting by the gate which leads into a tiny chapel . . .'

'. . . Only it is not a chapel, Jacquiz.'

'It has long since disappeared, if ever it was there. Dismantled for its stone, no doubt, after the Revolution. So we cannot tell what it was.'

'Not a chapel, Jacquiz. We know what it was. We know, because the shadowy guests, in that painting, are urging the couple towards it, because the bride is cringing back in despair and looking out from the picture, her face, tiny as it is, pleading to us to save her from this horror.'

'Another exquisite detail.'

'We know, because over the ridge, to the east, a first, dim, single ray of dawn is showing. Some of the guests, the shadows, are pointing to it and shrinking back. The others are urgent in their gestures. "Make haste before it is too late," their gestures proclaim, "before we the guests, and you the bridegroom, are powerless." Already it is almost too late for the shadows and the bridegroom. In a few minutes she would be safe from them. Already, because dawn is coming, the groom's face is changing back to a skull—'

'—Yet another exquisite detail—'

'—And he is labouring desperately, as he grows weaker every second, to drag her into the little chapel, which is not a chapel, before the sun comes to save her.'

Both of them sat in silence as the evening sun sank towards the eastern ramparts of Montreuil.

'The vision of Richard Van Hoek,' said Jacquiz at last.

'What did he mean by it? And why did poor potty Auguste think that it would help us? What is that painting doing, there in the attic?'

'That at least we can answer. The attic could have been Van Hoek's studio "within the Castle Gate". The painting could have been one which he left when he died. Someone, with a sense of the appropriate, could have had it placed on the wall of the room in which he worked, could have fitted that panel to protect it. And there it has stayed ever since.'

'Valuable, surely?'

'Not really. Valuable enough to guard from the hostel's young guests with a padlock, but beyond that, no. Van Hoek was unknown, or almost. His style is standard for Dutch painters of the time and largely undistinguished. His method – that of rendering successive events from left to right of the canvas – is not altogether uncommon, even at this late period, and constitutes no more than a curiosity. No, not a valuable picture.'

'Valuable enough for the Vibrots to take care of down the generations. I wonder why M'sieur or Madame didn't show it to us. Here we were inquiring about Constance, who was once engaged to Van Hoek. They must have known we'd be interested.'

'Tax. In France, if you are seen to possess a conspicuous object, somebody tends to come on you for tax.'

'But we hardly resembled tax narks, French tax narks.'

'The French trust nobody. But they needn't have worried. The fiercest of tax men could hardly squeeze them for having a Van Hoek.'

'I think that picture was better than you say. What about those "exquisite details" – *your* phrase first time?'

'Ah. When Van Hoek did those he was working way above his usual form. He must have been, as they say, possessed. It is here that we might look for an explanation of the painting. He had something horrible to say, and he was so urgent to say it that at times his urgency lent him touches of genius.'

'He was dying? Or knew he was doomed?'

'Something of the kind. He returned from the bed of the Countess, remember, having taken the jewels which were now due to him, and found that there was plague in Montreuil. He feared lest the plague would get him, perhaps – as indeed it did pretty soon – and he fell to, with great energy, to compose his last utterance.'

'But what did he mean by it?'

'The picture is obviously an allegory. The Woman in White, all youth and purity, has been tempted to walk by night with a specious young gentleman in black and a hint of scarlet. He persuades her, against all instincts and judgment, to marry him there and then; after all, he urges, the Church nearby will be lending its auspices to their union. But marriages should not take place at night after brief courtships under the deceiving moon. This she realizes only when it is too late, only when she finds that the monks – past and present – have assisted at her marriage to a corpse, with whom she, still living, Marigold, must now consort. The whole thing is a ghastly warning.'

'To whom and against what?'

'To the world in general and to Constance Fauvrelle, his betrothed, in particular. In case he did not survive the epidemic of plague, he was leaving Constance a piece of advice. One can read it several ways. For a start, he could be telling her not to dedicate herself to his memory – "don't marry the dead". Secondly, he could be warning her against marrying someone who looked like a good prospect but might turn out, too late, to have brought her to live, so to speak, in a charnel house. Although he didn't live to know it, such a warning would have been all too appropriate, in view of her later marriage to Comminges.'

'We don't yet know for certain that she was unhappy with Comminges.'

'Her first letter from that front – the one retailed by the old *veuve* Vibrot to Constance's father – cannot be called sanguine. If Van Hoek *was* warning her about marriage, she'd have done well to listen.

'But there is no need to insist that his concern was in that area, though it would quite likely have been. There are dozens of other possible interpretations of that painting – a warning against threats posed by the Romish Establishment, as represented by the Abbey, to protestants like Constance and her family; or against the wiles of the Papist Priesthood, for perhaps Constance had shown signs of wanting to make life easier by becoming a Catholic; or even against the external lures of splendid buildings which are insufficiently lit and the evil influence that can be exerted on the present by the past – an influence symbolized here by the cowled ghosts who urge the consummation of this hideous marriage. Any or all of this might be intended. But the important point, for us, is simply that Van Hoek was saying, more or less, "You watch out what you do with yourself, my dear, because the world is a very disagreeable and deceitful place, and I do not want you to end up with worms feeding on your flesh".'

'All right, I'll buy it,' said Marigold. 'but why is this allegory set, so particularly, in the Abbey of Jumièges?'

'A place famous for its beauty, its music and its learning, only two days' journey on horseback from Montreuil. It is only natural that a visiting Dutch painter should have been there and been impressed. It's even possible that they made up a party, so that Constance could go too . . .'

'. . . Yes,' said Marigold. 'In the early days of their courtship, perhaps. And since it was a memorable outing, he decided to use Jumièges as an image when he issued his warning.'

'Thus adding yet another level of meaning,' Jacquiz said: ' "Remember this beautiful place to which we went last summer, and already I am dead''. All of which is plausible enough,' continued Jacquiz after a pause, 'but why was Auguste telling us to go there?'

'I'm glad you're getting round to that at last,' Marigold said.

'We agreed, after we'd left him,' Jacquiz pursued, 'that he *was* telling us to go there, and we agreed that we would go if only *faute de mieux*. But why, Marigold? What should we look for when we arrive? Does the painting give us any clue about that?'

'Like all dons,' said Marigold, not unkindly, 'you are being too clever and complicated. Whatever that painting may or may not have meant, and whether or not you and I have interpreted it correctly, none of that can have anything to do with what Auguste was telling us. All *he* was saying, in his simple way, was, "I hope you recognize the place in this picture; please go to it." He knew we'd been disappointed, and that it was his fault because he'd destroyed the letters, and he also knew that there was still *something* at Jumièges which might help us and which his parents, for whatever reason, were not going to tell us about. So he waited till they were asleep, and then for the first time in his life dared to bring someone into the house without their knowing, because he liked us, I think—'

'—Because he liked you—'

'—And was sorry we had been disappointed. He then told us, in the only way he could, where we should go next. The fact that that picture was crammed with beastly allegories is beside the point: all Auguste was saying was, "Go on to Jumièges".'

'But how much did he understand? He understood that we wanted those letters, but did he have any conception what they were about?'

'I shouldn't think so for a moment,' said Marigold patiently. 'All he knew was that anyone interested in those particular pieces of paper, which had by now been flushed down the students' loo, would be interested in something still to be found at Jumièges. He risked his parents' anger to tell us that – remember how jumpy the poor dear was – and we owe it to Auguste, Jacquiz, not only to go to Jumièges, but to have a bloody close look when we get there.'


'Well, whatever else comes of it, I'm glad to be seeing this again,' said Marigold.

She looked up at the only remaining wall of the lantern tower of the Abbey of Jumièges, and watched it sway in the wind as the clouds swept over its summit. Then she passed under the arch, out of the nave and into the broken chancel.

'If only we knew where to start looking, said Jacquiz rather peevishly. 'Have you got those indigestion tablets of yours?'

'Too much lunch,' said Marigold, fishing in her bag.

They had started sharp at nine that morning from the Hôtel du Château de Montreuil, by the gate of which Auguste had been anxiously lurking.

'*Maintenant nous irons à Jumièges*,' Marigold had said to him, whereupon the idiot had clapped his hands and capered, then waved them gaily off.

They had driven in silence as far as Abbéville, past its gasworks and chimneys, along its canals, and on to the Forest of Eu. There,

'We're in Normandy now,' Jacquiz had said, as the car ran between the dense trees on either side. And then, as they rounded a corner and came over the brow of a hill, to see their road floating down from the forest and away through a wide and coloured valley past Fourcament and on to the ridges of Eawy,

'It's grand being with you on this trip,' he said.

'Nice Jacquiz,' Marigold answered, and blinked as she looked along the valley. 'Christ, how marvellous,' she said.

When they turned right for Tôtes and Yvetot, the country had become smugger, less dramatic, of a smaller scale, but still such, with its soft meadows and rustling autumn poplars, as to make a man give thanks to whatever gods there be and wish the day of his death long deferred. This they told each other in a roundabout way, by talking of the dull tasks which their Cambridge acquaintance would now be performing against the imminent beginning of the Michaelmas Term and congratulating themselves, by inference, on their escape into this world of exquisite sights and enchanted leisure.

At Yvetot they turned left, drove for a while past little farm houses arranged among their fields with the regularity of toys beside a child's railway, and then wound down, through tall, cool trees, still green, to the demure river-front of Caudebec, where they had lunch, in their euphoria rather 'too much lunch' as Marigold was later to remark, in a restaurant which overlooked the Seine. After this they had hurried through the prosaic townships which lay along the river towards Rouen and turned right, through a dormitory village and then into dreaming Jumièges, just as the guardian opened the gates of the Abbey to afternoon visitors. And now, under the soaring walls of the Church of our Lady, where the nave ceased and broken shafts encircled what had long ago been the sanctuary, Marigold fished in her handbag and said,

'Here they are. Gelusil or the other sort?'

'Gelusil. I think I'd better have three.'

'*Three?* I hope they're not addictive.'

She passed him three white tablets. Jacquiz crunched them, then burped loudly. Marigold primmed up her face and walked down the short passage into the smaller Church of St Peter.

'If only we knew where to look,' grumbled Jacquiz behind her, 'or what we were looking for.'

'Just look,' said Marigold.

'I'm not sure,' grizzled Jacquiz, 'that we shouldn't have gone straight on to Sens.'

'Why Sens?'

'That was the place from which Constance Fauvrelle – or Comminges as she was by then – first wrote to the widow Vibrot ... according to that account book your father

showed me. At least we know that the newly married Comminges actually *went* to Sens. With Jumièges, as far as we
know, they had nothing to do at all.'

'Constance came here with Richard Van Hoek.'

'She *may* have. What's that got to do with where she went
with Comminges months or even years later?'

'Auguste must have had some reason for sending us here.
We'll have plenty of time to go to Sens, if we need to, later
on. Just stop fussing and *look*.'

Her body suddenly tensed.

'Ouch,' she said.

'What is it?'

'Lunch. Oh dear. Much too much lunch.'

'Have a Gelusil.'

'No good. It's not that. Number two.'

'It can't be as sudden as that.'

'All that cream in the sauce,' Marigold said. 'It brings on
those quick, hot, runny ones.'

'Oh. I see.'

'After a bit you can hardly walk with it. We must find a
loo. Quickly.'

'Through the garden and on the terrace? You know, the
little ridge in that picture where—'

'—Yes, yes, yes, come on,' Marigold said.

They left the Church of St Peter by the South Door, turned
left through a garden of shrubs, and walked up some steps
on to the terrace.

'No sign of one anywhere. Eeeeeh.'

'Hang on, old girl. The old Abbot's Lodge is a Museum.
Perhaps there . . .'

'Where?'

'Back through the little church and then the cloister.'

Marigold scuttled ahead with quick, short, anxious steps,
into St Peter's, out of the West Door, past the yew tree in the
cloister, through the skeleton of the Library, across the grass
to the Museum.

But the Museum, whether or not it contained a loo, was
tightly closed.

'The guardian in the Gate House?'

They shot across to the entrance and into the guardian's office. The guardian listened indifferently to Marigold's breathless request, considered it coldly, shook his head in absolute and heartless negation.

'Jacquiz . . . I *must*.'

'I think I saw a café across the road.'

Marigold tottered out of the gate and then crossed the road with long, desperate strides, calculating that speed was now even more important than constriction. As Jacquiz followed her into the café, she squawked at a man behind the bar, then plunged through a tiny door by a juke box. Jacquiz started to order coffee and cognac for two, hoping that the preparation of this refection would distract the man from the celebratory noises which issued from behind the narrow door.

After quite a short while Marigold came out and said:

'Only a pair of feet. No paper. I had to use four pages of the Green *Michelin*. Unsuitable texture.'

'I hope we shan't need them.'

'Don't worry. It wasn't the Normandy *Michelin*. For some reason I had the Pyrenees one in my bag as well, so I used that.'

'They don't come cheap, you know. But on the whole it was a very good thing you got taken short like that.'

'What do you mean, a good thing? It was torture.'

'I think we've found what we came for. Look behind the bar.'

Marigold looked. The man there was pouring himself a glass of red wine.

'Dead spit of M'sieur Vibrot,' breathed Marigold, 'like a horrible creeping Jesus.'

She sipped her cognac.

'He has to be a brother or a cousin. Direct approach is best, I think.'

Jacquiz rose and went to the bar.

'M'sieur Vibrot,' he said.

The man nodded, without any sign of surprise, and gulped some wine.

'I think you can help me.'

'Indeed.'

The man drained his wine-glass, refilled it from a huge and villainous bottle, and said to Jacquiz:

'That will be one franc, m'sieur.'

Jacquiz gave him ten.

'I am looking for some old letters which I believe to be in your family. I am told they have been destroyed. But I am also told that you may be able to help me.'

'Who told you that?'

'The son of the Vibrots who live in Montreuil.'

The man tapped his temple but looked expectantly at Jacquiz, who now produced and examined a hundred-franc note.

'Can you tell me anything about those letters or what was in them?'

'I know nothing about what was in them.' A long pause. 'I only know that they are very old and three of them are in my possession.'

Jacquiz rustled the note.

'They will cost you two hundred francs each or five hundred for the three of them.'

'How much just to look at them?'

'Sale or nothing.'

'How did you come by them?' said Jacquiz cautiously.

'I was visiting my brother. I wished to go to the *cabinet*. The *cabinet* was full of my cow of a sister-in-law, who is always in the *cabinet* when someone else requires it. So I go to the *toilette* for the Youth Hostel, and there, in one of the cubicles, are these three letters in a rack where there is normally newspaper. I notice the difference, I remember about the story of the letters which my brother has inherited, and I take them away. I do not tell my brother and my sister-in-law, because they would have demanded them back, even though they did not care enough about them before to keep them safe. Such stupid sluts as they are, with that booby son Auguste. Just as I am going from the *toilette*, that son, that booby, comes in to do the cleaning and makes a great fuss about the letters, not because they are valuable but because there is now no paper in the rack for the pigs of students in the Hostel. So I give him the *Rouen Matin* which I am also carrying and the idiot is content.'

'Dear, conscientous Auguste,' said Marigold from across the room. 'That must be what fixed the subject of the letters in his mind. When we asked for them, he remembered his uncle had taken some away. His parents couldn't tell us that even if they had wished to help us, because they didn't know. So he showed us that picture, meaning we were to go to his uncle in Jumièges. Dear *clever* Auguste.'

'Where are the letters?' said Jacquiz.

'Where are the five hundred francs?'

'Here. You shall have them when I see the letters are genuine.'

'What a lot of loos in this story,' said Marigold brightly, hoping to relax the tension between the two men. 'The Vibrots' *cabinet* which this gentleman couldn't get into, and the Youth Hostel rears where Auguste had put all the letters—'

'Show me the five hundred francs—'

'—Show me the letters—'

'—And the pair of feet in this café which I had to do a job on – and a very good job I did have to do a job, because if I hadn't we would never—'

'—Here,' said Vibrot, slamming some thick sheets of what looked like parchment on to the bar.

'Here,' said Jacquiz, slamming down a 500-franc note but keeping his hand over half of it while he peered at the top sheet.

'By Jove,' he said, 'I think it's all right, old girl. The writing could be right, and the paper's certainly right.'

'How do you know?'

'Years and years in the Chamber of Manuscripts at Lancaster. You get a nose for this sort of thing.'

'I'll buy that,' said Marigold. 'Give him his cash and let's have a dekko.'

Jacquiz passed the note to Vibrot. Vibrot passed the sheets to Jacquiz. Vibrot drank and shrugged. Jacquiz crossed the room to Marigold. He placed the sheets on the table, lifted the top one very carefully, and began to read and translate aloud.

' "To the Esteemed Dame Vibrot",' he read slowly and with difficulty to Marigold, ' "Within the Castle Walls of Montreuil, at Her Lodging. Honoured Madame: Since sending to you from the City of Sens . . . I have been carried on South . . . to the City of Orange, where I am penning this letter . . . in the Hostelry of the Arena. Madame . . . I am the victim of my own most formidable error. Dear Madame, you must know that . . when we quitted Sens, my husband . . . hired a coach whereby we . . ." '

Jacquiz' voice faltered and ceased.

'Go on,' commanded Marigold.

'No good. She's crossed the page too clumsily.'

'You mean . . . you've paid out five hundred francs for two and a half sentences?'

'No. I'll be able to read it all right. But not straight off like this. It'll take time and a magnifying glass. So what we do now,' said Jacquiz, rising and tenderly lifting the sheets, 'is make camp for the night and then apply ourselves to our home work.'

'M'sieur,' called Vibrot as they left, 'it is fifteen francs for the coffee and cognac.'

Jacquiz returned to the bar and fished out the money.

'And another fifty centimes,' said Vibrot, 'for use of the *toilette*.'


'Perhaps you could just give me a rough idea of Doctor Helmut's routine when he's here,' said Ivor Winstanley to the Under-Collator of the Manuscripts of Lancaster College.

'He hasn't got a routine, man,' said the Under-Collator, a graduate research student of submissive yet venomous aspect.

Winstanley sighed and looked round the walls of the Chamber of Manuscripts. Not a book or a manuscript in sight, he thought wearily: just rows of metal filing cabinets and a portrait of the last Provost but three which (and who) had been considered too bad to hang in Hall or even the Junior Common Room. But I'm not here to complain on aesthetic grounds, he thought: I'm here, on the Provost's instructions, to take over Jacquiz Helmut's duties and to try to impugn his past performance of them – on pain of being myself impugned. To work, to work.

'Well then, how does business get done?' he inquired meekly.

'Like someone wants a document; like I find it; like Doctor Helmut looks at it and says it's too valuable (or not too valuable) to go out of the room, so the guy who wants it must suss it up in here (or not, as the case may be).'

'Not a very exciting task for either of you.'

'We have to make sure that all the lousy manuscripts stay in good condition,' said the Under-Collator defensively.

'And are they?'

'Help yourself, man,' said the Under-Collator. 'Look where you will.'

'I'm sure there's no need,' said Winstanley feebly. 'What else do you do?'

'We have to keep the Catalogue in order, like filling in cards for new acquisitions.'

'When was there last a new acquisition?'

'Shepherd bequest came through last June. Letters he had like from Rupert Brooke and Maynard Keynes saying come to tea next Wednesday but keep your hot hands to yourself.'

'And these letters have been filed and recorded in the Catalogue?'

'Just so, man. Matter of routine.'

'You've just been saying Doctor Helmut hadn't got a routine.'

'I meant, there isn't enough of it to call it a routine. So let's say it was a matter of course. Once a fortnight or so there's something to do as a matter of course and we do it. The rest of the time I sit here between ten and one and two and four in case there are visitors, and if they want something too tricky for me to handle, I call Doctor Helmut on the telephone and ask him what to do.'

'Suppose he isn't there and it's urgent?' said Winstanley desperately.

'The last time I had to call him about anything really urgent was ten months ago, man. He was there.'

This was ridiculous, Ivor Winstanley thought. The Provost's briefing, though it had intrigued him at the time, had clearly been quite absurd. Everyone knew that the Collation of the College Manuscripts was a light and simple task which carried a large honorarium. The custom had always been to give the post of Collator to someone who had spent several years discharging one of the more disagreeable College offices as a reward for conscientious completion of his labours. This was exactly what had happened in the case of Jacquiz Helmut. Years ago Jacquiz, as a junior Fellow, had been allotted the hideous task of supervising the renewal and modernization of the drainage throughout the entire College. Not only had he overseen this very efficiently, he had also managed the arrangements so deftly that, despite the crookedness of dilatory contractors and the villainous recalcitrance of their so-called workmen, a bare minimum of inconvenience had been suffered whether by Fellows, undergraduates or menials. Jacquiz had then been given the Collatorship, in recognition of his services, and had settled down, with everyone's blessing, to enjoy the prize. Whatever one might think of Jacquiz' scholarship or his lack of it, however much one might resent his personality or deplore his moral evasions during recent years, the plain fact remained that he had done a superb job over the drainage, had amply earned the sinecure he had been awarded, and had conducted himself, in regard to it, just as every Collator had always done – which was to say he left what little drudgery there was to the impoverished research student who was, by charitable tradition, appointed to the Under-Collatorship. And now, thought Winstanley, here was the Provost trying to get up some notion that Jacquiz had been in some way careless or inadequate. That the Provost should wish to discredit or put down Jacquiz was fully understandable; but that he should set about doing so by questioning Jacquiz' performance of his duties as Collator was the most pure and perverse of nonsense. The duties were so simple, the responsibilities so plain, that it would be impossible to make a hash of them save out of absolute malignance, and his worst enemy in the world would not accuse Jacquiz of that. Even this very nasty young man, who would obviously say anything he could to disoblige or injure anybody, did not and could not accuse Jacquiz of incompetence or negligence in his function.

But stay, thought Ivor Winstanley: my own survival is at stake here and no stone must be left unturned. He briefly rehearsed to himself what he could recall of his interview with Lord Constable. What was it the Provost had particularly suggested that he should look for? Irregularities, that was it, 'dubieties' in the Catalogue. Well, the assistant had already deposed that the Catalogue was promptly and properly kept in respect of new acquisitions; but it was just conceivable that something might have gone wrong, if only through sheer bad luck, in the case of some of the more obscure or ancient items. *Something* he must try to turn up in order to give adverse substance to the report awaited by the Provost, and in this area, if anywhere, something might be found. The long undisturbed, the boring, the unwanted, the uncalled for – these were the Manuscripts that might, just might, be misleadingly recorded in Jacquiz' Catalogue.

'Let's see,' he said to the Under-Collator. 'Suppose I were to look at the accounts of the stewardship of the College's manor of Pigs' Runton in Lincolnshire . . . for the year of 1754.'

The Under-Collator went to the Catalogue Cabinet, opened a drawer marked 'R/S', looked at a slip of cardboard and then looked at Winstanley.

'Bursar's office,' he said. 'Most of the old accounts are kept there.'

'Very well. Let's try . . . the original autograph of Provost Lauderdale's dissertation *De Pueris Apte Puniendis* – on the Fitting Chastisement of Students.'

The Under-Collator opened a drawer marked 'L'.

'Cabinet Fourteen,' he said quite soon, 'Section B, Drawer Beta – the top right-hand drawer of that Cabinet under the portrait.'

Winstanley applied as directed; the MS in question came directly to hand, clearly labelled, neatly enveloped in cellulose.

'We can play this game all day,' the Under-Collator remarked. 'It's all in order, man. The whole works.'

'I'm very glad to hear it.'

'No, you're not,' said the Under-Collator. 'You want to do Jake Helmut down. I can smell it.'

'Is that what you call him? Jake?'

'Yep. And he calls me Len. What do I call you?'

'My Christian name is Ivor,' said Winstanley reluctantly.

'Well, listen here, Ive. You'll find nothing wrong with this place, because Jake is too smart, see? This is a good thing for him and he wants to keep it. It's a good thing for me too, and I want to keep it. But if you want to do Jake down, and *if* you'd promise to see me all right – and I mean *all right*, Ive, like with a Fellowship guaranteed when I send in my thesis – then we might work something out, you and me, about how to fuck all this up and make it look like Jake was the cunt to blame. What the hell, I don't mind old Jake so much, but he's a snooty sod at times, and I've got my future to look after. So you just make the price right, Ive, and *then* we'll see, shall we?'

'Like you say, Len,' quavered Winstanley, thinking of the days racing by and bringing him ever nearer to the date when his Fellowship would come up for renewal; thinking of his edition of Cicero's Poems, not one third complete; thinking of an old age spent in exile from beloved Lancaster. 'Like you say.'

'I think that's about it,' said Jacquiz. 'There are several passages in which I can't make out the words very well because the pages are crossed so messily, but I'm sure I've got the drift.'

After they had left the Vibrots' café the previous afternoon, they had purchased a magnifying glass from a junk shop and moved into a nearby hotel. There Jacquiz had set to work immediately, and by midnight, crossed-eyed, exhausted and one third drunk, he had 'cracked' (as Marigold put it) the first of the three letters and had come to fair terms with the second. After a restless night, he had risen at seven a.m. and tackled the third, which, it appeared, he had now deciphered.

'Let's have the message,' said Marigold.

She stood behind him and began to stroke his hair.

'Poor baby,' she said, 'you look worn out. Poor baby. Nice Jacquiz.'

'Marigold?' he said, turning in his chair and reaching for her.

'At nine-thirty in the morning? I'm ashamed of you.'

'But some time?'

'Yes.'

'Some time soon?'

'Not long. Sweet Seine, run softly, till I end my song,' she murmured thoughtfully, as if the inconsequent words had special private meaning.

'What's that about the Seine?'

'Nothing.' She scratched his scalp lightly, then moved away to sit on her bed. 'Let's have the message.'

'Well, as I told you yesterday afternoon, the first of the letters is written from a pub in Orange. Constance tells *la veuve* Vibrot that her husband hired a coach to carry them on from Sens to Orange – which was pretty extravagant behaviour, since they could perfectly well have taken the public diligence, or ridden on horseback, as they had *until* Sens, with one of the numerous companies of travellers who were taking the main road south. No mention is made of the exact sum which Louis Comminges paid for the coach, or where he got the money from, but the implication is that since he was now in possession of the Rubies he wasn't too worried about blowing his other funds.'

'Does she say he'd actually taken the Rubies away from here?'

'No. She says nothing precise about that. She doesn't even mention the Rubies as such at all. But what comes over is the anxiety of an heiress who sees her new husband spending money recklessly and is afraid for her fortune. She refers to his liking for *Vins et viandes les plus chères*—'

'—Rather your sort of style—'

'—And his *hauteur*. I hope you would not accuse me of that.'

'You can look quite formidable when you try,' said Marigold, 'but never mind that. So Constance is a worried girl?'

'Yes. And of course it makes no difference which of them is actually carrying the Rubies. She was his wife and under his protection, and for all practical purposes they were his.'

'No women's lib in those days. Poor Constance.'

'Poor Constance indeed. Because quite apart from the way he's exploiting her and her treasure, she has another reason to be afraid: he refuses to tell her where he's taking her. They've already been two days in Orange, and she hasn't a notion about what's to happen next. When she asks him, he simply doesn't reply, and for that matter he hardly talks to her at all about anything. He's out all day, apparently *en poursuite de ses affaires*, and when he comes in he indulges in the *vins et viandes* aforesaid, makes love to her impersonally as if she were a common whore – she is, incidentally, less than enthusiastic about his physical attributes – and falls asleep. And that,' said Jacquiz, 'is the news from Orange.'

'And the second letter, you said last night, is even more depressing?'

'More depressing but also more dynamic. They are just about to leave Orange and a lot of things are happening. To start with, Comminges has now grudgingly revealed their general direction – which is to be West from Orange towards the Pyrenees – though he still refuses to specify their exact goal. He has also been at least passably candid about something else. Perhaps *les vins* account for that. Their journey West is going to be a little awkward, he has told her, because all members of his family are wanted men in all the big cities on the main route West, and to the North of it as well. Avignon, Alès, Millau, Nîmes, Montpellier and Lunel – all are out of bounds.'

'Why on earth?'

'It seems that a long time ago the Comminges family had been prominent Albigensians. For some reason which isn't quite clear the taint of the heresy still clings to them and the thing is very much held against them. When Constance asks why, in that case, they didn't make for the Pyrenees *via* Bordeaux and the West, he tells her that matters are just as bad for him in that area too. What it boils down to is that they must somehow get from Orange to Béziers, an old Cathar town where they will be safe, without using the main road. From Béziers on to the Pyrenees, *via* Narbonne, is no problem, but to get to Béziers itself without being arrested they must take a detour East by Carpentras and Cavaillon, then circle round to Arles (which apparently is not hostile), and after that proceed along the coast until they are almost due South of Béziers and can safely head North to the main road again.

'Now, this means that they must go from Arles to St Gilles, then across some very wild country from St Gilles down to Aigues Mortes (in order to avoid Lunel), then through an area of lakes and sea-marshes West of Le Grau, past Sete, and right on to Agde. Constance, writing to the widow Vibrot, tells her what is still almost true today – that much of that counry is *terra incognita*, where be dragons and probably worse. Constance is therefore very frightened and very depressed by, among other things, her diminishing stock of clean underwear.'

'I didn't know they worried much about that in the seventeenth century.'

'Perhaps they did in the type of protestant household in

which Constance was brought up. At all events, this second letter ends with the information that the Comminges are to set out for Carpentras the next morning at five. A coach has again been hired, despite the element of self-advertisement in such a proceeding, and in this they will go as far as Arles. After Arles they must rough it.'

'And the third letter?'

'Very brief and dated nearly a month later, from Narbonne. She simply says that they managed to journey safely to Aigues Mortes, that they stayed there more than a week because Comminges developed a marsh fever, and that they then moved on through the lakes to Béziers, where, mercifully, she had been able to get her undies washed.'

'I'm relieved to hear it.'

'Relations between Louis and Constance have improved during the journey – a certain camaraderie had arisen in the face of common dangers, one supposes, and perhaps the brute was grateful to her for nursing him through his fever. But she still hasn't been told where they are going, only that they may be passing through Toulouse and will definitely, quite definitely, spend some days in Pau. Pau, it appears, is as far West as they can go without Louis Comminges' again being in danger of arrest as the descendant of Albigensians.'

'There's a lot of explaining to be done about that. The Albigensian heresy had been wiped out centuries earlier. Why was anyone still worried because the Comminges had once adhered to it?'

'A very good question, I'd say ... the answer to which, along with the answer to many other questions, is reposing in the plumbing of the Youth Hostel in the Castle of Montreuil.'

'So the only thing we can do, I imagine, is to follow their route to Pau, hoping to pick up something on the way. Carpentras, Aigues Mortes, and so on. Those marshes. Béziers, Narbonne, Toulouse . . .'

'No,' said Jacquiz. 'We go straight to Pau. We can always go back along their route later on if we need to.'

'Straight to Pau? Isn't that rather precipitate?'

'I have reasons. Pau, for a start, is the place about which Constance is most emphatic.'

'But what can we be looking for in Pau?'

'What can we be looking for anywhere, come to that? In Pau, of all places, there should be thread which we can find and follow.'

'What thread? What thread can we conceivably pick up in *Pau*? Pau,' announced Marigold in disgust, 'is a spa-town with nothing in it except stuffy hotels and dying oldies.'

'*Rich* dying oldies,' emended Jacquiz, 'who go there for the superb view of the Pyrenees and to benefit from the salutary climate. A climate whose medicinal virtues were discovered by the Romans and have been appreciated ever since ... by, among others, retired merchants from Bordeaux and their vain and purse-proud wives. Such people were much the same in the seventeenth century as they are now, probably even more so. Now then, Marigold: if you had a valuable necklace to dispose of, a necklace to which your title was at least questionable (because your wife had it from a dying painter who had it in dubious circumstances from a Countess who had only a life interest in it, if that), a necklace which might at any minute become what in modern parlance is called "hot", what better place could you choose to dispose of it than a remote spa-town, to which news of its "hotness" should be slow in coming, full of rich, worldly, bored, ageing and self-made men, who would not be too scrupulous in asking the precise provenance of something which they or their nagging wives were eager to possess?'

'All right,' said Marigold. 'So Comminges wanted to flog that necklace in Pau. But that still doesn't tell me what we're looking for there. There'll hardly be a receipt in the local museum, or a plaque on a wall saying, "This is the house in which Louis Comminges sold the Roses of Picardie to Monsieur and Madame Frump." '

'Retired merchants,' said Jacquiz, 'may not be too scrupulous about provenance but they are very exacting about quality. Anyone who had a mind to possess that necklace would have wanted it valued by a master jeweller. Any master jeweller who had sight of such a piece would record a description of it and the details of any sale over which he presided – together with the amount of his commission. So we are looking in Pau for a house of antique jewellers which has connections, by inheritance or transference or sale or amalgamation, that reach back to such a house as might have existed in the seventeenth century. In short, a house whose anterior records go back three centuries.'

'Back to a master jeweller,' said Marigold, 'who, had he set eyes on the celebrated Roses of Picardie, might well have spotted what they were, even if he did live in a remote province, and then have denounced Comminges to the police. In one word, Jacquiz, Comminges would never have taken the risk of letting those Rubies he valued in Pau or anywhere in France, nor would he have tried to sell them – not until he got abroad somewhere. That must have been why he was now heading West – to take a ship from the Atlantic coast.'

'I've just told you: according to Constance he wouldn't be safe if he went anywhere West of Pau.'

'He could have gone skulking down by-roads – he'd done a good bit in that line already.'

'If Comminges had wanted to go abroad,' said Jacquiz, 'he could have taken ship from the North of France, within walking distance of Montreuil. Or he could have turned left from Orange for Italy instead of right for the Pyrenees. Or he could have gone South from Narbonne and crossed the border into Spain. He did none of these things. He went to Pau. Why? Perhaps because he knew of a jeweller there whose ... tact ... he could rely on in assisting him to a sale; or who would break the necklace up for him into smaller and more easily saleable lots. It is now almost certain that the Comminges family lived somewhere in that part of the world – a Gascon family, perhaps. Gascons, being poor, were always taking service under the French King. Hence Comminges' own quasi-military career. This was now over, so he was coming home to Gascony with his loot and calling on someone he knew in the area who would have the necessary skills, knowledge, associates and discretion to help him dispose of it — and that in a town full of rich potential buyers.'

'Very plausible,' said Marigold, 'very donnish.'

'What else would you suggest?'

'Nothing really. I just liked the idea of some of the other places. Aigues Mortes . . . the name and the marshes.'

'We'll see those one day. Later on this trip, perhaps — we may well have to go back in our tracks. But first of all . . . Pau. All right?'

'Yes. Pau, Pau, Pau. Very much all right.'

'Even with all those stuffy hotels you complained of?'

'I've only heard from Papa. Never been there. And anyway, you can show me the view of the Pyrenees.'

'Happily.'

He came towards her, but Marigold slid off the bed and away.

'Shall I start packing?' she said.

'Please.' He sighed, made towards her again, and then thought better of it and returned to his chair. 'Where's that map? I want to look out the route . . . We'd better go into Rouen, for a start, and cross the Seine there.'

'No,' said Marigold. 'I know of a better way across the Seine.'

'Quicker?'

'Maybe. Anyhow, better. My present to you, Jacquiz. Something *I* can show to *you*.'


Marigold directed Jacquiz to drive back into Jumièges.

'There again? It's a dead end.'

'Oh no. You remember I told you that Papa once took me to see the Abbey, years ago? He also showed me something else.'

They drove past the Abbey on their left and the Vibrots' café on their right.

'There's a small right turn,' Marigold said, 'here.'

For about half a mile they drove down a straight and

narrow road, which the Rolls occupied comfortably all to itself. At first there were depressing bungalows on either side.

'Those weren't there before,' Marigold said. 'I hope they stop soon.'

They did, giving place to small, very flat fields, heavily hedged. Then the car rounded a bend.

'Ah,' Marigold said.

On the bank of the Seine was a small office and just beyond it a stone ramp which led down to the river. The far bank of the river was 300 yards away; it rose almost sheer from the water for 300 or 400 feet, and was totally obscured, except for two white patches of cliff, by tall, swaying trees, which spread right along to where the river curved away North out of their sight, about half a mile from where they now stood. Enveloped by the trees above and on either side was a small inn which stood on a wooden quay. Surely, Jacquiz thought, the inn could be come at only by water, so closely was it contained (all but submerged) by shimmering foliage.

At first the only sound to be heard was the rustling of the leaves on the South bank, a rustling which carried clearly, in the quiet of the place, to Marigold and Jacquiz on the North. But after a while there was a light chugging. A small open motor boat was crossing the river, bringing with it a square and shallow barge lashed alongside.

'The ferry,' said Marigold. 'Every hour and on the hour.'

'Ferry? Where to?'

'South.'

'There's a way up that bank? Out of those trees?'

'You'll see.'

'I'd better get a ticket then.'

Jacquiz turned towards the office.

'It's free,' said Marigold.

'*Free?*'

'Papa said this was the ferry the monks and scholars used, visiting or leaving the Abbey. There is a sort of . . . right to be carried over free. Hildebrand came this way and Fulbert of Chartres, he told me; Marbod of Rennes and Peter Damian; Abelard, perhaps, when he went South to meet Heloïse, having stayed in the Abbey for the night to debate with the learned Abbot and examine the new books from Rome. Oh, Jacquiz,' said Marigold, 'to ride on the same ferry as Abelard.'

'The Rolls seems rather incongruous . . . and rather shaming.'

But the two men who worked the ferry seemed pleased enough to nurse it down the ramp and into the barge. They even refused a tip.

'What's got into them?' said Jacquiz.

'Be quiet,' said Marigold. 'Just for once, even you be quiet.'

On the far side of the Seine a little road led from the landing place, round the back of the inn, and zig-zagged up the steep river bank through a tunnel of trees.

'Thank you,' said Jacquiz. 'That was a good present.'

She put one hand on his knee and let it rest there. They came over the crest of the slope and then, sometime later, out of the trees. The road lay straight ahead of them over a flat, yellow plain; two spires, one to left and one to right, rose out of copses in the distance.

'The Plain of Neubourg,' said Marigold. 'Straight on for the South.'

# 2. Garden with Cypress

Ivor Winstanley, tacking to and fro and up and down on the back lawn of Lancaster, from Sitwell's Building to the Cam and back to Sitwell's Building, striking obliquely towards the Provost's Lodge, crossing thence to the North and so to the walled garden of Tertullian Hall, wheeling South and back to the Provost's Lodge, setting full sail West by North for the river and there heaving to on a commodious bench – Ivor Winstanley, voyage as he might, could find no answer and no comfort in any quarter of the compass.

The position, as he told himself for the hundredth time, was this: the Provost wanted something damaging that he could use against Jacquiz Helmut in the latter's absence, in return for which 'something' he would ensure the renewal of Ivor's Fellowship in January next; there was, however, no 'something' to be found in Jacquiz' very competently ruled department; *unless*, that was, the Under-Collator and assistant archivist ('Call me Len') could be heavily enough bribed to find it, or rather, since it was not there, to cook it up.

Now, thought Ivor Winstanley, leave aside any moral repugnance which he himself might feel at employing such methods against a colleague who had once been his close friend, there were two very formidable and immediate problems (to say nothing of the long-term difficulties, which latter, however, could wait). In the first place, the 'something' must be so cleverly cooked up that the Provost would accept it as genuine; for Lord Constable was too scrupulous to be unscrupulous except on what he considered to be grounds of total authenticity. And in the second place there was the oppressive matter of the Under-Collator's reward. This he had indicated must be substantial, and he had suggested the guarantee of a Fellowship. But Ivor was in no position to guarantee Fellowships; only Lord Constable could do that, and there could be no question (*vide* Problem I) of inviting His Lordship's accomplicity.

What it all boiled down to, then, was this: what bribe could he, Ivor, dredge up that would be sufficient inducement to Len to do such a job on the College manuscripts (a very high quality job) as would lend Lord Constable a good conscience when and if he came to scupper Jacquiz?

Money? As to that, he could raise £2000 in cash but no more, and he himself had exigent need of over half of it. In any case, it was clear to him that Len was out for something durable – something comparable at least with the Fellowship for which he hankered. Expertise? Could Ivor provide Len with advice and assistance that would make the Under-Collator's dissertation, when presented, of such excellence as to win through Ivor's intellectual contribution what was not to be had through Ivor's mere machination? Ivor doubted this. He himself was a Latinist, while Len, he understood, was some sort of social scientist. The only help Ivor could give would be in matters of style and taste, the very last commodities which would recommend Len's thesis to the sociologists who would assess it. Affection then? Could Ivor make a friend of Len, and induce him to render for love the services for which Ivor could not pay in kind or cash? Absolutely not.

But there must be some answer, thought Ivor, as he rose from the bench and paced the grass by the river. He was a man of long experience and, by Cambridge standards at least, intricate worldly knowledge. There must be something within his skill or within his gift which would meet the price of Len's treachery.

But what it was he must discover very soon. It was high time he looked in on the Chamber of Manuscripts again, and it was also nearly time for lunch, which he would take that day in Hall. The Chamber of Manuscripts lay on his direct route to the Senior Common Room and his aperitif; he would drop in on Len for a few minutes first. A little diplomatic probing might establish at least the area of possible negotiation.



'Well, that's about that,' said Marigold on the balcony of the Boulevard des Pyrénées in Pau. 'Jewellers in plenty, antique jewellers in profusion, but none of 'em with records that go back more than eighty years. So what do we do now?'

'Look at the view,' said Jacquiz.

Leaning on the balustrade, they both looked down on the invalids' funicular railway, which ran all of a hundred yards, from the *Boulevard-Balcon* down to the gardens opposite the main line station. Beyond the station was a complacent strand of suburbs, beyond these were ridges of green which rolled in towards Pau, flecked with an occasional white foam of churches or farmhouses, like waves in the light breeze, and beyond these again the mighty breakers of the Pyrenees, a murderous grey under a green sky, for ever threatening to engulf the city but for ever keeping their distance, respectful of bourgeois Pau, of its trim *Boulevard-Balcon*, of the comfortable tourists who lounged along with Marigold and Jacquiz. Over all these the sun dispensed a soothing yellow benison, while somewhere a clock struck twelve, taking twice the usual time to do it.

'We might start thinking about lunch,' Marigold said.

'The Curse,' said Jacquiz.

'I beg your pardon.'

'The Curse of the Roses of Picardie. When they came to Pau, Constance and Louis Comminges had been in possession of the necklace for some weeks. And yet apart from Louis' marsh fever at Aigues Mortes, no misfortune . . . no serious misfortune . . . had befallen them.'

'Why should it have?'

'Because in the whole history of the thing there is a tendency, a definite tendency, for the Curse to inflict a pretty savage blow on new owners of the necklace shortly after they acquire it. Probably not a fatal blow, for usually the possessors are given a reasonable length of time in which to enjoy the Blessings, and in order to allow this the first and most immediate disaster inflicted by the Curse must be something less than lethal ... though it *was* sometimes a killer (witness the case of the last Clovis) and it could have been so with Comminges. But my real point is this, sweetheart: in any case at all, by the time the Comminges reached Pau we would expect that one or both of them should have suffered something far more injurious than a mere bout of marsh fever.'

'And so?'

'And so, Marigold, it is at least possible that something very nasty happened to Comminges while they were actually in Pau. It was *due* to happen, don't you see? Overdue, in fact.'

'To be sure, to be sure. And how do we hope to find it out, without any kind of clue to follow, some three hundred and twenty years later?'

'The Resort of Pau,' said Jacquiz teachingly, 'is chiefly famous for the curative qualities of its climate. But it is also celebrated, in a lesser way, for the properties of its waters. After lunch we shall go and drink them.'

'And do we imbibe second sight along with them?'

'Not quite,' said Jacquiz. 'We conjure the Hamadryad, the nymph of the Spring, and ask what she has to tell us.'

'How do we go about raising *her*?'

'If my memory serves me,' said Jacquiz, 'it's far more easy than you might think.'


'So here we are again, Ive,' said the Under-Collator of the Manuscripts to Ivor Winstanley. 'Nice to see you back.'

'I'm just on my way to luncheon,' said Ivor, who could think of no other observation.

'At quarter past twelve, man? Now take me – I can't leave till one.'

'We can't always do as we'd like while we are still very young,' said Ivor sententiously.

'Pity. That's when we enjoy it most.'

'I take your point.'

'So by extension, Ive, have you been thinking about what I said? About a Fellowship an' all if I do what you want and bitch Jake.'

'I've been thinking, Len.' Ivor brought out the odious vocative as if he were gagging on a fish bone. 'A Fellowship I can't guarantee for you. Though I could help you with your thesis.'

'Like hell you could. What do you know of creative therapies for the mentally deprived? That's my subject – God help me.'

'God help you? You chose the subject. I should have thought that you'd have found it . . . very affinitive.'

'That's what you would think, Ive. Here's that grotty Len, you think, just a typical lower-class student, choosing one of those absurd new subjects which we have to let them do because they're too stupid to do anything else and we've got to go with political fashion and find some excuse for letting them stay here. So this Len, we let him write a thesis about some rubbish called creative therapies, which keeps him happy and stops him making trouble. That's what you think, isn't it, Ive?'

'Roughly . . . I must admit . . . yes.'

'You don't understand a thing, man. You don't understand that what I really want . . . what a lot of us really want . . . is to be just the same as you. Only we can't be, see? We weren't brought up to it; we weren't taught the right things. We weren't taught the ancient languages, nor even the modern ones so's you'd notice. We weren't told about French Painting or Classical Music, or how many balls on a baron's coronet, or what to wear or how to talk. We weren't even taught proper history, only the Tolpuddle Martyrs and the crappy-arse labour movement; no kings or battles for us, no Borgias and no Caesars. In the old days we might have been taught these things – in some of the old Grammar Schools; but not now. *Now*, Ive, we were just crammed full of balls about self-expression and equality and the new society, and told to go forth and build the bloody thing. And since it was the only way out, since it was that or the shop floor, we obeyed: we went along with their terms, Ive, which for most of us meant strictly social studies. Science or medicine we were allowed if we had a bent for them, but your sort of Latin and Greek palaver – never.'

The Under-Collator paused. He took a long breath and his body twitched *cap-à-pé* with frustration.

'So all we could do,' he went grinding on, 'is the kind of shit I'm doing. The only way we could talk or behave is the kind of way I'm talking and behaving, and that was *it*, man, we were stuck with it. Yet it was you we dreamt about, *you* we wanted to be like: fruity guys like you, living in tall rooms looking over a lawn and a river, eating and drinking like Lucullus himself. And those of us who got places at Cambridge, rather than Essex or Sussex or Warwick, thought we might have a chance, because Cambridge was where *you* hung out. But we found you had no time for us, quite rightly, from your point of view, because we were dirty and boring and ignorant of all the things you cared about, and it was too late, it would take too much trouble, to turn us into anything different. So like I say we're stuck with ourselves, and don't think it makes us any nicer.'

'Where is all this leading?' asked Ivor.

The Under-Collator's eyes glistened with treachery and aspiration.

'Well, one answer might have been a Fellowship. If I got a Fellowship and lived long enough near your level, some of you might rub off on me and it might not be too late after all. But I'm not likely to win one, and you can't arrange one for me. So I've been thinking of another little scheme, man; something which might just raise me up where I want to be, and teach me what I want to be taught . . . might give me the good life, man . . . and it's something which you could help me with, in exchange for my helping you to down Jake.'

'I've no money, if that's what you mean. None to speak of.'

'I've got a cleverer idea than using your money, Ive. We're going to use your credit.'

'I don't quite follow you. If you mean that you want me to guarantee accounts for you with the tradesmen—'

'—Don't be so fucking dim, man. Here I am, cracking you up as my kind of culture hero, and all you can do is squawk like a grocer. I mean credit like "credit in heaven".'

'I still don't follow.'

'Well, come one o'clock, Ive, you can take me out somewhere and buy me a nice spot of food and drink for what you call luncheon, like you've been taught how and what and I haven't, and I will then make it all very plain . . .'


The Pump Room at Pau, as Jacquiz had correctly remembered, was a kind of vestry to the Casino's Cathedral; and in it were several copies of the official booklet about the hygienic history of the resort and the efficacy of its winds and waters. As they drank the revolting stuff out of huge jars, Jacquiz translated for Marigold's benefit. The Romans had discovered the Springs and noticed that their waters, applied whether internally or externally, induced a sense of peaceful well being: hence the name Pau, a corruption of *Pax Fontana*. During the Dark Ages the reputation of the Springs had been kept before the public by the rumour that they had cured the impotence of the Vandal Prince Sphintrax, while the relaxing powers of the waters, on the other hand, had been much praised by Sphintrax' contemporary, the Abbot Digitalis (596 to 672 A.D.) of Oloron.

'The Prince apparently drank the waters, while the Abbot bathed in them. It's the old advertising technique of having it both ways, telling the client that whatever he wants your product will effect it. A prince made ripe for the pleasure of love, an Abbot saved from its temptations. Yer pays yer money and yer takes yer choice.'

But it was neither as an aphrodisiac nor as an anaphrodisiac that the waters of Pau had achieved the wide celebrity which was to be theirs in the Middle Ages. This had been accorded by the comparatively late discovery that the

waters (like the climate) were especially beneficial in cases
of malaria or marsh ague, such as were frequent in the Cam-
argue to the East and the swampy pine forests of Bordeaux
to the West. Rich people convalescing from malaria or
threatened with fresh bouts of it, noblemen, merchants and
prelates, came in ever increasing numbers to drink and bathe
in the Fountains of Notre Dame de la Paix, as they were now
known, a plausible and expedient theological association (a
shepherd boy's purported vision of Our Lady riding side-
saddle on a goat and leading him to a new source) having
been hurriedly devised for them just before the visit, in
1477, of the Cardinal Archbishop Arnando di Chiusi. This
Prince of the Church was suffering from rheumatism consequent upon ague consequent upon keeping a foolish tryst in
a tower in the Maremma. The waters and the climate
together did wonders for His Eminence, who lingered in Pau
for three years and assured the fortune of the city for the
next hundred.

'Until well into the second half of the seventeenth century,' Jacquiz said to Marigold. 'You see what this means for
us?'

'Not really.'

'Think, my dear, just think. Even though Pau was going
out of fashion a bit by the time Louis Comminges was born,
he would certainly have known, if he was born anywhere in
the region, that the waters of Pau had recently enjoyed
high esteem as a cure for marsh fever. And now, here he
was, barely recovered from just such a fever himself and
possibly feeling fresh twinges. So perhaps he did not come
here on business after all. Perhaps he simply came to take a
cure.'

'Which made him sexy like the Prince,' said Marigold, 'or
doused him down like the Abbot?'

'What happened, sweetheart, what I very much hope happened, was that the cure, as a cure for fever, failed, and that
Louis Comminges died here in Pau.'

'Why should he have done that?'

'Because the fever at Aigues Mortes had been a bad one,

let us say, and because in those days such fevers, cure or no cure, were very often fatal.'

'If,' said Marigold, 'he was coming to Pau for a cure, why didn't he tell Constance? They were now on better terms, you say, and yet he gave her no reason why they were to come here. If the reason was his health he would surely have taken her into his confidence.'

'Perhaps he left her in the dark just *because* he was now fonder of her. Perhaps he didn't want to worry her by letting her know that he still felt ill. Perhaps he thought that things were difficult enough already and that such knowledge would damage her morale.'

Marigold thought carefully.

'You said not long ago,' she remarked, 'that the Curse of the Rubies was not usually fatal straight away. It often did something nasty to new owners, you said, but it seldom killed them until later on, after they'd had reasonable time to enjoy the benefits of Blessings. So why should it have killed Louis so quickly?'

'I also said that there were exceptions to the general rule. Louis could have been one.'

'What about Constance?'

'Perhaps something happened to her too. But by this time, remember, Louis was the real owner of the necklace because he was the owner of Constance. So it would more likely have been Louis that the genii or whatever was after – and I very much hope it killed him.'

'Why are you so keen for the poor bastard to have died here?'

'Because where there is death there is often information, and the obvious place to find it. Let's go and see if it's there.'


Out of the Pump Room and along the Boulevard; round a proud Château (pepper pot towers and grey, square keep, machicolated 'Fourteenth-century Donjon,' said Jacquiz, 'meaning business; the rest was done up for comfort by

132

Gaston de Béarn later on'); across a bridge and into neat public gardens; out of the gardens, across a main road lined on the far side with solid provincial houses, between two of these and up a steep, narrow street, every other shop in which was a seedy *alimentation*, over a cross road and into a graveyard:

Acre upon acre of mausoleums, buttressed or battlemented like forts, fantastically moulded into flamboyant chantries or squat miniature basilicas; canopies of crumbling tin over rusty, jagged crosses; shiny black slabs engraven with gold arabesque and resting on piles of chunky white chippings, Roman columns artificially broken at the midriff, plastic flowers in Perrier bottles or filthy jam jars.

'Only the English have proper churchyards,' Marigold said.

'We're looking for the old part. That will be better.'

'How do you know there is an old part?'

'There was an old church here once. Look.'

Marigold looked, and saw low sections of two broken walls of flint, which traced a skeletal nave. Jacquiz led the way down the nave, through another maze of mausoleums, down an avenue flanked on either side with cypress, through a slit in a hedge and into a little glade of stunted pines. Big, sunken box tombs ('Are they inside,' whispered Marigold, 'or underneath?') lurked like submarines, awash with weed.

'A bit better than the modern part,' said Jacquiz, 'though the gardener needs a good flogging.'

'Bend him over one of the tombs,' suggested Marigold. 'Rather fun. He's a dish.'

'Whatever do you mean?'

'Over there. That fair, smooth boy in the funny overalls, with a hoe.'

'I can't see him.'

'He was just over there.' Marigold walked away and stood under one of the less stunted pines. 'Here. He seems to have gone somewhere.'

Jacquiz joined her. Marigold sat down on a square stone of convenient height. Jacquiz watched her carefully.

'Open your legs,' said Jacquiz.

'My *dear*. Now if only you were that little gardener—'

'—I'm serious. Open up.'

Marigold parted her trousered thighs and calves.

' "Louis Comminges",' Jacquiz read, and stooped to look closer. ' "Louis Comminges, *de la famille* Comminges de la Seigneurie de Saint Bertrand-de-Comminges. 1600–1654." '

'Not very precise. No relations specified.'

'Precise enough. Saint Bertrand-de-Comminges? It's famous for something.'

'M. R. James wrote a ghost story about it,' said Marigold. 'About a greedy canon who stole treasure from the Chapter House. A thing like a demented monkey came and carried him off. Something like that.'

'I remember. There's a little cathedral with superb wood carvings in the choir. I read about it and meant to go there . . . one year just after the war . . . only I ran out of currency and had to go home instead. Near Luchon, I think?'

Marigold fished in her bag and brought out the Green *Michelin* for the Pyrenees.

'Bugger,' she said.

'Why bugger?'

'It must be on one of the pages I tore out in that café at Jumièges – in the loo.'

'Silly *cow*,' said Jacquiz venomously.

'I wasn't to know we'd need this particular page.'

'You shouldn't have torn out any pages at all.'

'What was a girl to do?'

'And what are you doing with the Pyrenees *Michelin* in Normandy?'

'I told you. It just happened to be in my bag. I'm *sorry*, Jacquiz, but I'm sure we can buy another.'

'You should have done some travelling just after the war like I did. You didn't buy another *Michelin* just like that in those days. You were so short of money that you rationed yourself to one meal a day, you never had a room with a bath, you never had a bath at all if you had to pay for it, even a small vermouth was a luxury—'

'—For Christ's sake belt up—'

'—You just don't know how spoiled you are—'

'—And do you mean to tell me there was no way of fiddling a bit extra?'

'Plenty of ways – and a stiff prison sentence if you were caught.'

'I see. So you were windy.'

'You don't know how spiteful the socialists were. If they could catch anyone having more of anything than anyone else—'

'—They're just as bad now. Much worse. You were windy.'

'It's a different sort of spite now,' said Jacquiz, at once raging and rational, both furious with Marigold and longing to expound an interesting point to her. 'In those days the socialists tried to stop all expensive forms of pleasure by making them illegal. But this turned too many even of their own people against them, so they shifted their ground. They allowed us to do things again, and then made vicious propaganda out of those that overdid them. Instead of forbidding and punishing the pleasures of the rich, they now merely denounce them publicly and whip up a lot of envy and malice in the process.'

'Clever don,' said Marigold. 'I'm not sure whether I buy it or not. Poor little Jacquiz, not having enough money to go to Saint Bertrand-de-Comminges. But we can go now, can't we? I've found it on another page – on a map.'

'We shall still have to buy another *Michelin*,' said Jacquiz, resentment not yet extinguished, 'to find out what's there.'

'I thought you'd read it all up – so you said.'

'Quarter of a century ago. We'll need to know details.'

'Come to that, what are we looking for?'

'I'm sick of being asked that question.'

'I thought I saw that gardener again. Face like a seraph.'

'Never mind him. Clearly, if Louis died here in Pau and left Constance all alone in the world, she had to go on to St Bertrand and claim her place among his family.'

'You reckon she knew about them by now? He was pretty cagey about them earlier on.'

'Yes, but he'd told her, you remember, that they were *personae non gratae* because they were or had been

Albigensians. He probably told her where they lived at the same time. He must have told her at *some stage* (possibly when he was dying) or she wouldn't have known enough about them to have all this carved here. "*De la famille* Comminges de la Seigneurie de Saint Bertrand-de-Comminges".' He rapped the words under her pelvis. 'Now then. Here she was in Pau, having buried Louis. She couldn't go back to Montreuil after the way she'd broken with her own family, so she simply had to go on – since life as a lone female for one of her age and class was in those days almost unthinkable – to her husband's family in Saint Bertrand-de-Comminges. And since they seem to have been a pretty substantial family' – he rapped the epitaph again – 'there could well be records of them in Saint Bertrand, and perhaps of Constance too. And now what's all this?' Jacquiz said, brushing aside the wide bottoms of Marigold's trousers.

'What's all what?' Marigold rose from her tomb. 'I think I'll peek about for that heavenly gardener.'

'No. Look at this. Down at the bottom here. Carved letters in a different style – it must have been done later. "S", "A", "C" ... SACERDOS. SACERDOS EXORAVIT ET ADJURAVIT TE. The priest has exorcized and adjured thee. "T", "A", "N" ... TANDEM TACETO ET MANETO. At last be silent and be still.'

Marigold's cheeks froze over with goose pimples.

'Let's go and buy that *Michelin*,' she said.

'Perhaps a word with that gardener first? He may know if there's any story attached to the grave – something that explains that inscription.'

'It's all too clear to me. If you want me to stay with you on this hunt, Jacquiz, let's get out of here and go to Saint Bertrand. Maybe you'll find the full story there in those family records you spoke of – at a safe distance from this thing. To think I was sitting on it for all of five minutes.'

Marigold shivered and wrapped her arms about her shoulders. Then she ran off in the direction of the avenue of cypresses. Jacquiz followed her at a walk, looking about him for the gardener, whom he did not see.

# IV

# Landscape with Hermits

'Stavros Kommingi?' Balbo Blakeney said.

'If you please.'

'I have a letter from your sister's husband.'

Kommingi held out a small, brown, filthy hand. Balbo passed him the letter. Kommingi began to read and Balbo looked about him.

He was standing in front of a wooden shack, set down between two rows of stone blocks and broken pillars which had once, Balbo supposed, been one side of a cloister. Parallel to it and some forty yards away, divided from it by an area of dry earth and yellow weeds, ran a wall, still intact, which doubled as the opposite or North side of the cloister and the South wall of a church (or basilica, since it had no transept) the apse of which was visible beyond some tumbledown arcading that still stood at the cloister's North-East corner.

To reach the cloister and Stavros Kommingi's shack, Balbo had walked a good half mile from a jagged gap, which had once been a gate, in the old wall of Nicopolis, through piles of collapsed masonry, over hillocks covered with spiked grasses and ankle-wrenching tendrils, past an elegant odeon (a tiny area of civility in this stricken heath of savage flora and flinty soil), and finally through an orange grove which smelt of sweet decay. He had been warned when he left Previsa that morning (and indeed also warned by a couple of peasants on the boat from Heracleion to Patras) that Nicopolis, so far from being a decorative antiquity for tourists or a well ordered archaeological site for scholars, was a neglected wilderness; but he had still not been prepared for the desolation of the tract which he had just traversed or for the villainous decay of the holy edifice at which he had now arrived. Wind, dust and stone, thought Balbo;

a waste land. All we need now is the rattle of dead men's bones.

'So,' said Stavros Kommingi, handing back the letter, 'you will like some lunch?'

'Very kind of you.'

'There is not much.'

Nor was there. Half a glass of wretched white wine, a few wizened olives, some exceedingly tough sausage.

'They forget to pay my money,' said Stavros complacently. 'The wage for this job is quite good, as wages go in Greece, but no one can be bothered to come from Arta to pay me. When I am desperate, I shall go to them. Meanwhile' – he indicated the cracked basin of scrawny olives – 'I manage as I can and I enjoy my work.'

'What exactly is your work?' said Balbo.

'I show the place to visitors. I try to stop it falling down any more than it has. I take care of the mosaics. We will see them. Come.'

He led Balbo across the cloisters, then along the south wall of the basilica and through a door into the nave. Between where they stood and the massy but battered screen which hid the sanctuary were several areas marked off by rope. Pausing by the first of these,

'Birds, plants, beasts,' Stavros said. 'Simply but effectively done. Very durable.'

Balbo looked down at a smiling, waddling duck. 'Sympathetic,' he said.

'Yes. Sympathetic.' Stavros pronounced the word as though testing it, then screwed up the small, round, black eyes in his big, round, brown face. 'Why have you come here, good Kyrie Blakeney?'

'Didn't your brother-in-law's letter tell you that?'

'He says you are interested in some French people who are – or were – called Comminges.'

'And I think it conceivable that they may be the ancestors of the Kommingi. The Kyrios Pandelios says that you are knowledgeable of the family genealogy. I wondered if you could provide a link.'

'Only that is not all. You are treasure-hunting,' said Stavros flatly.

'Did Pandelios tell you that?'

'No. You yourself. You have that faint look of desperation that characterizes treasure-hunters. I too once had it – but now I have become a mere dreamer. More restful and scarcely less futile.'

'Will you help me?'

'Why not? I have no doubt you would be generous if you were successful. It will give me something else to dream about.'

'Before I hunt for treasure,' said Balbo, 'I must hunt for the Comminges who may have it.'

'I know of no Comminges,' said Stavros. 'All I know is that as my family goes back it seems to have been richer and richer the longer ago we are thinking of, and to have been established further and further to the North and to the West. Conversely, you might say, time, which has made us poorer, has drawn us to the South and to the East.' He spread ten filthy finger nails for Balbo's inspection, and cackled. The only word for it, thought Balbo: cackled.

'How far North and how far West,' he said carefully, 'have your researches taken you?'

'My speculations have taken me boundless journeys, good Kyrie Blakeney. But my knowledge only takes me to Kerkyra.'

'To where?'

'Kerkyra. Corcyra. Koryphos. Corfu. Look. A stork catching a snake.'

'What about Corfu?'

'That is as far as I go back with certainty. I know that we Kommingi once lived on Corfu, and that we had come there from further North and further West, though I do not know from what place. I also know why we left Corfu and when.'

'When? Why?'

'Look: the poet Virgil. The Greek characters under the portrait say so clearly.' Stavros stooped to examine the mosaic more closely. 'No pretence, no explanation. A pagan poet in a Christian church. Why?'

'I don't know. Tell me more about the Kommingi on Corfu.'

'Why,' insisted Stavros, 'is a pagan poet on the floor of a Christian basilica?'

'Perhaps because he wrote an Eclogue which some think foretold the birth of Christ.'

'Correct.'

'What has all this to do with the Kommingi?'

'It has to do with the Komiki. Another family who lived on Corfu. The Komiki had an heirloom: a beautiful manuscript volume, illuminated, of the poems of Virgil. The illuminations at the beginning and end of the Eclogue to which you refer, the Messianic Eclogue, were the finest of all. So fine were they that the Venetian Governor of Corfu coveted the volume for these alone.'

'But what has this to do with the *Kommingi?*'

'Patience, good Kyrie Blakeney. I think you have been a scholar – so Pandelios says in his letter.'

'A scientist.'

'Then had you not better begin by asking about my sources of information? Treasure-hunting is an unreliable livelihood at best and much more exacting than merely dreaming. You must be satisfied that the information on the strength of which you proceed is sound information. Otherwise you will only waste what little money and energy yet remain to you.'

'A very fair point. Well then: what are your sources of information?'

'Dust and ashes.' Again Stavros cackled. 'Volumes of local history and gossip in the library of the town of Corfu. Burnt when the library caught fire some years ago. Are you going to believe my account of them?'

'I have no choice.'

'Oh, but you have. You can just go home and abandon the whole thing. That is what reason advises. Why should you set out on a long trail, on the strength of information provided by a half-crazed curator of antiquities – who will be telling you, from his most unstable memory, what he thinks that he might once have read in books of light-minded tittle-tattle which no longer exist? Cease to be a treasure-hunter and stay at home dreaming like me.'

'I have no home to dream in.'

'Nor had I. I made one here.'

'I have promised to search. There is a bargain.'

'Ah-ha. So Pandelios is supporting the expedition. I might have known it. And you, the English man of honour, feel that you must give him value for his ill-gotten money?'

'That's about it.'

'Poor Kyrie Blakeney. Chasing one illusion in deference to another. Pursuing fairy gold in the name of honour. But one must respect you. Oh yes. That mosaic down there is the Empress Theodora,' he said, 'a whore who took up virtue because she found that it paid better and was a great deal more comfortable than vice. She did the right thing for the wrong reason, as your English poet says. But you, Kyrie Blakeney, are doing the wrong thing for the right reason. Therefore one must respect you. So much must one respect you that I shall try to tell you only what I believe to be strictly true. Let us sit down.'

They sat side by side on a set of twelfth-century sedilia. A piebald dog wandered up the nave, snarled rather slackly as it passed them, and scrabbled its way through an ugly hole in the screen and into the sanctuary.

'It keeps its bones there,' said Stavros. 'Now then: Corfu. The family of Komikos, who are, in the plural, Komiki. Unlike the Kommingi, who are Kommingi whether they are one or many.'

'Because, we hope, they are descended from the Com-minges, who are also plural whether they are one or many.'

'That is as it may be, good Kyrie. Meanwhile we have Christopheros Komikos and his family, the Komiki, and their beautiful illuminated manuscript of Virgil. What, we ask ourselves, have any of them to do with my ancestors?'

'To start with, they are very similar in name, I suppose.'

'Quite right, good Kyrie. Much, though by no means all, of the tale I have to tell will turn on that. Listen and ponder. Two families lived in the city of Corfu, the Komiki, at the head of whom was Christopheros Komikos, and the Kommingi, at the head of whom was one Andreas Kommingi. Both families were wealthy, owning ships which traded all over the Levant, owning gorgeous Venetian houses, almost palaces, in the city, and villas with large estates in the country. The only difference was that, whereas the Komiki had always been there, the Kommingi were quite recent arrivals. They had come from the North and West – it is impossible to be more precise, for that is all that they themselves ever gave out – they had come from the North and West, in their own ship, in the first decade of the eighteenth century. We are now speaking, you should know, of the year 1728 and for all that the Kommingi had been on the island for more than twenty years, no one knew one iota more of the history of their line and their riches than had been learned on the morning when they first put into Corfu harbour, in their ship *Cathar*, with a cargo of silks, perfumes, fine clocks and young blackamoors, "from the north".'

'The cargo suggests Venice.'

'But they hadn't come from there. The Venetian authorities on Corfu, glad to see wealthy newcomers but anxious to check up on the provenance of both them and their wealth, inquired of them by the next packet to Venice, and drew blank. All other inquiries in all other places – Genoa, Naples, Amalfi – drew blank. The Kommingi had just sailed in from nowhere – probably, the authorities thought, from some shadowy region where their wealth had been far from licitly acquired and which they were much too prudent to divulge. In the end, the administration decided to respect their reticence. For there was much to recommend the Kommingi: their money was copious and good; the silks and blackamoors they offered for sale were in prime condition and reasonably priced; and when they were all sold, the good ship *Cathar* sailed away none knew whither, and returned laden down with more merchandise of similar quality and appeal . . . none knew whence.

'Now, while the Kommingi were in general made welcome, there were certain Corfiot merchants who regarded them with suspicion as parvenus and with envy as rivals. Foremost and fiercest to take this view were the Komiki, who lost no opportunity of thwarting and blackguarding the Kommingi, but for a long time fought a losing battle. Every day the Kommingi gained in wealth and influence on the island, and by the time of which we are speaking they had long had the ear of the Governor himself, whom they used to supply, *gratis*, with the most succulent blacks of either sex from successive cargoes.'

'Is this the same chap that coveted the Komiki's manuscript Virgil?'

'Alas, no. Listen and learn, good Kyrie Blakeney. This is the *immediate predecessor* of the bibliophile, a man called Lorenzo di Burano, a man of debauched life but undoubted administrative talent, particularly keen and busy on the afforestation of the island.'

'When not keen and busy on young niggers of either sex?'

'Right. As time went on the Kommingi made it clear that they would very much like to be ennobled. As you know, at that time, although Venetian noblemen bore no title – only the appendage to their names of the letters NH (*nobilis homo*), – the Venetian Council often saw fit to ennoble eminent men in their foreign dependencies with the title of baron or count; and the Governor of Corfu now informed the Kommingi that he could arrange with the Council in Venice for the elevation of Andreas to the latter and higher dignity, on two conditions: first, that the supply of tender black flesh should be kept up and stepped up, novelty now being a necessity to a middle-aged man whose powers were waning; and secondly, to make it appear ἐν τάξει in Venice, that the Kommingi should contribute abundantly to the funds for afforestation. All this having been agreed, application was made by the Governor for a patent – a patent which was duly forthcoming and duly despatched from the

Serenissima. But it was at this very promising stage, alas, that the affair began to turn sour.'

'The Komiki?'

'The Komiki.' Stavros emitted a long cackle and spread his cracked and filthy palm just under Balbo's chin. To listen to Stavros, thought Balbo, was like listening to a lecture from a Regius Professor issue from the lips of a tramp.

'Oh dear me, yes,' said Stavros. 'Those Komiki. The rumour that the Kommingi were about to be ennobled was more than they could bear. They considered reporting the Governor to the Doge for depravity, in the hope that this would invalidate his recommendation on behalf of the pimp who had supplied him, but they abandoned the scheme as several members of their own clan were open to retaliation in kind. They considered a deputation to the Governor, to urge that the Kommingi were unworthy; they considered a bribe; they even played with the notion of assassination. But they need not have troubled themselves so sorely: for on the day before the patent was expected to reach Corfu, the Governor slumped dead as a stuck pig while sitting at stool on a choice commode and inspecting a new consignment of choice piccaninnies.

'Whereupon his Deputy or Lieutenant took over until a new appointment could be made from Venice – and it was this Deputy, now Governor in substance, who so admired the Komiki's Virgil. A deal was quickly done. The new Acting Governor would return the Kommingi patent to Venice, with the comment that it had been wrongly drawn – that by an easily understandable confusion the name "Kommingi" had been erroneously inserted in his predecessor's application instead of the correct name, which was "Komikos". In return for this service, the Komiki would present the Acting Governor, on the day the revised patent arrived in Corfu, with the illuminated Virgil.

'All of which was done. For Christopheros Komikos' county was in due course ratified in Venice and the emended patent returned to Corfu. It was now the Kommingi's turn to be unhappy.'

He paused as the piebald dog scrambled through the broken screen into the nave and slouched past them. A tile fell to the floor just behind it and was totally ignored both by it and by Stavros, who now continued:

'They had lost their main ally, the Kommingi, in the dead Governor. The new Acting Governor had always disapproved of them because of their influence with and easy access to the old, and he, like the Komiki, was scared lest they should raise a row about the doctored patent of nobility. Added to all this, was another factor: the new Acting Governor was a man of curious integrity. Although he had accepted the Virgil for his services, he would accept nothing else, no money, no jewels, no houses, no favours from the Komiki women. The fact was that the Virgil was the only thing he had ever yearned for so fiercely as to desert the paths of virtue, and that, in so far as procuring the altered patent was the only corrupt act he had ever committed, he was that much the more anxious to dispose, effectively but without committing a further crime, of those who might bear witness against him. There were, as the Komiki now informed him, excellent and strictly licit grounds for disposing of the Kommingi. For the Komiki were conducting investigations from which it had recently appeared that an indictment of piracy could almost certainly be laid against their enemies. Not all those skills and black ephebes had been acquired in the fair course of commerce. Let the Acting Governor now take over the investigations himself, with the ampler resources available to him, and no doubt hard proof of the Kommingi's delinquent methods of trading would soon be discovered – whereupon the Kommingi themselves could be summarily suppressed.

'So the Acting Governor turned his spies and informers on to the investigation. This was more difficult and prolonged than he had expected, as the Kommingi had covered their tracks with some skill. Indeed it was necessary to send to Venice itself and request the Venetians' experienced assistance in the matter, which turned on issues too delicate and distant to be resolved by a mere Acting Governor of a small island in the Ionian Sea. It was at this stage – five days after the collected evidence had been sent, in the care of a special Commissioner, to Venice – that the Kommingi vanished. One and all, root and branch, lock, stock and barrel. One day they were living with every refinement in their magnificent house, which overlooked the harbour and three of their ships at anchor in it. The next morning the house was a shell and the ships were gone.'

'Why hadn't they been arrested? I mean, if the Acting Governor had got as far as sending the evidence against them to Venice, one would expect them to have been detained.'

'Ah-ha. They were given a chance to slip away because that was what the Acting Governor really wanted. He wanted them out of the way, not volubly defending themselves in Courts of Law, where they would certainly have retailed at length his own motives for pursuing the investigations against them. A trial might have been the ruin of everyone, as both the Acting Governor and the Kommingi were sensible enough to see. As it was, a satisfactory solution had been reached. The Kommingi had departed South and East and would not be heard of again in Venetian territories whether for good or ill; while the Commissioner, who held the evidence against them, had been instructed not to make too much bustle about it in Venice – whither he had been sent only in order to delay the proceedings and give the Kommingi the time to gather up their effects and depart at leisure.'

'I should have thought the Acting Governor would have liked them to depart hugger-mugger – leaving their effects behind for official confiscation.'

'Why? The confiscated property would not have gone to him, since he was an honest man, but would have escheated to the state. He was not, furthermore, a man to bear animus. Although he may have disapproved of the Kommingi, he didn't hate them. He had the one thing he ever wanted – the Virgil – and he wished everyone well, including the Kommingi, provided only he could be sure that they wouldn't make injurious remarks, so to speak, in his own parish. The

Kommingi were now gone – to Lycia, as he later learned – *et voilà* . . .'

'All very interesting,' Balbo said. 'But as you must realize, what I want to know is not where they went after Corfu but where they came from before.'

'I am coming to that, good Kyrie Blakeney. As I say, before the Kommingi departed the island inquiries had been made about them and evidence had then been sent to Venice. But never forget that the persons to initiate the inquiries were the Komiki. So it is at least possible that the Komiki discovered where the Kommingi had come from when they first arrived in Corfu, and that the information is available to this day in their family records.'

'The Komiki never published it?'

'Neither then nor ever. But they are still there on Corfu, the Komiki, and it is possible that their records of this affair are still there with them. But your approach to them would have to be delicate. I myself tried to win their acquaintance, at a time when I was as not dirty as I am now' – he spread his fingers before his face – 'but was spurned because I was not a gentleman. You, good Kyrie, they will know to be a gentleman, and so it could be easier for you. But do not count on that. They have some family secret or catastrophe – nothing to do with what we have been talking of but something that came to them much later – and this makes them wary of strangers.'

'If the Komiki were not communicative,' said Balbo, 'there might be something to my purpose in the official records of the Island and City of Corfu, dating from when the Acting Governor of Corfu took over the inquiries from the Komiki.'

'Which was a very long time ago. Wars, revolutions, plagues and massacres have intervened. It is not only the Library of Corfu which has been destroyed. Official archives and records have likewise perished from time to time. Fire has gutted them or damp has rotted them or the prudence of man has buried or sunk them. Besides, the abstract of the inquiry which the Commissioner took to Venice may well have been the only copy and may well have stayed there. I do not think you will find what you want in Corfu unless it be in the private possession of the Komiki.'

'Who may not be willing to talk. What then?'

'Then . . . Venezia will be your only chance. We know that the Special Commissioner appointed to carry the evidence thither was instructed not to be . . . officious . . . in the matter. However, it is possible that at some stage the report was actually handed over to the Venetians, and if so, whether or not anything was ever done about it, it may well still be in the official archives – since those of the Serene Republic are less vulnerable and more carefully preserved than those of Corfu – and it may well contain the information you wish.'

'I. e.: where did the Kommingi live and operate before they went to Corfu.'

'So there it is, good Kyrie Blakeney. You should proceed first to the Komiki in Corfu, whom you will find unwelcoming of strangers; then to the official archivists of the City, who will almost certainly be unable to help you; and last to the official archivists of Venezia, who can throw open to you, should they be in a good mood, miles and miles of corridors crammed to the ceiling with documents among which you may seek a hundred years for the ones you desire – only to find them useless.'

'That's about it, I suppose.' Balbo sighed. 'Thank you, Stavros.'

'And thank you for thanking me, good Kyrie Blakeney. But if you ask my advice, you will not trouble to do any of these things. You will cease to be a hunter of treasure . . . which you find exciting but upsetting, destructive of tranquillity and grating on the nerves . . . and you will become, like me, a dreamer at home.'

'What home?'

'My home. Here.'

Balbo looked slowly round the crumbling basilica, up at the gaps in the roof and down again at Stavros Kommingi as he sat by his side on the sedilia. The proposal was preposterous but not, somehow, embarrassing. Stavros was neither importunate nor grovelling; he was merely making a modest invitation and in the mildest manner. The only problem was how to refuse him with a good grace.

'If you stay, I will find you drink,' said Stavros. 'I see that this is what you need, and I will find it for you. I am good at finding people what they need.'

'How is it,' said Balbo, temporizing, 'that you speak such fluent and idiomatic English?'

'I had an English friend. Here. Until not long ago. I found him in Corfu, when I was there reading in the Library of which I told you. Unlike you, he did not need drink, but he wished to be assured. He was travelling in search of assurance, and he thought that I might provide it.'

'Assurance of what?'

'He had been, for a time, a Franciscan Friar. Before that he had been a student. As a student he had witnessed something ugly – he never told me what – for which he was in part responsible. Although at first not much affected, he had been belatedly tortured by dormant remorse, and had fled from England. Eventually he had taken refuge with the Good Brothers in Italy, who at first calmed and soothed him by their gentleness and love of God's creatures, but later annoyed and disgusted him by their naïvety and ignorance.'

'But what assurance did he seek that you could possibly provide?'

'The assurance that he had been right to despise and desert the Good Brothers. He wished passionately to disbelieve in God, and he thought that this basilica – which I described to him one day – would help him. "Ah-ha," he said when I spoke of it, "the mouldering coffin of God, cast amid thistles upon waste land." So he came here with me and seemed to derive satisfaction from the spectacle of this poor church and from our life here in its shadow. For myself, I did not care what his motive was, only so long as he stayed with me. For I loved him, in a sort, and my hands were not dirty then.' He spread his hands before him. 'If you stayed, good Kyrie Blakeney, I would make them clean again.'

'What happened to your Englishman?'

Just perceptibly Stavros flinched before answering.

'In time, he went. One morning I awoke and he was gone. It would be the same with you. You would be quite free to go, you see. So why not stay, just a little while, and try what dreaming can do? If only for one night . . .'

Balbo looked at the morose and degraded piebald dog, which had apparently returned to the sanctuary unnoticed while he was talking with Stavros and was now emerging from it once more through the hole in the screen. 'It keeps its bones there,' Stavros had said. And now it was carrying one of them out. Not without difficulty; for the bone, a shin-bone by the look of it, kept getting stuck. Where, thought Balbo vaguely, would the dog have found a shin-bone? Too long for a goat and too short for a cow. Balbo, though a bio-chemist, had once done a short course on the anatomy of mammals in preparation for his wartime duties, which had at first comprised other matters than plague rats; and so he could with confidence pronounce that the shin-bone, which the dog was now at last carrying down the nave, was too long for a goat or a sheep, too short for a horse or a cow. The right length for a calf then? Perhaps . . . except that one slight bulge, just below where the shin would have fitted the knee-joint, stirred Balbo's distant memories of his wartime course and produced a flickering vision in his mind of an old man in a white coat who was pointing with a long, white wand at the knee-joint of a human skeleton.

'A man to see you,' said Elvira Constable, poking her nose into her husband's study and instantly withdrawing it.

'What do you mean, "a man"?' said Provost Constable of Lancaster College.

'I mean, not a gentleman,' said Lady Constable, prodding her nose through the doorway again.

'I wish you wouldn't make remarks like that. One of these days some wretched student will hear you and make trouble. What's his name, this – er – man?'

'I shouldn't think it matters, should you? Anyway, he hasn't really got one.'

'Stop being silly, Elvira. Of course he has a name.'

'I was speaking metaphorically. In fact his name is Jones, and here's his card to prove it.'

Syd Jones, said the card; and unexpectedly added an address in Jermyn Street and a West End telephone number.

'Ask Mr Jones to come in,' said Lord Constable.

'Go in,' said Lady Constable at once, shooting her nose back and forth through the doorway like a woodpecker working on vacancy. A man, who must have been standing just behind her the entire time she was talking to the Provost, worked his way round her and through what was left of the entrance. Luckily he was a very small man.

'That will be all, Elvira.'

'Thank you, my lord.'

Lady Constable curtsied and withdrew.

'My wife is rather eccentric,' said Lord Constable to Mr Jones.

'Just so long as she ain't dangerous,' said Mr Jones in a high-pitched and good-humoured Australian accent. 'Nah then: you're Lord Constable of Reculver Castle, life only, first and last; and you're also Provost of this College ... which means yer run the place?'

'I do, sir. What do you want with me?'

'Information, Lord Constable of Reculver Castle. I come from Jermyn Street, as my card states. Yer know what all *that* means?'

'No. Why should I?'

'"Cos you've got a knowing sort of look. But since yer don't ...'

Mr Jones tapped the top of his ginger head with four fingers of both hands.

'Intelligence,' he said. He lifted the lapel of his coat and huddled behind it. 'The old cloak and dagger game.'

'Do you possess ... rather more adequate means of identifying yourself than this card?'

'No, Lord Constable of Reculver Castle. If yer doubt me –

and I agree my Oz accent may strike yer funny – ring the number on my card. They'll put yer straight. And then, ever when y'er ready, we'll talk.'

'Shall we indeed?'

'Yeez,' said the chipper little man. 'Suit yerself whether yer ring the old firm first. Yer've forgotten to ask me to sit down, but I'm not a man to take offence.'

He perched his scanty bottom on a hard chair, took some notes from a briefcase, held them right up in front of his face, and began (presumably) to read them.

'Why are you working for a department of the British Government,' said Constable, 'when you yourself are Australian?'

'I'm not Australian. I went there to play cricket. I liked the accent and brought it home with me.'

'Syd Jones,' said Constable, reading from the card. He put it down and went on in a sing-song voice, like a big child telling over its lesson. 'Otherwise Jones, S., of Glamorgan, capped in 1946 and retired in 1957, all rounder, one tour of Australia and one of South Africa, best Test Match performances five wickets for seventy-three runs and a hundred and three not out, both in the same match – versus Australia at Lords in 1951.'

'Good going, sport. You a cricketer chap yerself?'

'No, but I have a passion for *Wisden*. I never played the game, not even at school, and I never watched it,' said Constable; 'but I have every extant volume of *Wisden* and one or other is always by my bed.'

'What's the attraction if yer don't like the game?'

'Figures. Records. Averages. Number of centuries scored, number of hat-tricks taken. Aggregate of runs made by such or such a man (a) in Test Matches, (b) in First Class Cricket as a whole. To me,' said Lord Constable, 'there is fascination here. Like a rare and powerful drug. *Wisden* both soothes and stimulates me.'

'Sounds a bit whacky from where I sit.'

'I know, I know. There is a strain of madness here. I have never before confessed this taste to anyone. No one knows save my wife, who dusts the volume currently on my bed table. But since you yourself figure in that magic compilation, I can surely confide in you. I was reading of you only the other night. You made a nought in both innings—'

'—A pair of ghoolies—'

'—Against Derbyshire at Chesterfield in 1948. Oh, how infinitely satisfying those two chaste symbols appear with your name, twice in the same line of the page. Jones (S.) caught and bowled Sligsby ... nought. And then, in the column for the second innings but, as I say, on the same line: Jones (S.) lbw bowled Bowles ... nought. I think it is my favourite entry in the volume – if not in the whole great work.'

'It wasn't so bleeding lovely when it happened, I'm here to tell yer *that*.'

'And so how is it, Jones, S., of Glamorgan, that you come to be doing ... the very different work ... on which you are now apparently engaged?'

'I knew a chap who knew a chap who asked me to run a message to a chap in Jo'burg when I went there on the S.A. tour. Nasty complications but mission accomplished. Department grateful, see? Took me on when cricket left me off, and shunted me into the Jermyn Street branch, which means home affairs. Home affairs include dicey dons. One of yer dons is dicey.'

'Which one?'

'The one that's gone straying off over Europe.'

'That'll be Doctor Jacquiz Helmut,' said Constable with relish.

'Never 'eard of that bastard. Try again.'

'None of my dons, except Doctor Helmut, has gone straying off over Europe.'

'Pardon me, Lord Constable of Reculver Castle. What about a certain Balbo Blakeney?'

'He is no longer one of my dons. Dismissed his post in the University and consequently deprived of his Fellowship of this College. For drink.'

'He's still on the list, sport.'

'He won't be on the next one. What do you want with him?'

'Rats. During the war he worked with rats. Right?'

'I dare say.'

'And I do say. Nothing much came of it, but he had a hand with rats. We think he knows something . . . which we'd rather like to know but don't. Rats are back in fashion, see? Read me, do yer?'

'I read you, Jones, S.'

'Dinkum so far then. But you tell me this Blakeney number is a wayback boozer?'

'Dismissed for it.'

'That's bad, him being a boozer. He may have forgotten what he knew. Where is he?'

'As you said, Jones, S., of Glamorgan: straying over Europe.'

'Please be more precise, Lord Constable.'

'Why should I be? I had to dismiss Blakeney, but I bear him no malice. Why should I allow him to be badgered about by you?'

'You don't like me?'

'I like you well enough, in so far as I know you. It's your department I don't trust. I don't think your department is going to be very kind to Balbo Blakeney. He has plenty to endure just now without unkindness.'

Lord Constable was a hard and resourceful man who, in the interest of Lancaster College as he conceived it, would stop at nothing to get his way. In the interest of the College he would deceive and exploit (as he was presently exploiting Ivor Winstanley), he would lie, betray and cheat (as he intended to cheat Jacquiz Helmut), and he would crush without mercy (as he had recently crushed Balbo Blakeney). But once he had had his way for the College's sake he bore no ill will for his own. His victims, once they had been so disciplined or disposed of that they could no longer fail or harm his College, could remain his friends, if they would, and, even if they would not, could expect from him nothing but courtesy and kindness. Lord Constable, so far from being vindictive, was of all men *ceteris* strictly *paribus*, the most considerate. He was therefore very sorry for Balbo and wished that Balbo might suffer no more than he had to; Balbo had been his man once, a bad man but his man, and in so far as he still could he would protect him now. And so,

'Balbo Blakeney has plenty to endure,' Constable repeated to Jones, S. 'I want him left alone.'

'He won't be left alone. When the likes of me comes prying, no one we want is left alone. You know that, Lord Constable of Reculver Castle. We'll find out where he is whether or not you tell us. And in the latter event we shan't be very pleased with you.'

'Don't you threaten me, man. I tell you, I have—'

'—Friends. Friends in high places. Friends in high enough places to piss on the department. Like enough, Lord Constable. But Balbo Blakeney hasn't any friends in high places any more, ever if he had. It's Balbo Blakeney we're really threatening, sport. And you can make it easier for him. Which, if I mistake not, is what you want.'

'How can I make it easier for him?'

'By telling me where he is. Blakeney, the dicey don, comes under home affairs, like I told yer. And so, even if he's abroad, a home affairs man goes to talk to him – provided we know where to find him and can go straight there. But if there's got to be a silly buggers' hunt, they'll send a foreign affairs man, because a silly buggers' hunt in Europe comes under foreign affairs, see, and once that happens we can't be at all sure who might be sent after poor boozy Balbo.'

'What difference does it make?'

'The difference between a foreign affairs man, perhaps a mean man, Lord Constable of Reculver Castle, and perhaps made even meaner by the trouble he'll have being all buggered up by the search – the difference between such a ratty-arsed sod as that bastard might prove to be and a *home affairs* chap, perhaps quite a nice chap, like me.'

Constable grunted noncommittally. Jones, S., rose from his chair and lightly sketched a forward defensive stroke with his wrists and arms, left elbow well up and prominent.

'Yer know what that is, sport?'

Constable shook his head.

'It's a straight bat. That's how I always tried to play, and how I still do. I think you know that much about me already. When you realized that I was a cricketer chap—'

'—A name out of *Wisden*, that's all—'

'—All right. When you realized I'd come out of the pages of your *Wisden*, you didn't bother any more with checking out my credentials. That's what I mean.'

He picked up his card from Constable's desk and put it in his pocket.

'You're trying to persuade me,' said Constable, 'that I can trust you.'

'Yeez. That you can trust me to be kind to your chum, or at any rate not such a bastard as someone who lives and hunts among foreigners and has picked up all their dirty foreign habits. And another thing: cricketing chaps often take to the drink – Tennyson, Chapman, Hammond, to mention only a few – and so they're well disposed, as a body, to poor old battered bottle-hoovers like this Blakeney seems to be.'

'But you said it was bad, from your professional point of view, his being a drunkard.'

'So it is. Very bad. But I could still be well disposed, personally, whether others might not be.'

'Will they send you . . . personally?'

'If I know where to find him . . . yeez. If not, it could be anybody – anybody from foreign affairs. Help me, Lord Constable of Reculver Castle; help me, help yer chum.'

'Balbo Blakeney,' said Constable, 'has not yet given us a forwarding address. But I believe him to be in Crete. In Heracleion.'

'What makes yer believe that?'

Constable hesitated.

'He was good enough to send me a postcard not long after he arrived there. He was settling down in Heracleion, he said, and had found a paying pupil to whom he gave lessons in English.'

'And how come he was sending chatty postcards to you

'. . . you who'd put him through the squeezer and poured him away down the pan?'

Constable blushed.

'When . . . he was disgraced . . . I knew he wanted to go away. I also knew that he'd recently lost his private fortune and had next to nothing of his own. So I asked him where he wanted to go, and he said Crete, and I . . . arranged for him to have a ticket.'

'Bought it with yer own bangers and mash, yer mean. Good on you, cobber.'

'So I suppose he thought it was only polite to send me a line or two to say how he was getting on.'

'And he was getting on – or getting by – in Heracleion. But no address?'

'No address.'

'Heracleion's a small place with a lot of bars, as I recall, for its size, but that don't make more than a conscientious investigator can cover in a day. They'll know of him in one of those – mayhap the first I walk into. That's the one good thing about piss-artists: it's no problem to find them if you've got less than a hundred square miles or so to look in.'

'There's a photo somewhere – my wife took it in the Fellows' Garden – if it would help.' Constable fumbled in a drawer. 'Here.'

'We've got one. But I'd like another.' Jones, S., looked at the photograph which Constable handed to him. 'Jeeze,' he said, 'when was this taken?'

'About two years ago.'

'Jeeze,' said Jones again. 'For someone who was sucking it out of a hose, this Blakeney looks very pretty.'

'*Pretty?*'

'Yeez. Not handsome – too soft. Not beautiful – too round. But pretty. See that smooth forehead? Like a small child or a puppy. Something you want to pick up and fondle – even though yer know bleeding well that at any mo it'll do a runny yellow crap down yer clobber.'

The taxi rumbled round the bends and down the hill towards the Port of Kato Korax and the country villa of Count Komikos on its quay. The expense of the taxi was much resented by Balbo, but there was no other practicable manner (or so he had been told) of making the journey. What made it worse was that he had been incurring unlooked-for expenses ever since he left Nicopolis. Two seconds after seeing the human shin-bone borne away by the piebald dog, he had realized the various possible implications of the spectacle (which ranged from the unpleasant to the unspeakable) and had felt a panic urge to be gone immediately. After a blind, panting rush from the basilica and a desperate long-distance race from Stavros (who had pursued Balbo, screaming that he was a nobleman by right and commanded Balbo to remain and make obeisance, well beyond the old city and almost into the nearest village) he had hailed the first car to pass him, a small farmer's van, and had bribed the driver to take him back to his hotel in Previsa. He had then celebrated his escape with a costly dinner of crayfish, drunk a great many glasses of French cognac from the only bottle of the stuff to be found in all Previsa, felt sick and guilty the next morning, decided notwithstanding to proceed straight to Corfu, and had been too tired, when he disembarked from the ferry that evening, to look for a cheap hotel. Indeed, the one into which he had booked himself, just over the road from the harbour, had been, by his standards, quite outrageously luxurious. It was here that he had been told that no approach to the villa of Count Komikos was conceivable save by hired car or taxi – one of which they had officiously insisted on procuring for him, no doubt on a handsome commission. And so now here he was, on a light bright Corfiot morning, circling down to the little port of Kato Korax, burning money, and passing at every hundred yards, or so it seemed, a perfectly satisfactory coach or bus on which he might have made the journey.

According to a slim guide book on Corfu, which he had purchased at a kiosk in Igoumenitza before boarding the ferry boat, the Komiki had for some generations been ardent and noted amateur natural historians. Balbo had therefore introduced himself, when telephoning the previous evening for permission to call at the villa, as a bio-chemist from Cambridge who was interested in the secretions to be had from local herbs and flowers. Count Komikos, at first very wary (as Stavros had said he would be), warmed a little when Balbo announced the ostensible purpose of his visit, bubbled slightly when Balbo turned a neat compliment about the distinguished contribution of the Komiki to Greek botanical studies, and eventually, though still with a trace of his initial reluctance, invited Balbo to lunch.

Although a free lunch would be most acceptable after his recent occasions of heavy expenditure, Balbo was for several reasons too troubled to take pleasure in the prospect of this agreeable economy. His first source of worry was the reflection that since Stavros Kommingi was plainly and dangerously disordered, anything or everything which he had said about the connection between the Komiki and the Kommingi might be untrue; in which case Count Komikos would have no information to give him, his journey would have been wasted, and his visit highly embarrassing. Balbo's second anxiety was that his visit would almost certainly be highly embarrassing in any case, this because of the difficulty he must undergo in turning the conversation from botanical secretions to the corrupt proceedings of the Komiki 200-odd years earlier, a pretty wide arc over which to switch compass. And a third and eminently justifiable fear which Balbo entertained was lest the Count, though indeed having the information which Balbo sought and having been brought by Balbo's dialectical skill to admit as much, might nevertheless refuse to come across with the goodies and have Balbo ejected for prying and treacherous abuse of hospitality.

All in all, then, it was an unhappy Balbo who climbed out of his taxi on the quayside of Kato Korax, went up an elegant flight of steps central to a charming if rather worn baroque façade, and knocked on a large, unpainted, panelled door with a brass grotesque of Gluttony affixed there for the function.

After rather a long delay, the door opened.

'Good morning,' said a voice in an Oxford accent with the slight bubble of catarrh which Balbo had noticed on the telephone. 'You, I expect, are Mr Blakeney from Cambridge. I am Count Komikos.'

Balbo was aware of a small hand which was reaching out as if to stroke his knee. For what Stavros Kommingi had not told him, if indeed he had ever known, was that Count Komikos, while perhaps seventy years old, grey at the temples, intellectual and authoritative in countenance, gentlemanly in bearing, and immaculately dressed as for breakfast in an English country house on a morning in 1912, was little more than three feet high.

'It is most kind of Your Excellency to receive me,' said Balbo, reckoning that an old-fashioned style of address was called for. With a deep bow he contrived to take the nobleman's proffered hand.

'I have always regarded it as my duty and privilege to receive learned gentlemen from foreign countries,' said the Count. 'Pray to come in.'

The Count led Balbo through a narrow hall flanked on either side by ill-painted portraits of otherwise distinguished and intelligent faces which surrounded narrow but normally sized shoulders. Was his host the first Komikos to have been born a midget, Balbo wondered; or had the portraits, or some of them, been blown up, so to speak, to conceal an hereditary disability? They passed into a study which looked out, through a bay window beyond a miniature desk, on to a grove of young cypress trees.

'Pray to be seated,' said Count Komikos, pointing to a chair between globes of heaven and earth.

Now or never, Balbo thought. I cannot play at games of deception with this exquisite old gentleman. In face of such courtesy and courage I cannot prevaricate and distort.

'Your Excellency should know at once,' said Balbo, not taking the chair which he was offered, 'that I am an im-

postor. I could indeed be called a learned man, a *quondam*
Fellow of Lancaster College, Cambridge' – Count Komikos
bowed very slightly – 'but I am now disgraced. I have come
here because I am engaged in a forlorn hope which is sub-
sidized by charity. I am, you might say, on a treasure-hunt.'

'You will find no treasure here.'

'I seek only information, Your Excellency, information
which may be in your family archives, about a rival family
with which your own family had to do ... and treated
somewhat less than honourably ... many generations ago.'

'Then it could be one of many families,' observed His Excellency equably. 'The important question must be ...
which. Some families we have treated so vilely that I could
not think of discussing such matters with a stranger, and
indeed might be inclined to confine or put down any
stranger who even mentioned them, on the ground that
he was already on the way to knowing more than was desirable.'

'Confine or put down?'

'You think I could not?'

'I don't know what to think.'

'You will soon be clearer. Now then: some families, as I
say, you would mention at your peril. Of other families to
which you might refer, I should tell you that although we
acted with enmity towards them we did not behave so dis-
creditably as to preclude frank and current discussion. Very
well, then. Name your family, Mr Blakeney, and we shall
very soon see in which category I place it.'

'I think I'd rather not.'

'Oh, but I must insist. You came here of your own will, Mr
Blakeney, purporting to have scientific business with me
which you now repudiate. Please to state what your
business really is. Then I can either take you in to luncheon
with an undisturbed mind ... or take you wherever else may
be necessary.'

The little figure gazed calmly up at Balbo and took out a
gold and onyx snuff box.

'Which family ... of all those with which the Komiki

have had dealings over the centuries ... which family interests you, Mr Blakeney? Pray to answer my question, sir.'

'The ... the Kommingi,' Balbo faltered.

Count Komikos nodded neutrally, walked to the wall of books behind Balbo, removed Volume 1 of Motley's *The Rise of the Dutch Republic*, and spoke into a tube that protruded from the back of the bookcase.

'Send Theodoraki,' he said.

'Who is Theodoraki?' inquired Balbo.

'My servant,' said the Count. He replaced Motley and took a pinch of snuff from his box.

'Why have you summoned him?'

'To serve me. And to serve you, as you deserve.'

'To luncheon, I hope?'

'That will be for Theodoraki to decide. When he has questioned you.'

'I have already answered *your* question. You said that would decide the thing.'

'Your answer hit on a marginal case. I am unsure.'

'Unsure of what, for Christ's sake?'

'Whether you wish simply to know more of the Kommingi for your own purpose – for your "treasure-hunt", as you allege; or whether you wish to impugn the honour of my ancestors. If the latter, you probably know enough already to do so, and Theodoraki will deal with you as he sees fit.'

'Confine me or put me down?'

'On the other hand, if Theodoraki thinks your motives for inquiring in this quite delicate area are innocent as far as *we* are concerned—'

'—I assure you they are. I only wish to know where the Kommingi originally came from. That's *all*.'

'So you say. Theodoraki will decide if you speak the truth.'

'How? How can this mere servant of yours decide anything?'

'Be quiet, Mr Blakeney. You might offend him. He is nearly here.'

Although Balbo had heard nothing from the hall outside the study, there was now a scrabbling on the other side of the study door, followed by an announcement in a croaky voice, 'Theodoraki. 'Sti Theodoraki.'

'Open the door to him,' said the Count.

'I don't usually open the door to servants. Tell him to come in.'

'Be careful not to offend him, Mr Blakeney. I have already warned you once. Now then, sir. Open the door to Theodoraki.'

As Balbo drew the door in towards him, a squat, chunky figure, dressed in a green robe which resembled a full-length nightdress, ambled through. It turned a bloated face and eyes bloodshot purple on to Balbo, then seized him, with hands like two clusters of barbed hooks, around the throat.

'So 'ow come you come 'ere?' said the Kyrios Pandelios. He glared out of his window at the Venetian well-head in the centre of the little square, as he always did when he felt in need of reassurance, and then turned back to the small figure which sat on his sofa.

'I asked at some of the bars,' said Jones, S., of Glamorgan, 'and they didn't know where he'd gone, but they said that you employed him and you might.'

'Might what?'

'Know where he's gone.'

'God love a duck. Why you want to know?'

'I've got some important questions to ask him.'

'What questions?'

'I'll level with you, fella,' said Jones, S., dramatically. 'Questions about rats.'

The Kyrios Pandelios began to giggle furiously. 'Holy arse-holes,' he said.

'Who taught you *that* bit of English, sport?'

'Kyrios Blakeney. What ees all this ballocks about rats?'

'Mr Blakeney did research for the British War Office during the last war, see? Some of that research was about rats, and the Government thinks it may come in handy in view of recent developments.'

'The war,' said Pandelios, 'was thirty years ago. What a damn thing will Kyrios Blakeney remember?'

'We may be able to jog his memory.'

'You going to pester 'im?'

'We simply want to consult him. Any objection?'

'Yes. Ees too nice a gentleman to be pestered. Nice, humourful gentleman. But 'e drink too much. You pester 'im about bloody rats,' said the Kyrios Pandelios, 'and 'e go drink even more.'

'You protecting him, bazza?'

'I don't want 'im pestered, is all. He is doing a mission.'

'For you?'

'And for 'im too.'

'So you know where he's gone?'

'I know where 'e was going.'

'Well, where?'

'I'm telling you, I don't want 'im pestered. He 'as work to do. I pay 'im.'

'What work?'

Pandelios pondered.

'Art work.'

'You commissioned him to paint pictures or something?'

'No. To find and evaluate.'

'Find and evaluate what?'

'No damn biz of yours.'

'Listen, cobber,' said Jones. '*Somebody*, pretty soon, is going to find Mr Balbo Blakeney in order to talk to him about bloody rats. Believe it or not, these rats are serious. Now: if I'm the one that finds him, I shall be polite to him and not pester him more than I can help, because I'm beginning to like what I hear of him. But there's others less appreciative who might turn stroppy with him and won't give a one-time fuck about his being a booze artist who might flip or any other sodding thing. So if you know what's

166

good for Mr Blakeney, you'll tell me where to find him. Do you get the message?'

'Like one ton of turds, I get it. But can I believe it?'

Lord Constable, reflected Jones, had trusted the cricketer, or at any rate the statistic in *Wisden*. What *persona* could Mr Pandelios be got to trust?

'Can I believe it?' Pandelios repeated.

'Like you can piss in a china pot,' said Jones, rather wearily.

'What ees this funny speaking of yours?'

'Oz. Strine. Australian. I don't get it right, but I try.'

'Why?'

'Because I find it amusing.'

'You ever went there – to Afstralia?'

'Yeez.'

'Why you go?'

'I went to play cricket,' said Jones, S., feeling silly.

The Kyrios Pandelios looked puzzled.

'The English croquet?' he said at last, pronouncing the 't' hard.

'Sort of,' said Syd Jones, not wishing to complicate things.

'Then I make you one deal. I like this Oz English, this Strine. Kyrios Blakeney teach me good filthy English but only English filthy English. You teach me some Afstralian filthy English, and if I like, I tell you where the good Kyrios Blakeney was going.'


As Balbo began to come to, he was conscious that Count Komikos was hovering more or less benignantly about his head, offering a drink.

'Where is he? Where's Theodoraki?' muttered Balbo, flicking his eyes nervously around the library.

'He has gone back where he came from. He will not come again till he is sent for.'

'I'm glad you've got control over the brute.'

'He is not a brute. He is an old family retainer. Nearly two hundred years old, to be precise.'

'What rubbish is this?'

'No rubbish at all,' said Count Komikos. 'Is that drink to your liking?'

'Thank you, yes.'

'Then if you're quite comfortable, I shall now explain.'


' "Shit a bastard brick",' pondered the Kyrios Pandelios. 'Yes, ees quite funny. Also I am keen to "drain my snake" and "gobble a sheila's cherry". You are kind and humourful man, Kyrios Jones, and will not be hurting blessed Balbo. So I will now be telling you where he was going when he sailed away from Crete.

'Only it will be assisting you but little,' Pandelios went on, 'as he was going to see my brother-in-law, Stavros Kommingi, curator of the antiquities at Nicopolis . . . who is now dead, having been – how you say? – raped? – by his dog. His throat was torn out while he was sleeping.'

'Savaged rather than raped, I'd say,' said Jones, S. 'Some dog.'

'The bones of a man, a young man, they think, were found nearby. They make a theory that the dog had become accustomed to human meat, and after long deprivation (the commodity being hard to come by) did turn at last on Stavros. God 'e knows about all that pile of crap, but the essential point, good Kyrie Jones, is that Stavros Kommingi, being dead of dog-rape, will be telling you nothing of what passed between 'imself and blessed Balbo, or what intentions, if any, issued from the latter's cake-'ole.'

'I suppose I could go there and ask if anyone else saw Blakeney?'

'And so you could. But they are big shitty bastards in Previsa and all that quarter, and they make you some tale for two ouzos and the merry hell of it, whether they saw him or not.'

'Still, it's a trail of sorts.'

'So it is,' said the Kyrios Pandelios, 'and the best of Afstralian luck.'

'So you see,' Count Kómikos was explaining to Balbo, 'as a younger son's bastard by one of the family's maidservants, Theodoraki quite naturally grew up to become a privileged upper servant in the family household. In accordance with the custom of the time, he was brought up by his mother in the kitchen, put to simple tasks as soon as he could walk, watched for signs of intellect or vice (the former of which would have procured an education for him, in so far as one was then to be had, and the latter his prompt expulsion from the house as soon as he could fend for himself), and being conspicuous for neither so much as for a friendly and loyal disposition was given, at the age of ten, to the ruling Count's twelve-year-old grandson, as companion and body-servant, an appointment which in those days lasted for life.

'As the years went on and the grandson rose to become himself the ruling Count, Theodoraki rose with him to become his major-domo. He was also, as he had been since they were boys, the Count's most trusted confidant. But not long after the Count had inherited, when Theodoraki and he were fifty and fifty-two years old respectively, a terrible disaster came upon them.

'The year was 1824, the war against the Turks was in full force – and the Count, attended by Theodoraki, crossed to the mainland to pay his respects to the English milord Byron, who was encamped at Mesolonghi. Now, as you may know, Mr Blakeney, Mesolonghi then stood, indeed still stands, in the middle of a coastal swamp, the vapours from which undoubtedly helped to wind down the mortal coil of the already much debilitated milord. When Count Komikos and Theodoraki arrived, the Lord Byron lay dying; and around him a pretty curious crew was assembled, which included a lad from Ithaca, of noble birth, who was acting as a kind of esquire to his lordship, having been promoted to the office more for his comeliness than his capacities. It is, I think, common knowledge – you will certainly find it recorded in more than one reputable biography – that this boy subsequently robbed milord's dead body both of money and jewels. What is not so widely known is that he was observed leaving Byron's tent by Theodoraki, who followed him, questioned him, disbelieved his tale of a pious vigil by the bier, stripped him of every stitch he was wearing and uncovered the stolen goods which were secreted in the region of the boy's *privata*. However, the boy's family was important, the matter was hushed up, and the boy himself swiftly moved to Ithaca . . . but not before he had put the eye on Theodoraki in revenge for his humiliation.'

'The eye?'

'The evil eye. Some families tend to transmit through the generations the gift of casting it. This boy's family was famous for it – and for the use they made of it to amass money and purchase nobility.'

'I do not think any Komikos should comment on other people's methods of attaining to nobility.'

'Perhaps you are right.' The Count smiled softly. 'More of that later. Meanwhile . . . here was Theodoraki, smitten by the eye and knowing it, rapidly succumbing to the noxious fumes of Mesolonghi; and in a few days he was dead.'

His Excellency paused and pursed his lips, as though a little uneasy about what must follow.

'My ancestor, having buried his old companion with every office enjoyed by the Church of God and the charity of man, at length returned to Corfu. Having no stomach in him for the town, he came out here to his house in the country, and day after day he spent pacing the quayside and the shore, looking South over the waves towards Mesolonghi, where the heart of his heart lay rotting in the sea-marshes. Or so he thought. But Theodoraki was quick in his grave and heard the call of his friend and master, as it was borne over Mesolonghi by the wind from the North and West; and so he rose, and took passage in a ship over the sea to Kerkyra, though it is well known' – here the Count's nostrils gave a slight twitch of embarrassment and he stumbled in his period – 'though it is well known that vampires do not easily cross water, whether salt or fresh.'

'*Vampires?*'

'At this point,' said the Count primly, 'we must halt for a little lesson in Greek folklore.

'Greek vampires, you should understand, are not necessarily bloodsuckers. Nor are they necessarily malevolent. While they often nourish themselves on human flesh, most are quite happy with the flesh of domestic or other animals. When they move about, which they can do as easily by day as by night, they tend to beat or rip strangers or persons they don't like, but they are also capable of doing good turns, such as carrying heavy loads or ploughing fields, for their friends and families.

'Now, Theodoraki is a vampire of the amiable kind. The loyalty which he has shown in crossing the sea, a painful proceeding for all vampires whether Greek or other, made that clear from the start. So when he reached here, he was given a commodious tomb in the garden and a sheep a day for his rations, for though kindly disposed he tended to become ... obstreperous ... if given less. He was then put to work. Menial work, it had to be, for although he had enjoyed a post of honour while living, his brain seemed to have been very badly damaged since he had become one of the living dead.'

'Why didn't they just let him rest then?'

'When he was consuming a sheep every day? My dear Mr Blakeney, Greece is and certainly was a very poor country. No one who was consuming food on that scale could possibly be allowed to remain idle. Besides, Theodoraki was anxious to be of use. The trouble was that he had neither the discipline nor the intelligence which had characterized him before his death, and was capable of only the simplest tasks. But as time went on, it was revealed that the instinctive gift which he had always possessed for detecting hostility or danger to the Komikos family from any quarter, for scenting treachery threatened or even natural disaster pending – it was revealed, I say, that this gift was not only unimpaired but was operating more intensively and accurately than ever. Though he could not properly speak, he was capable of grunting an elementary warning; and during the first year after his return he gave notice, weeks before the events proved him correct, of three attacks by Epirot pirates from the mainland, a freak tempest at mid-summer, a freak drought in the autumn, and of the dishonourable intentions of a prominent suitor to the hand of his master's eldest niece. The latter prediction, which was totally disregarded because of the total probity, as it was conceived, of the young man in question, was sensationally vindicated and established Theodoraki as the honoured prophet and guardian of the Komikos family thenceforward and for ever.'

'But why,' said Balbo, 'did Theodoraki ever become a vampire? In most accounts of vampire genesis, you only become one if you've been got at by another one and contaminated by his bite. Now, you say Greek vampires don't bite—'

'—I said that not all of them suck blood. Most of them will tear or bite human flesh if given no other.'

'But there seems no reason to suppose Theodoraki was ever bitten, so how was he ever infected by whatever virus informs the . . . the living dead?'

'He could have been infected by some chance contact . . . without himself or anyone else's knowing of it. Or his bodily resurrection could have been caused, as is often the case, Mr Blakeney, by perturbation of the spirit.'

'By the voice of his master's grief, you seemed to imply just now.'

'No. He heard his master calling to him, but only after he had already awoken. It was not,' Count Komikos rather shrilly insisted, 'his master's voice that roused him.'

'Then what was it? Theodoraki doesn't sound to have possessed a perturbed spirit.'

'Most likely of all, it was the effect of the curse cast upon him by the young Ithacot. The evil eye often makes revenants of its victims.'

'As a former scientist,' said Balbo, 'or merely as a man of common sense, I must lodge another serious objection. How did he get out of his grave at Mesolonghi? I quite understand how he gets in and out of his tomb in the garden here, a tomb which is above ground, I presume' – a nod of assent from Count Komikos – 'and specially fixed up to make things easy for him; but a coffin buried in the earth – even in marshy earth – is another matter. You did say he was *buried* in Mesolonghi, I think?'

'I did,' said Count Komikos gravely, 'and of course you are right. One more highly disquieting mystery; how did he achieve his physical release? You will simply have to make an act of faith, Mr Blakeney.'

'Or not, as the case may be.'

'You may disbelieve if you wish, sir. I cannot compel you to accept this tale, and I don't much care whether you do or you don't. I have simply told you what we in this house and family believe, in order that you may understand the revered and mantic status – perhaps I should say, necromantic – which Theodoraki enjoys among us. That is why I called upon him to come to you – to determine your good or ill will and possible intentions. And now you have reason, Mr Blakeney, to be very grateful to him. For he has assured me that neither you nor your inquiries bode harm to my hearth or kin. He has authorized me to tell you whatever you wish to know in furtherance of your quest.'

'Did he say anything about that quest? Whether it was well or ill fated?'

'Theodoraki concerns himself only with the fortunes of the Komiki. All he said of you was that you could safely be told what you came to ask. So now, Mr Blakeney – go ahead and ask.'

'Thank you, Your Excellency. Now then. Your family was once . . . involved . . . with the family of the Kommingi. Is it true that a certain ancestor of yours fraudulently converted the Kommingi's patent of nobility to the name of Komikos and then got up an inquiry to discredit them?'

'My ancestor showed well-timed ingenuity,' said Komikos, 'and if only on that account, he fully deserved to be ennobled.'

'A debatable point, but it need not detain us. My concern,' said Balbo, 'is with what the inquiry revealed about the Kommingi.'

'The inquiry was never completed. The Kommingi decided to fly from this island, which was what was wanted of them, so the inquiry was discontinued. You may be interested to know where they went – to Lycia, it was later discovered.'

'Thank you, but I know where they went, or at least where they ended up. The question is, Your Excellency, *where had they come from?* Where had they set out from when they first came to Corfu early in the eighteenth century? Surely the inquiry at least established that?'

'Oh yes – but not very precisely. They had come from somewhere on the West Coast of Italy.'

'A long coast, Count Komikos. Can't you come a bit nearer than that?'

'I'm afraid not. The West Coast of Italy was at that time famous for its many ports which served ... mariners ... engaged in the dubious kind of trade favoured by the Kommingi. On one such port they were based, and near it they had their former home.'

'But that could mean anywhere from Nice, which was then Italian, down to Scylla.'

'It could indeed. But there is, Mr Blakeney, one circumstance which may help you narrow the choice. It is generally thought that when the Kommingi evacuated themselves from their house on Corfu harbour they left nothing whatever behind them. In fact, however, some time after their departure, a surveyor of the property found in the cellar a portrait made in oils, dated 1699, signed with the name "Giocale", and labelled "Andrea Commingi" – Commingi with a capital "C", the said Andrea, or Andreas, having been at the head of the family when it first arrived in Corfu (and adopted the Greek "Kappa"), and having ruled them there during the twenty-odd years before he took them on to Lycia. Here, then, was a picture of the man who had brought the family from Italy – and here, also, was a piece of landscape behind him. Now, Mr Blakeney, had anything been known of the painter Giocale, something might have been deduced about the provenance of the picture and so, perhaps, about the provenance of Andrea Commingi. But nothing was or is known of Giocale – except, on the evidence of the picture, that he was a better landscape artist than portraitist, as there is (I am told) a certain minor talent evinced in the view revealed behind the vilely painted Commingi.'

'You're told? Then the picture still exists.'

'It has been preserved, Mr Blakeney. When it was found in the Kommingi's house by the surveyor, it was first passed on to the Special Commissioner who was conducting the Kommingi Inquiry, in case it should be of value as evidence.'

'But by that time the Special Commissioner was surely in Venice, seeking assistance from Venetian experts in furthering the inquiry. Or rather, as it turned out, *not* seeking assistance, as the inquiry was already being tacitly abandoned.'

'Quite right, Mr Blakeney. The Commissioner was, at any rate, in Venice. He was called Baron Cuccumelli – his descendants still live on this island – and he was a distant connection by marriage of that noble and indeed dogal family of Venice, the Vendramin. So Cuccumelli was staying at the Palazzo Vendramin – whither came to him from Corfu the portrait of Andrea Commingi. It was, thought Cuccumelli, of no relevance, since the inquiry was, as you say, very soon to be abandoned. He therefore decided that he would give the picture as a parting gift of gratitude to his Vendramin host – who hung it in the remote corner of the Palace where it still hangs today, adorning the Salon of Chemin-de-Fer in the Winter Municipal Casino, which the Palazzo has now sadly become. Now, Mr Blakeney: some who have seen it have been charmed by the landscape view behind Commingi, but no one has been able to say what area it represents. But suppose it does represent a real area, and suppose you were ingenious enough, where others have failed, to recognize or discover what that area was; then surely you might have a clue as to precisely where, on the West Coast of Italy, the Commingi had lived before moving to Corfu.'

'Always assuming that the picture was painted near their home.'

'You will have to assume something, I think, in a quest of this nature.'

'Yes,' said Balbo bleakly. Then, 'How do you know the nature of my quest?'

'I don't know anything, Mr Blakeney, except that you are hunting back into the past. Quests back into the past must always depend largely on assumptions, as the mouths of most informants have been closed for ever by dust.'

Count Kómikos rose.

'Luncheon,' he said. 'I thought it as well to settle your business first. During the meal I shall give myself the pleasure of questioning you – about our old Alma Mater and how it marches in these troubled times.'

'Theodoraki will be waiting on us?'

'Alas, he is too clumsy these days. But if you wish another sight of him, you may observe him in the garden, I think.'

Count Komikos crossed to the study window, raised himself on tip-toe in order to peer out, then turned to Balbo and beckoned him. Balbo joined the Count and looked out over his head. A figure in a long, green night shirt, its back to Balbo and Komikos, was sawing very fast through a four-foot tree-trunk, using a huge double saw unassisted.

'As I told you,' His Excellency said, 'there is no one in the world like a well nourished and well disposed vampire for the performance of heavy menial tasks.'

Balbo loitered by the Corfu Cricket Ground in front of the arcaded Liston. He did not sit down, as he would have liked to, at one of the café tables by the boundary, because he could not afford an expensive drink. Although the September Cricket Festival (*TO KPIKET ΦΕΣΤΙΒΑΛ*) was long since done, a match between two teams of schoolboys was being tolerably well conducted out on the wicket. Not that Balbo knew whether the game was ordered well or ill, but he found memories which it brought, of long, dull Eton afternoons, drowsily comforting.

Balbo needed comfort. His problem was this: his search now clearly led to Venice, to the Winter Gaming Rooms in the Palazzo Vendramin, but the Winter Gaming Rooms did not open (so he had been informed in Hariocopoulos's Tourist Bureau) until November 1. This meant that Balbo would need special permission to gain access to the Giocale painting; that he must hang about in Venice for days, perhaps weeks, until he got it, or must else produce a large bribe. Both courses were costly and neither practicable; Balbo's money would run neither to bribes nor to lengthy sojourns, even at the cheapest rates, in devouring Venice.

But what alternative was there? He could, of course, return to Heracleion and say to the Kyrios Pandelios, 'Well, here I am back again, and here's a little bit of change for you, I had quite a good run for your money but got cold feet about going on to Venice – and after all I can't imagine that picture would have been much help, just as well I cut your losses for you.' But this would be feeble, just plain wet. The Kyrios Pandelios would nod politely and pretend to agree that Balbo had done the sensible thing, but he would in truth despise him, and justly so. But at least, thought Balbo, in Heracleion I should be safe: I know its ways by now, there would be just enough money, there would be the occasional trip to the bordel by the docks and enough cheap brandy to see me through. A choice then: did he propose to become a snug object of contempt in Heracleion, or a manly target for destitution in Venice?'

Balbo cared for neither. He lingered in his far from cheap hotel in Corfu, telling himself it was not worth looking for something humbler as he would have made his decision and be ready to depart the next morning. But the next morning became the next and then the morning after, and on the third afternoon after his visit to Count Komikos

Balbo was still in Corfu, watching little boys play cricket.

'Mr Blakeney,' said a rather high-pitched but definitely masculine voice. 'Mr Balbo Blakeney?'

'I suppose so,' said Balbo, surveying a tubby little runt of a man whose forehead was barely level with Balbo's chin. 'How did you know?'

'I got a snapshot, cobber. Lord Constable gave it to me. You're not quite as pretty as yer picture, but ye're obviously you – if you take me. Enjoying the cricket?'

'It's quite amusing.'

'Ye're not letting on, are yer? It's home.'

'What do you want?'

'A word about rats, Mr Blakeney.'

'Rats? Who sent you?'

'Them. Not the rats, I mean. My bosses in Jermyn Street.'

'Jermyn Street?'

'Headquarters of my Department. Very hush-hush.'

Balbo shrugged.

'How did you find me?' he said.

'I asked around.'

But it had not been quite as simple as that. When Jones, S., had left Kyros Pandelios in Heracleion, he had known that by all the rules in his book he should take himself off the case and hand it over to the Foreign Department which, and which alone, was allowed to conduct man-hunts (as opposed to mere interrogations) outside the U.K. Syd Jones's orders had been to find out, in England, where Balbo was, to go straight to him, and to ask him certain questions, note certain details of his physical and mental condition, and test his reaction to certain propositions. These orders permitted Syd to follow Balbo abroad (if it was known that Balbo was abroad) but only when and if he knew precisely where to find him. So much Jones had told Constable, and Constable had told Jones, enough, just enough, to enable his superiors to authorize his trip to Heracleion. But Balbo had not been in Heracleion or even in Crete; and by all the rules of his service Jones, S., must now desist.

He did not desist. He had very much liked what Constable

and Pandelios had said of Balbo; he wanted to be the one to find him; and he had told himself that provided Balbo might still be presumed to be in Greek territory and provided that he, Jones, S., knew pretty well where to look for him (Previsa), then he could justify himself in sticking to the case on the ground that he was still *travelling to* Balbo and not, in any serious sense, hunting him down.

Such casuistry, as he well knew, would be chastised as disobedience if he failed, applauded as professional initiative if he succeeded. And now, with a bit of luck, he had done just that. In Previsa, since the day was bright and his manner modest, he had been truthfully and immediately told what he wanted to know (*pace* all Pandelios' warnings of venal and mendacious Previsans): yes, there had been an English stranger there some days before, he had been chased from Nicopolis by the crazy (and since deceased) Kommingi, and he had taken a bus to Igoumenitza. In Igoumenitza, a clerk in one of the ferry boat offices had recognized Balbo's photo: yes, the English Kyrios had taken a ticket to Corfu. So, therefore, had Jones, S. Once there, he had wandered uncertainly about the town, had stopped, because he was a cricketer, to watch the cricket – as, it appeared, had Balbo Blakeney, for different but perhaps not entirely dissimilar reasons.

'I just asked around,' Jones, S., repeated.

'And you want a word about rats?'

'That's it, sport.'

'Not vampires, by any chance? I'm rather good on them.'

'Rats. They say you're rather good on them.'

'I don't think I can really help you.'

'I think I can help you. You need a drink.'

'I was putting it off as long as I could.'

'But if I'm paying . . .? Then we could sit down at one of these tables. The name, since you haven't asked, is Syd Jones.'

'Since you're kindly buying me a drink,' said Balbo, 'I think I shall call you Sydney.'

It really is a nightmare, thought Ivor Winstanley. He turned over, switched on the light, looked at his clock. 3.45 a.m. He put two Alka-Seltzer tablets in his glass of Malvern water, waited impatiently till they surfaced, and drank. There were nasty rumours, he was well aware, about what they did to the lining of one's stomach, but they were always good to knock him out for a couple of hours.

Not tonight. The waking nightmare raged on, spurning the opiate. Round and round it raged. One: Constable was going to do him down – unless he, Ivor, did Jacquiz Helmut down, by finding and demonstrating irregularities of past administration in the Chamber of Manuscripts. Two: if he were to meet Constable's order, he needed the help of Len, the Under-Collator; even if he didn't need Len's help, he would need his connivance, as Len knew very well that there had been no irregularities and was in a position to refute with ease whatever case Ivor might try to fake up. Three: he could have Len's connivance, and indeed his expert assistance, in return for Len's price; and Len's price, as revealed at luncheon the other day, *Len's price*—

It didn't bear thinking of. Sweat rolled over Ivor's neck, his shoulders, his back, his thighs. His pyjamas were soaked. Soon it would get through to the sheets, and then what on earth would the bed-maker think of him? He got up, went through to the bathroom, took off his pyjamas, towelled himself down in front of the looking-glass, detested the hairless white slug he saw in it, failed to find a clean pair of pyjamas in the bathroom chest of drawers, put on an old white shirt he had once used for Royal Tennis, went unattractively back to bed, and took two more Alka-Seltzers.

But the enormity of Len's suggestion, of the price he was asking if he were to help Ivor, still hammered at Ivor's brain. No, Ivor could never consent to paying it. There must be some other way out. Think . . . Accuse Provost Constable of applying foul pressures? No one would believe him, and they would probably consign him to a bin (there were several bins ready and willing to whisk a man away at the bidding of Lancaster College). Find some excuse for sacking

Len, and then manage the thing without him? But these days the Lens of the earth, however lazy or ignorant (and Len, to be fair, was neither), were quite unsackable. And never in a thousand years could Ivor conjure a trick dirty enough to discredit Jacquiz without Len's inside knowledge of the Chamber, its manifold contents and complexities.

Assassinate Lord Constable, the onlie begetter of Ivor's troubles? At least it would make a memorable end to Ivor's somewhat humdrum career. Better go out as Constable's killer than his jackal . . . But that way madness lay. Applied intellect, Ivor had always believed, must sooner or later triumph in any situation. Back to the beginning, then, back to first premises. One: Constable was absolutely going to do down Ivor, by depriving him of his beloved Fellowship, unless Ivor could contrive to do down Jacquiz Helmut. Two: if he were to oblige Constable, Constable the unrefusable and unaccusable, he must somehow procure to his cause the deadly arts of Len. Three: these were on offer, but the asking price – Oh God, oh God, oh God.

Balbo drained his first drink within seconds of its arrival, so that Syd Jones was able to order him a second before the waiter had left them. Balbo sat silent until this came and then took a stiffish swallow.

'Very well, Sydney,' Balbo said. 'What is it you want?'

Syd Jones looked out at the cricket and nodded slightly in appreciation of some arcanum that was for ever hidden from Balbo.

'These bleedin' rats,' said Syd. 'You worked with them . . . or on them . . . during the war?'

'Unsuccessfully. They wouldn't do as they were told.'

'Right. But now the thinking is that there might be a way to make 'em after all. And the thinking also is that you might find it. There's an old story that you had quite a hand with rats, that you might have got through to them if you'd been given a bit longer.'

'All that was thirty years ago,' said Balbo.

'Those concerned have a long memory.'

'Mine is shorter. If I was getting through to rats, I certainly don't remember how.'

'Probably not. The story is that ... that you had a kind of natural empathy. Not a conscious technique. Something in you, very rare, that might still be in you. Something which could still be used now.'

'What for?' said Balbo, and finished his drink. 'One thing I do remember – we were going to use those rats to spread bubonic plague.' He beckoned to the waiter. 'Now I'll buy you one.'

'Save yer money, sport. Have it on the old expenses.'

'Okay. But you're wasting the public money.'

Syd instructed the waiter.

'It is public money, I suppose?' said Balbo.

'Yeep.'

'Then as usual it's being wasted. I'm not interested, Sydney, even if I'm competent. I wasn't too keen on spreading bubonic plague then. I'm far less keen now.'

'This time it's not bubonic plague.'

'Then what is it?'

'They'll tell you ... if you come home and talk to them. That's why I'm here. To persuade you to come home and talk to them.'

'Who are "they"?'

'Friends of my bosses in Jermyn Street. People on the right side.'

'But you see, Sydney, I just don't want to come home.' Balbo paused; he handled his newly arrived drink but did not yet drink it. 'Have you ... money ... to persuade me?' he said.

'Not me, sport. Not beyond expenses to get us both home with. But *they* will be offering money when they see you. You can be sure of that.'

'I doubt it. I can't remember the chemistry involved, and I don't believe in this empathy bit.'

'They do. So do I, now I've met yer.'

'How can you know?'

'They told me one sign to look for. Now I've found it.'

'Found what?'

'Sorry, sport. Trade secret – for now at any rate.'

'Hmm. Handsome fee going, you think?'

'Pretty fair.'

'And positively no bubonic plague?'

'No bubonic plague.'

'Something even nastier, perhaps?'

'Something . . . necessary.'

'But you won't yet tell me what,' mused Balbo, as Syd shook his head, 'and in any case I don't want to come.'

'What's stopping you?'

'I'm on a mission.'

Now that Balbo had been offered a definite and perhaps profitable alternative, he had become perversely determined to stick to the enterprise of which, not many minutes before, he had been both weary and sceptical. Am I just being bloody-minded, he asked himself, or is it that I mistrust the moral flavour of these (otherwise not unpromising) overtures? He did not mistrust the messenger; but messengers were never told the whole truth, and however truthful Sydney Jones might be in himself, his assurances (no bubonic plague this time, nothing nasty, something necessary) were not worth the breath that conveyed them. Or could it be that he resented the impertinence of such a claim upon him, which came slinking out of the past like a blackmailing request from a long-forgotten acquaintance with whom one had once exchanged drunken and deplorable confidences? Or was it the bland authority he resented, *their* competence, logistical, mental and official, to trace him down after all this time? Or did the sheer *knowingness* offend him? 'He had this gift,' they had apparently told Syd Jones, 'and if he still does you'll see such and such a sign of it on him.' As it happened, this business of the 'sign' made a strong appeal to Balbo's curiosity; but not strong enough to outweigh his feeling (of whatever elements this might be compounded) that Jones must be refused. Besides, the drink he had just swallowed had made him feel more optimistic about his search (nothing very dreadful could happen to him, he now thought, if he ventured at any rate as far as Venice); and the peremptory demands of Jones, S., (though he rather liked the man) reminded him, by contrast, of the generous and spontaneous patronage of the Kyrios Pandelios. All in all, then, affection, endeavour and loyalty (if not perhaps his best practical interest) showed him his course very plain. He must soldier on under the banner of Pandelios; he must stand to his mission and proceed at once to the swamps and labyrinths of the Serene Republic.

'What mission?' Jones now prompted him.

'A search.'

'Animal, vegetable or mineral?'

'Mineral.'

'A hidden treasure?' asked Jones, with the affable frivolity of one engaged in killing time with word games.

'You might call it that. Hidden somewhere back in time. In the earth too, for all I know.'

'Ah well. None of my business.'

Jones's tone had suddenly changed to that of one who evidently thinks he is dealing with a nut-case but is too polite to say so. Balbo, who did not like to be taken for a nut-case, felt compelled to justify himself.

'This . . . this treasure,' he said, 'belonged to a powerful family in France but was stolen in the seventeenth century. Both thief and treasure disappeared. I think I have now found the descendants of the thief, and through them I hope to go back in time until I find somebody, between those alive today and the thief himself, who was known to possess the treasure.'

'What would you do then?' said Jones, patiently humouring.

'Try to find out what this somebody did with it, and then start working *forward* in time . . . until I come to where the treasure is now.'

'Sound enough. Except,' said Syd Jones, with the air of explaining a logical fallacy to a backward child, 'that you can't be sure that this original thief passed it on to one of his family. You say that he and the treasure disappeared?'

'I do,' said Balbo, trying not to feel like a total imbecile.

'He may have done anything with it, fella. Sold it, lost it, destroyed it . . . or been destroyed by it. Been killed for it by other thieves, perhaps. There is no reason ever what at all to suppose that any of his descendants, direct or indirect, ever got a sniff of it. And if they *did* inherit it, think of all the surplus by-blows, knocked-up sheilas or shagged-out fancy boys who might have been paid off with it anywhere along the line.'

Jones sat back with the patient self-satisfaction of a pundit who has finally disposed of a chunk of prime nonsense. Balbo sat forward with the desperation of a poor pensioner who, about to be committed to an old people's asylum as mentally and physically inadequate, pleads with the authorities to recognize his sanity and right to fend, however humbly, for himself.

'I simply hope,' he said, 'that if I go back far enough I shall hear news of what I seek. The original thief, or one of his successors, may indeed have done almost anything with it. But by following the line back I may eventually come to somebody who was close enough to my treasure to have heard at least rumours about what became of it.'

Jones, S., nodded, no longer as if patronizing an idiot but as if mildly congratulating a pupil on having passed a test. But only an intermediate test.

'Ever who you come to,' he now said, 'they'll be good and dead. How do you extract rumours from a corpse?'

'For an intelligent man,' said Balbo, much of his confidence restored, 'you can be remarkably obtuse. The dead leave records.'

'A lot of them couldn't write.'

'Not always written. For example,' said Balbo, wishing to cite a concrete instance that would fully justify his ways to Jones, 'I am now on my way to Venice to look at a portrait of a man whom I believe to be the original thief's fairly near descendant. It is thought that the portrait, which has a background of well painted landscape, may indicate where the subject lived, or at any rate a place where he was active, at a prosperous period of his life.'

'Or simply,' said Syd Jones evenly, 'the place he went to to have his portrait done, or some other place he just fancied enough to tell the artist to stick in behind him.'

'Even then, to identify the place might help. My point is,' said Balbo, 'that here is a record which *could* tell me enough to take me yet further back, or possibly to turn me aside, but in either case to take me one stage nearer to news of what I seek.'

'Or just rumours, as you said yerself. But you've sold it to me,' said Syd Jones equably. 'If it's all the same to you, I'll come along to Venice.'

'I'm not sure,' said Balbo, 'that it is all the same to me.'

'Of course,' said Jones. 'How inconsiderate of me. I'd forgotten that you no doubt like travelling in style, and having me, with only my grotty little Government expense fund, will be an embarrassment. You might even feel you had to stake me from time to time.'

Balbo hung his head.

'Mr Blakeney,' said Jones in a very gentle voice, 'I know all about you. That you were rich and are poor. Don't be proud. Don't be difficult, or ashamed. I'd like to come and I'll pay for the pleasure. This expense fund of mine – we both know it's not really so grotty but what it'll feed and water two. Besides, two pairs of eyes see sharper and wider than one. I am . . . sort of trained . . . in this kind of thing.'

Balbo looked up and smiled hazily.

'All right,' he said. 'Come. To be candid, I'm getting pretty sick of my own company. And it's a very long time since I've spoken with an Englishman.'

'Sorry, sport. Welshman,' said short-arse Jones.

'All cricketers are English under the skin.'

We won't bother to argue that one now, thought Jones, S., of Glamorgan. The thing is, this poor lonely sod is taking me on (or rather, letting me take him on) because he trusts and likes me (I think); and so I owe it to him to warn him straight off what he's in for. This business of the rats isn't going to go away. Even if I didn't go with him to Venice, he'd be hearing a lot more about it from somebody; and as it is, he's going to hear it from me. So now let's warn him, and try to work out a formula for making it all as friendly as we can.

'Look, Mr Blakeney—'

'—You may as well call me Balbo—'

'—Look, Balbo. We're going to have to do a deal. If I come, I pay—'

'—Will they let you?'

'I think they will, *providing* I go on talking to you about rats. Trying to persuade you to come home.'

'I've told you, Sydney. I've got my mission.'

'Sooner or later, either the trail will peter out, or you'll come to the end of it. Would you consider coming home then?'

'Are they going to be that patient?'

'I hope so ... if I ask them nicely. They could put on pressure, of course, and even get quite rough, but they won't want to do that. You know too many people to complain to.'

'I used to.'

'Still do, Balbo. That Provost man at Lancaster College would come buzzing to your aid like a fly after shit – begging yer pardon. If I remind them of him, I think they'll play it gentle. *But* you'll have to let me get on with my persuading.'

'I'm always happy to listen. I don't mind being told what they're up to.'

'Mind you, I'm a bit hazy about the scientific theory behind it. And like I've given out already, I'll have to be very cagey what I tell yer – until you've actually agreed to help them.'

'But why so cagey, Sydney? You assured me it wasn't nasty.'

'I assured you it was necessary. Balbo. There are aspects of necessity which gently-nurtured dons don't always care for.'

'I must say, you're making me very inquisitive.'

'I aim to, matey.'

'Balbo. I can endure cobber, sport or fella, but not matey.'

'Right, Balbo. Next step is to ring up Jermyn Street and put them in the picture.'

Syd Jones had left a lot out when telling Balbo the probable attitudes of Jermyn Street. It was true that they would prefer not to be rough with Balbo but not true that they would desist from being rough out of deference for Lord Constable. It was true that they could be patient and would be prepared to authorize quite heavy expenditure; not true that they would subsidize Balbo's travels indefinitely on the off-chance that he would prove compliant when these were over. It was quite true that Jones could tell him a certain amount about what he was wanted for, but not true that Jones had, as he implied, a general if not a scientific grasp of the whole matter. His understanding of all but the most rudimentary elements was very deficient indeed, though, to be fair to Jones, he himself could have no idea how deficient. Lastly, it was not true that Jones simply had to ring up Jermyn Street and 'put them in the picture' before wandering off to Venice with Balbo. Just as he had misrepresented the situation to Balbo, in order to gain his confidence, so he would now be compelled to misrepresent the situation to his masters in order to retain theirs. For while he never for a moment forgot his professional obligations to Jermyn Street, neither did he forget his duty to Balbo – which was to protect him from the less desirable practitioners in Jermyn Street's, or its associated departments', employ. This he could only do by remaining with Balbo, and neither Jermyn Street nor Balbo would assent to this unless he tempered the truth to both of them.

The best way to do this, he had decided, was to convince each of the relative docility of the other. To Balbo he had reported that time would be granted; to his masters he now telephoned that time would be needed. Blakeney, he said, though quite cooperative, was much confused by drink, disgrace and premature old age. It would take time to sort him out. If roughly treated, he would almost certainly end up unsortable. Yes, Blakeney had the 'sign' which Jones had been told to look for, the sign that indicated he might still have the special powers premised of him; what he did not have was comprehension, and this Jones could only undertake to induce if given *time*. Blakeney was anxious to see some picture in Venice, a picture which meant much to him, which he feared he might not see again in his lifetime; and Jones proposed to humour and accompany him, working on his poor shattered intellect the while. Would Jermyn Street approve and authorize this course, together with such expenditure as might be required in order to sustain and comfort an old man, not indeed debilitated beyond hope, but sadly vulnerable to physical circumstance?

No, we won't, said Jones's immediate superior; and what the hell are you doing in Corfu? Yes, we will, said the superior's superior, who had once, long ago, seen Jones make fifty-seven against fast bowling on a bumpy wicket in a rotten light; but don't go pushing us too far and report promptly from Venice.

So far, so good, thought Syd Jones as he rang off; but suppose my old Balbo finds his clue in Venice and wants to go on somewhere else? What shall I do then, tirra lirra? Head off poor Balbo, or fob off his nibs in London like I did just now? But the same ball won't beat him twice, dilly dilly, and I'll have to think of another.

The next morning Balbo Blakeney and Syd Jones took the ferry from Corfu to Brindisi. On the boat Syd taught Balbo gin rummy and Balbo taught Syd piquet. They then ate a long and very nasty lunch, during which Balbo told Syd everything which he himself knew of the nature and goal of his quest, and of the events which had decided him to undertake it. The lunch lasted till it was time for a late tea (Greek coffee laced with Greek cognac and a bar of chocolate). When dusk began to come down they went on deck and watched the guardian figure of God's mother loom closer and closer as they neared their anchorage.

'Time for preacher to do some converting,' said Jones.

'Go ahead. You've spared me all day.'

'I'll start by asking you a question. When you were working with those rats during the war, what went wrong?'

'I've told you. They wouldn't obey orders. The idea was to use them to spread bubonic plague behind the enemy lines. To do this, three things were necessary: to find a strain of fleas or lice which would carry plague in the climate of North-West Europe; to infect the rats' fur with these fleas, and to pack the rats off in the right direction, making sure they'd keep going. And that was the trouble. Rats are intelligent animals and pretty quick to get the idea you're trying to put over; but they are also independent and don't necessarily want to fall in with it.'

'Where did you come in on all this?'

'Originally I was running the flea circus. Poisoning the fleas and making sure they'd be cosy on the rats. Then one day they asked me if I'd like to take a spell at teaching the rats their work. They wanted a fresh mind on the job, they said. So I went along to the rat farm, and found they were still trying to train the brutes in the same way as you train a dog – you know, by demonstration associated with command or prohibition, these in turn being associated with action or performance, and performance being followed by reward or punishment. But rats, as I told you, are a bloody-minded lot, bless 'em, and although they soon got the hang of it all, they'd only deliver the goods when they felt like it. If they weren't in a giving mood, no bribe could make 'em and no fate could scare 'em.'

Balbo paused.

'Time for a drink?' he said.

'When we've finished our discussion,' said Jones, gently and evenly. 'So what did you suggest to the boys in the rat department?'

'Don't your people know all this?'

'Yes. And so do I. But I want you to tell me.'

'Then as you know bloody well,' said Balbo, 'I suggested that certain drugs might make the rats more obliging. The trouble with that was that all soothing drugs just made them damned idle while the stimulants made them more perverse than ever. Then we tried addicting them to heroin – withdrawing the dose if they didn't toe the line. But that was only a new variant of the reward and punishment routine, and they were far too proud and too tough to be had that way. So after that we tried setting up a King Rat and enforcing obedience to him. This worked well enough – except that we could never enforce the King Rat's obedience to us. He led his troops in a direction of his choosing, not ours. Still no drink, Sydney?'

'Still no drink.'

'If I'd been one of my rats, I'd have just gone off and bought one for myself.'

'Why doncha?'

'Somehow ... I value your approval. And believe it or not, Sydney, in the end it turned out to be rather the same with those rats. Under most of their instructors they got fed up and after a while they did the equivalent of going off and buying their own drinks ... *i.e.* they found something which they liked doing and paid no more attention to teacher. But there were some people whom they seemed to like, or whom, for whatever reason, they wanted to please – just as I find myself wishing to please you, you personally, quite apart from any money which you may give or withhold.'

'And for such people the rats were always ... in a giving mood?'

'Almost always. We called them Pied Pipers.'

'And you were one of them, Balbo boy?'

'No. With me it was different.'

'How was it different? Tell yer uncle Syd. What was so special about *you*, 'squire?'

'The Pied Pipers ... were most of them just lab. boys or assistants.'

'Oh dear me. Not officers and gentlemen?'

'Not real scientists either. They didn't know what any of it was about. Their job was to keep the rats in good trim and to feed 'em whatever drugs might be prescribed from time to time. Beyond that, to ask no questions and to sweep the floors.'

'But it was, as you say, different with the great Balbo.'

'Yes. And don't think the rats didn't know it. They have a very acute sense of caste and status. I'm told it's the same with gorillas. They know the difference between a load of plebs gawping at them through the bars and people ... people of ...'

'... People of what, Balbo?'

'People of quality.'

'Good on the gorillas. Now back to rats. They sensed that you were a person of erudition and authority. *And* they liked you. Mostly they just liked the pleby boys with the dustpans – I wonder why, Balbo – but they also liked superior and clever old you, as well as respecting your commissioned rank. So where did that get you?'

'It made me a kind of human King Rat. They could sense my will with the minimum of overt demonstration on my part, and they were eager to serve it.'

'So where was your problem? All you had to do was send them speeding off to spread the plague among the Hunskies.'

'As a matter of fact, policy was now reconsidered. If we spread the plague among the Hunskies, we would also be spreading it among the loyal French and Belgians whose countries they still occupied. Second thoughts all round.'

'But surely that scientific whizz-kid, the great Balbo, had the answer to that. *He* could teach the rats the difference between a Kraut helmet and a Free French beret, if anybody could.'

'That I might or might not have done. The trouble was, Sydney, that in order to control them at all I had to be with them, or at least readily accessible to them. It was no good my briefing them, so to speak, and then packing 'em off across Europe. I had to go along the whole way.'

'Oh dear. The great Balbo exposed to nasty bullets. That wouldn't do, now would it?'

'I volunteered to take my rats wherever anyone wanted them to go.'

'I know you did, old Balbo,' said Syd Jones softly.

'But I won't pretend I wasn't relieved when they put it all off. They still couldn't make up their minds about policy. And I don't think they had all that much confidence in my ability to control the rats as accurately as was needed.'

'They're prepared to put money on it now. But we're missing something out, aren't we, Balbo? We're forgetting something else you found out about yer relations with them rats. You were the King Rat on two legs, whom they liked, whom they respected, whom they adored . . . as a God. But the trouble is with a God King . . . say it, Balbo . . .'

'. . . That he has to die before he grows too old, so that his spirit may pass into his successor while he is still strong and quick. What is more, Sydney, very often his subjects eat him, so that they may inherit something of his wisdom and divinity.'

'Which is what those rats had in store for you. The King must die, sooner or later, to make his loyal subjects a dainty dinner. That's the message which came through to you, on whatever weird wavelength it was you listened in to your trusty rodents. Or so you hinted in the paper you wrote . . . the one which all the scientific journals refused to print, thereby pissing good and rotten on your regard for science and scientists and almost causing its extinction. But we got a copy, Balbo. One of the editors who rejected it was buddy-bazzas with us, and let us see it just on the off-chance we might be interested. Which we were, being more open-minded than scientific journals. And so were some of our friends. But let's go back a little in our memoir. What happened after you started to get the message, that you, the God King, would one day become the bloody sacrifice?'

'The war ended and I went.'

'And gave up rats for good . . . except, of course, to record your experience in that paper which nobody wanted.'

'Where is all this getting us, Sydney?'

'Once a King of rats, Balbo, perhaps a future King of rats.'

'Obviously not. The King-God of the rats has to be young and energetic. We've just been through that. After a time they kill him, whether or not they eat him, so that his spirit may enter into his successor while still in its prime. If I was presented to the rats again, they wouldn't want me. Too old.'

'You've gone through the Catechism, Balbo; now hear the Sermon. You are assuming that the rats, like any primitive people, confuse power of body with power of spirit. Now, we've been doing a bit of research . . . or rather, the department with which my department corresponds has been doing a bit of research . . . and we find that rats are far too advanced to make that elementary mistake. The rats know that the spirit may stay fresh in a stale body – and that all the time it is accumulating knowledge and wisdom. So the longer the God King can stay alive, the better . . . always providing his thinker is in good nick. Only when they scent the approach of mental deterioration do rats kill their king, whether he has two legs or four. He may not make such good eating, but they absorb a higher quality of wisdom, and they are serious enough to prefer enlightenment to *gourmandise*.'

'How do you know this?'

'Don't interrupt Preacher's Sermon. Let's just say that careful experiments have been conducted, many of them suggested by your pirated paper. And now, Balbo boy, we come to the real crunch. This "sign" I was told to look out for . . . it's the sign which the rats look for, which tells them a man is fit to be their King. First they like him; then they assess his cerebral quality; then, if they want him for King, they look out for this "sign", and if he is worthy it appears on him. Very few people are marked with it. You were marked with it. You still are. As long as it is there the rats will not reject you; only when it starts to go away will they know that at last your mind and your spirit are about to decline and that it is time, if you are their King, to kill you.'

Syd Jones looked up at the vast Madonna of the Shore, under whom they were now passing.

'*Ave Maria, gratia plena*,' he remarked. 'This sign guarantees to the rats that you have the special grace they require in their Sovereign and their Godhead. You have the sign, you have the grace. Amen. End of Sermon.'

'Hmm,' said Balbo. 'I knew they were snobs, both social and intellectual. But that they looked for special grace or any visible sign of it is a new one on me. What is this sign, Sydney? How does one spot it? Something in the eyes?'

'Such mysteries, honoured Balbo, are to be revealed only to converts – to those who have expressed a will to be initiated. For the time being at least you have other interests, you tell me, another mission. Enough for you to know that sign is on you . . . or in you, or somehow with you, as the case may be. Now then. You've been a good and patient fella,' said Syd Jones, watching the receding Madonna, 'and there's just time for a nice big drinkeroo before we berth.'

It was not until he was half way through his nice big drinkeroo that Balbo remembered that no more had been said about the nature of the 'necessary' task, to the fulfilment of which all this talk, effort and expense were presumably directed. Somehow it seemed indelicate to raise the matter. Syd Jones was now off duty, his mien indicated; further questions about the matters or 'mysteries' which his embassage served would have to wait until he called the next session.

From Brindisi they caught an aeroplane to Rome, and from Rome, only minutes later, an aeroplane to Venice.

'Quickest way,' said Syd Jones. 'I'd have brought us from Corfu to Brindisi by air if they still ran the 'plane.'

'What's the hurry? Trains are more soothing.'

'My bosses don't grudge money well spent, but they do object to loitering.'

But when, after they landed at Venice airport, Balbo suggested taking a speed-boat across the lagoon, Syd chivvied him towards the overland bus.

'We'll get the *vaporetto* from the Piazzale Roma,' Syd said.

'How's that for loitering? Your way will take four times as long as a water-taxi.'

'My bosses don't grudge money well spent, but they do object to extravagance.'

'What they object to,' grumbled Balbo, 'is any sort of pleasure or comfort.'

'On second thoughts,' said Syd, 'we will take our own speed-boat. I think the money may be well spent after all . . . because I want to know,' he said a few minutes later, 'what this lagoon reminds you of.'

Balbo looked out of the little cabin into the dismal night. The Marshes of Styx, he thought. Charon the Ferryman.

'Death,' he said: ' "oozy death." Bodies in the mud, or tangled in the reeds.'

'Very good sport. And not only in the mud or the reeds. There's one of these islands where they bury them; that's San Michele, on our way in. And there's another island, not on our way this trip, where they take what's left of 'em after they've spent such and such a time on San Michele. Because there's a lot of customers who want lodgings on San Michele, and after you've been a while there the law says you've got to move on, to let others have their turn. So then you're directed,' said Syd Jones, 'to this other island, which I've just been telling you about.'

'I've heard of it. Where the skeletons are dumped. The island of dead men's bones.'

Balbo lit a cigarette and coughed thickly.

'Why are we having this morbid conversation?' he said.

'To give my bosses their money's worth.'

'How does it help your bosses?'

Jones, S., pointed ahead of them. A clump of reeds swayed up out of the dark waters in the headlight of the boat, then gave place to a tiny island, on which a ruined chapel was perched above a narrow, muddy beach.

'Once a monastery,' said Syd. 'By day you can see that the monks had their own graveyard. They certainly wouldn't have wanted their dead to go on to San Michele. Oh dear me, no.'

'Why not?

'Trouble and expense. And then later, you see, the corpses of the good brothers, like those of every cobber else, would have been translated to . . . the island of dead men's bones, as you just called it.'

' "Where or in what manner he is buried",' Balbo quoted Lord Chesterfield, ' "must be indifferent to any rational man." '

'But that's just it, sport. When they got to the second island they weren't buried. To use yer own words again, they were "dumped".'

'And so?'

'They weren't only skeletons, either. Sometimes quite a lot of meat was left on the carcasses.'

'Sydney, what on earth has all this to do with you or your bosses?'

'Rats, man. Rats.'

'Rats getting at what was left . . . on the carcasses?'

'Right. That's what warned off the good brothers in that monastery back there.'

'I don't see why it should have bothered them unduly. I certainly don't see why it should concern you or your department.'

'What with one thing and another, Balbo, the rats got to chewing up the bones as well. The skeletons were broken apart. Dispersed.'

'Well?'

'Well, the good brothers would have believed in the Resurrection of the Body, Balbo. And being specially religious they would have set a lot of store by it. Now, you or I might think that the Almighty God would find it pretty well as easy to reassemble broken bones and get 'em up decent as he would to bring out something presentable from six foot down; but the brothers might not have seen it that way.

Simple men they were, mostly; peasants. To their crude minds, it might have seemed that a corpse on its own in a coffin had a better chance of coming up nice and neat on the Last Day than a heap of bust-up vertebrae and well-gnawed femurs which were anyways all mixed up with those of thousands of bazzas else. Peasants might think that even God might fit 'em out with some other bastard's pelvis or stick their swedes on the wrong fucker's neck. And being peasants, they wouldn't care for that at all.'

'*How does this concern you?*'

'Have a good think about the rats, Balbo. The rats.'

'No doubt they were tolerably contented.'

'Oh yes indeedy. Were, and are, tolerably contented. And will be – for a time at least. But what happens . . . when the amenity is withdrawn? The habits of those rats have become very thorough, very fierce and very entrenched – the good brothers knew all about *that*. Those rats were and are very bad news indeed, Balbo; but not quite so bad, as long as they stay in their own place. So what happens when supplies stop reaching them there?'

'Supplies, in this instance, are surely inexhaustible?'

'Not if the enlightened Municipality of Venice decides that from now on the remains removed from San Michele are going to be incinerated instead of dumped.'

'The Roman Church forbids cremation.'

'Not very volubly. Not nowadays. The Roman Church already lets individuals choose cremation in certain circumstances. It won't bother about a spot of quiet combustion *en masse*. Not if it's discreet . . . and for the social and sanitary good of the community. The Church, Balbo, is just as concerned with things like sanitation or finding plum jobs for niggers, these days, as it is with the word of God. So the Municipality goes ahead with the Church's blessing and burns its deados, as soon as their time is up on San Michele; and our rats, Balbo, our intelligent but narrowly specialized rats, have lost their long accustomed livelihood. My goodness, but they're going to feel deprived. Whatever are they going to do now? Die? Migrate? Migrate where? And

198

with what, precisely, in their sharp little rodent minds?'

'That's a problem for Venice – when and if it ever happens.'

'How very true, sweetheart. It's also a problem for England – where it is already happening.'


'Essex marshes. Saint Cuthbert-Juxta-Aestuarium,' Syd Jones said.

'What's that?'

'Saint Cuthbert-Juxta-Aestuarium. Saint Cuthbert next to the Estuary. Meaning the Estuary of the Thames, not twenty miles from the centre of London. I'll tell you over lunch. Harry's Bar for that. You'll need to be well nourished.'

Syd and Balbo were walking through the Campiello Barozzi, having just come out of the Europa e Britannia Hotel. They were in fact staying at the much cheaper (but entirely adequate) Pensione Flora, a hundred yards away, and their visit to the Europa had been the result of a simple piece of logistic analysis by Syd Jones.

'The Municipal Casino in Venice,' he had said, 'is partly owned by, or is at any rate closely connected with, the Company of Italian Grand Albergi, or CIGA. If we want permission to visit the Palazzo Vendramin before the Winter Casino opens up there, from CIGA we can get it. The nearest influential representative of CIGA will be the manager of the nearest CIGA hotel – the Europa e Britannia.''

Whither they had gone, and whence they were now bearing away a letter which would ensure their admission to the Vendramin for a private view of the apartments at any time after 15.00 on any or all of the next three days.

'Luncheon at Harry's Bar,' Syd Jones repeated, 'and a little look into the Church of San Moise on the way. It's just over the bridge and always good for a laugh.'

'Do you often come to Venice, Sydney?'

'Venice is my passion, Balbo. I first came here on a very simple mission as a messenger boy. I was only here three hours, but that was enough. From then on I've spent a large part of almost all my leaves in Venice . . . Yes, San Moise is still open. You can see why that façade annoyed Ruskin so much – and of course that loony reredos of Moses on the Mount. Ruskin would surely have been much keener on the Church of Saint Cuthbert-Juxta-Aestuarium, Balbo, sometimes known as Saint Cuthbert in Insula Paludis, Saint Cuthbert on the Island in the Marsh. Early English, Balbo. Plain and wholesome. And yet not so bleeding wholesome either, since the river-tides changed and the island subsided and the churchyard started sinking right into the swamp. And now I've seen enough of that bad-tempered old yid with his nagging Commandments, Balbo. Quick march for Harry's Bar.'

In Cambridge, Ivor Winstanley too was on his way to lunch. For the second time in only a few days he was to have this with the Under-Collator, Len, whom he was about to collect from the Chamber of Manuscripts. Last time Len had put up a proposition; he had told Ivor exactly how he could help him discredit Jacquiz Helmut and exactly what would be his price for doing so. This time Ivor was to say whether or not he would meet it.

Although he might be able to extract a few minor concessions from Len, the basic clauses of the deal were absolutely set; rigid, ruthless, unalterable – and horrible. Can I go through with it? thought Ivor, who still did not know what his answer was to be. Do I dare to go through with it? But do I dare *not* to go through with it? Is it really so awful? Yes, it is; it is a betrayal of every kind of trust; it is utterly vile. But in a few weeks now my Fellowship expires. Where would I go if my Fellowship were not renewed? Where could I then find warmth and company?

'. . . So the upshot is,' Syd Jones was saying to Balbo, 'that the graveyard of Saint Cuthbert's has begun pretty much to resemble that island out in the lagoon. Easy access for the rats. Get it, Balbo?'

'Very clearly.'

'So the local authorities stepped in and started to clean the place up, to cart away the – er—'

'—detritus?'

'Yeep. Cart away the detritus and pop it in the ovens somewhere. But by the time they'd cleared about a quarter of the churchyard, they were faced with another nasty little problem . . . to do with the rats who'd been feeding on the ground they'd cleared. It seems that the other rats in the rest of the graveyard wouldn't share the remaining provender. Not enough to go round. So the first crowd had to clear off elsewhere.'

'And by this time,' said Balbo slowly, 'they had developed rather rare tastes, I suppose?'

'Right, chum.' Syd Jones hooked a pale prawn from its pink shell. 'They'd got used to their victuals being quite unusually high. Like with those rats in this lagoon, they'd started on their particular diet because it was readily available, and they'd ended up with liking it. At fresher meat, which might once have been preferred, they now turned up their noses. But where were they to go on finding their dainty diet? Well, there were no sources as easy as the one they'd been forced to leave, but there were many quite as plentiful . . . if they were prepared to work hard. To do some sapping and mining, so to speak.' Jones, S., looked long and ruefully at Balbo. 'And here,' he said, 'we are coming to the heart of the matter. For whatever reason, you see, they began to prefer vaults to graveyards. Cosier to live in, I suppose, when they finally finished their dig. But I don't need to tell a cultivated gent like yourself, Balbo, that rats tunnelling into the vaults isn't the best thing for the fabric and the foundations of, for example, Canterbury Cathedral. You know about all that work they're doing there?'

'Yes. I used to contribute something.'

'Well, they won't have told you this when they wrote

round with their fund-raising forms, but a lot of it's got to do with repairing the damage done by Old Cuthbertian rats while they helped themselves to a late archbishop or two. They'd crossed the Thames from Essex by the Dartford Tunnel, paused for a while at Rochester but failed to get much joy there because the terrain was too tough, and then continued on their pilgrimage to Canterbury, where the system of canals and town-ditches gave them just the approaches they needed.'

'Why this obsession with cathedrals? Plenty of other churches en route.'

'Cathedrals,' said Jones, S., 'are bigger and fatter and warmer than parish churches.'

Balbo took a long drink of dry Orvieto.

'So,' said Syd: 'two immediate problems. One: get them out of Canterbury. Two: dispose of them. And later on, problem three: what to do with our little friends still at Saint Cuthbert's.'

'Leave them there.'

'Yip. After all, the church was always remote, it is now almost inaccessible, it has been closed without any complaint, and the health authorities have agreed to interfere no further. But,' said Syd Jones, 'that graveyard will not for much longer supply our furry friends there. Unlike the island in this lagoon' – he waved a hand South by South-East – 'it is not being constantly replenished. Before many moons those rats will have to leave Saint Cuthbert's, bound for Westminster, Saint Paul's, York Minster ... if they follow the same pattern of behaviour as the last lot. How to stop them, Balbo?'

'Poison them. Poison them in Canterbury too.'

'Balbo. Rats who have got used to eating what these rats have got used to eating are not easy to poison. And even before all this happened, these lot, like other strains of English rats, had become pretty much immune to all known kinds of rat poison.'

'Yes. I remember hearing about that. It happened only in Wales, I thought.'

'It started in Wales – in 1970. Time shifts frontiers, Balbo.'

'Time brings new rat poisons, Sydney.'

'Experiments with those, and experiments in other directions, have gone down the spout. So now they want you,
Balbo. The man with the Sign. Think on these things, cobber.
Coffee you'd like? And some kind of fancy rot-gut to go with
it? *Think on these things, fella.* And after we're done here,
we'll check in at the Palazzo Vendramin and see what's to
do about *your* little problem.'


'Coffee?' said Ivor Winstanley to Len.

'Yes, please, Ive. And some of that white raspberry mixture to go with it.'

'Framboise.'

'That's it: Fromboys.' Len leant foward over the table.
'Righty, Ive. Decision time.'

'Not here. Not in public. We'll go back to the Chamber of
Manuscripts after we've finished and discuss it all there.'

'Nothing to discuss, Ive. Either you say "yes" and I do it,
or you say "no" and I don't.'

'I must be quite clear, first, that I have understood exactly
what you want, and exactly how you will do . . . what you
will do.'

'Righty, Ive. So I'll tell you again. In the Chamber of
Manuscripts. *One last time*, Ive. Now be a good chap and
order that Fromboys.'


'Jeeze, Balbo,' said Jones, S., 'I wouldn't want to meet him on
a wet and windy night in the public urinal.'

Four feet above a raised chair, from which, later in the
autumn, the Chef du Parti would preside over the high table
of Chemin-de-Fer in the Palazzo Vendramin, hung a crudely
painted portrait of a hatless and totally bald young man,
whose cast of features bore some resemblance (Balbo

thought) to that of Stavros Kommingi. The resemblance was necessarily no more than general as the man in the painting was somewhat mangled in his particulars: he had one ear, one eye, and what looked like two noses, the lower half of that organ being vertically slit by a deep and narrow weal, possibly (thought Balbo) an old sabre cut delivered at an unusual angle.

The portrait ended about mid-way down the man's straddling thighs, between which was written, in neat gold letters,

ANDREA COMMINGI
*in anno aetatis trigesimo*
*Giocale pinxit MDCXCVIIII\**

As if to compensate for his ugliness, Commingi had clearly taken enormous pains with his dress, a saffron tunic girdled with a broad belt of scarlet, from which was slung, in an intricately embossed scabbard, a scimitar with unguarded hilt of gold and ivory. An even more remarkable feature was a scarlet plumed cod-piece protruding from breeches of white satin, all but a few inches of which were concealed by high black Marlborough boots.

While Commingi's costume had been painted with considerably more competence than his face, the landscape in the rear, as Count Komikos had told Balbo, had been painted with more skill than either, and also with love.

To Commingi's left the middle ground was occupied by a stretch of low, rocky coast from which a causeway carried by two arches jutted into the sea and disappeared behind Commingi's tunic. In the background were three snowy mountains, the tallest and middle of which was partly concealed at the apex by the filthy and jagged index finger-nail of Commingi's raised and commanding left hand. To Commingi's right was a large, sheer lump of rock, the landward end of which was presumably joined by the causeway somewhere behind Commingi's upper rump, while the seaward spur was topped by three Doric temples, these being side-

---

\* Andrea Commingi in the thirtieth year of his life. Giocale painted this in 1699.

ways on to the beholder and built along the spine of the ridge. The light was that of a winter's afternoon; and the effect of the whole was charming, hazy and romantic (as in some fantasy of a much inferior Claude) but at the same time chilling and desolate; for the coast of stone (one conceived) could never have nursed or housed a human being, the buildings had an air as of having been raised by deities or spirits, and the waves which beat on to the steep promontory of the temples had eaten into the base of the cliff in such a way as to leave a kind of diseased and skeletal nose of rock hung some fifty feet above them.

' "Faerie lands forlorn," ' Balbo said.

And telling me nothing, he added to himself. There was no such place as this one; Giocale had merely invented it to suit his mood or that of his patron. Furthermore, thought Balbo, even if the picture had indeed provided him with a hint where to go next in his search for the receding Commingi, surely it would nonetheless be his duty to give up that search, in view of what Sydney had been telling him at lunch, and help the authorities to save stricken Canterbury from the rats. If, that was, he still had any capacities in that area, and *if the story was true.* For Balbo, who had known people from Sydney's department and similar departments during the war, was well aware how deviously and malignantly they went to work. They told you they wanted you for one purpose, and you wound up serving quite another – one which you would have repudiated with shame or horror if given half a chance at the start.

Now then, thought Balbo: this story of the rats in the foundations, the rats who have developed a special tooth for long-dead human corpses – this is just the kind of story which might have been deliberately tailored to titillate what is left of my scientific bent and to appeal to my cultural conscience. And again, it has been delivered in too orderly, too leisurely, too literary a manner to be quite real.

Is Jones lying? Probably, but the lie is almost certainly for the most part *theirs.* Jones, that is, is aware only in slight degree of the extent to which they are trying to trick me.

He knows, perhaps, that they want me for something other than they have declared, but he still thinks it is much the same sort of thing, only rather more so. And yet again: clearly he believes that business of the 'sign', do *they?* Or have they just told him to look out for some personal characteristic of mine which they know of, in order to dupe him, and cause him to intrigue and flatter me? But in any case at all, Balbo concluded, if this enigmatic picture marks, as it seems to, the final frustration of my hunt for the Kommingi, Commingi or Comminges, why should I not take a chance on this rat business, which may give me money to fill my empty pockets, occupation to pass my ample time, and probably material (of however ghastly a nature) to engage and scour up my mouldering intellect?

'Weird,' said Jones, S., 'that landscape; beguiling – and poisonous.'

And you haven't seen the clue, he added to himself, have you, my poor old Balbo? But then, to be fair, how could you have seen it (even if you hadn't drunk a litre of wine and two large grappas) without a bit of my kind of training? Training in busting elementary codes, which can exist in pictures just as they can on the written page. The question is, though, what am I to do? If I interpret for Balbo, he'll want to go on with this hunt and I'll have extra trouble and delay in doing my clear duty and getting him back to London. And they won't like that at all. But I have promised to help him; if he would listen to my story, I said, I would help him with his quest. He has met his part of the bargain, he has listened very patiently – and now I should meet mine.

Anyhow, do I really want the old thing to fall for their spiel and present himself in Jermyn Street? He's certainly being tricked, as am I. True, he has the 'sign' they told me to be ready for; and from his own account, he appears to have the gifts which it signifies and bestows; but that's not saying they mean him to use these gifts in the way they told me to tell him. God knows what they've got in store for the poor old lamb. Anyway, one thing's for sure: if I help him now he'll trust me later, and that will make it easier for me

to push him whichever way I want him to go in the end . . .
their way, if needs must be. *That* argument might just persuade them to agree if I ask for permission not to bring him
in quite yet but to follow up with him on his trek for at any
rate one stage further. God knows, I want to: and they can't
kill me (or can they?).

Aloud, Syd Jones said to Balbo:

'You say that this bloke operated somewhere on the West
Coast of Italy before he went and set himself up in Corfu?'

'That's my information, Sydney.'

'And you think that this pic – more especially the landscape at the back of it – may tell you exactly where?'

'That's what I was hoping. But this place . . . it's nowhere I
recognize. It's nowhere on earth.'

'You can't expect things to be too simple. Now, that rock
with the temples on it – there's only one way of getting on
to it, by that causeway. Right?'

'Right. Like Monemvasia – only that's in Greece.'

'Never you mind Monemvasia. But hang on to that causeway, which is partly hidden by friend Commingi here . . .
who, incidentally or not so incidentally, is also concealing,
with his dirty great finger nail, the tip of that peak – the
middle one of the three. What does that do for you?'

Balbo shook his head.

'The Trinity?' he mumbled. 'The three crosses on Cal-
vary?'

'Don't be too precious, man. Three peaks, one blacked out
by a finger nail, means two of something, probably something lofty or important, where there were three before.
And since it's Commingi's finger nail, he's had something or
other to do with fucking up the third. Then these three
temples, on the left, mean three of something old-fashioned,
unreal, useless or superstitious. All this along with the one
causeway, the one road between the mainland on which the
mountains are and the hunk of rock which holds the
temples. It's a simple code of numbered or itemized allegory.'

'Why was he using a code?'

'Because he was a pirate who didn't want anyone to know where he worked from – or rather, where he *used* to work from. He knew he was off to somewhere else, to Corfu, fairly soon, he'd be taking this portrait as a souvenir of the old days in another place – but it might not quite suit him if his new neighbours rumbled where that had been just as soon as they saw his pretty pictures. Besides, like all his kind he enjoyed little mystery games. And so, old lad, reading from his left to right, what we have is this. One: three eminences, one of which is almost deleted by Commingi's left-hand index finger – that is, *not* the finger on his sword hand but the finger on the hand which would grasp the scabbard when he unsheathed that ratty cutlass with his right. Two: the one and only causeway or bridge from the shore out to an islet, just a heap of rock, part of the said bridge being hidden behind chummy's anus. And three: three outdated and rather pretty buildings, of pre-Christian or anti-Christian religious significance, all in a row atop the rock or islet. Getting any warmer?'

'No.'

'Well, as you say, it's nowhere on earth. But if we read the code aright, it will tell us a good deal. It *will* tell us where the Commingi came from, and it *will* tell us, when we get there, a lot about the place itself, though not in direct physical or geographical terms. The whole thing is a pictorial pun.'

'But before we can enjoy the pun we must get to the place How do we deduce the name or whereabouts of *that*?'

'Look closely at those temples. At the cornices.'

'Letters?'

'Can you read them?'

' "P" . . . "O" . . . on one cornice. Short for Poseidon, I suppose, meaning it's his temple. Very appropriate – the God of the Sea.'

'Just stick with the "P" and the "O". On the cornice of the next temple?'

' "N" . . . "A" . . . "O" . . . "S'. Naos. Greek for a temple. And on the next "I" and "T". Short for Italianus? That gives us a sort of dog mixture of Latin and Greek. "The Italian

Temple of Poseidon." All right. They *are* by the sea, and we know the place we're after is on the Italian coast. But why "naos" in the singular when there are three temples?'

'Crude collective image, Balbo. All three constitute a multiple shrine in the God's honour. But it's the letters that matter, not the phrase. The phrase just fits in loosely with the overt sense of the picture, and that's all. Forget the literature, sport, and stick with the literals.'

Balbo gazed at the three groups of letters. At last,

'No good,' he said sadly. 'My wits aren't what they were, sorry.'

'Never mind. I've got the message. Where to go, that is. The rest of the interpretation must wait, like I say, till we arrive there. I'll just make a rough copy – and not so rough either. The little details may be important when we go to work on Giocale's jokes.'

For some minutes Syd Jones traced lines on the back of an envelope.

'Right, Balbo. Time to be off.'

'Where?'

'Where those letters tell us. I'll give you till we get there to go on trying to crack it. You need practice. All right, cobber? Ready to come along with me for the next round?'

'I suppose so. Yet I have a feeling . . . that it's my duty to go back to England for the next round. After all, if I could really help with those rats . . . Canterbury, places like that – they mean a lot to me.'

'I'm the expert on when to go back to England,' said Jones, S. 'You leave that to me. For the time being we're carrying on with your hunt back through time, old Balbo; it's not often I get the chance to horn in on something like this.'

'If you say so, Sydney.'

'I do say so. We'll nip along to the Piazzale Roma right away, and hire a car to be ready for collection early tomorrow. We'll need a car on this lark. And then,' he said with more confidence than he felt, 'I'll give the boss in Jermyn Street a still, small tinkle on the telephone, and tell him please to let Jonesy boy know best.'

# V

# The Abbé Valcabriers' Scrapbook

'Okay,' said Len to Ivor Winstanley. 'Here we are, back in the Chamber of Manuscripts, as snug as two lice in the woodwork. And now, for the last time, Ive, I'll tell you what I will do and what I shall want for doing it.

'There are these two books in here, see? Hand-written books: a Breviary and a transcription of Vergil's Georgics, both fourteenth-century, both exquisitely illustrated. Here they are, Ive.' He unlocked a small safe, which stood beside his desk, and took out two bags of white oilskin. 'In a minute you'll get a last look at them. Make the best of it, Ive. Because very soon they're going to vanish, these books. And nobody any the wiser, for the time being, except you and me . . . and a certain private collector, who lives in Bavaria. The one who's been writing to us to buy our stuff legit., but can't have it because of the silly old statutes, so he'll be glad to grab it this way: being as how he's an old nutter who wants to keep everything pretty just for himself, all screwed down under lock and key where no one else can ever get at it (like we keep the stuff here, come to that), so that he's prepared to pay a very large sum for the exclusive right to gloat over that Breviary. Which very large sum, Ive, is part of my price; the second part being that handsome MS of the Georgics, which *I* shall have the exclusive right to gloat over – until, that is, I feel the need to turn it into cash. Which I hope won't happen for a long, long time; because my aim, Ive, is the good life, and for the good life I don't only want money, I want something, like that Georgics, to look at and nourish my soul with, and tell myself I'm the only person entitled – which I suppose makes me pretty much like that nutter aforesaid to whom we shall flog the Breviary.'

'Well,' said Ivor, who had heard all this before but was even now uncertain quite how to read Len's attitudes and whether or not accept the deal which Len was offering, 'at least you seem to want culture as well as cash.'

'And *you* to help me appreciate the culture. To teach me how to set the good life up. That's the third part of my price.'

'So. You want one book to sell, another . . . to look at and "nourish your soul with" – or to sell at a future need. And you want counsel. What service do you offer in return?'

Although Ivor very well knew the answer to this question, he sat forward, eager and alert, hoping, this time, to find that Len's scheme for discrediting Jacquiz Helmut was not quite as hideous and treacherous, as murderous, as it had hitherto appeared, that there might after all be some element, previously overlooked by himself or omitted by Len, which would temper the wind to Jacquiz enough to allow him, Ivor, comparative ease of heart.

'You know what service, Ive. You know how it's all planned. These two items, with certain others, are usually kept in this safe' – he rapped the safe by his desk with his foot – 'and very carefully packaged in oilskin.' He lifted one of the oilskin bags, which was labelled 'The St Gilles Breviary', untied a lace which secured the top of it, and slid out a slender volume bound in dark, floppy leather. The second bag (labelled 'The Wandrille Georgics') he passed to Ivor Winstanley.

'Come on, Ive. Get involved.'

Ivor unfastened the second bag and took out the volume similar in binding to the Breviary but somewhat smaller.

'Now,' said Len. 'First we find new homes for the loot.'

He opened a drawer in his desk and took out two wash-leather pouches, labelled respectively 'B' and 'G'. ' "B" for Breviary,' he said, ' "G" for Georgics.' He took up the Breviary and eased it into the appropriate pouch. 'Your turn, Ive.'

Ivor picked up the Wandrille Georgics. He remembered that years ago, when he was still Jacquiz' friend, Jacquiz had shown him the volume. There was a haunting illumination which showed Eurydice as she was being snatched back to

Hades from Orpheus, who had just turned and was stretching out his arms to her. 'I'll just have a last, quick look at that,' thought Ivor. 'But oh no, I won't,' he thought. 'I can't bear the sight of this beautiful book, knowing what's going to happen to it, knowing what it's being used for.' He worked it hurriedly into the wash-leather pouch labelled 'G', and shuddered as Len reached out to take it from him.

'This is the one I'm keeping,' Len reminded him. 'The Breviary goes to our friend and patron, the crazy bibliophile from Bavaria. I'm meeting his agent in London tomorrow. The Chamber must be closed for a couple of days, Ive – unless you want to man it.'

'I haven't yet agreed to the plan,' said Ivor.

'Meanwhile,' said Len blandly, 'we must find something to take their place in the safe.'

He opened his desk drawer again, took out two floppy leather-bound volumes, superficially similar to the fourteenth-century ones, and put one of them in each of the white oilskin bags. These he laced firmly at the necks. He then unlocked the safe and put them inside.

'So what have we got?' he said as he locked the safe. 'We have two packages, labelled "The St Gilles Breviary" and "The Wandrille Georgics", both in their right place in the safe, where they have been for years. We have the key to the safe, also in its right place.' He put the key of the safe in a cash box and locked the cash box with another and smaller key, which he then placed in the left-hand breast pocket of his denim jacket. 'And we have the real books out here on this table, ready to go on their travels. I shall take both of them to my digs this evening, and the Breviary to London tomorrow. If the agent is satisfied with its authenticity and condition – which he will be, Ive – he will telephone his principal in Bavaria, and this latter will immediately authorize the payment of thirty-five thousand pounds' worth of German marks into an account which I have had the foresight to open in Geneva. As soon as I am properly notified of this credit, I shall hand over the book. Until then, we shall have rather a nasty, suspicious time, the agent and I, sitting with the book half way between us, waiting for the bank to wire me in the agreed code at the agreed address. Do admit, Ive, it's all been very well got up. You would never have known where to find a buyer.'

'I would never have wished to sell. I'm still not sure that I'm going to allow you to.'

'You've got no choice. Unless you fuck Jake up, the Provost means to fuck you up. This is a sure way – and the only way you've got – of fucking up Jake.'

'Tell me again: how does that bit of it work?'

God, how I loathe this, Ivor thought. Jacquiz and I have long ceased to be friends, and it was his fault our friendship died, but that I should be helping to subject him ... to this ...

'Easy. For two, three weeks from now we say nothing. Then comes round the first routine monthly check since you took over as Temporary Collator. As usual, the Third Bursar is present as witness. I take the key of the money box from my pocket' – he did so – 'I unlock the money box and give you the key of the safe' – again he did so – 'and you unlock the safe. Go on, Ive,' said Len, 'unlock the safe.'

Ivor unlocked the safe.

'Take out the two oilskin bags.'

Ivor took them out.

'Now then. Think yourself into the part. You're conducting a monthly check. Your first. You know – you think you know – that everything was in apple-pie order when Jake left for Europe. Mind you, there was no formal take-over – there couldn't be, because the Provost appointed you after Jake had left. But you have the certificate signed by the Third Bursar, as witness, that everything was as it should have been at the last monthly check-up. But yet again, Ive, that was in August.'

'In August?' said Ivor, simulating a surprise he no longer felt, so often had they been through this before.

'Yep, August. Although it's called a monthly check, there's one month in which it isn't made. September. Because September falls outside any University term. In

August the Long Vacation Term ends; not till October does the Michaelmas Term begin. September is a non-month in this University, Ive, the only mouth when nothing at all happens, so nor does the routine inspection of the Chamber of Manuscripts of Lancaster College.'

'And what difference does that make to me?'

'Think, Ive. Think yourself right into the part. Here you are, doing the October inspection, knowing that the last one was over two months ago. Your first inspection too, like I say. So although you still reckon it's all really okay (for what could possibly go wrong in Lancaster College, Cambridge?), you decide to play it safe, and you get all officious. You say, "I think we'll open up those oilskin bags and check the contents." And I say, "Excuse me, Sir," I say, "we only do that every six months, on account of it being bad for the books to be taken in and out, old and fragile as they are, and passed around and pawed at and in general exposed to the air." And the Third Bursar says, "Yes, that's right, Ivor, every six months, in March and August. I saw them in August with Jacquiz, and that's good enough." And you say, "No, I'm new in this, and I want a look at what I'm responsible for. However delicate those books are, they ought to be taken out of those bags and checked more often, being as how they're worth a stack of bread, especially if no one has been through the safe for nearly ten weeks." Real busy-body bippering, see, Ive, and the Bursar and me, we're frightfully impressed at such conscientious behaviour, and then you open up those bags – open them, Ive – and what do you find?'

'Fakes,' said Ivor, taking one out of the bag labelled 'The Wandrille Georgics'. 'Bad imitations that would fool nobody.'

'Now look inside that book.'

'Blank pages.'

'Right. Probably intended as a commonplace book or diary. Something of the kind. Not exactly fakes or imitations, Ive, just books of the right size, thickness, and texture of binding to fool somebody who didn't open up the oilskin bags. But you *have* opened them up; and now you say, "If this is 'The Wandrille Georgics', then I'm a wet fart", or some choice expression of that kind, and you pass it over to the Bursar.'

Oh the shame, thought Ivor, oh the vile shame. He handed the volume he was holding to Len.

'Something seems to have gone wrong, Bursar,' he said.

'Yes. Not bad. If you can only get it as natural as that on the day, we'll be all right. Meanwhile, no point in over-rehearsing.'

Len replaced the dud Georgics in its oilskin, replaced both oilskins in the safe, then took the key of the safe from Ivor and locked it. Once more he placed the key of the safe in the money box, locked the box with its own smaller key, and put this in his left-hand breast pocket. He then took the wash leather pouches which contained the genuine volumes and placed them in a blue British Airways grip.

'And then the balloon goes up,' said Len. 'In theory, of course, it could have been an outside job. But the easy access evidently enjoyed by the robber, and the obvious knowledge displayed of administrative custom – like putting duds in the oilskins in the expectation of fooling people at all the checks till next March – all that indicates an insider at work. Who? *Not* honest Ivor, who scarcely knows his way into the place and hadn't even got a key to the money box where the safe key is kept, seeing as how Jake never turned his keys in when he went off, and the Under-Collator has to hang on to the only set left to keep the place running day by day. All very amateur and gentlemanly, all very typical and upper class and congenial – if only sixty-five thousand quids' worth of manuscript books hadn't been pinched. So who had 'em? Obvious candidate: that nasty, ungrateful, scruffy little prole, the Under-Collator, Len. He's been in there morning, noon and night, he has all the keys, and *he* knew that since the stolen books were examined in August, the bags that contained them wouldn't – or shouldn't – be opened again until March. Well, Len's come unstuck, they all say: send for the boys in blue.

'At which stage, up gets Len. "Mercy, kind gentlemen," he cries, "I can prove it wasn't me. Or at least, that it *needn't* have been me. *Who* took off last September at a moment's notice? *Who's* at large in Europe with his dainty new wife, and nobody knows where? Who had all the keys? Gentlemen, I gave you the name of – Doctor Jacquiz Helmut.'

'He's a very rich man already,' objected Ivor.

'Rich men like getting richer. Or perhaps he just fancied the books because they were so pretty.'

'Thin,' said Ivor.

'Very thin, Ive. But just thick enough to get Provost Constable's ears twitching. What does he really want? He wants *out* for Helmut. The old puritan doesn't give a damn for the pretty books, and now he sees his way to downing Jacquiz and finally ridding the college of his contaminating influence. So: "Let us all keep very calm," says His Lordship, in his best King Solomon manner. "First, let us *not* call the police and make a nasty scandal. We want no publicity. Least of all do we want to look silly – as we certainly shall, *if* it turns out that our own chosen Collator has scarpered with this load of loot. Let us remember that traditionally this College settles its own internal affairs. Indeed, as Provost, *I* am the law within these walls, *I* am the Queen judicial Bee to buzz, and there are plenty of statutes to prove it." '

'There are,' agreed Ivor. 'In theory at least the Provost can investigate and try any offence, even murder, committed within this College.'

'So I thought,' said Len. 'And so this is what he says: "Let us tell ourselves," he says, "that the books are probably beyond retrieving, and let us quietly disembarrass ourselves of the two men, in practice the *only* two men, who may have taken them, thus purging our beloved College of dishonour, greed, corruption and all that shit. The student Len we will unload on some grotty but well paying polytechnic (for who cares what Len may whip from a polytechnic?) lest he sue us for wrongful dismissal. As for Doctor Helmut, we can demand his resignation on grounds of incompetence, for whether or not he stole the books, it was his absolute responsibility to ensure they could not be stolen, and the system under which he administered the Chamber (a system which poor Mr Winstanley had not time to reform, so let's have no bugger blaming him) was clearly a real turd-heap.''

'And so, man,' said Len, 'a happy issue all round. Ivor sent for and covertly congratulated, for of course the Provost is shrewd enough to see his cute little prick somewhere in all this, and then triumphantly re-elected to his Fellowship in the New Year. Lousy Len, now with ample capital and the means of raising more, quietly easing himself out of the academic scene and living the good life, with the assistance of constant bulletins of advice from his friend, Ivor Winstanley.'

'Why will you be needing that.'

'I told you. Part of my price. I want to keep up the connection. You may not believe this, Ive, but I've got to be rather fond of you ... What other beneficiaries? Oh yes, my lord Constable, of course, happy to have disinfected his realm of the worldly parasite, Helmut. Smiles all round, Ivy man.'

'Not on Helmut's face.'

'That Jake was smug. He could do with a bit of a jolt. And it's not as if he'll actually be charged or tried or jugged or anything of that. He'll just have to resign. He will be ... mildly humiliated.'

'He'll be totally destroyed. There will be rumours and much worse. No one in his world will ever give him reputable employment again.'

'Like you just said, Ive, he's a very rich man.'

'He'll be ruined as a scholar. It's a damned shame, what you're doing to him.'

'What *you* are doing to him. What Constable is doing to him. I'm just ... taking my chance when I see it.'

'It's ... it's the *untruth* of it all that tortures me. I may not amount to much as a man, Len, but the idea of falsehood victorious, even if it is only at the expense of a sod like Helmut ... it makes me squirm.'

'Your sentiments do you credit, Ive. Do we go ahead? Yes ... or no?'

After a while,

'Yes,' said Ivor in a very small voice, and thought of the good days, not, after all, so very long ago, when he and Jacquiz had played Royal Tennis and walked home together through the Fellows' Garden.


'According to M. R. James's story,' said Marigold Helmut, 'the Canons of the Cathedral lodged in there.'

She pointed to a square and dismal edifice of grey-blue stone which bore the indistinct legend *Femmes*.

'Things seem to have moved on since then,' said Jacquiz. 'But I expect that's about right. They'd have a nice view over that meadow ... and easy access to the cloister.'

' "Ancienne Cathédrale Sainte Marie-de-Comminges",' Marigold read from the newly purchased green *Michelin* on the Pyrenees: '*Entré: deux francs*. How mean to charge people.'

'I don't know. The carvings in the stalls of the chancel are said to be magnificent.'

'They get two stars in here. But they're not what we've come for, are they, Jacquiz?'

'We'll have a look at them, of course. But no, they're not what we've come for. They were done in the sixteenth century. They can't, as the phrase goes, *refer*.'

Marigold and Jacquiz walked along the South wall of the Cathedral leaving the *Femmes* to their right. Jacquiz paid five francs for each of them ('Goodness, sweetie,' said Marigold, 'our new *Michelin*'s out of date already') to a guardian seated in a sentry box, and they were waved briskly on and into a small cloister.

'This is the Pillar of the Four Evangelists,' said Marigold, halting in front of it. 'One carved at each cardinal point of the compass, you see. I can't feel that they *refer*, poor poppets. What *have* we come for, Jacquiz?'

'The Comminges, as their name tells us, were an important

family in Saint Bertrand-de-Comminges. Remember that gravestone in Pau? "The family of Comminges of the Lordship of Sainte Bertrand-de-Comminges." That being the case, there will surely be some mention of them somewhere in this Cathedral. But it is important that we concentrate on monuments and so forth of the *seventeenth* century. We are concerned with Constance Comminges, the widow of Louis Comminges, who died and was buried in Pau. Constance must have come here from Pau to seek out her relations-in-law sometime in the middle 1650s. Comminges of before that date are of antiquarian interest only.'

'I wouldn't be too sure of that,' said Marigold. 'If you ask me, there's a lot still to be filled in about that Louis Comminges, and it will help to know about his ancestors.'

'Provided we keep our research priorities absolutely clear.'

'Silly old don,' said Marigold kindly.

She looked out from the South side of the cloister. Open arches in the wall gave on to fields and foothills.

'Such a beautiful place,' she said. 'I wonder why M. R. James had to write such a horrid story about it. He was a silly old don too. A twisted old bachelor, obsessed by boys and medieval manuscripts.'

'At least you will acquit me of boys.'

Marigold giggled. They passed along the Southern walk of the cloister, then turned left and up to its Northern side. This was lined by three sarcophagi, beyond the westernmost of which was a small door into the Cathedral.

'Perfectly harmless, those sarcophagi,' Marigold said. 'Not at all fierce or devouring, like they sometimes are. M. R. James really did get this place wrong.'

They passed through the little door. Immense faces confronted Marigold, grinning and leering, one of them snarling at her, at first from among the others, then eyeball to eyeball, occupying her entire vision.

'*Jacquiz.*'

'I'm here, love.'

He grasped her hand. The snarling face receded to its

place between two others; all three swam backwards and upwards, to become three of the corbels which lined the outside of the chancel screen.

'Didn't you see anything, Jacquiz?'

'Nothing.'

'I think I was a bit premature about M. R. James.'

'Oh? Want to see the carvings in the choir?'

'No more carvings for a while, sweet. Let's just look around.'

'All right. The ambulatory. If there was a family chantry or anything, it would have been in the ambulatory.'

'Funny. That verger behind us, Jacquiz. By those steps, in the long gown. Just like the pretty gardener at Pau.'

'What pretty gardener?'

'The one in the old part of the cemetery.'

'I never saw him. Only you did. Where's this verger?'

'Gone up the steps, I think. There's a sort of raised chapel up there, the new *Michelin* says. What a *hideous* picture. Why is it behind the altar?'

'It's all about the Saint. This is his mausoleum.'

'Oh dear. More carving. But this time . . . unobtrusive, I'm glad to say.'

She sighed with relief.

'Fifteenth century. Long after Saint Bertrand died.'

'I dare say that accounts for it. That verger's watching us.'

'Good. I'm going to make an inquiry. Where is he?'

'Just round the corner where we've come from.'

'That's not a verger. It's a priest.'

'It was a young verger. In one of those long gowns with a high collar.'

'It's a young priest in a dark suit and a dog collar. *Bon jour, M'sieur le Curé. Peutêtre vous pouvez m' aider. Est-ce qu'il y a un tombeau de la famille Comminges?*'

'A vault, sir,' said the young priest courteously. 'You will allow me to introduce myself. I am the Abbé Valcabriers. Not an officiating priest of this Cathedral, simply a resident here in the town. But of course I take an interest in this beautiful building.'

223

'We thought you were a verger,' Marigold said.

'The custodian is away today – attending his grand-daughter's wedding in Luchon. I undertook to stand in for him, madame.'

'The Comminges vault,' said Jacquiz impatiently.

'Sealed since 1656. We don't really mention it, certainly not to strangers. But since you already know of it, you may see the entrance, if you wish.'

The Abbé Valcabriers led the way round to the North of the ambulatory, then westward along the North screen of the Chancel.

'There.' He pointed to the last Chapel in the ambulatory. 'The Chapel of the Virgin. The tomb of Hugues de Châtillon, who made notable Gothic additions to the Cathedral. And at the East end of the tomb – in the wall there – the entrance which you seek.'

A very low doorway in the wall . . . or what had been a doorway. Now it was sealed by a marble slab which fitted exactly into the frame. Only the lintel protruded. Below this, some words engraved on the marble. Words indecipherable in the dimness. Jacquiz lit a match.

' "*La Famille comminges*",' he read aloud before the match went out.

'They say that before it was sealed,' said the Abbé Valcabriers, 'there was a much more elaborate inscription. Going into the historical glories of the family. They fell on bad times, you know. "La Famille Comminges" was all that was left to be said when they blocked that doorway.'

'There's a bit more than that though,' said Jacquiz.

'Just the formal declaration of closure.'

Jacquiz struck another match.

NUNC EST CLAUSUM HOC SEPULCHRUM
IN SAECULA SAECULORUM
AMEN
MDCLVI

' "Now this sepulchre has been closed," ' he translated, ' "for ever and ever. So be it. 1656." '

'I told you. A formal declaration.'

'Sounds more like a prayer. That "Amen"; as if to say "Let's hope so at any rate." There's even more, in smaller letters.'

'Since you are so determined, let me save you from exhausting both your matches and your eyesight. The sentence in smaller letters reads: "Noli aperire ne surgat Constantia." '

' "Don't open it",' said Jacquiz, ' "lest come forth Constance." '

There was a long silence.

'You are interested in country legends?' said Valcabriers at last.

'Particularly in this one.'

'I will show you a . . . local chronicle. A rare volume.'

'Thank you. But we have rooms booked at Saint Girons. We must return there this evening. How long will it take me to read this chroncle?'

'Such of it as pertains to the Comminges – to study it properly – four or five hours. But you may take the book to Saint Girons. I can see you are a man who respects books.'

'I will bring it back tomorrow.'

'Tomorrow or later. It makes no difference. Please wait in the cloister. I shall bring it to you there in ten minutes.'


Just for the look of the thing, Ivor Winstanley had decided to open up the Chamber of Manuscripts for an hour each morning and afternoon on the two days during which Len would be in London. On the afternoon of the first day, an undergraduate in a blue College blazer and a crested College tie, a rather unusual tenue these days, arrived in the Chamber five minutes before Ivor meant to leave.

'My name is C. A. A. Symington, sir,' the undergraduate said. 'A Freshman this term. Son of F. A. A. Symington of 'forty-six.'

'How do you do, Symington,' said Ivor, shaking hands. 'I remember your father well.'

As prim and proper as you are, Ivor thought; not but what I'd sooner have you than some horror in leather trousers and a sleeveless vest.

'My father told me,' said Symington, 'that there was a marvellous book in here. The St Gilles Breviary. May one ask to see it?'

Ivor began to sweat. Just like his father, Ivor thought: a dim little man of no importance always getting in somebody's way – taking ten minutes to make up his mind what kind of sherry he wanted from the Buttery when five more people were waiting.

'I'm afraid the key is in London,' Ivor said. 'I've only taken over very temporarily from Doctor Helmut, who is on Sabbatical leave. So naturally I leave all the details to my Under-Collator – who is presently in London on business.'

'Never mind, sir,' said Symington. 'I can come another day.'

'The trouble is,' said Ivor hoarsely, 'that the St Gilles Breviary has become . . . very delicate and brittle . . . since your father's day. It is no longer to be taken out and shown,' he said wildly, 'without a special order from the Provost.'

'I understand, sir,' said Symington politely. 'I shall call upon the Provost to obtain such an order. Good afternoon, sir.'


In the cloister at Saint Bertrand-de-Comminges the Abbé Valcabriers handed Jacquiz a brown paper parcel.

'You should return this to the last house on the right before you come to the Porte Lyrisson,' he said, 'a house with a gable protruding slightly over the street. Now, if you will excuse me, I must return to my duties as guardian inside.'

As they drove downhill out of Saint Bertrand Marigold said:

'I wonder what he does if he's not a priest of the Cathedral.'

'He could be at another local church. Or he could have private means. There *are* ordained priests who have no cures.'

'This is the Porte Lyrisson we're coming to,' said Marigold, consulting the green *Michelin*. 'That must be his house. What a quaint house.'

Jacquiz slowed the Rolls.

' "Comminges aed. 1567," ' he read. 'Above the door there. One way and the other Monsieur L'Abbé seems to make quite a hobby out of la famille Comminges.'


Oh God, oh God, thought Ivor. Whatever is going to happen when that wretched boy appears before the Provost and asks him for an order to view the Breviary? Constable will think that I've gone off my head. At best he'll think I've made a silly mistake and just tell Symington that no such order is necessary. Then Symington will come back here – and whatever shall we show him? I'll never be able to stall him a second time, not after he's seen the Provost.

The telephone rang.

'Ivor,' said the Provost's voice, 'Mr C. A. A. Symington has been to see me.'

'Already, Provost?'

'Son of F. A. A. Symington of 1946, whom we both remember. A very persistent man, Ivor. Like father, like son.'

'Quite so, Provost.'

'Well, of course you know what he came about. He wanted an order to view one of your more valuable manuscript volumes.'

There was a long pause.

'Are you there, Ivor?'

'Provost.'

'I only wanted to say that I think it's very sensible of you to introduce this new system – making people get an order to view. We can't have every student in the place pawing at rare manuscripts just because the idea suddenly takes his fancy. *But*, Ivor . . .'

'Provost . . .?'

'I do think you should have warned *me* that you were going to do this. After all, I've got to sign the things.'

'An oversight, Provost. I've had a lot to do in this new job . . . as I think you know.'

'Yes, Ivor. I know. And because this is the case I've refused this Symington an order to view—'

'—*Provost*—'

'—And I shall refuse any similar requests for some weeks to come. We can't have you overworked, Ivor. You've got enough on your plate without mealy-mouthed boys like C.A.A. Symington – er – messing you about.'

'I am most grateful, Provost. I hope Symington wasn't too disappointed.'

'He was very obstinate. He seemed to think he had some sort of right to look at that Breviary, however busy you were. So to keep him happy I said as soon as you'd settled in properly – some time in the New Year, Ivor – I was going to get you to organize an exhibition of the College documents, manuscripts and whatever, in conjunction with the Librarian, for all to gaze upon. Of course I fully realize, Ivor, that this too may create problems for you . . . but I think we can manage them when the time comes. Good-bye for now.'

'Good-bye, Provost, and thank you . . . very much.'

'Not at all, Ivor. A loyal man deserves all the support I can give him.'

So that was it, thought Ivor as he rang off. Clearly, Lord Constable had sniffed the air when Symington made his odd request and had got some kind of whiff in his nostrils of what was afoot. He smelt trouble brewing for Jacquiz as requested and for the time being at least he was going to play along with Ivor. One problem solved, Ivor thought. The disappearance of the Breviary cannot now become known until it suits Len and me that it should be – *i.e.* at the next monthly check with the Third Bursar, this to occur, as provisionally agreed with him this morning, on October 30.

Marigold stood at a window and looked down on the stable yard of their hotel at Saint Girons.

'Nearly dark, Jacquiz. Come and take a look before it's too late.'

As he joined her, she took hold of his hand and gently scratched the palm with the nail of her second finger.

'How are you getting on?' she said.

'It's a kind of scrapbook. The Abbé has evidently made copies of local documents ranging from official proclamations in scurrilous broadsheets, anything which has been preserved in museums or public records, and from these he has cut out all the most striking or amusing sections and stuck them into this book.'

'And la famille Comminges figures largely?'

'Yes.'

'As striking . . . or amusing?'

'So far . . . as picturesque. The entries which concern them are more prominently placed and mounted than any others. I suppose the Abbé is especially interested in them because he happens to live in their house.'

'Perhaps he's a descendant. Or some kind of connection.'

'I shall certainly ask him when I return the book.'

'What does it say?'

'I've only managed the earlier entries as yet. The first of them is in monk's Latin – rather more difficult than usual because there are a lot of bastard words made up out of Provençal roots and Latin inflections. The author seems to have been a Canon of the Cathedral at Saint Lizier, writing towards the end of the fifteenth century, and his theme is the extirpation of the Albigensian heresy, to which a lot of locals subscribed. This Canon raises a great paean in praise of the triumph of orthodoxy in the Crusade led by Simon de Montfort the Elder nearly three hundred years before he wrote, and he then goes on to gloat over the humiliation of some of the grand families who protected or sympathized with the Cathars ... first of all the Counts of Toulouse, of course, then the related Trencavels, Viscounts of Carcassone, and then, sweetheart ... sweetheart, it is a pleasant thing to look out into the evening with you.'

'And with you. Go on, nice Jacquiz. After the Counts of Toulouse and the Viscounts of Carcassone ...?'

'... The next lot to catch it were – guess whom – a famous family of Albigensians, the Vidames of Comminges. They didn't just protect or sympathize with the Cathars, they were fully paid up subscribers to the heresy.'

'The Vidames of Comminges ... *Vidames*, Jacquiz?'

'A Vidame was a French nobleman who held lands from a bishop or Prince of the Church in return for defending and representing him in secular matters. Sometimes, of course, a grateful bishop would make an absolute gift of lands or estates to his Vidame, or the Vidame would blackmail the bishop into handing them over. In that case the Vidame would come to hold the lands in question direct from the King of France – or far more probably, in this part of the world, from one of the semi-sovereign dukes or counts, such as Toulouse, or from the Holy Roman Emperor, who was Otto the Fourth at the time we're talking of. As far as I can make out, however, our Vidames of Comminges claimed to hold their territory, which was a good third of what is now known as the Comté du Comminges, as an independent or palatine Barony, acknowledging no overlord at all. From time to time their cousins, the Counts of Comminges, who held the rest of the region, tried to get the Vidames to pay homage for their piece, but without any success.'

'So these Vidames were pretty big bugs in this particular rug,' said Marigold.

'Until Simon de Montfort came on the anti-Albigensian Crusade. He captured the reigning Vidame, Roger-Raymond-Louis de Comminges, shoved him in a dungeon in Carcassone (which he had taken from the Trencavel Viscount) and tortured him to death while putting him to the question about his fellow Cathars. The Vidame's lady, who seems to have been a woman of resource, somehow smuggled her three sons clear and lay low in Saint Gaudens – but with little enough to hope for, as most of the family's castles and estates were sacked or ravaged during de Montfort's Crusade and the Royal Crusade which followed, their lands were declared forfeit to the King of France – who now began to gain some control down here – and their titles were pronounced invalid. Total disgrace in short. However, by some freak the Royal Clerks omitted the Seigneurie of Convênes later to be known as Saint Bertrand-de-Comminges, from the Warrant of Escheat. So although the family was no longer noble, since the Royal Warrant ordained that such vile heretics must forfeit even the use of the particle "de", they did remain Esquires of Convênes – or Saint Bertrand as it was soon after renamed, in honour of the famous bishop. Eventually Roger-Raymond-Louis's widow brought her sons back to live there, in a farmhouse just outside the town, and from 1229 onwards the family scraped a rough and ready living as low-grade gentlemen farmers. The monk's chronicle ends with them still in this sorry condition nearly two hundred and fifty years later, in 1470; but at least they'd done better than their cousins, the Counts of Comminges, who were bled dry by Louis IX's Seneschals after the Royal Crusade and vanished into a pit of debt and degradation well before the end of the thirteenth century. A bit hard on them, really, because although they'd supported the Counts of Toulouse against Simon, they'd never been heretics and they'd switched to the King's side well before the end of it all.'

'Turncoats deserve everything they get,' said Marigold. 'Anyway, *they'd* had their lot, while the Vidame crowd had managed to hang on – after a fashion and up till 1470. Do we know what happened to them then?'

'Yes. The story of the "Vidame crowd" – now, you remember, without any kind of title – is continued by a priest of Saint-Bertrand, who was apparently writing in about 1670, in part as local historian, in part (at the later stages of his narrative) as an eye-witness. According to him, the surviving branch of the Comminges went on living virtuously and very humbly on their farm right up to 1515. Then, after nearly three hundred years of obscurity, they began to become famous again – or at least notorious.'

Jacquiz paused, kissed Marigold, felt her squeeze his hand three times in quick succession, then proceeded:

'The point to remember is that the Comminges, although they had declared themselves converted to orthodoxy in 1229 (in order to forestall any attempt to take Convênes/Saint Bertrand from them), had in fact continued secretly as Albigensians. Now the Albigensian heresy amounts, very roughly, to saying that the material universe has been created by the Devil, and that everything in it must be eschewed by those who aspire to know the true God and to pass into the realm of the spirit. Most Albigensians therefore led pious and ascetic lives, shunning all fleshly gratification. But there were just a few who held that the Devil of the physical world was by no means inferior to the God of the spiritual (for if he were he would not have been permitted to operate) but was in fact equal to and independent of him. In this case, they said, the Devil's creation must be equal to and independent of God's creation – and hence arose Albigensian sub-sects of great dottiness and depravity, and many brands of neo-paganism.

'Back to the Comminges in their farmhouse outside Saint Bertrand. Having lived blameless lives, ostensibly as orthodox Christians but in truth as pious Albigensians, for almost three centuries, they suddenly deviated to a more than usually perverse variant of the heresy, and declared – publicly – that the Devil was not just equal to and independent of God, but was positively victorious over Him and had in every way supplanted Him. From this it followed that Evil was now paramount, not only in the Devil's terrestrial kingdom, but also in the spiritual kingdom formerly ruled by God; and that there was therefore an absolute religious obligation both to practise Evil and to worship it. The Comminges now emerged overnight as Satanists, Conjurers and Necromancers – and, quite incredibly, were allowed to get away with it. Partly because Saint Bertrand was at that time very remote, partly because the Church there had gone into a steep decline since the days of the Saint, partly because they terrorized their neighbours and petty tenants into covering up for them whenever outside inquiry threatened, they were able to continue and thrive in their Diabolism for two generations. By spell and subterfuge they ruled Saint Bertrand, became rich, acquired more and more property in the town itself (their previous "lordship" having mostly comprised poor land outside it); they built fine houses – like the one in which the Abbé now lives – and they became hated. Finally, when they became more hated than feared, someone sneaked on them to the Inquisition, an organization which was a match even for the Comminges. In 1597 they were purged and broken by a special Commission which came all the way from Avignon for the purpose. There is a copy of the Convening Order in the Abbé's scrapbook.

'But once again, a resourceful woman saved the family. A wife of a younger brother secreted, in the mountains above the Vallée du Lys, one son, one daughter and herself. In due course she returned with them to Saint Bertrand, professed innocence of the crimes of which the rest of the family had been convicted, induced both the Bishop and the Prefect to believe her (on pain of sleeping with both), and established herself, with their aid, in one of the Comminges mansions in the town. Her son and daughter grew, married, prospered – apparently by the uses of virtue. Her son's son, however, was a bad lot, given to dicing and, what was worse, to losing, and was finally dispatched to serve the King in the North, supposedly as an Officer, in fact as a low-grade Commissary. This was the Louis Comminges who came to Montreuil and married Constance Fauvrelle.'

'So now we know,' said Marigold, 'why Louis had to be so careful what towns he went through on his way home. Presumably the case in 1597 made such a splash that the Comminges were still widely suspected and liable to be persecuted.'

'Yes. Except in the old Cathar strongholds, where

traditional hatred of the Inquisition would guarantee sympathy for those pursued by it – even for those who, like the Comminges, had disgraced and perverted Cathar doctrine. Thus Louis couldn't go to Avignon, where the Inquisition was established in strength, but he could go to Arles, where any victim of the Holy Office (however vile) was seen as a martyr who had suffered in the same cause as the sons of old Provence.'

'And from Arles he came at last to Pau, where he died. But to judge from that inscription on his gravestone, Jacquiz, the family was still given to Diabolism ... Necromancy ... or something in that area.'

'The inscription was adjuring him to rest.'

'Exactly. Implying that at one stage he must have been restless. Who raised him? Or did he raise himself? At best, it can be explained as mere rumour or illusion. But even that is hardly wholesome. Not wholesome at all, nice Jacquiz.' She twined her fingers in his. 'But go on. What happened next? What did poor Constance find in the way of family when she got to Saint Bertrand?'

'I don't know. The Priest and I have only got to Constance's marriage.'

'You know all that bit.'

'I want to check his account against our other sources. And then I shall get on to ... what *exactly* happened in Pau.'

'And after.'

'And after,' said Jacquiz, rocking slightly as she squeezed his hand (once, twice, thrice).

'But an interval now,' she said. 'Dinner.'

'Only dinner?'

'Only dinner ... now.'

'And then ...?'

'More reading for you. I want to know about Constance. We are, after all, related.'


I wonder, thought Len, if something has gone wrong.

He looked over at the agent who had come from his client

in Bavaria. The agent nodded back and then went on reading the *München Tageblatt*, which the hotel had specially procured and sent up for him that morning. Len looked at the Breviary, which lay cushioned on its wash-leather pouch in the middle of a low table half way between himself and the agent. No, he thought: the man was satisfied when he examined the merchandise; I heard him telephone the authorization; nothing has gone wrong, it's just that the bank in Geneva is taking its time about sending my wire.

And yet, he thought, we have both been sitting here since yesterday lunch-time – that is, for well over twenty-four hours. Surely the money should be in my account in Geneva and I should have had my telegram by now. It's ridiculous, this situation, ridiculous and horrible: we distrust each other so much that every time one of us wants to piddle, we both have to go to the lavatory, each holding a corner of the Breviary. Thank heaven that neither of us has yet wanted to crap.

I want to get home to Cambridge, Len thought. Ivor will be worried if I'm not back after two days. I want to get back to the Chamber and talk to dear old Ivor, learn more of the things which he teaches me without knowing it. I want to have a long private look, in my own private room, at my own private edition of the Georgics, my exquisite 'Wandrill Georgics'. I hope it will be safe where I've hidden it: inside the folding wooden chess set, with a label on the pouch saying 'Correspondence Games in Progress'. I know that old slag of a landlady sniffs around when I'm away, but I don't think she'll stick her snout into Correspondence Chess.

And now what next? he thought. How soon can I cut the painters and sail away into the good life? Be patient, Lenny boy; there's no hurry; you'll have quite a happy time in Cambridge, looking at 'The Wandrille Georgics', learning things from old Ive. If you fuck off too fast, you'll fuck the whole thing up – and if you do that, quite apart from anything else, you'll be letting down old Ive. Just sit there, Lenny boy; yes, Lenny; just sit down, as Ivor would say, quiet, and let the thing go on.

But I don't want to sit down in *here* much longer. Tick-tock goes the marble clock. Funny, you don't often see a clock on the mantelpiece (sorry, Ive, mantel-*shelf*) of a room in a hotel. But then this isn't just any old hotel, now is it? But oh Christ, I wish I was out of it. Tick-tock, tick-tock. For Christ's sake, God, for God's sake, Christ – where is my wire from Geneva?

Marigold sat by the window, looking down on the stable yard as it lay in the moonlight and wondering why the universe should ever have come to exist. If one looked at it logically, she thought, there should never have been anything, not even empty space ... just nothingness, like a sleep. Who or what had wakened nothingness, and how?

A chair squeaked. Jacquiz rose from the dressing-table in the far corner of the room, and came across to her. He put both hands on her shoulders.

'Jacquiz. You're trembling.'

'It's not nice, Marigold. What's in that scrapbook.'

'You're frightened.'

'Well. Rather appalled. I think ... that we should give this whole thing up.'

'No,' said Marigold.

'When we started, you said ... that if there was ever a nasty smell ... you'd sheer straight off.'

'There have already been nasty smells, sweetheart. But I haven't sheered off, have I? I'm not going to. Whatever I may have said at the start, *now* I want to see it through.'

'Of course.'

'Go on then, tell. Tell about that scrapbook.'

'Not now.' The palms of his hands were sweating through her dress. 'In the morning. Time enough then.'

She sighed. 'Love now, Jacquiz?' She put a hand up to clasp one of his hands, where it gripped her shoulder. Even the back of it, she thought, seemed to be sweating; but perhaps that was her. 'Sweet love.'

'Quiet love.'

'Not like you, Jacquiz. You used to make such a production of it.'

'I was silly. Sweet love, quiet love. I see that now.'

'Love. And then, in the morning, you shall tell me what you've read in that scrapbook.'

Jacquiz shivered and pressed his lips down on to her hair.

# VI

# The Gods of the Shore

'Very pretty,' said Balbo Blakeney.

'Magnificent, I should call it.'

'No, Sydney. Imposing at first sight, I agree, but only theatrical if you look at it a bit longer.'

They stood on a beach and looked up, as from the stage of an ancient odeon, past tiers of terraced houses and up again into a narrow re-entrant of rock.

'Yes, theatrical,' Balbo said.

'Still, I'm glad Jermyn Street allowed us to come here,' said Syd Jones.

'Were they keen?'

'Not at all. But I said I must have more time to talk to you, and that meanwhile you must be humoured.'

'Thank you. But if you ask me, you seem to believe in my search rather more than I do. I sometimes think that I'm humouring you.'

'Well, do that. Remind me, Balbo: exactly what is this treasure we're looking for?'

'Rubies. Rubies with a curse on them.'

'Rubies are supposed to be lucky . . . to confer prosperity and distinction.'

'So do these. They also have a curse on them. Every now and then they turn nasty with their owner. If, that is, they still exist.'

'You said . . . that you were searching back into time for them.'

'Searching back to the time . . . and the place . . . at which they were last known about. And for the person who knew about them.'

'Well. Here we are at the place at which Andrea Commingi was probably painted in 1699. Or rather, the place indicated, not by the picture itself, but by the literal part of

the code in that picture, which was painted in 1699. Therefore a place which was important to him, almost certainly
the place in which he lived, and from which he operated,
before he moved on to Corfu. Now then, Balbo: what can
this place tell us about Andrea Commingi – if we use the rest
of that code right, I mean the *visual* parts of it?'

'It may show us his house, if we look. His . . . habitat.'

'And might we see the glitter of rubies in all this? The
ghost of their glitter, perhaps?'

'You go too fast, Sydney. I see nothing yet. Are you *sure*
we're in the right place?

'Yep. The letters on those temple cornices. "P", "O" . . .
"N", "A", "O", "S" . . . "I", "T". Wanted: a sea port on the
West Coast of Italy, as per previous instructions. Answer,
the anagram of the letters – POSITANO. And here we are.'

'It almost seems too simple.'

'It always does – once you've got the answer.'

'Even I got it – after a time. That makes it very simple.'

'You solved the anagram, when you'd been told what the
letters were. You wouldn't have seen them, tucked away on
that musty old canvas, if I hadn't shown them to you.' Then,
as Balbo looked hurt, 'Sorry, old man,' Syd told him, 'but we
have our professional pride.'

'So here we are. What now?'

'The picture, Balbo.'

Syd Jones took from his pocket the envelope on which he
had copied the Commingi portrait and its landscape.

'Remember: we are not looking for a direct resemblance.
We are looking for a code of visual clues or puns.'

Balbo looked up at the re-entrant.

'There are three famous heights along the coast,' he said:
'at Sorrento, at Amalfi, and here. This town is between the
other two. Perhaps the forefinger that blocks out the *central*
height in the picture indicates that Commingi had control of
the height above this, the central town. Perhaps it had an
observation post or a fortress. He'd have had a lot of enemies
after him – not least the exise men.'

'Yes,' said Jones, S. 'Coming at him both by land and sea.

He'd need a tower looking out to sea and at the same time tactically situated so as to deny access by land. But what about the snow on the heights?'

'A way of telling us that he was particularly prone to operate along the coast by winter? The whole picture had a wintry feel. Bold pirates favour rough weather.'

'So far, so good, Balbo . . . may be. But this is getting us no nearer to the man. There *is* a ruined tower up there which could well have been his fortress and his observation tower; but it tells us nothing of what we want to know about him.'

'We don't so much want to know about him,' said Balbo; 'we want to know what he knew about the Rubies. Which member of the family, if any, had possession of them; or when, where and by whom they'd last been sighted.'

'Yep. Not the sort of thing you find out in a ruined tower. But we're not done with that picture yet. We agree that the finger nail blocking out the central peak probably confirms Positano (the central town with a famous height above it) as his base, and also tells us that he had control. What does the rest of it tell us? What a pretty little girl.'

'Where?' said Balbo.

'Just gone behind that rock. Long dress and a basket of flowers. About fifteen.'

'An interesting age, I've always thought. Physically nubile yet still so innocent.'

'Let's keep our minds on our work. That picture. It must tell us more about him – him and his ways of going on.'

'The two Sicilies,' Balbo said.

'What about them?'

'When Commingi lived here, this coast was part of the Kingdom of Naples – which was the second half of the Kingdom of the Two Sicilies, the other half, of course, being Sicily itself. That causeway in the picture – it could symbolize a route or voyage between the mainland and the island of Sicily.'

'Why should that island be Sicily?'

'The temples. They could stand as a conventional sign for Sicily. There are celebrated groups of temples all along the

Sicilian coast, notably at Agrigento and Selinunte in the South.'

'Come to that, there is a celebrated group of temples at Paestum – just down the coast from here,' said Jones, S.

'Then Paestum is another place he might have been sailing to. Wherever it was, that causeway, the one and only way to it, could indicate that Commingi had a special route, known to him alone, a route suitable for winter, since winter is so strong in the picture. Or that he, and he alone, ran a special line in goods.'

'Yup,' said Syd. 'The picture could mean that and a great many other things beside. None of them is bringing us any closer to Commingi, or helping us to find out what, if anything, he knew about the Rubies.'

Balbo twisted the toe of his left shoe in the sand.

'If those temples do indicate Sicily,' he said, 'or Paestum, for that matter, why are the letters which make up Positano written on *them* rather than elsewhere in the picture?'

'Because it's a natural place for them to be. Carved on masonry, to which, on the face of it, they bear explicit reference. Remember? PO, NAOS, IT – Poseidon's temple in Italy. *Your* translation. All quite obvious and above board; nothing there to invite suspicion.'

'But it did invite *your* suspicion.'

'Oh yes, cobber. The serious codebreaker, as opposed to the casual nosey-parker, is bound to see through the camouflage, and the chap who devised the code would have realized this. So he arranged that as soon as the trick had been found out it should start to operate on another level – his intention being no longer to reassure but to confuse. If anyone gets as far as realizing that those letters are an anagram of Positano, he is then faced, as we are, with the question of why they are carved on the cornices of temples which, we think, stand for Sicily or possibly Paestum. But once again, Balbo, even if we answer the question, we shan't be getting any nearer to what we want to know about Commingi, which is what, if anything, Commingi knew about the Rubies.'

'I just saw that girl.'

'What girl?'

'The one you said you saw. With the flowers. Sitting on a rock, she was, arranging them in her basket. "Rose girl, bearing your posies",' Balbo quoted,

> ' "What are you coming to sell?
>     Is it yourself or your roses,
>     Or yourself and your roses as well?" '

'Was it roses she had?'

'I think so. She's gone now.'

'This is getting us no further at all,' said Jones, S.

'Hardly surprising. Why should the ghosts talk to us? Just because we've been clever enough, or think we have, to discover where Commingi lived before he came to Corfu, why should that tell us anything about the Rubies?'

'If only we could find out *something* about his life here . . . We can't just give up now. It would be such a shame, old Balbo, to give up now.'

How sad he sounds, Balbo thought. I wish I could come up with something for him. I like this man. I'd like to impress him. I'd like to give him pleasure – the pleasure of going on with this hunt. I can't really believe in it myself, but clearly it excites him, and anyway I'd like to go on leading this kind of . . . wandering life . . . with him for a while longer. I wish I could find a clue for him, a clue to tell us where to go, what to do, next. Desperately, he said,

'That crumbling nose – which the sea had formed out of the rock . . .?'

Syd Jones shook his head.

'Don't clutch at straws,' he said. 'Try to reconcile the contradiction. Letters which make up Positano . . . carved along the cornices of a group of temples which symbolize Sicily.'

'Or Paestum . . . which isn't far from here.'

Keep it going, Balbo thought. Something may turn up.

'Where's the map?' he said.

'In the car,' snapped Jones S.

'Never mind. There's one that'll do in the guide book.'

Balbo took a paperback edition of *The Companion Guide to Southern Italy* from his coat pocket and consulted the table of contents. Keep it going, he said to himself; just a chance I may find something for him. And then aloud,

'Map One. No,' he said a few seconds later, 'it gives out just too high up. On to Map Three . . . page 182.'

'What the hell good is all this?' grumbled Syd Jones as Balbo turned the pages.

'You may well ask,' said Balbo, and plucked with one hand at Jones's sleeve, balancing the guide book on the other. 'Oh, Sydney, you may well ask. We have been very silly, Sydney. We have been far too clever and very, very silly indeed.'

In a first-floor room above a famous perfumer's shop in Jermyn Street, a thin, ratty man said to a smooth, plump one:

'He can't go on chasing all round Europe at the department's expense.'

'It is very important,' said the plump man, in a voice brittle with suppressed irritation, 'as you have been repeatedly instructed, that he should bring Blakeney in gently. For it is important that Blakeney should cooperate, and Blakeney is the kind of man who requires, as a necessary condition of cooperation, civil and civilized treatment. This he is receiving from Jones, who must be allowed some licence in such very tricky circumstances.'

'So you have said before, sir. Allow me to remind you, once again, that time is running out.'

'We have a good five weeks before the start of Operation Falx.'

'We shall need at least one week for the precise training of Blakeney. And a week before that to set him in the right frame of mind, sir. We also need time for medical check-ups and so on.'

'Jones will bring Blakeney in when he's ready to come. He will be of little use to us unless he *is* ready to come. Jones will be a sound judge of that.'

'I sometimes think, sir,' said the ratty man in a rich, level tenor, 'that your life-long partiality for county cricket has caused you to overvalue the capacities of Jones in our own very different professional sphere.'

'And I sometimes think, Q,' said the smooth man with a bland look but jagged utterance, 'that your life-long dislike of the game has caused you to undervalue them – and to resent Jones's presence here. But let us not argue about that now. As things are *now*, Q, Jones is in the field . . . "preparing" Blakeney, who, he reports, is rather disturbed and very intrigued by the story he has been told about the mutant rats, but must nevertheless (in Jones's view) be allowed to settle his own personal obsession with some private piece of antiquarian research before he will be fully ready to join us. So let Jones watch over Blakeney while he settles his obsession – no better or more patient man for the job – and then bring Blakeney quietly in.'

'And suppose Blakeney is still pursuing his obsession three weeks from now – by which time it will be essential to us that we should have him here within hours?'

'Then, said the plump man, lightly but tightly, 'we *shall* have him here within hours. It would be a pity, because Blakeney would not be at his best under compulsion, but it would be our only course. However, I don't think we need worry. Jones knows the schedule; that is, he knows when we need Blakeney.'

'He was told to bring him in straight away if he could.'

'And we must certainly keep up our pressure on him. But he must still have licence if he makes out a good case for it.'

'I yearn,' said the ratty man with a throb in his voice, 'to have Blakeney safe here, under our hand and eye.'

'It will certainly be a great relief. Jones will have prepared him, with his account of the rats from the marshes, for something pretty disagreeable; but we shall need quite a lot of time and tact to reconcile him to the – er – detail of Operation Falx.'

'Map three,' said Balbo, 'is on page 182. By the Grace of God my eye strayed to page 183 opposite.'

'God has nothing to do with it,' said Jones, S., as he edged the hired car on to the coast road and turned right for the South. 'It's just that you're improving.'

'Thank you, Sydney. Page 183 explains that Paestum was originally a Greek colony called Poseidonia, that it is famous for three magnificent temples by the sea, and that one of these, though in truth dedicated to Hera, has for many centuries been wrongly but universally called the Temple of Poseidon.'

'Yer going well, sport.'

'Now, consider that inscription in the picture: "P", "O"; "N", "A", "O", "S"; "I", "T". *Poseidonos Naos Italianus*. Normally the Latin for the Temple of Poseidon would be Templum Neptuni, but since this one was built by Greeks it is named in Greek – Poseidonos Naos – albeit in Roman letters. However, to make it quite clear to all that, though Greek, it is situated in Italy, we have the epithet Italianus. The clue is then complete. A Greek Temple of Poseidon – commonly so called – but situated in Italy. It must mean the famous one at Paestum or Poseidonia. And just in case we're still in doubt, the picture tells us that it is by the sea-shore and one of a group of three. Where else in Italy, other than at Paestum, are there three Greek temples, by the sea-shore, one of them a reputed Temple of Poseidon?'

'I'll buy it, sport. So Paestum is in some way very important to this Commingi. But do those letters *also* mean Positano, like we thought at first?'

'Perhaps, and perhaps not.'

'And our interpretation of those three peaks – do we still think we got them right?'

'Again, perhaps, and perhaps not. Perhaps we were right,

in which case the causeway now definitely stands for a voyage from Positano to Paestum ... in those days far more convenient by sea than by road ... a voyage of singular importance to Commingi. Perhaps we were wrong, and Positano has nothing to do with any of it, the anagram being purely fortuitous. What we *do* know,' Balbo concluded his exegesis, 'is that Commingi, beyond any doubt, must have had associations with Paestum.'

'Which brings us back to the old question, Balbo. What do we look for in Paestum? What is there, in Paestum, which can tell us anything about Andrea Commingi or about his knowledge, if any, of the Rubies?'

'I'll tell you that when we get there – *if* my hunch is right. If it's wrong, I shall be so disappointed and embarrassed that I shan't want to talk any more about it, in case you laugh at me.'

'I wouldn't do that, old Balbo. Not after the way you're trying.'

'Even so, I'd prefer not to tell you about it ... unless I'm proved right.'

Jones, S., looked curiously for a moment at Balbo, then quickly turned his eyes away, before Balbo could notice them, and concentrated on the road to the South.


When Q had finished his conversation with his superior on the first floor above the perfumer's shop in Jermyn Street, he returned to his own office on the second floor and decided to use the rest of his afternoon completing certain simple but tedious preparations for Operation Falx.

First, he telephoned the Brigadier who commanded the 17th (South Eastern) Lorried Infantry Brigade, quoted a mandate recently granted to his department by the Ministry of Defence, and on this authority requisitioned the services of two battalions of fully trained infantry for 'unspecified fatigue duties', these to last for seven days commencing on 29 November. He also requested the Brigadier to confirm that the personnel of the Ministry of Works in Dover Castle (where the Brigadier had his headquarters) had received instructions from the Minister to close Dover Castle to the public during the same seven days that had been named for the performance of the unspecified 'fatigue duties'.

The Brigadier said that these instructions had indeed been received by the personnel of the Ministry of Works, who had already (as also instructed) caused notices to be posted in the area to inform the public of the proposed closure, this being attributed to a fictitious project of 'Reconstruction'. Comprehensive measures had also been taken to inform tourist agencies, *etc.*, *etc.* The officials had obeyed their orders without any question, said the Brigadier, because they were sound and responsible men, many of them old soldiers; but they were rather puzzled at being required to engineer such a deception and would appreciate some sort of briefing about what was going on. So, for that matter, would he himself. To take two battalions away from their normal duties for seven days was no light matter, and it was playing old Harry with the arrangements for the administrative inspections due in early December.

To this Q replied that the Brigadier and the two Lieutenant-Colonels commanding the battalions on requisition would be fully briefed before very long. As for the officials of the Ministry of Works, they were simply to be told that the closure was required by the exigencies of the public service. If, as the Brigadier maintained, they were responsible men, many of them with military records, then they would understand by this that they were to mind their own business and not to ask annoying questions.

Q made his next telephone call to the Dean of Canterbury. A date had been fixed, he told the Dean, for the performance of the necessary task of which the Dean was cognizant. Work would begin on 29 November and would last for seven days. No, it would not be necessary to close the Cathedral, only the Crypt and the South-East Transept.

Next, Q addressed a memo to 'Lambda of Bio/Chem.' which ran:

I cannot persuade Theta to compel Jones to bring Blakeney in immediately. Theta points out that there are still five weeks (exactly, as it happens) before Operation Falx and he is sure Jones will produce Blakeney in plenty of time. I am not so sure. I hope you can continue the necessary research for Falx without Blakeney's help. Theta says that in any case Blakeney won't be of much help until he is ready and willing to come. Theta could be right about this. He is at least ready to adopt tough measures should time become really short.

I will let you have the latest set of figures *re* Blakeney tomorrow.

                                                            Q of Home.

This memo Q put into a buff envelope, on which he wrote 'To the Assistant Manager, AltoMarine Products Ltd'. He then summoned a messenger and instructed him to deliver it at the offices of AltoMarine, which were on the third floor two doors further down Jermyn Street.

'Thank God that's done,' he said aloud. And then,

'Is Theta a sentimental fool, or a man of sound intuitions?'

Since he received no answer, he put on the greatcoat which he had bought second-hand in Oxford, when an undergraduate of Hertford College, thirty-two years before, and walked down the street to dine alone and very elaborately at the Stafford Hotel.

'There is a story,' Balbo said to Jones, S., of Glamorgan, 'that even long after the Greek colony of Poseidonia became the Roman city of Paestum the citizens continued to remember their Greek origins, and once a year used to call on their Gods by their Greek names and weep as they remembered they had once been Greeks.'

'Who told you that story?'

'*The Companion Guide to Southern Italy*,' said Balbo honestly. 'Another thing it says: Paestum was famous for its roses, from which they used to make scent.'

'Roses?' said Syd. 'They seem to be featuring today. First on the beach at Positano . . . But none of this has anything to do with your hunch, Balbo?'

'Not as far as I am aware.'

Balbo looked up at the Doric capitals and broken pediment of the Temple of Poseidon, then away through tall, waving grasses towards the sea.

'Pity you can't actually see the sea,' he said. 'It used to come in much closer, of course. So much closer that a pirate or shady merchant . . . like our friend Commingi . . . might have found it a very handy area in which to store things . . . to *hide* things, Sydney.'

Balbo led the way along the road of broken stone. After a while they came to a crossroad. Behind them was the Temple of Poseidon, which they had just left, and beyond it another Doric temple, archaic, squat, sprawling. Before them was a third temple. Otherwise nothing but scattered stones in coarse grass? Nothing? It must be possible to see the village from here, Balbo thought in a momentary panic, the Museum, the Church of the Annunziata, the numerous restaurants and hotels mentioned in the *Companion Guide*. Yes, of course he could see the village; just for a moment it had been obscured by a mound, that was all.

'Remains of the Roman Forum,' said Balbo, gesturing at the stones. 'The Greek Agora is underneath it. If we walk a little further . . . by this mound, Sydney, is a subterranean chapel. Dedicated to Hera, the *Guide* says. Think of that picture, Sydney. The causeway, representing some special kind of voyage, leaves the mainland, passes behind the figure of Commingi, and at some point, unseen by us, passes on to, or *into*, the islet on which those three temples are placed.'

'Careful, Balbo. You're telling me about your hunch before it's been proved right. You didn't want to do that, you said. You might feel silly if it turned out to be a dud.'

'It has been proved right. Sydney. Already.'

'I thought I saw that little girl again.'

'Don't be absurd, Sydney.'

'Slipping round that mound. There were roses in her

basket and something else. Small flowers like a cross. White.'

'Alyssum. Sweet alyssum. Funny.'

'What's funny?'

'Coincidence, that's all.'

'You're not being very plain, Balbo.'

'Let me explain, step by step. My hunch, Sydney, now proved right, was that the causeway, which disappeared unseen into the islet below the temples, signified a voyage – possibly from Positano but no matter – a voyage from somewhere which *ended* in or near some cave or grotto, unseen in the picture and therefore secret in fact, in the region of, and in a sense underneath, the three temples of Paestum. In that cave or grotto Commingi would store his loot. All right?'

'All right – as a hunch. I don't see that it's been *proved* yet.'

'Sydney, the cave or grotto which I hypothesized now turns out to be this underground chapel.'

'How do you know that?'

Balbo was breathing heavily with excitement.

'It fulfils all the conditions. It is near the three temples and it is underground – *i.e.* beneath their level. It *must* have been Commingi's secret hiding place, Sydney, because there is a sign scratched in that stone, near what must have been the entrance to the shrine, a crude sign of a face with only one eye and only one ear, characteristics, or rather deprivations, which distinguished the portrait of Andrea Commingi.'

'Where . . . is this sign?'

Balbo pointed to a stone supported horizontally, like a lintel, by two shafts which protruded some six inches from the ground.

'But it's tiny, Balbo. How on earth did you spot it?'

'Scientists . . . who have spent long periods in laboratories scrutinizing arrangements of cells or patterns of corpuscles . . . develop a sharp eye, Sydney.'

'Then why didn't you spot those letters in the picture?'

'Because my eyes were still dull, as they had been for years. It must be you that have begun to quicken them.'

'Me?'

'I like to please you, Sydney. I very much want to impress you.'

'Well, fella, you certainly have.'

Syd Jones bent down and examined the inscribed face once more.

'No doubt of it. One eye, one ear. Obviously there to mark the spot clearly for Commingi's confederates and so on – but too small for anyone to see unless he had biz here and had been told whereabouts to look. To small for anyone but you, that is. But now comes the old question, Balbo: this tells us "Commingi was here"; but what does it tell us of his knowledge of the Rubies?'

The evening breeze raced through the grasses to the sea. Somewhere a bell was rung.

'They want us out . . . What does this tell us, Balbo, about the Rubies? Or about Commingi himself, for that matter?'

'Nothing new.'

'Could the Rubies be hidden in that shrine?'

'No. It was excavated very thoroughly some years ago. They'd have come to light then if they'd been here. Anyhow, if Commingi himself had the Rubies, for which supposition there is no positive reason whatever, he wouldn't have left them here, he'd have taken them on to Corfu and thence to Lycia. But if we assume, as we've had to, that we must just go on searching back into the past, hoping eventually to hear news of the Rubies, then, Sydney, this place does tell us something . . . something which might just keep us in the hunt.'

'I'll be buggered if I can see what, sport.'

The bell rang again, more urgently. They turned and walked back towards the two temples to the South of the Forum. The dying sun struck through cloud and gilded the columns of the Temple of Poseidon as they passed.

'It's very simple,' said Balbo at last. 'Quite a good next step back for us would be to Andrea's mother or father . . . uncle or aunt . . . or whatever.'

'Granted.'

'So where are they living – while Andrea is racketing up and down this coast?'

'You tell me.'

'Safe at home somewhere. Being a good son (why not?) he makes sure they have every comfort for their old age, and he carries with him some little token of their love. Like a medallion, or a crucifix, or a charm against the evil eye – like this one.'

Balbo held up an oval slab of shoddy plastic, perhaps two inches long. On one surface was carved an attenuated figure in skirts, hands raised in adjuration; on the reverse, a creature with the body of a rhinoceros and a head that was encased in scales and bristly with spikes and fangs.

'Where did you get that?'

'At the little shop by the entrance. When we came in, while you were having a pee. It's a copy of a stone found in the subterranean chapel when it was excavated. The carving on the stone had been dated to the late seventeenth century, the advert on the counter said, and the stone's presence in the chapel was unexplained. Now I'm explaining it. That stone was – or could have been – a charm once the possession of Andrea Commingi, who was constantly in and out of that chapel during the last years of the seventeenth century. It was a present from the old folks at home, or at any rate it came from a region with which he was in some way connected.'

'Begging a lot of questions?'

'Yes, but this could be so, and if we're to continue in business we've got to believe it is so, because it's all we've got to go on. You know what those little carvings are?'

'No. Do you?'

'Oh yes. At one time I spent several holidays in the part of the world from which they came – and to which we are now going.'

'All on account of a plastic souvenir?'

'A copy,' emended Balbo, 'of a stone carved in the seventeenth century. That brute on one side is the Tarasque.'

'The what?'

'A monster that lived in the Rhône and came out from time to time to terrorize Tarascon. It also captured respectable washer-women and made them act as wet nurses to its puppy, the Drac. Many noble knights of Provence were sent against it. All were humiliated and most devoured whole.'

'Are you sure you've got the right monster?'

'Absolutely. I've seen pictures and models of it in the museum of folklore at Arles. *That* is the Tarasque, and on the other side is Saint Martha, who came to Provence from Bethany with Lazarus and the three Maries, and subdued the Tarasque with Holy Water and commanded it to stay at the bottom of the Rhône till the end of time. But the thing is, Sydney, whoever possessed the original stone – and why not Andrea? – must have had connections with that part of Provence ... Tarascon, Beaucaire, Arles, Avignon or Nîmes perhaps.'

'First,' said Syd Jones: 'that stone might just as well have belonged to one of Andrea's crew.'

'We've agreed to make an act of faith that it was Andrea's.'

'*You've* agreed. Let's say I join you. *Which* part of Provence is that stone aiming at? You've just named Tarascon – and a great ring of towns all round it.'

They passed out of the enclosed site and turned right towards the hotel at which they were to spend the night. The sun flashed for the last time through the Temple of Poseidon. The bell rang, slowly and without insistence; no longer a warning that the day was dying but a lament for its death.

'The funny thing is,' said Balbo, 'that girl you saw with roses and alyssum.'

'What's funny about her?'

'Peculiar. The coincidence. Provence is famous for alyssum, particularly Arles. *Dans Arles, où sont les Alyscamps,*' Balbo quoted. 'And the Alyscamps are also famous for their roses: *Quand l'ombre est rouge, sous les roses.* Alyssum and roses in that girl's basket; an appropriate mixture, in view of our own destination.'

'So you think we ought to take the hint and go to Arles?'

'Certainly. But first I think we should go to Tarascon. After all,' said Balbo holding up the plastic oval and peering closely at it in the dusk, 'it was the jolly old Tarasque that gave us the clue.'

'Two days' drive from here.'

'I look forward to them, Sydney. Let's go and drink to the Tarasque—'

'—And its puppy the Drac.'

On the whole, quite a satisfactory outcome, thought Syd Jones, as he bought Balbo a Campari and soda – nothing stronger, Balbo had said – in the bar of their hotel. The trail was getting cold. From a personal point of view he was sorry, as he was enjoying Balbo's search, indeed was rather fascinated by it; but there could be no doubt that its termination would make the performance of duty very much easier. If they drew a blank in Provence, there would be no alternative but for him to take Balbo back to England and deliver him in Jermyn Street. The whole matter, thought Syd, would have been decided for him: he need have no conscience at all about deflecting Balbo from a mission which would by then be dead, and none about handing him over, because Balbo, when all was said, would be needing occupation and livelihood, and with both of these the Department would assuredly provide him. True, the task which awaited Balbo might not be a very wholesome one, but at least it would provide him with something to exercise his mind, and that, once his search had to be abandoned, Balbo would surely need – if he were not to fall back into the state of mental atrophy and moral torpor in which Sydney had found him.

That the search would have to be abandoned, Syd was almost certain. The reasoning which was now taking them to Tarascon was tenuous (to say the least of it) and the evidence on which that reasoning was based was almost worthless. *If* Andrea had used that chapel to store his merchandise, and *if* he (and not someone else) had dropped that stone there, and *if* that stone was a gift from close relations or a reminder of a place of importance to Andrea (as opposed to a trifling curio which he had casually picked up), *if* all these most unlikely conditions were true, then there might just be some clue in Tarascon or that region to take them on another step. But what sort of clue, for Christ's sake? And precisely how and where should they look for it?

No. The thing was as good as over. The wonder was they had come as far as they had. Luck had certainly been on their side . . . And so what, thought Syd, if the luck holds, if we *do* find something in or near Tarascon, if the trail should grow warm once more . . .? Could he bear to leave it? Could he bear to drag Balbo away from it? Would Balbo consent to be dragged away from it? What would Jermyn Street do if they both stayed with it? How long, in the end, would Jermyn Street hold its hand? Well . . . these were questions for which he did not expect to have to find an answer; he would trouble himself no more with them at present; he would simply look forward to a pleasant two days' drive, up the Italian coast and into the heart of Provence, with his good friend, Balbo Blakeney.

I suppose, thought Balbo for his part, that it's all turning out for the best. I never really believed in this search; I'm only keeping it up to please and amuse Sydney (I like pleasing Sydney – I hope he's noticed how I'm knocking off the hard stuff); and some time it'll have to end, probably in Tarascon, because although the thesis which I put up to Sydney could be true, I'd lay 10,000 to 1 against.

Well, so be it, Balbo thought. We shall have a lovely drive together to Tarascon, and when we draw a blank there I can tell myself I've done everything in my power to give Sydney pleasure and to keep faith with the Kyrios Pandelios. This being so, it will then be time to go back to England, where Sydney says I'm needed to help them cope with some extraordinary plague of rats. Sydney will have done his duty in getting me home, which will be good for Sydney. As for myself, I may or may not enjoy what work they have for me to do, but I shall certainly benefit, mentally and financially, from the employment, and if, as Sydney says, this has something to do with saving the fabric of Canterbury Cathedral, then I shall be proud to be of service in this way. If, on the other hand, this talk of Canterbury and the rest is official cover for something else, something really disgusting which *they* have thought up . . . well, as to that, there is no more to be thought or said until I know precisely what it is. After all, the operations which they think up, while more often than not disgusting, are apt to be necessary as well. But suppose, just suppose, they are up to something which I would regard as criminal . . .? Well, you just wait, Balbo Blakeney, you just wait and see.

'No, thank you,' he said aloud. 'Nothing more now, Sydney. A bath, I think, before dinner.'

'They're moving north to Provence,' said Q to Theta. 'Tarascon and Arles. Jones thinks that Blakeney's inquiries are going to fizzle out. The scent's going dead, he says.'

'Provence,' said plump Theta. 'Already half way home from where they first met. I told you we could put our trust in Jones.'

'Can we put our trust in Blakeney?'

'In his competence, you mean, or in his cooperation?'

'Both.'

'His competence depends on some . . . charisma . . . rather than on intellect. From what Jones says, the charisma is still there.'

'And his readiness to cooperate?'

'My dear fellow, how should I know? Jones thinks that he will only cooperate after he has finished with these inquiries of his. Well, it seems they have almost finished with him. Therefore no further obstacles.'

'The influence he is supposed to have with rats must mean that he has some affinity with or affection for rats. Which in turn means that he might not be too pleased by the plans that we have in store for you.'

'He will obviously have no objection to clearing them out of Canterbury Cathedral.'

'But it's not as simple as that, is it?'

'There is, as you indicate, another dimension to it all. The question is, will Blakeney find it out?'

'He'll have to be told certain things which would make it *possible* for him to find it out.'

'By that time he should be so far committed that he won't be able to back down . . . or make public complaint.'

'He's a drunk, remember. Drunks don't always see these things quite straight.'

'Perhaps it's better he shouldn't. Perhaps we want him confused . . . charismatic and confused . . . in all things accepting the advice and instructions of Jones, S., who has nursed and protected him all across Europe.'

'You mean,' said Q, 'that he'll do for Jones what he might not do for us?'

'Jones seems to be soothing him along quite well so far. It seems that Blakeney is becoming increasingly attached.'

'Perhaps Jones is too. In which case . . .?'

'. . . In which case, Jones knows his duty to us, and also his duty to his friend, which will be to prevent Blakeney from annoying us and bringing our odium upon him when everything might be so comfortably and profitably arranged.'

# VII

# The Relict

'Nothing more we can do now, Ive. Nothing except wait for the monthly check-up on the thirtieth.'

Len and Ivor were walking in the Fellows' Garden of Lancaster College.

'You're sure no one will get wind of that Swiss bank account of yours?' Ivor said.

'As sure as a man can be. I employed no intermediary when I set it up. And the money from our friend in Bavaria was paid direct by banker's credit from his bank in Munich.'

'Which means that the bankers know and our friend in Bavaria knows.'

'Hell, man, somebody had to know. Our friend in Bavaria is going to keep very quiet, because he has been receiving stolen goods and will not wish to draw attention to himself. And the bankers will keep quiet because that's bankers' etiquette.'

'Not, alas, as strictly observed as formerly. Bankers are beginning to get twinges of social conscience. Even the Swiss.'

'They won't get many twinges about a mere thirty-five thousand pounds.'

'I expect you're right,' said Ivor, 'but this sort of thing is enough to make anyone nervous.'

'You can say that again. While I was waiting in that hotel in London to hear the credit had been lodged I could have screamed the place down.'

'The other volume ... The Wandrille Georgics ... it's safely hidden in your lodgings?'

'Yes. Snug as a snake in winter. Now then, Ive. When can the good life begin?'

'*That* is a problem.' Despite himself, Ivor was rather enjoying the mechanics of the plot. While miserable about

263

what was being planned for Jacquiz, he was nevertheless anxious to ensure Len got full benefit of his enterprise and was finally stowed away with his loot in safety and comfort. 'You see,' Ivor went on, 'if everything goes to plan, the Provost is going to arrange – or so we think – for you to be quietly shoved off into inferior academic employment, probably at a polytechnic. Now, even Lord Constable can't arrange this with a mere snap of the fingers; it will take time; and during that time you'll have to hang about in Cambridge.'

'I can't just vanish during next vacation – around Christmas, say, when nobody's looking?'

'No,' said Ivor. 'If you disappear before you've taken up the new job which Constable is going to procure for you, everyone will get suspicious.'

'They'll already be suspicious.'

'But content, on Constable's instructions, to let the thing lie. If you suddenly disappear, however, you will make it quite blatantly obvious to all and sundry that you, and not Jacquiz, are the guilty party.'

'Right. So I stay around until a new job's found for me. What then?'

'You take it up,' said Ivor with relish, 'you then begin to show signs of mounting discontent, and after a year or so you drift away, apparently searching for more congenial employment, but in fact just – well – losing yourself. No one, forgive me, is going to care what happens to you once you are gone, and your exit will have been so gradual as to excite no notice. What you *must* avoid is a sudden and dramatic vanishing trick within a few weeks of the theft's being discovered.'

'That I see, Ive. But I don't like the idea of staying a whole year at whatever dump Constable gets me consigned to. Especially as it may be months and months before I'm even sent there.'

'I fear, Len, that patience is one of the necessary pre-conditions of the good life which you envisage.'

Len giggled. 'I love it when you say things like that,' he

264

said. 'Your voice all plummy with worldly wisdom.'

'You must also see that I'm right?'

'Yeah. Yeah, I see it, Ive. Well, what the shit? Suppose I wait around for even as much as two years before I scarper, it's a small price to pay for the good days that are coming. I shall let *you* know where I've gone, Ive. You'll come and see me sometimes?'

'I rather think I might. I don't know what it is about you, Len. By all my rules I ought to loathe you, but somehow . . . I'm becoming rather attached. I have a delicious sense of complicity. Now, I think we had better sit down on that seat under the Judas tree and go through the drill for the day of the check-up just one more time.'

'Right,' said Len, as they sat down. 'I pass you the key of the cash box, and you open it and take out the key of the safe. You open the safe and with my assistance, since you're new to the job, you produce several items, which are duly checked off on his list by the Third Bursar, and then you produce the two oilskin bags. "The St Gilles Breviary," you say, looking at the labels, "and The Wandrille Georgics." "Right," says the Third Bursar, and ticks them off on his list – hardly looking at the bags, he's done it so often. "But I think," you then say, "I think, as it's the first inspection to take place during my tenure, that we'll open up those oilskin bags and check the contents . . ." '

'It turns out,' said Jacquiz, depositing the Abbé Valcabriers' scrapbook on the back seat of the car, 'that the priest's account of Louis' marriage to Constance and of their journey as far as Pau is pretty vague. I should have expected this. After all, he wasn't there, and none of it, in itself, was of very much interest to him. What he does tell us squares absolutely with what we know already. Obviously he was merely repeating what Constance told him – they became quite thick later on, as we shall see. But they never became thick enough for Constance to tell him about Van Hoek the painter, or the Rubies, or the precise circumstances under which she married Louis.'

Jacquiz started the engine and eased the Rolls out of the stable yard, through the arch, and on to the road.

'As far as the priest was concerned, Louis and Constance met and married while Louis was in Montreuil. Constance had cast off her family and embraced Louis' nominal Catholicism, and then they had come South. Constance admitted to bringing some unspecified "dowry" with her, and this, along with profits which Louis had supposedly made as a Commissary, was enough to explain Louis' decision to abandon the King's service and return home. The priest learnt of Louis' illness at Aigues Mortes and of his death at Pau, after which, he tells us, Constance had come more or less straight on to Saint Bertrand to seek out the Comminges, doubtless requiring their protection.'

Jacquiz drove the Rolls over a bridge, turned sharp right and crossed another bridge, and then accelerated gently down a long avenue, heading out of St Girons for St Gaudens.

'I don't think we shall ever know,' Jacquiz said, 'quite when Louis told Constance of their ultimate destination and of his family there; probably when he told her of his Albigensian ancestry, possibly as he lay dying – but at some stage he must have told her, and to Saint Bertrand-de-Comminges she duly came after he was dead. And what she found was this: Louis' father and Louis' aunt were still alive. (These were the two children of the woman who had rehabilitated the Comminges in Saint Bertrand after the trouble with the Inquisitors.) Louis' mother was dead, but his father, now getting on for sixty years old, had recently married again, taking a young peasant girl from the plain below the town ... who, when Constance arrived, was already six months pregnant of her first child. Brothers or sisters Louis had had none (his mother had been sickly and given to dropping her children stillborn) so the household, situated in one of the Comminges' properties in Saint Bertrand, consisted of Louis' father, the new and pregnant wife,

Louis' widowed and childless aunt – and now Constance, who, I need hardly tell you, was regarded with manifest suspicion by all of them, particularly by the new wife, Constance's step-mother-in-law though in fact even younger than Constance.'

'Their house – was it the same one as Valcabriers lives in, the one we saw yesterday?'

'No. It was much nearer the Cathedral, just across the square from it, in fact, and facing its West façade. Indeed, this propinquity contributed very materially to the ... subsequent undoing ... of poor Constance.' Jacquiz shivered slightly and slowed the car so much that it almost seemed he would stop. But at the last moment he accelerated again and drove on, though with evident reluctance. 'Anyway,' he continued, 'there was Constance living with, if barely accepted by, her new family, and at this juncture the priest, our narrator, first comes on the scene in person and makes her acquaintance. It seems that one day he was accosted, in the Cathedral, by a "wild-eyed and trembling woman" who said that she was being haunted and could only escape the ghost that haunted her by coming into the Cathedral. This was Constance speaking. She went on to say that for some time she had had a feeling, an increasingly strong one, that before very long the spirit would overcome whatever power kept it out of the Cathedral and would be able to torment her there too. Having listened while all this was being gabbled at him, the priest very sensibly led Constance away to a vestry, sat her down, gave her a glass of wine, and asked her to tell him her story slowly and from the beginning. Which she now did. Of her marriage and journey Southwards she gave the sketchy version of which I've already told you, but became a great deal more detailed and precise when she reached the events which had followed her arrival in Saint Bertrand.

'When she had first presented herself to the Comminges, she found that they already knew of her existence. At some point during the journey from Montreuil, it now appeared, Louis had written them a letter and paid a courier to carry it to Saint Bertrand. The letter had told them that he had taken a wife in the North and had thereby bettered himself, since his wife was in possession of a private fortune. They should expect to see him and her in a matter of months or even weeks, the letter had continued, but before he finally returned he had an important affair to settle in the matter of his wife's property.'

'But he did not tell them what this property was?'

'No. After all, the loot was still very "hot" indeed. The letter might well go astray, Louis would have thought, and the last thing he wanted was for anyone to know that it was he who had the Rubies. For almost certainly he meant to dispose of them in Pau, as we surmised earlier, and total discretion was needed.'

'Then why did he write to his people at all?'

'Pretty natural, I'd say. He intended to come home, the bad hat made good, with a fortune in money, and like many before him he could not resist the temptation to do a little boasting first.'

'And so Constance was greeted with two simple questions,' said Marigold: 'where was Louis? and where was her fortune?'

'Right. To the first there was a very simple answer. To the second she returned some evasion about being heiress presumptive to an estate of her father's near Montreuil.'

'And of course nobody believed her.'

'No. It seems that the priest, to whom she was now telling her tale in the vestry, pressed her to tell *him* what her fortune actually consisted in, and she so far broke down as to hint that it was something easily portable. But neither to him nor to the Comminges did she breathe a word about the Rubies – which are therefore never mentioned, *as such*, in the whole of the priest's narrative. He refers to Constance's fortune as her "dowry" or her "treasure", and evidently had no inkling of its nature or its fabulous value. His tone is that of a man who thinks she probably has a box tucked away somewhere with fifty or a hundred gold pieces in it, a very tidy sum in those days, but not up to a ruby necklace.

'But back to the Comminges. When they heard that Louis had died in Pau, they reasoned very much as you and I did, that he must have been in Pau to sell something (which would have been consistent with the statement of intent in his letter) and something that was most unlikely to have been land, whether near Montreuil or elsewhere. So they badgered Constance. Although the fortunes of the Comminges, which had nose-dived after the trial in 1597, had been somewhat restored under the tutelage of Louis' grandmother (the lady who slept with the bishop *et al.*) there was certainly room for more. A stiff injection of money always comes in handy – and so *where*, they wanted to know, and *what* was the fortune about which Louis had written to them in his last letter? When she repeated that she was heiress to an estate in Picardy, her father-in-law beat her up – helped by his sister and his wife.

'At this point, as Constance told the priest, she decided to leave. Travelling alone might be very awkward for a woman, and she didn't really know where to go, but anything was better than sitting in Saint Bertrand being bullied by the Comminges, and she supposed that "her dowry" would provide her with means of support.'

'Where do you suppose she had the necklace hidden?'

'A very good question.' Jacquiz slowed the car as they came into the suburbs of St Gaudens. 'Clearly, nothing was safe in the Comminges household, not even hidden on her own person, as they stripped her naked whenever they beat her up. I'm afraid we shall never know, as she didn't even tell the priest. She simply told him that after some days in Saint Bertrand she was still in possession of her "treasure" despite the strippings and whippings, at the onset of which he had determined to take both her "treasure" and herself off somewhere else, anywhere else, forthwith.'

'But she didn't, because here she was in the vestry.'

'She couldn't.'

Jacquiz drove past some handsome gardens (cascades and Aleppo pine) and turned left for Luchon.

'They locked her up?'

'No. She couldn't move more than a furlong from the Comminges' house.'

'They followed her and brought her back?'

'No. She literally could not move her limbs when she got to a distance of two hundred yards or so – "two hundred and fifty paces", the priest quotes her as saying – from the Comminges' front door. She was, she thought, bewitched. The priest, who knew the history of the Comminges family, thought so too. But this was by no means the worst of it. She was, she said, haunted by the spirit of her husband. He did not appear to her but he was constantly whispering in her ear—'

'—Telling her to hand over the goodies to his relations, I suppose—'

'—And threatening to come bodily from Pau if she did not. This was the real horror of it. The voice said that it was only the spirit of Louis but it insisted that, if Constance did not do as she was told, the actual corpse would rise and come to her from Pau. Only when she was in the Cathedral, Constance informed the priest, was she safe from the voice, and she was no longer sure, as she had already told him in her first outburst, how long even that immunity would last. Alternatively, she said, she was afraid lest she might be the victim of a second spell which would prevent her from walking as far as the Cathedral (only a hundred paces odd from the Comminges' house) and enjoying the protection and solace which it yet offered her. But this, as you'll soon see, lovely Marigold, was certainly not going to happen. It was no part of the Comminges' plan to keep Constance out of the Cathedral – quite the reverse, for reasons which will later become very plain.'

Marigold looked through the windscreen at the ranks of the Pyrenees, huge white knights on dappled chargers, now advancing towards her at a steady walk across the plain, the foothills going before them like so many esquires holding their masters' bridles. Would the trumpet ever blow for the charge, she wondered idly, would the esquires release the harness and back off, one fine autumn morning, and the white knights come thundering and trampling over the vasty fields of France?

'What on earth did that poor priest do?' she said.

'First, he asked her what made her think that the spirit would soon be able to follow her into the Cathedral. To this she answered that every time she entered the Cathedral she felt that the spirit was clinging yet closer to her, and that its capacities of adherence were steadily increasing – to the extent that when she had come in that very day she had sensed that the spirit had been separated from her by the powers of sanctity at the door only with enormous effort, and that soon those powers would be unable to control the spirit at all. This impression was borne out by the words with which the spirit habitually took leave of her as she passed on to holy ground. "I have friends that work within," the spirit would say; "soon I too shall enter." Or, "Only a little while now, Constance Comminges, only a little while and your faithful husband will follow you even here." '

'Certainly,' said Marigold, 'there is something not at all wholesome about the church. I had a *very* odd feeling when I went in.'

'Constance told the priest that the spirit seemed to be telling her that certain diabolical forces were conspiring, as it were, with the weaker agents of holiness in the Cathedral to subvert Godhead and prepare the ground for the penetration of evil.'

'All I know is that yesterday I was mocked ... scorned and mocked ... by something malignant and obstructive. Faces loomed and leered and mouthed at me, and what they were saying was that I should never find what I came for, but that if by some miraculous chance I *did* ... well, I'd better watch out.'

'Watch out for what?'

'The consequences of finding out what I wasn't meant to know.'

Jacquiz slowed the car.

'We'd better turn back,' he said. 'Forget Saint Bertrand, forget the whole thing.'

'We must return the Abbé's book.'

'All right. And then go straight back – to England.'

'What a waste of a Sabbatical year. No,' said Marigold. 'I've already told you: whatever I may have said at the beginning, now I mean to see the thing through. It's totally riveting.'

'I am starting to think that it's also extremely perilous.'

'So is anything exciting. So now go on. Constance told the priest that the spirit of Louis was in continual attendance on her and was soon, as she thought, going to gain access to the Cathedral. What next?'

Jacquiz drove doubtfully on. The road took a long curve towards the East. To the left of them spread a flat, yellow plain, to their right the white knights of the Pyrenees still paraded slowly towards them, and straight ahead, now, was a tiny, distant ridge, like a cardboard cut-out, on which stood a two-dimensional town of tissue and at its centre a Cathedral of silver foil. St Bertrand-de-Comminges.

'What next?' said Marigold.

'The priest asked her about the spirit's threat that the actual corpse of Louis would rise from its grave at Pau and come to Comminges. How often was the threat made? What form did it take? She replied that the threat was by now being made daily and that it was totally clear and straightforward, begging no questions whatever. How, one might well wish to know, was Louis' body to get out of its coffin and dig its way up past the stone? This interesting question had been anticipated by Louis' spirit, which had early informed Constance that it could claim the service and loyalty of certain living associates, who would, at his spirit's command, disinter his body and help it on its way to Saint Bertrand. Not that it would need much help once it was clear of the grave: for as soon as the corpse had been disinterred, the spirit would rejoin and reanimate it. You thus get the extremely powerful and disagreeable concept, to be found also, I believe, in Voodoo doctrine, of a corpse that is propelled and controlled by its own returned soul.'

'Good grief,' said Marigold. 'How soon was this going to happen?'

The town on the ridge ahead, from being a mere silhouette of coloured paper, had now acquired a third dimension and with it rather more reality. But it was still only a toy town on its little citadel, no more to be taken seriously than a child's castle with lead soldiers on its ramparts.

'It was going to happen soon,' said Jacquiz, 'but the spirit refused to be precise. Constance told the priest she thought the spirit was doing this to increase the terror: after all, she pointed out, it's bad enough expecting the arrival of a living corpse at a definite and stated hour, but only to know that it may, or may not, turn up at any time at all over the next fortnight is more than flesh and blood can bear. The priest took a different view: he said that the paramount reason for the spirit's imprecision was that, even given the Comminges family's talent for necromancy, this kind of resurrection was very difficult to arrange and might prove impossible. So the spirit was in no position to make an exact engagement on behalf of the cadaver.'

'Which view do you take?' asked Marigold.

'Neither. I try to take the rational, the scientific view. Obviously the whole thing was somehow being faked by Louis' father, in order to frighten her into giving up the wealth to which Louis had referred in his letter. For if the spirit of dead Louis *had* been capable of reaching Constance, it would also have been able to communicate with his father, in which case it could have gone straight to him and told him exactly what to look for and also (spirits being traditionally omniscient in such matters) where: no need for all this haunting and threatening of Constance. But as it was, I tell myself, of course there was no ghost nor spirit, only a clever and greedy old man playing conjuring tricks; a lot of ventriloquism, I expect, with hypnotic suggestion thrown in, which would account for how they stopped her walking more than two hundred and fifty paces. Of course the old man would have had to play it very carefully: he did not know what he was looking for, whereas the spirit he was purporting to be *did* know, which meant that he would have to choose his words very carefully to disguise his ignorance. But I dare say he was shrewd enough to manage that; and once he got a firm grip on Constance, which he clearly had by the time she approached the priest, she wouldn't have been asking very many logical questions. So there we are: reason says the whole thing was a try-on and that the threat of Louis' bodily resurrection was the big-time bluff by which poppa Comminges helped to compel Constance, who was badly scared already, finally to chuck her cards in.'

'Did the priest ever show any signs of taking a rational line?'

'Most definitely not. The nearest he came to that was to inform Constance, as I told you just now, that resurrection was heap big magic and hard to encompass. In principle he was with her, ghosts, rising corpses and all, every inch of the way. If priests took a rational line, sweetheart, they'd soon be out of a job.'

'But you, Jacquiz . . . you are *sure* of your rational line?'

'I'm just a dreary don, as you've so often reminded me. We tend to be rational.'

'You seemed to be . . . rather nervous . . . just now. You said this whole business was beginning to seem perilous.'

'I'm not denying that it's becoming very peculiar. By "perilous" I only meant that I thought . . . it might badly upset you. Just because the story is so horrid.'

'I'm not upset by horrid stories, Jacquiz. What *might* have upset me badly, if anything was going to, was what . . . what I saw and felt . . . when I went into the Cathedral yesterday. Would you like to give me your rational line about *that?*'

Silence. The car slunk on between tall hedges.

'I suppose you're going to say I was hysterical,' Marigold said.

'Imaginative.'

But two large drops of sweat were standing on Jacquiz' forehead, just under the line of his hair.

'You're only trying to reassure me,' Marigold said. 'You do think there's something . . . abnormal . . . here.'

'Unusual ... perverted, yes.'

'No. Abnormal ... unnatural ... *super*natural, Jacquiz.'

'There are elements ... which are very difficult to account for. So far as we have come, one can make a rational explanation. But for what is about to happen ... for all that I'm going to tell you now ... it is not at all easy to account in everyday terms.'

'Go on.'

'Well, the next thing Constance told the priest was that the spirit said that when his corpse *did* arrive from Pau, then either Constance would have to hand over her "treasure", or, if she refused ...'

'Go on.'

' ... She would be compelled by the corpse to submit to its ... marital attentions.'

'Jesus.'

'In fact, the spirit said, once the cadaver had made the effort necessary to rise and come to Saint Bertrand, even if Constance handed over her "treasure" to the family straight away, the cadaver might feel that after its prodigious journey it deserved to embrace its lawful spouse in love. And once it had done that, of course, and relived earthly delights, it might not be at all willing to return to the place whence it came.'

'Jesus,' said Marigold again.

'All of *that*,' said Jacquiz, 'rather supports my rational explanation. Obviously, I could say, old Comminges was putting on heavy pressure in order to scare Constance into handing over the loot as soon as possible.'

'That certainly fits.'

'But what makes me uneasy is the memory of that picture by Van Hoek which we saw in the castle at Montreuil. The circumstances in which Constance now found herself are beginning to resemble, quite closely, those dreadful scenes which Van Hoek painted using Jumièges as background. You remember: the bride and ... and whatever it was she had married ... moving through those cloisters attended by cowled monks. The similarity between the fate of the bride in the painting and the enormity with which Constance was now being threatened is too near for comfort. It is as though Van Hoek, in his death throes, had had some satanic vision of Constance's future. And the quality of that vision somehow seems to ... to guarantee ... the reality of what Constance was now in fear of, until one feels that the threat against her cannot merely have been a random piece of nastiness faked up by a rapacious old mountebank, but that it must have been genuine, must have come from where she thought it came and *must*, actually and faithfully, have promised what she thought it promised.'

'The resemblance could be coincidence. That there is a resemblance does not mean that there has to be a connection. Van Hoek's maniacal picture does not rule out your rational explanation.'

'No; but it shakes one's confidence. And other things,' said Jacquiz, 'come very near to destroying it.'

'What other things?'

Jacquiz slowed the car and parked by the side of the road. The town and the Cathedral were close above them now, occupying all the narrow segment of vision defined by the tall hedges.

'I'll read you the priest's account of what followed,' he said, leaning over and lifting the Abbé's scrapbook from the back seat. 'Of course, it may well be just a prime instance of superstition, panic, misapprehension or sheer gullibility. But somehow, as I think you'll agree, it rings true.'


Len passed Ivor the key of the cash box. Ivor opened it and took out the key of the safe. He opened the safe and with Len's assistance, since he was new to the job, he produced several items, which were duly checked off his list by the Third Bursar. He then produced the two oilskin bags.

'The Saint Gilles Breviary,' he said, looking at the labels, 'and The Wandrille Georgics.'

'Right,' said the Third Bursar, and ticked them off on his

list – hardly bothering to look at the bags, he'd done it so often.

'But I think,' Ivor then said, 'I think, as it's the first inspection to take place during my tenure, that we'll open up those oil-bags and check the contents.'

'Excuse me, sir,' said Len, 'we only do that every six months, on account of it being bad for the books to be taken in or out, old and fragile as they are, and passed round and pawed at and in general exposed to the air.'

And the Third Bursar said,

'Yes, that's right, Ivor, every six months, in March and August. I saw them in August with Jacquiz and that's good enough.'

But Ivor said,

'No, I'm new in this, and I want to look at what I'm responsible for. However delicate those books are, they ought to be taken out of those bags and checked more often, being as how they're worth a stack of bread – sorry, I mean, considering how valuable they are – especially if no one has been through that safe for nearly ten weeks.'

Real busybody bippering on Ivor's part, the Bursar thought, and was duly impressed at such conscientious behaviour; and then Ivor opened up the bags, and took out two floppy leather-bound volumes, superficially similar to the fourteenth-century originals, and opened one of them.

'If this is The Wandrille Georgics,' Ivor said sweatily, 'then I'm a wet fart. I'm sorry: I mean, of course' – handing the volume to the Bursar – 'something seems to have gone wrong.'

'Woow-eee,' the Third Bursar said.

On the morning of the day of the monthly check of the Manuscripts of Lancaster College, Ivor had been remorseful, fascinated and extremely nervous.

First, Ivor was remorseful because of what he was helping to do to the absent Jacquiz. Jacquiz was a pig and a coward, a glider away who had once glided away in the most vilely treacherous manner at a crisis in the College affairs which closely concerned himself and Ivor; but for all that, Ivor thought, he is a scholar and a man of taste, and he does not deserve this.

Secondly, Ivor was fascinated and curious because he loved a plot and he dearly wanted to see whether this one would work. As far as he could make out, the mechanics of the thing were pretty sound (provided he could play his own part plausibly) up to the time when the substitution of the fakes would be discovered. What was in doubt was whether or not Lord Constable would react as Len had predicted, whether he would exculpate Ivor himself, that was to say, then accuse Len but accept Len's plea that Jacquiz must be at least equally suspect, decide to keep the whole business quiet, 'unload Len on a grotty polytechnic' (in Len's words), and demand Jacquiz Helmut's resignation. Constable was, as Ivor knew, in general very much on Ivor's side in this intrigue and had already been of material assistance; but whether Constable would condone the actual method which Ivor had adopted (and in particular whether he would tolerate the very considerable element of profit which, as Constable would surely realize, must have accrued either to Len or himself or to both of them) was another matter. Lord Constable was an old-fashioned socialist from way back, and he did not approve of anyone's making a profit, even though such a person might at the same time be furthering his (Constable's) designs.

So what with, first, remorse and, second, curiosity, Ivor was, thirdly, nervous. There was another reason too for this. On the success or failure of this day's work depended the renewal of his Fellowship. Remorse was one thing and curiosity another, but a man's livelihood (not to say his entire *raison d'être*) was something else again. Food, drink, friends, hearth, servants, occupation and (more or less) honour, all of these, in descending order of importance, were guaranteed by his Fellowship. Without its renewal he would be nothing. It was enough to make any man nervous, and it had made Ivor so twitchy that he had all but made a hash of his lines. Luckily the Bursar, who had been half asleep most of the morning, did not appear to have noticed.

But now he was really sitting up.

'Wooow-eee,' he said again: 'that's torn it. What had we better do?

'We must finish the routine check, gentlemen,' said Len respectfully but authoritatively, 'in order to see if anything else is missing; and then we must go to the Provost.'

And *then* we'll see, thought Ivor: I wonder if, once my Fellowship *has* been safely renewed in January, there is any-thing I could do to help Jacquiz; it would be so very agree-able to have my cake and eat it, particularly at the expense of Lord Constable.

' "Having heard the wench through",' Jacquiz translated to Marigold from the Abbé Valcabriers' scrapbook, ' "I be-thought me what I should now do, both as a priest of God and a servant of man. And first I did make this Mistress Comminges walk two hundred and fifty paces from her own door towards the wall of the town, that I might see with mine eyes whether she was truly hindered in her going or was but making pretence of it, the which I might tell from the manner of her walking and her arrest, and from what at that time should be revealed in her face and eyes.

' "Surely enough, when she had walked two hundred and forty paces, the flame of hope, which had burned strong till then as she walked with a holy priest, flickered and faded in the windows of her soul; and her breath came forth in sharp gusts; her limbs dragged; she did utterly halt; and it was as though, she said, her legs and whole body had come up against an unseen wall of stone. 'I can march no more, good father,' cried she; and when I, being a man of ample arm and girth, did urge her body from behind with all my might, I could not budge her but one inch nor the smallest part thereof. And so it seemeth to me that in this thing the woman spake truth, and wherefore not in else?

' "For certain true it was that she was mightily plagued by a spirit, who vaunted itself to be her husband, at many times, and most wickedly of all when she would fain enter our sacred Cathedral of Mary of Comminges: for I myself heard the voice of the spirit—" '

'—Poppa Comminges' ventriloquism?' Marigold interrupted.

'One would like to think so. There is a reference to his hanging about the place later on. "For I myself heard the voice of the spirit",' Jacquiz continued, ' "how it did rail at her that soon it would come with her into the holy place that should be holy then no more. And I went with her, a score of times, around the screen that doth hedge the chancel, and did hear the muttering and chuckling (but not the words) of divers voices, which issued as from the mouths of the corbel-heads that beautify the screen but must surely have no place in God's church, so sly and odious were their cacklings to mine ear.

' "And so I determined in my heart that this woman spake truth; and first I went to Master Comminges, her father-in-law, and asked him to his teeth what he knew of such hauntings and estoppals, for I had seen that he was often in attendance upon this woman (not by her wish, as she told me, though he came not into the church." '

'But could presumably throw "mutterings" and "chucklings" from outside it,' said Marigold.

'From the South door to the screen? Perhaps. At least to the South side of the screen ... or to the West end of the screen from the West door,' Jacquiz said. 'But the priest implies that the noises came from all round it.' He turned his eyes down to the book ' "And he returned word",' Jacquiz read on, ' "that he knew nothing of such foolishness; that his daughter-in-law was free to walk whither she would; and that if she feared ghosts, let her seek sanctuary in holy church, as for many hours each day she did. Then I asked him why he came not into holy church himself, and gave him my cross to kiss, and he shrank from me and sucked in his lips between his jaws, and said that he would come and go whither and whence and when and how he listed, and that our Cathedral of Saint Mary was little to his liking, for that it was sumptuous with ornament and vanity and was an affront to the True God and King." '

'By which he, if he was a Comminges off the old block, presumably meant the Devil?'

' "All of which matters standing thus",' Jacquiz translated, ' "I did resolve in my soul on these acts: I must cleanse the Cathedral, cleanse the woman, and chase the spirit back to Hell which brewed it; and I must command the body to stay fast in its grave at Pau. And yet my heart misgave me lest my lord the Bishop should hear of this and be wrath; for he was a prelate of high blood and haughty mien, who scorned to believe that the Devil and his works could dare walk forth to defy him in the domains of his spiritual governance. Therefore, I counselled with myself to say nothing of this to my lord the Bishop, lest he should forbid me quite, but to act as my Lord Jesus would exige of me and do his work by stealth.

' "Therefore did I keep fasts and watches by night within the church; and where and whenever the evil voices muttered or trilled, I did sprinkle fair holy water and command the demons to be gone *in nomine Patris et Filii et Spiritus Sancti*, and of our sacred Mary of Comminges. As the water made wet the wood of the screen, there was a loathely noise of hissing and slithering, as of vipers; and when I had done this on many nights, there was no more muttering or screeching from Saint Mary's chancel screen." '

'Round One to Mother Church,' said Marigold.

'On points,' said Jacquiz. ' "Next did I confront the spirit which assailed the woman",' he read, ' "bidding it begone to its Master and cleansing the woman herself with a powder made of a precious relic of Saint Bertrand his body (to wit the tip of his great toe) which she swallowed in a gruel of grass grown in our cloister. And the woman said that the spirit's voice and railing had ceased, and I heard them no more with mine own ears, and I thanked Our Blessed Lord that he had given me the strength so to prevail.

' "Then did I tell my lord the Bishop (falsely, for which God forgive me, but I was about God's business) that I must hie me to the town of Pau where mine Aunt that had reared me from an orphan babe lay dying. And my lord gave me leave, for though he was a proud man in spiritual dominion he yet was of tender kind in the things of this world, and he made me loan of his own ass. To Pau then I came, and to the grave of this Louis Comminges that had been the woman's husband, and there I did sanctify the grave, that no evil being of body or spirit might defile or open it, and I besought the spirit and the body of this Louis, that the body should lie quiet till the Last Day and the spirit should stay in Hell and pray for God's mercy at the time of Judgment.

'"And I returned to Saint Bertrand, and told the woman all I had done, and she said that no sounds or voices had besieged her and she was still at peace. And I told all that I had done to Master Comminges, the father of Louis; and he professed gladness that his daughter was no longer troubled, and urged her to go into the Cathedral yet more than even before, that her peace might be abiding: for the place, he said, was passing grateful to her, albeit that vanities of which he spake before did rankle much with him. As for my prayers and exorcisms at the tomb of his son, here too he declared himself well pleased; and he said it was his wish that the True God and King might in all things conquer." '

'By which, being him, he meant the Devil,' said Marigold for the second time. 'But Mother Church has simply walked right over Lucifer in every round so far.'

'Mother Church has not walked right over anybody,' said Jacquiz. 'As I said just now, so far she has won – or seemed to win – on points. There are several more rounds still to run.'

'Lucifer makes a come-back?'

'Listen and learn,' Jacquiz said grimly, and bent his head again to the Abbé Valcabriers' scrapbook.


'So what it amounts to is this,' Lord Constable said: 'some time between the previous count, which was in August, and the count this morning, both The Wandrille Georgics and

The Saint Gilles Breviary have been taken from their respective coverings and two worthless paper volumes placed there instead.'

'That's about it, Provost,' Ivor said.

'No question of it,' the Third Bursar said.

'Spot on,' said Len.

Provost Constable went to the window of his study and gazed down on the Great Lawn of Lancaster.

'In August,' he said with his back to them, 'the count was conducted by you, Third Bursar' – he jabbed a finger back at this functionary without turning to aim – 'and by you, Under-Collator' – a similar blind but accurate jab of the finger – 'and by the Collator of the Manuscripts of Lancaster College, that is to say Doctor Jacquiz Helmut?'

'That's about it, Provost,' Ivor said.

'No question of it,' the Third Bursar said.

'Spot on,' said Len.

'And on that occasion the books were taken from their coverings and absolutely recognized as the genuine volumes?'

'That's about—' Ivor began, but the Provost turned from the window and held up a hand.

'Now then,' Lord Constable said: 'who had access?'

'I did,' said Len, 'all the time. Ive here didn't, because I kept all the keys. But Jake did, because he had his own set – what he's taken away with him.'

'Very succinctly summed,' the Provost said. 'Well, Third Bursar, you have played your part, I think. It is now a matter for myself and the incumbents of the Chamber of Manuscripts ... present and past. A very good morning, Third Bursar.'

'A very good morning, Provost,' said the Third Bursar, and reluctantly retired.

'Pray be seated, gentlemen,' said the Provost to Ivor and Len, gesturing at two low stools which were placed in front of his desk. With some difficulty Ivor and Len sat down on the stools, while Lord Constable seated himself behind the desk.

'I am disappointed in you, Ivor,' Lord Constable said. 'Officers are meant to do the work assigned to them themselves, not to bribe semi-menial underlings to do it for them.'

'Who are you calling a semi-menial underling?' said Len.

'Thank you, Under-Collator. I suspected but was not sure that you and Mr Winstanley were in collusion. By rising so swiftly to so crude a bait, you have confirmed my suspicions. So now we know exactly where we stand.'

'Maybe you know, Prov,' said Len, 'but I'll be buggered if I do. What are you going to do about it all? And anyhow, how did you suspect that Ive and me was in collusion?'

'From the very obvious glances and grimaces which you have been exchanging ever since you came into this room. A truly amateur performance.'

'All right, all right,' said Len, miffed. 'But what are you going to do?'

'Make the best of a bad job, Under-Collator. As Mr Winstanley will doubtless have told you, I consider that the present state of Doctor Helmut's private life and private fortune renders him . . . of dubious value . . . as a Fellow and officer of the College. I should like him . . . gracefully . . . to retire, and I asked Mr Winstanley to find and show me good reason why he should be required so to do.'

'Well, now you've got it. Things were so badly organized in the Chamber, you can say, that two of the star items got snatched.'

'Very good, Under-Collator. But who snatched them? If Doctor Helmut retires under the present circumstances, he will be suspected, not merely of incompetence, but possibly of crime. I cannot allow any such suspicion to attach to him. That would not be just. I may – I do – wish him away from this College. But I shall not allow him to be savagely and unfairly defamed. Doctor Helmut will be . . . pressed to resign . . . on grounds of inefficiency; but guilt for the felony must be definitely fixed elsewhere, for all to see.'

'You mean on us, Prov,' said Len good-naturedly, 'on me and Ive?'

'No, Under-Collator. Not on you . . . and Ive. That would be to stain the honour of the college. That such a theft of College treasure should have been perpetrated by established members and beneficiaries of the College would be very shameful. The unspeakable ingratitude of it . . . No. The blame must be fixed elsewhere.'

'But to fix it on the innocent would be unjust by your tenets,' Ivor Winstanley said.

'Precisely, Ivor. Perhaps you now understand what a thoroughly nasty muddle you have made? Whom can I find who can justly be compelled to bear the burden of this guilt *without* at the same time impugning the honour of the College? Nobody, I think. The next best thing is to find someone who will *willingly* take the blame for this crime, though it be not his by right, either because he wishes to be of service or because he is offered a suitable reward. It must, remember, be someone who has nothing to do with the College, and yet somebody to whom the guilt for the theft can plausibly be imputed.'

'Very tricky job to find such a person, Provost.'

'Yes, indeed, Ivor. And to whom, in all the circumstances can I more fairly depute the job of finding him . . . than to you? You have bungled very badly, Ivor, but you need not give up all hope of re-election in January. Provided you find a suitable person or persons who will accept blame and punishment for this robbery, thus enabling the College to preserve its dignity and honour, if not its property, then you shall be duly re-elected. Meanwhile I shall inform the College Council in confidence of the larceny that has occurred, and say that for the moment the inquiries will be only of a private nature. And one thing more.'

'Provost?'

'If, as I suspect, one or both of the two missing books have been disposed of for money, then I would suggest that this money might fitly be used to persuade and reward our scapegoat.'

Len and Ivor exchanged dismal glances.

'Never you worry, Ive,' said Len. 'We'll find a way.'

'I hope so, indeed I do,' said Provost Constable pleasantly: 'I shall be very interested to know what it turns out to be.'


' "For a sennight after I had ridden back on my lord's ass from Pau",' Jacquiz translated to Marigold as they sat below St Bertrand in the Rolls, ' "the woman Constance was tranquil and the chapels of the Cathedral were still. Then, one morning, the woman was not at her accustomed place in the Cathedral, at prayer in the Virgin's Chapel as was her wont. At first I thought nothing of this, thinking she had business else to attend to; but seeing Master Comminges, as he loitered in the square by the West door, I did question him of his daughter-in-law, to which he returned answer that she had come early to the Cathedral, with the first light of the day, and that he had not seen her since she went through the portal.

' "Then did I hasten back into the Cathedral, thinking it exceeding strange that the woman should have been that many an hour inside without I myself had clapped eyes on her. And still seeing her not, I did make question of one and another, till at last an old sacristan said that he had seen her kneeling in the Chapel of the Virgin and kneeling by her side a figure, a man, as he thought, dressed and hooded all in white, as it were a monk, and thinking it no ill that she should be praying with a holy man he had passed by, but that when he passed again they were no longer there. Then went I to the Chapel of the Virgin and found that which most I feared, that the door to the Vault of the Family Comminges, which is in the wall of that Chapel and hard by the tomb of Hugues de Châtillon – that this door was loosed and swung open at my touch.

' "And beneath, at the bottom of the stairs, among the sepulchres, was this Constance lying on a stone slab as for dead; but yet did she live, for she turned her head and smiled at me, and babbled that her husband had lain there with her not an hour past and she had had great delight of him, and he was now gone to get her treasure (for she had told him, in her pleasure, where it was hid) and would come soon again to her that they might take their joy of love." '

'It must have been Poppa Comminges,' said Marigold. 'If he got himself up in a shroud, and if it was pretty dark, as it was yesterday in that Chapel, and if she was terrified, as she must have been at first, and if he remembered how his son spoke and acted, he could have passed himself off as Louis – as indeed *vocally* we think he already had.'

'A lot of "ifs" and "ases",' Jacquiz said.

'It can't have been Louis, because Louis, quite apart from being dead, was a rotten lover, you remember, on Constance's earlier showing, and now here she was "having great delight of him". It must have been Poppa, who was perhaps more talented in that department, who'd maybe learned a thing or two from his young bride, and was now giving Constance the benefit.'

'The priest thought something of the kind – to begin with. "At first I chided her, that this could not be, and that being a widow and grown riggish she had taken some peasant or prentice boy into the tomb to do her wanton business, and being now all thing disordered and ruttish, her juices all awash, she did boast, in a mood of knavery, that it was her husband had come for her. 'Indeed it was he,' she crieth, 'for should I not know the body and flesh of my own, and wondrous it was that though I had no happiness of him before, his very touch now maketh me to tremble as I would swoon.' 'Come, wench,' said I, 'he has been these many weeks agone in his winding sheet, and can be no object of desire.' And then she did look at me, with a sly and crooked pravity, and smiled at me, and bared her teeth, and showed her tongue betwixt; and then did I know what foul and most unnatural lust had come upon her and what monstrous congress she had had in that place and looked to have again ere long. Blindly I ran forth from the Vault, and forth from the Cathedral of our blessed Mary, and thence to my lodging, where I fell asweating and apraying and could not venture forth until the hour of the last office." '

Jacquiz looked up from the book. 'You see what he's saying,' he said.

'Yes. He was saying that Constance was a necrophiliac and that her husband had had to die to arouse her. But *I* say,' said Marigold, 'that she was simply mistaken about identities. She thought she was coupling with her husband because of certain superficial similarities, and though she'd dreaded the idea previously, when it came to the point she found it very exciting; but the person with whom she in fact coupled was her father-in-law obscured by a shroud.'

'What do you say she was aroused by? Her father-in-law's amorous skills? Or the notion of doing it with ... with a revenant?'

'Both, I dare say ... so long as we are absolutely clear that the latter *was* only a *notion* or delusion. And another thing. She was obviously so crazily randy with what had happened and what was going to happen, with being aroused for the first time ever, that she didn't know what she was saying. I bet she went back on it later.'

'She didn't get the chance, sweetheart ... " ... When I came out from my lodging the bell was ringing for Compline" – that is, "the last office" referred to above – "and I made haste towards the Cathedral. As I came into the place before it, a group of people came forth from the West door, of whom some two or three were supporting a body, the body of the woman, Constance Comminges. Not half an hour agone, they said, there had been a great squealing from the Vault of the Family Comminges, and those who had gone thither had found the woman, her legs splayed and her robe lifted ready to make the beast with two backs, and her throat rent from jaw to jaw. There was none other there among the sepulchres whom they might charge with this foul murder, and so now they were taking the corse to her father-in-law's house, and would then make report to the Praefect. And at that minute Master Comminges himself, roused by the crowd and the commotion, came forth from his house to receive (though he knew it not at first) his daughter's corse." '

'He knew it all right,' said Marigold. 'He'd done her in, and then hidden in one of the family tombs in the Vault. In those days they often didn't seal the slabs down, you know. So he'd hidden with the remains of one of his ancestors, slipped out when they'd taken her up the stairs, and whizzed round and home by some side door (through the cloister perhaps) while they were carrying her out of the main exit.'

'Why should he have wanted to kill her?'

'She told him where the loot was during their first bout – remember? He'd now got the necklace safe. Henceforth Constance could only be an extra mouth to feed – or an extra mouth to blabber about the Rubies – and in general a big embarrassment. Perhaps his young wife knew that he'd rogered her, and though allowing it once – in order to get the treasure – had come down very firmly against second helpings. Perhaps she herself killed Constance in jealousy—'

'—But Constance was all arranged for more coupling when she was killed—'

'—Perhaps she heard the wife's footsteps and was so over-excited she mistook them for . . . her lover's. Perhaps it was indeed her lover – Poppa Comminges, that is – who'd been persuaded by his young wife that he must kill her while she was still down there waiting. Perhaps the young wife came too to make sure that Poppa did a good job. Perhaps he came alone and had her again before he cut her throat.'

'A lot of perhapses.'

'All of them quite sane and rational when compared with your apparent belief, that it was Louis Comminges come from Pau. Why are you so anxious to believe in the impossible, Jacquiz?'

'I'm not anxious to. But . . . perhaps it's a reaction against a lifetime of donnish logic and routine . . . I find myself somehow convinced by the priest. By his tone. And I find something very significant in Van Hoek's . . . anticipation of the theme. Van Hoek's picture is so powerful in its way that I feel that what he prophesied must have happened. Why are you anxious *not* to believe this tale, Marigold?'

'I believe it all right . . . but not the priest's interpretation. I believe it can all be explained quite naturally.'

'But you used to be far the more superstitious of the pair of us. It was *you* had the experience when we entered the Cathedral.'

'I know. I'm prone to superstition. I *did* have a beastly experience when we went into that church. For that very reason,' Marigold said, 'I am determined to cling to reason, to face the demons down with common sense. I want to stay sane, Jacquiz.'

'So did our priest,' said Jacquiz with a sombre chuckle. 'So he insisted that after Constance had been buried in the family vault it should be sealed for ever. At first, he says, they made a crude job of bricking it up, then, later on, he raised money to have a pukkha arrangement done – the one we saw in the Virgin's Chapel yesterday. "And this I did, not only that she might not come forth, but that her husband might not come to her. For such lusts as these, once consummated as this had been, do lend the dead the will and the desire to come to each other in their hellish congress, and also, if they be not closely mewed up, to go forth and couple with those yet quick upon the earth, thereby befouling and perverting them too and ever increasing the tribes of the living dead. I went also to Pau, once more to adjure the body and spirit of this Louis (of which there is now record carven there), and to cause his stone to be strengthened and widened and most deeply and firmly sunken, that nevermore, whether by his own might or by the help of his familiars, should he be able to rise and rove. And all this I did with monies raised from the good burghers of Saint Bertrand-de-Comminges, who had taken heed of Constance Comminges her shameful and hideous passing." '

'A family matter, one would have thought, paying the special undertaker's bills.'

'The family had left. Poppa Comminges, his sister, and his now very pregnant young wife went away . . . "to live, and to prosper, as they say, in the city of Arles. For not all men thought as I did (and sware before the Praefect), that the wench was slain by her dead husband so that (having parted with her treasure to his people) she might be with him among the living dead. Some men thought that Master Comminges had slain her for her baubles, of which there hath been much chatter but no man knoweth the real nature thereof; and though this could not be proven, yet did Master Comminges, knowing how he was by some men regarded, decide to remove elsewhere." '

'Thank God at least "some men" had a bit of sense,' Marigold said.

'I'm not going to make an issue of it, sweetheart. We've heard the priest's story and we must both interpret it in our own way. But there is one more thing of interest. "... Albeit, as I recorded heretofore, that the family Comminges are said to wax fat in Arles, in a fair, tall house near to the Priory of the Knights of Malta, it cometh to my ken that two fine men-children, of which the young trollope hath lately been delivered, were stricken by sore misfortune, being crushed by a cross-stone which fell as they played in the ruin of the antique theatre. So true it is that any gain which is founded on evil practice (for howsomever men may opine that the true facts fadge, it remaineth that Mistress Constance her treasure was won from her by means that was all thing evil) – that any gain, I say, which is the fruit of wickedness, will bring other fruits to ripeness with it that shall poison to the death ..." You see?' said Jacquiz. 'If, as we obviously hope, the "baubles" or the "treasure" which Poppa Comminges somehow got from Constance was indeed the necklace, the Roses of Picardie, then it is in absolute accord with the legend that the Comminges should prosper in Arles and yet lose "two fine men-children" in an ugly accident.'

'The Roses up to their old tricks again? Dispensing power, money, reputation – and spilling blood all over the place as well?'

'Right.'

'So now we go,' said Marigold, 'to Arles.'

'Right.'

'And what do we look for there?'

'For a start, a fair, tall house near the Priory of the Knights of Malta.'

'A pleasant destination,' said Marigold. 'Do we leave today?'

'Yes. A night in Albi, or somewhere round there, *en route*. But first we must return this book to the Abbé.'

Jacquiz started the Rolls and they sailed up the hill to St Bertrand.

'Rather a long order,' said Ivor to Len in the Chamber of Manuscripts. 'To find someone who'll take the blame for stealing those MSS, and thus keep bright the good name of the College . . . Why *should* anyone be willing to take the blame?'

'If we pay them good,' said Len.

'What with?'

'My loot. *And* there's the Georgics still to sell.'

'But then what would you have?'

'You,' said Len. 'You re-elected a Fellow, which is how I like you.'

'But how would you live?'

'Not the good life, that's for sure. But I'd manage.'

'No,' said Ivor. 'I can't accept such a sacrifice. I *want* you to have the good life, Len, and to hang on to that edition of the Georgics for the sheer pleasure of it for as long as possible. We must find another way.'

'A long order, Ive, like you say. But you know what? I think I might, just might, have an answer. What I've got in mind – it's as bent as a bad penny, Ive, but it might just slip down the slot and set the pretty birdie singing . . .'

The Rolls stopped outside the gabled house near the Porte Lyrisson.

'Buck up,' said Jacquiz as he handed the Abbé Valcabriers'

292

scrapbook to Marigold: 'I'm rather blocking the road.'

Marigold scampered across to a solid wooden door. As there was no bell or knocker, she rapped with her fist. Very soon the door opened.

'*Excusez-moi,*' she began, and then stopped, silenced by the beauty of the acolyte who stood before her.

'You – you were in Pau,' she cried: 'the gardener.'

The boy put the index finger of his left hand over her lips and with his right hand took the book from her. Then he closed the door.

# VIII

## The Cloister of Saint Trophîme

'Lagadigadéu! La Tarasco!' sang Balbo Blakeney. 'Lagadigadéu! La Tarasco du Castel!'

'What's all that in aid of?' said Jones S.

'I was hoping to summon the Tarasque.'

The two men gazed down into the great river from the ramparts of the Castle of Tarascon. The Tarasque did not appear. A thin whisper of autumn sighed through the pines from the North.

'The Tarasque was commanded by Saint Martha to stay below the waters till the end of time. Or so you said at Paestum. Why were you so drunk last night, Balbo?'

'Little lapse. Sorry. Please forgive.'

'I'll forgive. I just wanted to know why. I thought that you didn't seem to be needing the hard stuff – or not so much of it . . . during these last few days.'

'I didn't. Driving up from Paestum to Santo Stefano I felt fine. And that night at Santo Stefano. Marvellous, that was. Langoustine on the terrace, and your talk about being a cricket pro in the days when amateurs went out to bat through a special gate of their own. A vanished world . . . And then, thinking of that world, I started to get sad. Cambridge in the forties and fifties. That poor sod Clovis du Touquet coming to a May Ball. Still some zest in science then.'

'What was that?'

'Science. I still took an interest . . . about the time you were walking in to bat from the non-amateur gate.'

'No. Not science. The May Ball . . . somebody coming to it.'

'Clovis du Touquet. The one I told you about who was . . . smashed to death. In any case, a vanished figure from one's youth. Sad. That night at Santo Stefano I got sad.'

'But you didn't get drunk. It was *last* night you got drunk.'

'The Santo Stefano sadness wasn't real sadness. It was a delicious melancholy. Poetic self-indulgence. But the next morning ... as we started the run up to Menton ... the delicious melancholy turned sour on me, as it is apt to, and started to hurt. "Last day," it said to me, oh, very sharp and concrete now, no more vague evocations of misty autumn mornings at Cambridge, a straight, fierce, personal pain: nag, nag, nag, "your last day out with Sydney, tonight you'll be in Menton and tomorrow you'll drive on to Tarascon and possibly Arles, and what the hell to do you think you're going to find in either?" So when we got to Menton—'

'—You got arseholes drunk. Pretty feeble, I'd say. Flat out on the quay, like a sailor. Good thing I came to look for you.'

'Sorry, Sydney.'

'Why didn't you say what was bothering you?'

'Too embarrassed.'

'You're saying it now.'

'With a certain type of hangover a man will say anything. He'll even try to call up the Tarasque.'

'It's four in the afternoon. You can't still have a hangover.'

'It's about four in the afternoon that *this* sort of hangover begins. Lagadigadéu! La Tarasco!' Balbo shouted from the rampart. 'About as much chance of raising the Tarasque,' he grumbled, 'as there is of finding the clue we need to carry on.'

'You were very persuasive in Paestum.'

'It was all improvised. You knew that. To keep the show going. But the show's over, isn't it? I'll come quietly, Sydney. Back to beastly London to talk about these rats.'

Yes, thought Jones, S.: he still has the sign. In fact it's particularly clear this afternoon. They'll be glad to see him. Pleased with me for bringing him in without any fuss.

'I dare say,' he said carefully, 'that we'll be seeing quite a lot of one another ... in these next few weeks.'

'As far as that goes, good. But it won't be the same – will it, Sydney? – as, well, being on the trail together?'

'No, Balbo. It won't be the same. For a start, we'll have to turn the car in now and fly home . . . since we're going.'

'A clue in Tarascon. Where, for God's sake? What ever was I thinking of? A clue in Arles? In a bull's pizzle.'

'Come on, Balbo. The show's over, as you say. It was an intriguing idea . . . to hunt back through time until you heard the news you wanted. I wish we could go on hunting. There may be a voice somewhere, for all I know, still telling the news out loud and clear, but I think we've lost the wavelength.'

'Too bloody true, sport,' said Balbo, badly imitating Syd. 'So what now?'

Both men turned and started down a narrow stone stair.

'Pop into Saint Martha's Church,' said Sydney, 'her what tamed the Tarasque. Her tomb's in the Crypt. Fine work, the book says.'

'Yes. I expect it will open again about now. But I meant – what later, Sydney?'

'Drive on to Arles this evening. Hand the car in at the Avis office tomorrow morning. Book two seats on the next plane from Montpellier to London.'

They crossed a courtyard surrounded by walls so high that Balbo imagined he was a rat crossing the bottom of a dried out well.

'Decent dinner in Arles tonight, anyway,' he said. 'I shan't get drunk again. There's a good little restaurant down by the bull-ring.'

They walked through a grey tunnel and came out into the October afternoon.

'Funny,' said Jones, S.: 'October here feels rather like England.'

Across the road an old woman was opening up the Église Sainte-Marthe.

'Seventeenth-century Genoese work this tomb of the saint is going to be. They seem to have left it rather late,' said Jones, S., 'before getting round to doing her the honours.

After all she'd done for the place. There's gratitude for you.'

'At least they did get round to it in the end.'

'South door, this. Romanesque.'

'Sydney. Oh, Sydney, Sydney,' blabbered Balbo: 'look, *look at that notice on the wall.*'


'Any further word from Jones?' said Theta to Q.

'No. I'm beginning to get worried.'

'Why? His progress is westward, homeward . . .'

'That's just it.' Q went to the window and looked along Jermyn Street towards the back of Fortnum's. Caviar, he thought, fresh foie gras, gulls' eggs (when in season), lobster mousse. Having with some effort regained his self-control,

'That's just it,' he repeated. 'I'm worried he'll want to move East again. Or stay where he is.'

'Why on earth? His last report as relayed to me by you stated that they were *en route* for Tarascon – and that he thought Blakeney's personal search was finished.'

'Not finished. *Foutu.* Dead scent.'

'As far as we are concerned, finished.'

Smoked salmon, thought Q, game pie.

He slammed the window shut and turned back into the room.

'Tarascon,' he said to the serene, almost Buddhesque Theta, 'was to be the next place and the last where they might find a further clue to help them in this hunt of Blakeney's. Jones was going to take two days on the trip from Paestum to Tarascon – much too long, but I gave my consent because they *were* moving in the right direction and he said that Blakeney must not be hurried.'

'Quite right.'

'But the point is that even if they take their full two days from Paestum to Tarascon they should have been in the latter by last night or this morning.'

'This morning.'

'All right. This morning. It is now eight o'clock in the evening. Why have we not yet heard that they are coming on to England?'

'They will still be looking for their clue. In this context, I think that Tarascon designates an area rather than just the town.'

'I dare say. But Jones was very clear about what would happen. There would be no clue, he said; there couldn't conceivably be. They would just take a turn round Tarascon and another turn, perhaps, round Arles, more or less for the sake of it, and that would be that. Now they have had plenty of time, my dear Theta, to take turns round half Provence. But still no word. You and I are still here, at eight o'clock in the evening, because we are both hoping that Jones will come through and assure us that tomorrow they are flying home. That is what we are waiting for, that is what should have happened. Why has it not?'

'Perhaps he thinks it's too late to get us.'

'It is never too late to get the duty officer.'

'The duty officer has no powers to instruct him.'

'He should not need instruction. He should merely be announcing that he is coming home as already instructed. Since he has not yet been in touch to announce this, it is now safe to assume that he is not going to announce it. He has another footling and time-wasting request.'

'If he has, there is still plenty of time. We can give them another ten days.'

'No. No, we can't.'

'What do you mean, "We can't". I know of no intention to bring forward the date of Falx.'

'It is a question of Blakeney's fitness for Falx.'

'If we have him in ten days, there will be three weeks to make him ready. Time enough,' said Theta in his thin, tinny voice, with a rapturous smile.

'On the contrary, if he has ten days more at large before he gets here, he will almost certainly be unfitted for his task altogether,' purred Q very gently, looking like a stoat.

'What *can* you mean?'

'This morning Lambda and I discussed the latest sets of figures. Those which deal with the danger levels at the Cathedral were, if anything, rather reassuring. Those that concern Blakeney are quite the reverse.'

'Can we trust them? I mean . . . so soon?'

'Yes. Lambda is quite clear about that. Jones has now been with Blakeney long enough for the figures which Jones sends in to be more than a mere random selection. They are consecutive over a period sufficient to give them validity. And all of a sudden, sir, they are very disturbing.'

'I thought the main thing was his forehead. The fact that it is unlined.'

'All we can tell from the forehead, sir, is whether or not he actually has the Sign. A completely smooth forehead means he has it, even the slightest furrow would mean that he had lost it. But we cannot, from the forehead, gauge the strength of its operation, whether it is waxing, waning or remaining constant. For this we need a more complicated calculus.'

Q produced a sheet of figures.

'Now then, sir. These are the figures which have been sent daily by Jones since he has been in Blakeney's company. Jones records them very precisely on a system in which he was long and arduously briefed by Lambda. To speak very broadly they provide shorthand descriptions of certain aspects of Blakeney's behaviour, diction and appearance which have important bearing on the strength, or otherwise, of the godhead he carries within him. I cannot properly interpret them myself; for an exact and scientific assessment we depend, of course, on Lambda.'

Theta pursed his lips but nodded to Q to proceed.

'The important point is, sir, that these figures, these symbols of Blakeney's condition, showed a hideous deterioration some seven days ago followed by an even more spectacular *improvement* as from three days ago—'

'—The time when Jones rang in from Paestum?'

'Right, sir. Now, this very extreme contrast, this huge arc over which the matrical pendulum has so abruptly swung both this way and that, must give us, in Lambda's view, the gravest cause for anxiety.' He pointed delicately to the figures at the bottom of the page. 'Figures like these, the most recent, suddenly quite superb after a long run of very poor ones, constitute a statistical freak and indicate an imminent collapse.'

'Collapse of Blakeney?'

'Of the Sign, and its validity, within and upon Blakeney. The figures will stay good, Lambda thinks, for the next two or three days after that lot – a final flare-up, as it were. Then they will peter out.'

'Today? Or tomorrow?'

'Precisely, sir.'

'Peter out for good?'

'Lambda doesn't know. In the only other case he observed closely, the fading of the Sign was arrested – for a time at least – by injections.'

'*Injections?*'

'Rodent plasmas.'

'Cher-ist.'

'We must get him back at once, sir. Whatever Lambda can or cannot do, he can only do it if he has Blakeney to hand.'

'To needle-point. But after all these years . . . why should the Sign leave him now?'

'It has to leave him some time. Why not now?'

'Is there no one else?'

'We know of no one else at the moment, Theta. I think I must have some dinner. Will you join me? They do one quite well at the Écu de France, down the street.'

'Rather a waste – when all I can manage is a glass of milk and a biscuit.'

In all the years he had known him, Q had never eaten a meal with Theta. He had often wondered why his superior had never suggested it. Now he knew.

'In any case,' Theta continued, 'somebody must be here in

case Sydney rings the office . . . somebody with the muscle to tell him he must now bring in Blakeney at once.'


'Molluscs,' said Balbo, 'are becoming dangerous. Especially if they're out of the Mediterranean, like these.'

He tucked into a large plate of Praires with relish.

'Hangover gone?' said Jones, S.

'Since we saw that notice in Sainte Marthe's.'

Syd Jones looked through the window of the restaurant across the street at the outer wall of the sunken arena of Arles. Damn that notice in Sainte Marthe's, he thought: it's going to complicate everything.

A girl walked along the street and glanced briefly towards the entrance of the restaurant. Where have I seen her before? thought Jones. Damn that notice. Where have I seen that girl? Gone already.

'Balbo,' he said, 'we must think very carefully what we must do.'

'It's quite clear, what we must do. That notice said that a certain Monsignor Bernard Comminges, Canon Resident of the Cathedral of Saint Trophîme in Arles, would be giving an address next Tuesday, on the Role of Satan under God, in the church of Sainte Marthe at Tarascon. That means that there is someone living in Arles called Bernard Comminges. In Arles, Sydney, where we are this minute sitting and eating our dinner, some five minutes' walk, if that, from the Cathedral of Saint Trophîme.'

'The clerk at the hotel didn't know him. He shook his head as if we were mad to ask.'

'A typically nasty French habit, to dissimulate ignorance by imputing perversity or insanity to the questioner. I once tried to buy a bottle of Delamain cognac in Dieppe. Two old women who didn't have it in their shops denied that such a cognac had ever existed and looked at me with disgust, Sydney, as though I had proposed to them some particularly evil form of sexual congress. In that case it wasn't ignorance they were trying to conceal, it was the inadequacy of their stock; the underlying technique, however, was the same. But be all that as it may,' said Balbo, 'you are not going to tell me, because one hotel clerk shakes his head and shrugs his shoulders, that a person with the title of Canon Resident of the Cathedral of Saint Trophîme is not to be found here in Arles.'

'And what if he is to be found?'

'Sydney, you're really being very peculiar tonight. We are looking for a necklace of Rubies that was last heard of as being in the possession of someone called Comminges. Furthermore, we are now very near that part of the world in which my friend Clovis du Touquet, who may have been looking for the necklace, or may even have been summoned by someone to collect it, died a very strange and horrible death. The combination – a Canon Comminges, living in Arles, *i.e.* within a short distance of Aix-en-Provence – is too strong to ignore. So tomorrow, when the Cathedral is open, we step inside and ask the nearest priest, verger or pious old woman where we can find Monsignor the Canon Resident.'

'Who will certainly think we are mad the moment we start asking for ruby necklaces.'

'The question has to be put sooner or later. If he is a member of the Comminges family we're looking for, he will almost certainly know the legend.'

'Suppose he does. Suppose he even knows where the Rubies are. What makes you think he will tell us?'

Balbo mopped up the last of the Praire juice with a piece of garlic bread.

'Of course, we may have to keep on at him,' Balbo said. 'He may crack; or he may inadvertently give us a hint. Not necessarily a direct lead to the jewels, but something helpful.'

Syd Jones heaved a very deep sigh.

'Time, Balbo; time. If I don't bring you in soon, *they're* going to get angry.'

'I thought you were prepared to play them along for a while.'

'I was. I am. But the "while" is nearly over.'

'Surely it can extend to a chat with the Canon tomorrow?'

'And if that keeps us in the hunt?'

'Surely, just a day or two more ... And then we could suspend operations, if we weren't through, till after the rat business is finished with. But at least, Sydney, now we are here, we must talk to the Canon.'

'So we must,' conceded Sydney, 'I will telephone the duty officer in Jermyn Street and tell him we need up to three days more ... allowing us time to act on any information this Canon character may put up.'

'Thank you, Sydney.'

'Not at all, sport. I'm enjoying it all, as you know. It's just that I'd got into the way of thinking that the hunt *must* be done with at last—'

'—That's what I thought too—'

'—And that's what I've told them in London. So it's been an effort working myself back into the former frame of mind, that's all.'

'What about *them*? What will be *their* frame of mind?'

'We'll see when I telephone. I think they'll go along with me all right.'

And that was what he really thought, and what he really wanted. Reluctant as he had seemed a few minutes earlier, he knew that the hunt could not be abandoned now that a new line, against colossal odds, had been opened up to them. Nor did he think it likely that Theta would quarrel over three more days. For a moment he thought of ringing London there and then in order to dispel any doubt or anxiety immediately. Then he remembered that his latest set of figures about Balbo must be relayed during the call, and these were in a notebook in his briefcase back in the Hôtel Jules César. Ah well, he thought; the call can wait. Balbo seems happy enough guzzling his frogs' legs; it's good to see him eating so well and looking so fit, even after last night's dismal performance; he's a different man from what he was a week ago. So let's just enjoy our tucker.

Anyhow, it will be much easier to telephone from the hotel.

'Urgent news for you,' said Theta when at last he heard Jones, S., on the telephone. 'But first let's have the latest figures on Blakeney.'

Syd Jones read them out; Theta read them back as a check.

'Now wait,' said Theta.

Syd Jones waited.

'Sorry,' said Theta after ten minutes had passed. 'You'll have to hang on a little longer.'

'Would you like me to ring again later?'

'No. We're nearly through. Just hang on.'

In the office in Jermyn Street, Theta laid the telephone receiver through which he had been talking to Jones, S., gently down on his desk, then turned to Q who was holding the receiver of a second telephone.

'You've checked that Lambda took down the right figures?' asked Theta. 'They absolutely correspond with the ones on that paper, the ones which Jones has just relayed to me?'

'Yes,' said Q, 'they do. Can I go back to my partridge in the Écu de France? Partridges are very expensive, you know.'

'Ask Lambda if he is *quite sure* that his interpretation of Jones's new figures is correct. Tell him to check his findings.'

Q told him. They waited. Q thought about his partridge, of which he had eaten only one mouthful when summoned back to the office. I'd better order another, he thought: start again from square one. The telephone started to quack. Q listened carefully.

At last he replaced the receiver.

'Lambda says there can be virtually no doubt at all,' he purred at Theta.

'Right,' yapped Theta. 'Go back to your dinner.'

'What are you going to do?'

'I'll tell you later.'

Q went. Theta picked up the telephone receiver from his desk.

'Are you there, Sydney?'

'Yes, sir. If we've finished with those figures, I have a request.'

'Just listen, Sydney. If your return is correct, and if Lambda of Bio/Chem has not gone off his head, by this time tomorrow morning Blakeney will have lost it.'

'Lost what?'

This charisma or whatever he has. The Sign with it.'

'What do you want me to do?'

'Observe. If his forehead is still unlined, then he still has it, in however weak a form, and you must rush him straight back to London, where we shall see what we can do. But if lines, however faint, are beginning to form on his forehead, then *it* has gone, and that is that.'

'You mean, he'll no longer be any good to us?'

'No. I don't mean quite that. Even if the charisma has gone – indeed just *because* the charisma has gone Lambda says he may still be able to serve us, though in an altogether different way. What you must do is this: if the Sign has gone tomorrow morning, *i.e.* if his forehead is beginning to crease in the normal fashion, you must just hang around with him wherever you happen to be—'

'—Arles—'

'—Hang around with him there, or let him move about if he wants to, and ring in to the duty officer twice every day to report where you are.'

'Twice?'

'Twice. If anything out of the ordinary has happened, tell him to put you through to me.'

'Or Q?'

'If I'm not there.'

'If neither of you is there?'

'One of us will be, from nine a.m. to nine p.m., seven days a week. We may well have special instructions for you.'

'What's going on, then?'

'You'll be told, when and if you need to know. No point in complicating your life until we have to, Sydney. Meanwhile, just telephone in twice a day, as near as you can to noon and seven p.m.'

When Theta had finished talking to Jones, S., he broke his rule of many years and joined Q at his table at the Écu de France.

'No, no food or drink,' he said with distaste. 'There is something I want to discuss with you. Something that won't wait.'

'You mean . . . what will now happen to Blakeney?'

'And what we should do about it. What . . . and how. But first, *why*? To begin with, why has the Sign left him? On Sydney's showing, he is in many ways a fitter and better human being now than he was when Sydney first met him. Yet to explain the disappearance of the Sign, of the charisma, we must posit some process of debilitation or decay.'

'Puzzling, I agree. My own theory is that this search in which he has been engaged, while not bringing about any obvious personal deterioration, may nevertheless have affected or changed his mental processes in such a way as somehow to dissipate his qualifications for – er – Kingship or Divinity or whatever he was endowed with.'

'We know almost nothing about this search – except that it is very important to Blakeney. It's a line we might pursue if we want to know what has brought about this sudden deprivation.'

'But do we really want to know? Surely the plain fact that Blakeney has lost, or is just about to lose, his charisma, must be enough for us. I don't think we can waste time on "why". It is an academic exercise.'

'An enjoyable one.'

'I thought the need was for decision rather than enjoyment.'

'*Touché,*' said Theta. 'Very well. What are we to do? He himself will not know he has lost the Sign – any more than he knew he had it, before Sydney told him. It could be our duty to warn him and protect him against the consequences of his loss.'

'But here,' said Q, examining with satisfaction the cheese soufflé which had now followed his partridge, 'the emphasis at once shifts to "how". How should we ensure his protection? And this in turn leads us to the question: How will *they* go about their – er – part of the business?'

Theta nodded.

'We must also ask ourselves,' he said, 'the question "who?". Will the job be attempted by *their* local representatives, wherever Blakeney happens to be? Or will there be delegations from all over the world?'

'We then remind ourselves,' said Q, 'that they are not so much doing a job as taking part in a sacrament . . . a sacrament of a therapeutic nature. We may therefore assume that as many of them as possible would wish to be present. This could be a very great number, since one may presume that even a crumb of this particular feast will have the desired effect; as with the Christian Sacrament of Holy Communion.'

'We are going too fast,' said Theta. 'We have forgotten to ask an important and elementary question: given that for many years he has not been active in his role and has had nothing whatever to do with *them*, will *they* still be concerned about *him*?'

'When we decided to recruit him, we predicated such concern. On the best advice. Which was, that once he had been given Grace in *their* eyes, so to speak, the Grace would be valid and applicable (even if not applied) until the disappearance of the Sign. *Their* concern would therefore last until the latter event – which would precipitate the consequence of which our experts informed us.'

'In short,' said Theta, '*they* will act. But before they can act, they must know. Will *they* automatically divine what has happened to Blakeney by some process of second sight? Or is it necessary for one of their number to observe him and spread, so to speak, the word? If so, how widely would it be spread?'

Q very carefully applied a nugget of mustard to a forkful of soufflé and inserted the combination.

'If you remember,' he said, 'we toyed with the idea of asking Blakeney to exercise his influence from a distance, *i.e.* from wherever he happened to be, in order to save time and trouble and avoid staging a confrontation. We thought he might *will* them to leave Canterbury Cathedral and take themselves off somewhere convenient. But we were advised that this was beyond his powers. In order to exercise his influence, he must be present. From this incapacity . . . from the fact that he could not reach them through the psychic ether, as it were . . . we must deduce, by corollary, an incapacity on *their* part to pick him up through that medium. And if they can't do that, they certainly won't know what is happening to him now unless they see for themselves or are told by somebody who has.'

'By . . . somebody?' said Theta.

He poured himself a glass of Q's Evian water and put two large yellow tablets into it. While these dissolved,

'By somebody?' Theta repeated. 'You mean, of course, by one of *their* own number?'

'So I did. But if one comes to think of it . . .'

Theta's pills had now vanished in the Evian water, which had turned into a syrup like gaseous hair-oil.

'Yes,' said Theta, and took a sip of the hair-oil. 'Yes,' he said, and took a gulp. 'Yes,' he said, and drained his glass, 'if one comes to think of it, there should be some way in which we could inform *them* . . . those of them, that is, who are occupying Canterbury Cathedral . . . of what has happened to *him. They* would then emerge, instinctively drawn to the performance of their rite on the person of their God who is God no longer, with the object of crossing the channel by whatever means and seeking out Blakeney . . . of whose whereabouts we should have told them to give them additional impetus. Meanwhile, Operation Falx could be brought forward, all known exits from the Cathedral blocked by the troops, drains and canals intensively watched over, all of *them* slaughtered as they departed in accordance with the original plan, and their remains taken to Dover Castle for disposal and research. There are just two snags. First, how are we to put over the necessary information to *them*?'

'A hypnotist?'

'He would have to have powers comparable to those which Blakeney used to have. Rare.'

'We can consult Lambda and his people.'

'Yes. First thing tomorrow. We want some method of making *them* understand that their God-King, or one of their God-Kings, has lost his Grace, and that they may find him, in order to perform their rite, in Arles. And this brings us to the second snag . . .'

'Yes, Theta?'

'Suppose . . . some of them actually get through. Get through the cordon of troops, get on to boats across the channel, track down Blakeney in Arles . . . or, if he's left, find and follow his trail to wherever he goes? What then, Q?'

'Then . . . Jones's report of what occurs should be extremely interesting.'

'Of course, we needn't say he's in Arles. *If* we succeed in getting through to them, we could misroute them. So long as we are sufficiently convincing to get them out of the Cathedral . . .'

'I've an idea that in order to be that convincing we must believe what we're saying – and that means telling the truth.'

'In any case,' mused Theta, 'once they've been told about Blakeney's loss of Grace – and that is the bare minimum they must be told in order to get them moving – once they've been told about *that* and the hunt is on, they'll make their own inquiries among their own – their own, er, people, who will be on the alert, as word spreads, over wider and wider areas. Even if only one of them escapes the cordon he could, given a little time and luck, start a hue and cry all over Europe. In which case, wherever Blakeney was or wasn't, and wherever we'd originally told them he was or wasn't, sooner or later he'd be having visitors.'

'Then let us hope the soldiers do their duty,' said Q, 'and there are no survivors. Meanwhile, it very much remains to be seen whether we can get through to them. After all, that was what we wanted Blakeney for.'

'We wanted him to command or cajole them to get out. A difficult task, any attempt at which was bound to encounter strong resistance and even arouse violent hostility. The thing needed either very substantial authority over them or a very subtle insight into their idiom, both of which Blakeney might have had and we definitely had not. What we are now trying to do is something far easier: merely to inform them of something they are well equipped to understand. There must be some way of doing it.'

Theta poured more Evian. He took out a phial and shook some green powder into the glass.

'By the by,' said Q, 'could we not recall Jones? We're short-handed as usual, and there's no need for him to stay with Blakeney now.'

Theta patted his luxuriance of malfunctioning stomach.

'It will be useful to know where Blakeney is for the time being, and what he is up to. Furthermore,' he yapped in his poky little voice, 'as you yourself remarked, Jones's report of anything that might happen in the region of Blakeney could be extremely interesting.'


'The first sensible person whom we meet,' said Balbo to Syd Jones as they walked through the West Gate of the Cathedral of St Trophîme.

Outside the church the early morning had been bright and blue, with a light, dry chill of autumn; inside the building the chill became heavy and dank. It was almost as though a mist rose from the floor, crept upwards, crawled about the vaulting and down the walls and columns again, making dim the ranks of candles before the side-chapels.

Balbo and Syd Jones walked up the southern side and into the ambulatory. In front of the second chantry a black, cowled figure placed a lighted candle on a spike in the rack, crossed itself and backed away with bowed head. It started to mutter.

'Funny,' Balbo said; 'it sounds like Hebrew.'

'What do you know of Hebrew?'

'Only what it sounds like. At Cambridge I had a Jewish friend who used to take me to a synagogue. He didn't believe in it any more than I did, but we were interested to see and hear what went on. The rabbis sounded rather like that old woman, only in a lower register of course.'

'Why should an old lady who crosses herself be talking Hebrew in a French Cathedral?'

The figure ceased muttering, turned East and continued before Balbo and Jones round the ambulatory. Balbo took three or four long, rapid strides until he had caught up with her, then looked down into the cowl and said:

'Excusez-moi, madame. *Je cherche le Monsignor Comminges. Où puis-je trouver?*'

The figure halted and pulled back the cowl. A pretty face, thought Syd Jones as he came up with them, a girl's face, almost a little girl's face, the same face that had peered into the restaurant last night, the same face (only of course it couldn't be) that had looked gravely down into the basket of roses on the beach at Positano. What was a girl like this doing, dressed in a monk's habit, lighting candles, muttering Hebrew (or so Balbo maintained) in this dismal basilica?

'You are sure you want the Canon?' the girl murmured in English.

'Oh yes indeed.'

'I think you cannot know until you see him. And when you see him it will be too late.'

'Too late for what, mademoiselle?'

'Too late . . . for you not to have seen . . . what you will already have seen.'

'Come, come,' said Jones, S. 'He can't be that awful. He's giving a public address in Tarascon before long.'

'He may give the address but nobody will attend it, except

myself and perhaps one other. Do you still wish to see Monsignor Comminges?'

Balbo looked at Syd Jones, who looked back. They both looked at the girl in the black habit and nodded.

'Very well, gentlemen. Kindly follow me.'

Lambda of Bio/Chem was six feet and seven inches tall and as broad as a barrel. He smoked small cigars made with holders attached and laughed a great deal, even when what was being said, by himself or another, was not in the least funny.

'We must remember,' he said in Theta's office, 'that we are dealing with a new strain. More intelligent, probably, but in some way ... alienated.'

'So alienated as not to be interested in Blakeney and his fall from Grace?'

'The last God-King we know of,' said Lambda merrily, 'died of injections we gave him in order to resuscitate his Sign and charisma when they were fading.' He guffawed loudly for several seconds. 'He was promptly cremated. So we cannot know what would have happened to *him*. Nor can we know how the new strain reacted to his loss of Grace, as we did not, in any case, know of the new strain at that time. Our discovery of the new strain is even more recent than our discovery of the class of human God-Kings, which God knows is recent enough.' For some reason he found this fact hilarious. 'But what we *do* now know about the latter is that human God-Kings, recognized as such by *them*, have existed since very ancient times, are exceedingly rare, are often not conscious, or fully conscious, of their own power and position (or of having the Sign), and are ... immolated and consumed ... by their subjects when their charisma, for whatever reason, dies away. I should add that this rite accounts for a number of ugly and hitherto unexplained deaths and disappearances (skeletons found in woods or quite literally in cupboards), such as those of

Thyrios of Phocis in 29 B.C., Alexander Bishop of Tyre in A.D. 984, John Coneycatcher of Norwich in 1569, and, quite lately, a certain Mrs Fisher of Tring, which have puzzled the historians or the authorities right down the ages. As to the God-Kings, then, we are comparatively knowledgeable. But as to the new strain of *them* we are still abysmally ignorant. We do not know whether the new strain recognizes and obeys the authority of such as Blakeney, whether they will be interested in his loss of Grace, or what action they will take about it. But having made this profession of ignorance, let me put on record my *belief* that the new strain will react to the failure of a God-King much as the old strains have always done. If those in Canterbury Cathedral are made aware of what has happened to Blakeney, then they will, in my view, wish to go after him.'

Lambda laughed very heartily indeed.

'Has Blakeney finally lost the Sign?' he inquired.

'We are expecting a telephone call from Jones at any moment. But it is surely safe to assume,' said Theta, 'on the strength of your interpretation of the figures, that he will lose it?'

'Yes. Probably within hours.'

'Very well. Now to the nub. When Blakeney has lost his Sign and his Grace, *they* will wish to track him down – *if* they are made aware of his condition. *They* will leave the Cathedral and can then be destroyed by the soldiers in cordon . . . *if*, I repeat, they can be made aware of Blakeney's condition and so enthused to a pursuit. But can *they* be told, Lambda? Can they be made aware?'

'Yes. By a direct presentation to them of Blakeney himself.'

'That is no good. We want to bring them out, not take him in.'

'You could take him in briefly, then remove him rapidly, hoping that they would follow.'

'Take him in where to? *They* are all skulking underneath the Cathedral or the precinct. Among the antique carrion . . .'

'Take him into the crypt. They'd be aware of him then.'

'Too dangerous. If *they* suddenly swarmed in that low and confined crypt, no one could protect or remove him. They'd pick him clean there and then.'

'Then you've only one chance. If you can get hold of some part of his clothing, better still some part of his body, nail parings, hair, a piece of skin, they will be aware of this as having belonged to one who once had the charisma and now has not. A sort of superannuated Grace or Godhead still hangs about him, you see – that is why they want to absorb him into themselves – and this would almost certainly show in even a small piece of his body or accoutrement . . . which should also be enough to give them a scent and put them on the trail, especially if you get hold of other such oddments and lay a regular spoor for them.'

'We don't want to lay a complete trail. We just want to get them out of the tombs and the fabric, so that the soldiers can kill them.'

Lambda laughed until he shook. 'Well, I guarantee nothing,' he said, 'but I still think one small piece of Blakeney or his underpants would interest them enough to get them moving. It's certainly worth trying.'

'It certainly is,' said Q. 'When Jones rings in we can order him to procure some such fragment and despatch it to us.'

'No,' said Theta. 'Jones will . . . smell a rat, if you'll forgive the phrase. He is fond of Blakeney. He won't do it – not this. I know my Jones.'

'But if we explain that *they* will never actually reach Blakeney, that they'll all be killed as soon as they come out into the open . . .?'

'He wouldn't trust the soldiers to be one hundred per cent competent. Any more,' said Theta, 'than we do. No. We must send another agent to fetch a piece of Blakeney or his kit. It shouldn't be difficult.'

Lambda applauded with a volcanic laugh.


Balbo and Syd Jones followed the black figure, which had now once more covered its head with the cowl, out of St

Trophîme, to the left for fifty yards and to the left again down the Rue de Cloître. The figure then turned left yet once more, through an open gate in a high wall, past which Balbo and Jones followed it into a narrow courtyard. Then the figure halted, turned back towards them, and held up a hand.

'Stay until I come again,' the girl's voice said.

Balbo and Sydney nodded, then turned towards each other.

'What do you make of her?' Balbo said.

The lines, thought Jones, S.; the lines are on his forehead. I can only just see them, minutely tenuous and shallow creases, but they are there. I must let Theta know as soon as possible. That beautifully smooth and unmarked forehead ... alabaster, the poets would say ... the Sign of Grace ... now rumpled, ruffled, coarsened and cankered by the touch -- the touch of what? Time, age, fate, unworthiness? But if ever he was worthy, he is worthy now.

'Did you hear me, Sydney?'

'Yes, Balbo. I don't know what to make of her. She is very young.'

The girl in black came out of a low door in the wall to their right. Her cowl had again been pushed back. Black eyes looked out of a small, slightly asymmetrical face, the chin being deeply cleft and rather crooked, its right bulb hanging lower than the left.

'Now come,' she said.

They followed her through the door, up a flight of stone steps and through a low arch on to a balcony that overlooked a plot of grass and faced across it towards a similar balcony, underneath which was a gallery arcaded in the early Gothic style.

'The Cloister of Saint Trophîme,' said Balbo.

Their guide led them along the balcony to a point where it made a right angle with another such. She opened a door which faced them, went up three or four steps, turned right up more steps, knocked on a stanchioned door, opened it without waiting to be commanded, and held it while Balbo and Jones, S., passed through.

They were in a long, high, splendid chamber, which must run parallel, Jones thought, to the balcony over the West gallery of the Cloister. Along the walls were tapestries of mythical scenes; all down the room were marble statues of slender goddesses and piping fauns; in the centre was a fountain, in the form of a little boy pissing a high arc of water on to the inner thigh of a laughing nymph. At the far end a figure in a cassock sat with its back to them, looking into a cavernous fireplace in which burned a large, blue fire.

'The two English gentlemen, Monsignor,' said the girl.

The figure slowly turned its head, the back and top of which seemed to be closely hooded in white, until it was at last facing its guests. It did not rise.

'Good morning, sirs,' it said in a somewhat muffled voice: muffled, because its face, like the rest of its head, was entirely concealed, all save two red eyes, by a mask of white linen irregularly dappled by small bright stains of red.

# IX

## Au Bord des Tombes

'She'll never do it,' said Ivor to Len in the Chamber of Manuscripts. 'Why should Marigold Helmut take the blame for stealing those books? What's in it, as your generation would say, for her?'

'She likes me. Once she let me tongue her – right here in this room, on this very table. So you see, I've got quite a way with her when I'm trying, and I think, given a fair chance, I might persuade her. And then she likes annoying Jake – that's one reason why she let me tongue her, so's she could rush back home and tell – and *this* would certainly annoy him.'

'But she won't, for Christ's sake, be prepared to go to *prison* for the pleasure of annoying him.'

'She won't have to. She can pretend it was all some kind of joke she rigged up at his expense – some kind of marital pay-off – and the law will go all soppy about her deprived womanhood and all that crap, and let her down light.'

'Only,' Ivor said, 'if she could produce and return the two books. If she could do that, I agree with you that a case could be got up to the effect that she'd done it simply to score off a cruel and domineering husband. But as it is, though The Wandrille Georgics can be returned, the Breviary's gone for ever. If she couldn't give that back, she'd be bound to go down for a stiff sentence.'

'No. She could say she'd destroyed it in a fit of rage or frustration. Out of her resentment of something or other. Resentment's considered pardonable these days, Ive, even respectable. "Justifiable resentment", that's the phrase they always use. So if she tells them she's done it all because her husband is a big rich pig, and here's one book back but she's very sorry, she burnt the other to get her own back on capitalist society for nourishing fat cats like Jake and not loving the niggers enough, they'll not only let her go, Ive, they'll positively pat her on her pretty little bottom and tell her how beautifully compassionate she is.'

'*That* would depend very much on the judge and jury. There's been a swing the other way lately – thank God. But even suppose,' said Ivor, 'that you're right about that, remember that Constable has told us we're not to use anyone who's connected with the College.'

'She's not actually a member. She's hostile to all that it stands for, and Constable doesn't care for her one little tiny bit. I'm pretty sure he'd agree that if she were found guilty it would in no way dishonour the fair name of Lancaster – which is all he's really interested in, that and doing down Jake.'

'It would be nice to save Jacquiz as well as ourselves.'

'Difficult. Getting Jake sacked is very much part of the bargain. But if that's what you want, we might try what we can do later. Meanwhile,' said Len, 'if we get Marigold to take the rap in the way I've suggested, we've got a lot going for us. True, we'll have to give up the Georgics, but we keep the cash for the Breviary, and you keep your Fellowship.'

'But you assume far too easily that she will be ready to help us. You say that you can talk her over – that she'll be glad to fall in with your plan because she enjoys annoying Jacquiz. But is she so very malleable? Is her regard for you so very high – just on the strength of occasional conversations and one bout of cunnilingus? Might she not have been reconciled to Jacquiz during their travels? The mere fact that she consented to go with him at all indicates some extent of underlying loyalty. And above all, *pace* what you say about the possibility of the law's letting her down lightly, why should she be prepared to run the still considerable risk – about fifty-fifty, I'd say – of the law's turning up very nasty?'

'I just think I might persuade her, Ive. I know where to scratch her, so to speak.'

'You've got to find her first. God knows where they are, she and Jacquiz.'

'There, I admit, we have a real problem. I did say, Ive, that all I had was a notion. I never guaranteed anything.'

'Nor you did, Lenny.' Ivor patted Len lightly on the shoulder. 'And come to that, it's quite a clever notion. But, Lenny, but ... And then again, the more I think of it, the keener I am to turn the tables on Constable and somehow preserve Jacquiz, and I hardly think your scheme provides for that. Marigold's confession would do nothing to mitigate Constable's imputation of Jacquiz' incompetence.'

'You can't have everything, Ive.'

'Oh yes, you can,' said a voice.

Ivor and Len looked up. Elvira Constable was standing in the doorway.

'I know more about what's going on than you might think,' she said. 'Although my husband does not exactly confide in me, he likes to think aloud in my presence, in rather the same way as some people think aloud to their dogs or cats ... as a useful exercise in the precise formulation of the problem in hand. So I have heard all about your activities and your difficulties while metaphorically sprawled on the mat at my master's feet. Now then. I wish you to understand that if you will listen to what I can tell you, you can find a very simple solution to the whole affair.'

Ivor rose and offered Lady Constable a chair.

'But may one ask ... why you should wish to assist us?' he mused.

'Because I've been condescended to in the most insulting way ... treated like the dogs and cats I was just talking of ... for far too long. I suddenly find, Mr Winstanley, that I can bear it no longer. I want a bit of my own back after all these years, and with God's help and yours I mean to get it.'

On their way to Arles, Jacquiz and Marigold had stopped at Albi. By the time they had moved into their hotel it was still only four o'clock, exactly the same time on exactly the same day as Balbo and Jones, S., were visiting the church of Sainte Marthe or Saint Martha in Tarascon.

'Cathedral or Toulouse-Lautrec?' Jacquiz said.

'Toulouse-Lautrec. I've had rather enough of churches.'

So they went to the Toulouse-Lautrec exhibition in the fortified Episcopal Palace. Marigold disliked the pictures of the straddling old whores on sofas but was delighted by Coco Dansant. As she stood and admired the black dancer horn-piping in his deer-stalker, Jacquiz said:

'There's a young man over there who's very taken with you. Only a boy, really.'

Marigold turned. 'I see no one,' she said.

'In front of that picture of German troops marching along a street . . . He seems to have gone.'

Marigold went over to the picture. Leading the soldiers was a young mounted officer, whose golden hair descended six clear inches beneath the rim of his forage cap down the back of his head and his neck. His face, in profile, was set yet soft, arrogant, tender, with a small nose slightly hooked. The acolyte, she thought, the gardener. Aloud she said,

'What a pretty officer.'

'Exactly like the boy who was looking at you, though a little older.'

'I expect the boy had come to see the picture of himself. Rather a frightening coincidence for him.'

'It was you he was interested in.'

'I was once told,' said Marigold, ignoring Jacquiz' last remark, 'that I bore a close resemblance to Bellini's Madonna of the Meadow. I went to the National Gallery to see, and it simply wasn't true. The person I *did* look like was Cupid in the Bronzino – you know, the one where he's goosing his mother. Once I'd discovered this, I found myself going back day after day, appalled yet fascinated by my role in the painting. I expect it's the same with that boy.'

Why am I babbling on like this? she thought. Why don't I just tell him that that boy has been with us, on and off, ever since Pau? Because it can't be true and I won't have it, any more than I'll have dead men mating with their widows, it isn't tolerable or decent, it isn't, in one word, sane. Strange boys don't follow one all over France, flickering in and out of one's line of vision in multiple disguises.

'How was he dressed, that boy?' she asked.

'In a green track suit. Or rather, not quite a track suit. The bottom half was more like tights.'

'How exciting. Good legs?'

'Perfect. And a piquant bottom,' said Jacquiz. 'Just the very thing if only one liked boys.'

'What a pity I missed him,' Marigold said, praying she had seen the last of him, knowing she had not.


'In 1947,' Elvira Constable was saying (at about the same time as Jacquiz and Marigold entered the Toulouse-Lautrec gallery in Albi), 'my husband was Tutor of the College. He was known as a stern disciplinarian, as a determined and (for that period) very left-wing socialist, and as a man who despised the pleasures but intensely cultivated the uses both of intellect and of body. It was then I married him. I often wonder why. I think I was vanquished by his sheer physical presence. He was – indeed he is – an impressive man to look at.

'Now, when my husband had returned from the Army to Lancaster in the Autumn of 1945, he made the acquaintance of a young bio-chemist who had become a Fellow of the College while he himself was away at the war. I refer to Mr Balbo Blakeney, the unfortunate gentleman who recently had to leave us because of his addiction to the drink. In 1945, however, Mr Blakeney was a bright and promising young scientist, with a brilliant reputation for his war-time research into the nature and capacity of rats. My husband was fascinated by all he had to say on the subject, most of which had to do with achieving tight enough control over rats, both individually and in the mass, to exploit them for the purposes of contamination, occupation or destruction. It seems that Mr Blakeney had come very near discovering certain techniques, part scientific and part personal, that would have turned the common rodent into a formidable military weapon.'

'I remember about that,' said Ivor; 'but surely he gave it all up after the war and went in for some other line.'

'The effects of alcohol on the blood stream,' said Lady Constable. 'Very appropriate, as it turned out. But he still remembered his war-time work very clearly, and he had, so my husband said, a drawer full of notes of the experiments which he had made at the time. Robert often asked to see these, but he was told that he would be quite unable to understand either their substance or their implications – and just as well for him, Mr Blakeney used humorously to add, if he valued his sleep.

'Well. One day during the long vacation of 1947, not long after our wedding, I brought Robert a cup of tea at his desk and with my habitual clumsiness – much increased by nervous awe of Robert – I spilt a lot of it over a fawn folder which was thickly stuffed with documents. Robert said something quietly savage, and I leant forward to wipe up the tea with my handkerchee, and Robert snatched the folder away from under my eyes – but not before I had seen inscribed on it the words "B. Blakeney. Work in progress, Netheravon, April 1944".

' "So you've persuaded him to let you look at those notes at last?" I said. And he told me he'd been allowed to borrow them for the period of Mr Blakeney's absence in France, where he had gone to spend the long vacation.

'So of course I thought no more of it, until I discovered some days later, while snooping round my husband's study in the unpleasant fashion we females have, that he was in fact copying out all the documents in the folder, though these were in long hand and very hard to decipher. When I asked him for his reasons for undertaking this painfully laborious task, he told me to mind my distaff – an old-fashioned phrase of which I rather approved – and once more I thought no more of the matter . . . until Mr Blakeney came to dine with us at the beginning of the following term. Since the provision of food and drink which my husband allowed me to make for our guests was niggardly even for a notoriously sparse era, it was a wonder Mr Blakeney accepted the invitation; but accept it he did, and in the course of an otherwise unmemorable evening complained to us very bitterly of his bedmaker, who, he said, during his absence in France had poked her nose into a drawer which he had always forbidden to her and had spilt a large quantity of what looked like tea on a folder full of his war-time notes. Of course, he said, the wretched woman had denied it, but who else could it have been?

'It was then that I realized that my husband had been in possession of Mr Blakeney's documents without Mr Blakeney's knowledge or consent and must have returned them to Mr Blakeney's rooms, as stealthily as he had obtained them thence, some time before the latter returned from his tour. Since I was at that time very much in love with Robert Constable, I held my tongue in front of Mr Blakeney; and only after his departure did I tax my husband with the lie he had told me.

'His excuse for deceiving me was that he had not wished to worry me; his excuse for thieving from Mr Blakeney was that he had been, as he put it, about the world's work. It was possible, he said, that those records, if read and understood by the wrong people, might lead to the development of a rodent force which could be used against the working class in case of its protest or revolt. Perhaps such a development was already in hand. It was therefore essential to make the notes available to "correctly thinking people", by which my husband at that time meant left-wing elements only short of and perhaps partly comprehending the Communists themselves. This would enable them to anticipate the use of such a weapon against them and even, perhaps, to produce one themselves, to counter oppression and to further beneficent revolution. He had therefore, as a matter of socialist duty, "procured" and copied Mr Blakeney's notes unknown to Mr Blakeney and sent his copy off to "suitable recipients".'

'And who exactly were they?' asked Len.

'I never found out exactly, Mr Under-Collator, and I never

knew the exact scope of the information which my husband sent. Nor, as far as I am aware, has anybody, "suitable" or "correctly thinking" or of whatever other description, made any use of it. I have yet to hear of rats replacing soldiers. But you surely see the weight of what I am telling you? On evidence to which Mr Blakeney and myself can attest, my husband is guilty, at the very least, of stealing Mr Blakeney's notes, of copying and conveying them to a third party (no matter exactly to whom) without Mr Blakeney's knowledge or permission, and of illicitly entering Mr Blakeney's accommodation in order to replace the notes. Even if we leave aside any suggestion of crime or treason (and why should we?) my husband in any case stands convicted of flagrantly unprofessional conduct ... public knowledge of which would certainly bring about his ruin.'

There was a long silence.

'And you are prepared to ... show him up ... on this count? To *strip* him?' Ivor asked.

'I am prepared, with your assistance, to torment him. To let him know that if he wishes this matter to remain secret, he must obey my will and yours, Mr Winstanley, Mr Under-Collator, to obey anybody's will but his own will be to him a very grievous punishment.'

'Why have you chosen us as ... assistant chastisers?' said Ivor.

'*And* beneficiaries,' added Len.

'You will do as well as anyone. Your antics have considerably amused me. More important, I need someone to seek Mr Blakeney out, because without him to bear his part of the testimony, mine is useless. It would also be convenient if he could tell us where the stained notes now are. They would improve our case and add to our bargaining power.' She fingered and twisted the bright yellow beads on her necklace. 'They are not, by any chance, in this Chamber? He *could* have presented them to the College, I suppose?'

Len went over to the Catalogue.

'No,' he said. 'No trace of anything written or presented by Balbo Blakeney.'

'Try the College Library,' said Lady Constable.

Ivor rang up the Librarian.

'There's a typed copy of his paper on rats,' he said, 'the one he wrote when he returned here after the war.'

'That was the one that ruined his reputation,' said Elvira Constable, 'the one which nobody would heed or print, averring it to be lunacy.'

'I remember,' said Ivor. 'He produced it as a kind of memoir, long after he'd changed over to blood and alcohol.'

'In 1948,' said Lady Constable: 'about a year after the events of which I have just been telling you.'

'In any case, it can't possibly be what we're after?'

'No. We are looking for a fawn folder full of hand-written notes.'

'Then we're out of bloody luck,' said Len.

'Even if they were here,' said Lady Constable of Reculver Castle, 'we should still need Mr Blakeney himself ... to confirm that the tea stains were made in his absence, at a time when he had thought his notes were lying undisturbed in their drawer. Yes, gentlemen,' she pursued: 'Mr Blakeney must at all cost be found, and it needs someone shrewd and ruthless, someone with a snout well practised in truffling for misery and squalor, to find him. In a word, Mr Under-Collator, it needs you.'

'Lady, lady,' said Len, 'you slay me with your compliments. But I've no idea where to start.'

'He went to Crete,' said Elvira Constable. 'But more recent and accurate information is probably to be had at this address in Jermyn Street' – she passed Len a used envelope on which she had scribbled a number – 'an agent from which has been here to inquire after Mr Blakeney of my husband. One presumes that the agent must have got on his track by now, and that someone at that address can therefore tell you at least roughly where to look.'

'Why do these people in Jermyn Street want Balbo?'

'My husband quoted the agent as saying that "Rats are in fashion again".'

'That seems to fit all right,' Ivor said. 'They think he can

331

help them in something to do with rats – though he must be a bit rusty on the topic by now, and God knows why they should need such help.' He giggled foolishly. 'Perhaps "correctly minded" left wingers are at last making effective use of that information which the Provost sent them all those years ago. Did the agent seem at all suspicious of Lord Constable?'

'Quite definitely not. All he wanted was my husband's assistance in locating Mr Blakeney.'

'Perhaps it's him they suspect. Or perhaps, as Ive says, they just want his help in coping with some old rat situation, never mind what's caused it. But whatever their reason for wanting him,' said Len, 'they may also want to keep him to themselves. No way are they going to strain their ghoolies to help me and Ive.'

'If you present yourselves, and if Mr Winstanley explains in his best manner that Mr Blakeney is wanted for reasons of College business, I imagine they'll be pleased to give you what help they can.'

'I don't,' said Len. 'Organizations like this Jermyn Street don't rate College business as high as old-fashioned sweethearts like you. But' – he turned to Winstanley – 'it has to be worth a try. Find Balbo, confirm that he can support Lady C's story . . . though this, of course, will be the first he'll have heard of it, I hope he remembers those tea stains real good . . . find Balbo, I say, then blackmail His Lordship into keeping his cake-hole shut about those manuscripts and doing everything else we need to oblige us. And thereafter heigh-diddley-dee for the good life. What say, Ive, man? Surely worth a try?'

'Yes,' said Ivor: 'surely worth a try.'

'No time to lose,' said Lady Constable, swirling to her feet like a pre-Raphaelite apparition. 'I say, get cracking.'

'We'll spend the night in London,' said Ivor, 'and be at Jermyn Street first thing in the morning.'

'My god, these dreary Picassos,' Marigold said. 'Who would have thought the old man had so much shit in him?'

Marigold and Jacquiz were in the Picasso Room of the Musée Réattu, formerly a Priory of the Knights of Malta. The previous night at Albi had been restless. Marigold's sleep had been full of shadows and voices, of figures writhing on tombs and hideous cries of pleasure. By two in the morning she had been able to bear it no longer.

'We must leave now,' she said to Jacquiz. 'There is something or somebody that wants us to get on to Arles at once. That is why I am being tormented.'

So they had persuaded a reluctant and incompetent night-porter to make out a bill for them, and they had then driven on to Arles. When they arrived, at six in the morning, it had been too early, or so Marigold said, to book into an hotel. She had made Jacquiz park the Rolls by the public gardens and roam the streets with her, up the steps and past the Theatre, down the hill to the Arena, then across to St Trophîme and down again to the Baths of Constantine, where they mouldered by the River Rhône.

'Here,' she said; 'the house that Poppa Comminges came to with his new wife must have been round here.' She opened a green *Michelin* and consulted a plan. 'We know he lived in "a fair tall house" near the Priory,' she said. 'The Priory is a hundred yards along on the left.'

So they had walked down the street past the Priory and along the river.

'There are many fair tall houses,' Jacquiz said, 'and even if we knew which belonged to Poppa Comminges, how would that help us?'

'The family may still live there,' Marigold had said, and shivered fiercely.

Finally, Jacquiz persuaded her that they should go inside the Priory to the Musée Réattu, which had just opened, there to get warm and inquire of the curator, whether he knew of a fair, tall house in that neighbourhood which had once belonged to a *famille* Comminges.

But the curator, a woman with a short skirt and spindly

legs, had shaken her head stupidly when asked (in rather the same way, though they could not know this, as the clerk at the Jules César had responded to a similar question from Balbo Blakeney). Marigold had wanted to leave at once but Jacquiz had insisted on a quick round of the rooms. Other attendants, when questioned about the Comminges and their dwelling, had responded as sullenly as the curatrix, the attendant in the Picasso Room most sullenly of all.

'They all know something, I'm sure,' Marigold had said. 'My God, these dreary Picassos . . .'

'Let's find a hotel,' Jacquiz said.

They walked up the hill away from the river, through the Place du Forum, into a narrow street.

'Straight on for the main road,' said Marigold, wearily consulting her chart. 'Then we can turn left for where we put the car – which is almost opposite the Hôtel Jules César. I suppose we'd better stay in it. Though quite what we're going to do here, I don't know.'

'If we can't find the house,' said Jacquiz, 'we must hunt round all those places Louis and Constance went to on their journey to Pau. Aigues Mortes and the rest.'

'That would be going backwards. We want to move on . . . to wherever the Comminges went to when and if they left Arles. You know, Jacquiz darling, I'm sure those attendants all knew something. I'm sure the name of Comminges meant something to them. But they just weren't talking. They were trying to pretend, for whatever reason, that somebody or something did not exist. Perhaps a few hundred-franc notes might help.'

'There's the Museum of Christian Art,' said Jacquiz. 'Would you mind if we just popped in before going to the car? There's a sarcophagus I want to look at. It has a Christian motif on one side, Pagan the other; not altogether unusual, but a fine example.'

'Suits me,' Marigold said. She suddenly, for no reason at all, felt less defeated and depressed.

Inside the Museum, Jacquiz circled his sarcophagus warily.

'The last supper on this side,' he said, pointing to the low relief carving, 'and on the other Hermes guiding the soul of the dead man to the Elysian Fields.'

'Where do those steps go to? Marigold said.

'Down to the Cryptoporticus. Where a lot of these coffins once were.'

'There's someone coming up.'

But Jacquiz was more interested in Hermes. Marigold watched while a boy in a dark jacket, grey shorts and white knee socks emerged at the top of the steps. He stared at Marigold, briefly felt his penis, then turned away towards the exit.

'Surely,' she said, 'French schoolboys stopped wearing that rig years ago.'

'What can you mean?'

'The acolyte at Saint Bertrand.'

'Who? Where?'

'The gardener at Pau. We must follow him.'

Marigold hurried after the boy as he slipped out of the Museum; Jacquiz reluctantly started after Marigold. The white stockings turned left down the street, left down another, and left down another. Finally they turned left yet once more, into a portico.

'The Arlaten Museum,' said Marigold, glancing at *Michelin*. 'All the folklore. What a lot of culture for one morning.'

Inside the portico was a ticket office and inside the ticket office was a goitrous old man who said, disagreeably, that yes, a boy had indeed just come in and gone up the stairs, and, even more disagreeably, that no, he did not know of a local house belonging to anyone called Comminges, and, more or less civilly at last, that entrance was three francs a head for adults, which Jacquiz promptly paid.

'Did the boy pay?' asked Marigold, on impulse.

'No,' said the old man; and then, after a pause, 'He had a student's card.'

Jacquiz and Marigold went up the stairs and walked through several rooms which contained wax tableaux of

Provençal characters engaged in elementary activities. There was no sign of the boy in white stockings.

'It says in the *Michelin* that this place was started by a poet called Frédéric Mistral,' Marigold reported.

'He was potty. He wrote in the local lingo.'

'Not so potty but what he won a Nobel Prize. In 1896. That's how he got the money to set this up.'

'What are we doing here, Marigold?'

'Following the boy to see what turns up.'

'That's mad.'

'No. Frightening, rather. You see, it's the boy you saw yesterday in the Lautrec gallery in Albi.'

'How do you know? You didn't see him.'

'You said he was like the officer in the painting. So is this one. Younger, but almost identical. Anyway, I know. He's been with us for some time, you see.'

'No, I don't see . . . A very pretty boy?'

'Yes,' said Marigold. 'Frighteningly pretty. I think *this* must be Monsieur Mistral.'

On the wall was a huge canvas of the bull ring in the Roman Arena. A self-important man with a pointed beard and an operatic hat was arriving to take his seat, while everyone else stood up and clapped him.

'The French paying homage to letters,' said Jacquiz. 'I expect he commissioned it himself, in order to hang it here. Typical Frog conceit. Like Courbet painting that picture of local bigwigs bowing and scraping to Courbet.'

'Frédéric Mistral all right,' Marigold said, examining the black and white numbered diagram which hung beneath. 'Number One in the key. Jeee-sus, what a creep. I'm glad to say there's one man looking very sour and *not* clapping . . . and he is . . . Number Nine . . . Almighty God, Jacquiz, *sweet*, *sweet* heart, M'sieur Joseph Comminges.'

No, said the goitrous elder in the ticket office a few minutes later, he did not know anything about any Joseph Comminges, his forebears his house or his offspring.

'He was important enough,' said Jacquiz, 'to be very near M'sieur Mistral in the picture.'

The old man shrugged and pouted. His two goitres wobbled malignantly, rubbing against each other. Jacquiz produced a hundred-franc note. The old man hissed like a faulty tap. Jacquiz produced a five-hundred-franc note. The old man took it, then extracted the hundred-franc note from Jacquiz' other hand as an afterthought.

'It is our shame,' said the old man equably, 'and of it we do not speak. Of the Joseph Comminges in the picture all we need say is that he, like his ancestors, enjoyed some prosperity as a merchant but was subject to maladies, many kinds of which seemed much to afflict his family. He has sick headache, a migraine, in the picture. That is why he is scowling; no one would otherwise dare scowl at the great Mistral.'

'What's so shaming about any of this?' Marigold inquired.

'His grandson, madame. His grandson is still with us in Arles. He is a priest.'

'How eminently respectable.'

'He is a man of strange beliefs and strange arts. He has *les maladies de la famille* worse than any before him. He is . . . *maudit*, madame. And yet, despite all his traffic, despite the – the *visiteurs du soir* that come at his summons, the Church still respects him. He is the Right Reverend Monsignor Comminges, also the Very Reverend the Canon Resident of the Cathedral of Saint Trophîme. We do not understand it, and naturally we do not like to speak of it to *étrangers*.' He paused, then looked down at the banknotes in his hand, evidently decided that he had not yet given full value, and with a truly French respect for money proceeded to complete the package, just as a restaurateur might deem it only proper to throw in *petit fours* with the coffee for those taking any menu at over 100 francs. 'That boy who came in here before you,' he snuffled furtively, 'is Canon Comminges' nephew – or so he is sometimes called. There is also a niece. But how can there be nephew or niece when Monsignor Comminges is an only child of an only child, the only surviving Comminges of them all? The girl I have hardly seen, of the boy I know only this for certain, that he is – how do you say? – a familiar, a messenger of the Right Reverend Monsignor, and that he comes and goes, with or without message or mission, exactly as he pleases. It was not true, what I told you, that he had a student's card. I admitted him for very fear.'

'We didn't see him up there.'

The old man crossed himself over his goitres and spat; then told Jacquiz and Marigold where they might, at a need, find the Canon.


'So now we are all assembled,' said Canon Comminges, his voice buzzing and burring through his linen mask. 'Doctor and Mrs Helmut, welcome. Mr Blakeney and Mr Jones, my renewed greeting. You have all displayed ingenuity and persistence in order to come here, and I trust that your efforts will shortly prove to have been worth while.'

Well, well, well, Balbo Blakeney thought: Jewy Jake Helmut and a fizzing new wife. When Jacquiz and Marigold had been ushered in by the girl in black only a few moments after his own arrival with Sydney, Balbo's first feeling was one of amazement – what in hell was Jacquiz doing here? – and his second one of embarrassment. After all, Helmut would certainly remember the squalid scandal which had led to Balbo's expulsion from Lancaster. But after Jacquiz had greeted him quite civilly (though not without reciprocal surprise) and the new wife had given him a lively smile, Balbo felt reassured on the latter count and less resentful on the former. Helmut, he told himself, was known as an historical scholar with a strong inclination towards the rare, the beautiful and the bizarre; and the Roses of Picardie were therefore quite definitely his dish (as Sydney might have put it) though God alone knew how and where he had come in on the whole caper. And what, one might ask oneself, was his precise motive? Scholarship or pelf? There were also a good many more somewhat pressing questions (what about the little girl who had shown them up, for a start?); but surely there must now be every chance, Balbo thought, that if one could stomach the creature in the shroud for the next hour or two, either he or another would come across with the answers.

'Before I tell you anything further,' pursued the Canon, 'about the matter which has brought you all here, I shall say a brief prayer to God and His Servants to guide us to good intent and good understanding. *Audi nos, Domine, si tua est voluntas, vel iube Servos Tuos nos audire . . .*'

That Balbo Blakeney, Marigold thought: oh, those cherubic cheeks and kind, sad eyes. Yes I know I'm trying to love Jacquiz very much just now, but there are times, *there are just times*, when a girl feels like an hour or two's change.

'. . . *Igitur te precamur,*' droned the Canon, '*ut nos omnes sancta sophia Tua impleas ad gratiam Tuam penitus fundas in animas animosque . . .*'

The sheila fancies my old Balbo, thought Syd Jones: well, jolly good luck to both of them. That, as it happened, was the very least of Syd's troubles: for it had now appeared to him that all the elements were present of a very considerable muddle. What with this Canon character who couldn't or wouldn't show his physog (impetigo? deformity? pox?), and what with this nun-girl who seemed to have been popping up all over the place, and what with the appearance of Doctor Jacquiz come lately Helmut from Balbo's old College (what game was *he* playing? Sydney wondered) never mind his pert little madame – what with all this and Jermyn Street too, it was very important, Sydney felt, to arrange one's thoughts with care. Very well then. One: he must let Jermyn Street know, as soon as he got out of the Canon's lodging, that Balbo's forehead was starting to crinkle and that he had definitely lost the Sign. Two: he must not, however, leave in a hurry or before anyone else, in case he missed something. Three: if Theta meant what he said last night (that in the event of Balbo's losing the Sign Jones was simply to hang about with him and telephone in twice a day from wherever they might happen to be), then there was a very good chance of a ringside seat for whatever might happen next. Four: surely one had to face the fact that

Balbo's loss of the Sign could, just could, mean trouble for him with his rodent subjects-cum-worshippers; for even though he had broken his connection with them many years before, had they broken *their* connection with him? Five: one must therefore be very wary lest . . . well, lest exactly what? Since Jones could not answer this question, he settled for just wary. Six: one must also be pretty leery of the Canon, who, whatever his physical or facial disqualifications, was evidently pretty cute at working out arrangements – witness the almost simultaneous arrival here of all four of his petitioners, a consummation which his manner and tone implied to have been brought about by his deliberate contrivance. So watch your step, Jonesy boy, said Jones to Jones, S., and don't let yourself be fobbed off with fibs and fiddles when question time comes round.

'. . . *Neve obliviscamur,*' the Canon was saying in a very earnest voice, '*Comitum Tuorum, sub te, Domine, positorum sed plane Te Ipso editorum, Seraphorum et Cheruborum, Principatuum et Potestatium, Sedelium et Dominationum, Archangelorum Angelorumque, eorum qui viribus manibusque terrestrem mundun gubernant, Te remoto spectante. Sed Unius simus memores super omnes, in opere hoc ad quod iam accedimus, Illius qui pallidulas mortuorum animas ducere, vincere, condere, praebere, tandem de profundis solvere per Te potest. Per Christum et Omnes Dominos Nostros, Amen.*'

' "Nor let us forget",' Jacquiz translated to himself, ' "Thy Companions set beneath Thee, Lord, but surely sprung from Thee, the Seraphim and Cherubim, Principalities and Powers, Thrones and Dominions, Archangels and Angels, those who govern the physical world with their strengths and by their hands, while Thou dost watch from afar. But of One above all else let us be mindful, in this task which we now draw near – of Him Who, through Thee, is empowered to lead, bind, hide, show forth, and at last to loose from the depths the pale souls of the dead. Through Christ and all our Lords . . ." '

Eccentric, to say the least, Jacquiz thought. He thinks God

leaves the care of the physical universe to certain semi-divinities or underlings which he created, and watches only from afar. He believes in a Lord of the Dead – whom he has just invoked. Not quite the Devil, I dare say, but not far off it: 'empowered to loose from the depths ... *de profundis*'. The man's a raging Manichee: after all these centuries the Comminges are still Cathars, or near enough to be going on with if you bend a point here and there. Well, thought Jacquiz, it looks as if he's going to come to the meat of the matter at any minute. Listen hard now, and think about other problems later: poor old Balbo, for example, not exactly a problem, perhaps even an asset, but undoubtedly a new factor, to say nothing of his friend. And another thing: where's that girl who showed us in, and what's become of that boy – the 'nephew'? If he was appointed (as his 'uncle's' familiar or messenger) to lead us here, why did he have to do it in such a roundabout and chancy way? But never mind any of that for now: just listen to this abominable priest.

Monsignor Bernard Comminges, the Very Reverend Canon Resident of the Cathedral of St Trophîme, crossed himself after his concluding apostrophe and surveyed his audience through the twin holes in his mask.

'This' – he pointed to the speckled linen which covered his face – 'has been inflicted on me by the Curse which attends the Ruby Necklace known to us and to the world as the Roses of Picardie. It is not, as some of you may have assumed, the ravages of the Italian Lazar or the Raw-Boned Knight of England or whatever charming euphemism we may select to designate the American disease; it is the final stage of an undiagnosed sickness of the skin that has failed to yield to – indeed has positively been nourished by – all the most powerful drugs prescribed by modern science.

'At the same time, I should remark, I enjoy many benefits of the type traditionally conferred by the Roses. I am highly placed in the Church, I hold an office which accords well with my tastes and temperament, I am protected, or at least tolerated, by my ecclesiastical superiors despite my heterodox theories and the hostility of the local populace. I am also extremely well situated in all temporal and monetary matters. For all this I have the Roses to thank. After all, it takes a very powerful influence indeed to reconcile the Vatican to a Monsignor who habitually pronounces neo-Albigensian doctrines—'

'—Does anyone come to listen, sport?' said Jones, S.

'—Very few. But the doctrines are pronounced, and are known to be pronounced, alienating many of the faithful. Yet I remain, by favour of the Roses, a Canon-Resident of a venerable and beautiful Cathedral Church. That is much.'

The Canon paused. He quivered slightly, then suddenly clutched at his mask. After a few seconds his hands began to sink, slowly and painfully as though forced down by some huge effort of the will, and eventually clasped one another in the Canon's lap.

'It is much,' he growled through the linen, 'but it is not enough. Not enough to compensate me for the relentless torment and foul humiliation of my illness. In order to be rid of that evil, I will gladly be rid' – he gestured widely round the richly tapestried chamber – 'of this good. I must be rid of the Curse and if needs be of the Blessing as well. I must be rid of the Roses of Picardie.'

He thrust himself forward in his chair, picked up a poker and hacked viciously at the fire.

'So I said to myself,' he continued, 'I shall restore them whence they came. We know, from the old records, that they were once in the possession of the family of the Counts de la Tour d'Abbéville; it was not too difficult to trace the last survivor of that line who was capable of receiving, or rather of collecting, the necklace. I sent for the Vicomte du Touquet in order to tell him where it was and to bid him take it; for although it was not (and is not) here with me, only when it was removed, by another, from the place where I, its present inheritor, knew (and know) it to be – only then would the Curse be lifted from me. Or so I believed. And so I summoned du Touquet to do what I wished.'

'But before he even reached you,' Balbo said, 'he was battered to pieces in Aix-en-Provence.'

'After he had left me,' corrected the Monsignor, 'after he had been told where to find the Rubies and was already on his way to collect them – it was then that he died. Clearly, his knowledge and potential possession made him eligible for both Curse and Blessing, both of which, in his case, took a particularly swift and violent form.'

'Rather hard on him,' said Marigold. 'Knowledge or no, he hadn't even set eyes on them. Or could he have?'

'No,' said the Canon, 'he could not. The Roses are a very long way from here, much further than Aix-en-Provence. The reason why both Curse and Blessing operated so fiercely, on one who merely knew where the Stones were hidden, was probably that Clovis du Touquet came of a line whose ancestors had connived at the original theft of the Jewels from the Jew of Antioch *and* the Jew's murder. Later, when the Rubies came into their hands, although they well knew where to find the Jew's heirs, they kept the treasure for themselves. Morally speaking, it was as though Clovis's family had itself stolen the jewels from the Jew.'

'*Your* family also stole the jewels,' said Jacquiz, 'stole them from Constance, wife of Louis, after hideously murdering her one way or another. Yet neither Curse nor Blessing seems to have been so monstrous with the House of Comminges.'

'Yes, we stole them, Doctor Helmut. But not from a rightful owner. The last rightful owner, as far as we know, was the Jew of Antioch. Naturally, his Curse must be much more powerful against the line of those connected with the original thieves and murderers than against those who have merely come by the jewels through a chain of later thieves.'

'And the Blessing? How do you account for the varied intensity of *its* operation?'

'That the Blessing operates at all,' said the Canon, 'has always been and remains a mystery. Meanwhile, please let me continue. It seemed to me that the brutal death of Clovis du Touquet was a sign to me that it would not be enough to

343

give the Roses away just to anyone at all, or even to a descendant of previous possessors; if the Curse was to be lifted from me, the Roses must be restored to someone of the line of the *last rightful owner,* the Jew of Antioch aforesaid. But how was I to find any of his descendants? There was need of more than learning, more than mere detection here. So for many weary months I have been conducting certain . . . experiments; and I believe that very soon now I may have the knowledge which I seek.' He eyed them all and chuckled, like a frog cackling at the approach of rain. 'It was in the course of my search that I learned, incidentally but quite explicably, that, you Mr Blakeney, and you, Doctor Helmut, with your respective companions, were on your way.'

'How did you learn that?' said Marigold.

'It will all be made plain, Mrs Helmut, as time goes on.'

'That boy?'

'Pray be patient, Mrs Helmut. I learned of, permitted, and indeed in some ways assisted your approach; for I had decided that your assiduity and ingenuity made you all worthy of the honour of being present when I finally discovered the rightful heir to the Rubies and then bestowed them upon him. It might even be that someone among you . . . one whom I trust . . . being stronger and more able to travel than I, might assist me in the bestowal. As to that, we shall see. Meanwhile, the final discovery has yet to be made, the final experiment to be performed. Tonight? Yes, why not tonight? I invite you all to wait on me tonight.'

'There are one or two things,' said Jones, S., 'that we'd all very much like to know first. Like about that girl Balbo and I saw. And in Doctor Helmut's case there seems to have been a boy—'

'—A nephew of yours somebody said he was—'

'—And lots of other little matters,' said Jacquiz, 'which patently require elucidation.'

'All in good time, lady and gentlemen. Such questions must wait. I must retire to rest myself for what lies before me.' The Canon rose. How upright he stands, Marigold thought. 'Let all attend,' he said, 'at the Church of Saint

Honorat in the Fields of Alyssum at the last stroke of midnight. Attend me there or stay away for ever.'

'The Fields of Alyssum?' said Syd Jones.

'Otherwise called the Fields of Elysium, in either case Les Alyscamps.'

'But they're closed,' said Balbo, 'at dusk. Fenced in and the gate locked.'

'So that you frightful Frogs can charge admission, I suppose,' said Marigold; 'whatever one's being admitted to,' she added doubtfully.

'You will see what you are being admitted to, madame, in due course. Be worthy of it. As for you, Mr Blakeney, know this: the gates will indeed be locked but they will be opened on the password.'

The Canon now stalked to and fro among them, murmuring:

> 'Dans Arles, où sont Les Aliscams
> Quand l'ombre est rouge, sous les roses,
>   Et clair le temps,

> 'Prende garde à la douceur des choses,
> Lorsque tu sens battre sans cause
>   Ton coeur trop lourd,

> 'Et que se taisent les colombes:
> Parle tout bas, si c'est d'amour,
>   Au bord des tombes.

'There is your password,' said the Canon: 'Au bord des tombes.'

After the Canon had issued his invitation, he ushered his guests down the rows of statues to the door of his great chamber and remarked that they would know their own way out of the Cloister. There was no sign of the girl who had shown them all in, nor of the 'nephew'.

When they reached the street, Balbo offered to accompany Jacquiz and Marigold to their car and help them install themselves in the Jules César. The offer was well received, and everyone was glad that Balbo and Jacquiz were making intelligent efforts to turn what might have been an embarrassing encounter into a pleasant if unsought reunion. Presumably, thought Sydney Jones, Helmut and his wife will now ask Balbo for some explanation of myself. In all the circumstances, he felt that Balbo might as well tell the exact truth, and to this effect, in a brief aside, he instructed him; after which he announced to the party at large that he had an urgent telephone call to make, and then immediately went back to his bedroom in the Jules César to make it.

Theta took Jones's call when it came through from Arles. Having questioned Sydney very closely about the faint new furrows that had now appeared on Balbo's brow, and having conferred awhile with Lambda, he told Sydney that it must now be taken as certain that the godhead had deserted Balbo. He then repeated the instructions which he had given the previous evening. Balbo might now go wherever and do whatever he pleased, Theta said, but Sydney must accompany him closely throughout the day, insist on a bedroom adjacent to Balbo's at night, and telephone in to Jermyn Street every day around noon and seven p.m.

After he had given these orders to Jones over the telephone, Theta left Lambda and Q in his office and went to a small waiting-room, where Ivor Winstanley was sitting with Len.

'Let's get this clear,' Theta said: 'what do you want with Blakeney?'

'As Temporary Collator of the Manuscripts of Lancaster College,' said Ivor truthfully enough, 'I need information from Mr Blakeney about the present whereabouts and past provenance of certain important documents.'

'Important documents?' Theta's voice rattled like a bag of plastic draughtsmen. 'Scientific documents?'

'Yes. Rough notes on experiments.'

Theta thought very carefully. He looked at Ivor and he looked at Len and then he said:

'If you found out where these papers were, you would be prepared to let us have a look at them? In return for our assistance?'

'You haven't been of any assistance,' said Len.

'But if we were?'

'I see no reason,' Ivor said, 'why you shouldn't be shown them.'

'Yup,' supplemented Len; 'you goose us, we goose you.'

'Excellent. Now, would both of you go to Blakeney? If not, which?'

'Me,' said Len. 'Ive will be minding the shop.'

'Very well,' said Theta. 'Please wait a little longer.'

Theta returned to Lambda and Q. He told them of his conversation with Ivor and Len about Balbo's notes.

'It is at least possible,' said Lambda, 'that they might provide a valuable extension to his thesis, which is largely a theoretical afterthought. A few hard chemical and physiological details might be very helpful.'

'But surely,' said Q, 'Jones can find out for us about them. We don't need to let these dons loose in Arles.'

'Only one of them will go,' said Theta, 'the younger one, not yet a don, by the way, and he, to judge by the look of him, is just what we *do* need to let loose in Arles. We have, you remember, to procure a piece of Blakeney's bodily tissue or of his clothing.'

'Preferably both,' Lambda said.

'If we send one of our own men,' said Theta, 'Jones will probably recognize him and, with his knowledge of the affair, guess what kind of thing we're up to. In which case, being Jones' – a fond look flickered briefly on Theta's face – 'he would watch our man like a kestrel and protect Blakeney from him. But if we send someone who purports to be, who *is*, an emissary from Blakeney's old College inquiring about manuscript papers, Jones will suspect nothing and the emissary can help himself to Blakeney's hairbrush or whatnot at leisure.'

'You think this man will accept the assignment? And how will you explain our request? It is ... rather peculiar.'

'I shan't attempt to explain it. I shall tell him what we want and what we will pay in money down. I shall also tell him,' said Theta, 'that people who oblige us seldom regret it, and I shall then draw the obvious corollary. It is the kind of talk that he will understand.'

'So there it is, Provost,' said Ivor Winstanley, back in Cambridge some three hours after his visit with Len to Jermyn Street. 'We don't want to cause any scandal. We just want to settle things tidily.'

'Let us assume,' said Lord Constable, in the tones of a mathematician who states his data before proceeding to a formal proof, 'let us assume that Balbo remembers the incident (which he may not) and so can confirm that the folder was tampered with. Let us further assume that the folder and the notes can still be produced, despite all that has since happened to Balbo. If, Ivor, *if*, I say, these assumptions hold good then there is, I should agree, a very strong case to answer. Rather than try to answer it, I should be prepared to come to terms.' He gave the impression, Ivor thought, of being a lawyer who was representing somebody else, of being himself a man of total probity a million miles removed from any taint or sense of guilt. 'In that event,' Constable said, 'what would your terms be?'

'First, that the theft of the Saint Gilles Breviary and The Wandrille Georgics be ignored from now on and totally hushed up.'

'The Third Bursar already knows of it.'

'So may others, by now. But all that is necessary is for you to tell them that consultations have been made in the proper quarters, that the matter is in good hands, and that if there is to be any hope of recovering the volumes, the less noise the better. They will accept that from you without question and

348

aren't in the Chamber or the Library; but even if they no longer exist, Elvira and Balbo should be able to make the story stick – provided Balbo is cooperative. Well, I think I can see to that, Len thought, though the Jermyn Street guy who's already with him may be rather a nuisance. Let's have no botching, Lenny boy, because a lot depends on this: Ive's fellowship; Jake's tenure (not that I give a fuck for Jake, but if Ive wants him seen okay, then I want him seen okay); and your own secure enjoyment, little Lenny, of the money you've netted for the Breviary – to say nothing of the Georgics to gloat over. In time, of course, the Georgics may have to go for money; and that's why it would be good to do more work for these Jermyn Street operators – keep farm-fresh greenbacks floating into the kitty. But as to all that, we shall see. The job just now, thought Len, as he drove past the drowsy dun farmhouses in their twilight groves of umbrella pine, the job just now is to move in like a rattlesnake on Balbo Blakeney in the Hôtel Jules César in Arles.

'But what on earth is he going to do?' said Marigold for the seventeenth time.

Balbo, Jones, S., Marigold and Jacquiz were all about to dine together in the restaurant of the Jules César.

'One thing's certain,' said Sydney: 'he's not going to produce the sparklers. They're not here,' he said, 'or anywhere near here.'

'Not in his immediate possession,' said Balbo; 'but apparently deemed to belong to him by . . . by whatever does the cursing and the blessing.'

'If we're to believe what he said,' said Jacquiz, 'he is going to conduct some kind of experiment which will finally reveal the "rightful owner" of the necklace – *i.e.* some descendant of the Jew of Antioch. Now, if we consider the place, the time and the rather dubious reputation of the Right Reverend Monsignor, we conclude, I think, that magic is in the air.'

'Black magic?' said Marigold, making huge eyes.

'Not necessarily. Official Catholic doctrine condemns all magic, but in practice one may recognize that magic undertaken for a benevolent purpose can be classed as "white" or at least as "grey". The Canon's declared aim, to give the Roses back where they belong, is at any rate equitable.'

'He also hopes to shift the Curse,' said Jones.

'Off himself but not on to anyone else,' Balbo replied. 'The rightful owner will not be subject to the Curse.'

'Still, his motive is not wholly altruistic,' pronounced Jacquiz; 'therefore his magic will be grey.'

'That,' said Balbo balefully, 'may well depend on his method. As Jacquiz implies, his choice of venue is – well – *curious*.'

'What is this place, the Alyscamps?' Marigold asked.

'A pagan necropolis,' Balbo told her, 'which later became one of the most famous cemeteries in Christendom. Roland is supposed to have been miraculously transported and buried there. There used to be hundreds of sarcophagi, buried and unburied; but in the sixteenth century connoisseurs started picking them up cheap from the City Fathers–'

'–The coffins were *sold?*' protested Marigold. 'How shocking.'

'I don't know. Better be sold off to decorate an agreeable garden than left behind while the cemetery was cut to bits by railway lines and housing estates. That's what happened later. Small factories went up too – and they pushed through a smelly canal. All that's left of the Alyscamps now is an avenue with sarcophagi on either side, one or two of a score or so chapels, and the ruins of Saint Honorat at the end. "A broken chancel with a broken cross",' Balbo concluded abruptly.

'And yet there was that lovely poem he said to us,' said Marigold. 'I don't know much French but ... I wanted to cry. *Parle tout bas*,' she quoted, '*si c'est d'amour*–'

'–Evening all,' said a voice.

Everyone turned and looked at Len, who was standing behind Marigold. Of those present, Marigold had once and briefly known Len very intimately, but never well; Jacquiz had known him well, at least on a professional level, and for quite a long time, but never intimately; Balbo vaguely recognized his face; and Jones, S., did not know him from Adam.

''llo, Marigold ducks,' said Len, pressing her shoulder. 'How do, Jake? Didn't expect to see you here. No one said.'

Marigold grinned rather desperately. Jacquiz nodded. Len turned to Balbo.

'Having a fling with old chums, are we?' Len surmised. 'And who's this?' He looked at Sydney. 'No, don't tell me, you're Jones, S., of Glamorgan, I once saw your pic in the paper, when you retired.'

'Clever of you to remember,' said Syd.

'I'm good at faces, that's what it is,' said Len, who had in fact been told all about Jones by Theta. 'Make a hole somewhere, folks. Little Lenny is hungry for his dinner.'

Sydney and Marigold, who were next to each other at the round table, exchanged glances and shifted their chairs. Len seized a chair from a neighbouring table, rammed it into the gap, moved past Marigold with much contact of thighs, sat down, flicked his fingers at a passing waiter and smiled insolently round the table.

'What in the name of God are you doing here?' said Jacquiz.

'I might ask you the same question. I was sent here to see Balbo Blakeney. College business. Your office kindly obliged with his whereabouts,' said Len to Jones. He flicked his fingers again, and considerably to everyone's annoyance was promptly handed a *carte* by the Maître in person. 'Appropriate you should be here, though,' said Len to Jacquiz. 'We're trying to raise some old papers of Balbo's for inclusion in the Chamber . . . in a manner of speaking. Details after din-din, if anyone's interested.' He looked at the *carte*, then handed it across the table. 'I expect you speak the lingo, Jake. Just tell him I'll have the second most expensive item for each course – Ive says that's a sound way to play it. And a bottle of his second most expensive bubbly.'

Confronted with twice as many people as he had expected, Len decided that his business with Balbo had better be plainly stated to all four of them. After all, Jacquiz, and by extension Marigold, also stood to benefit and must surely be on his side; and as for Jones, an instinct told Len, before he was half way through his Terrine des Poissons, that Jones would go along with whatever Balbo wanted. So if Balbo was going to be helpful, that was fine; and if he wasn't going to be, well, things would get rough anyway and there would be no point in trying to keep anything from Jones, S., of Glam.

He therefore gave a clear account, over coffee and cognac, of what Provost Constable had been planning for Jacquiz and what part Ivor Winstanley had been bullied into playing. Then, omitting the theft of the two manuscripts, he described how Ivor had determined to revolt and how Elvira Constable had unexpectedly come to their aid with her tale of Constable's monstrous behaviour with Balbo's notes.

'So the question is,' said Len to Balbo, 'will you help us? Will you support Elvira's story, and can you put your hand on that folder with the tea-stained notes? I'll just pop off to the loo and give you a few minutes to think it over.'

Balbo had left his room key on the dinner table when they rose to go into the hotel lounge for coffee, and Len had loitered and snapped it up. He now departed to Balbo's room, opened it, took a dirty pair of socks from the bottom of Balbo's wardrobe, a few strands of hair from his comb, and a used strip of Elastoplast, which had a faint stain of blood on it, from the wastepaper basket in the bathroom. Blood they should appreciate, thought Len, whatever they may be up to; let's hope they'll be pleased with little Lenny.

He then went to his own room, put his pickings in a large envelope provided by Jermyn Street, sealed it with Sellotape also provided by Jermyn Street, and zipped it into the overnight bag which, complete with washing gear, fresh shirt, pyjamas, pants, socks, brush and comb; and tie, Q had obtained for him from a special store in the department just before he was driven off to Heathrow.

The envelope he would deliver to Jermyn Street when he returned the next day. Meanwhile, with his official mission now fully on schedule, he returned to the party in the lounge to see how his personal business was marching. He found that everyone, including Jones, was very amused by the notion of checkmating Lord Constable in the manner proposed.

'I always thought Elvira would rebel sooner or later,' said Jacquiz; 'for the last ten or twelve years she's been simply a servant.'

'What I won't forgive is his meanness to Ivor,' Balbo said.

'Hear, hear,' said Len.

'What about his meanness to me?' said Jacquiz.

'You can take care of yourself. Ivor, for all his worldliness, is too innocent.'

'Hear, hear,' said Len again. 'So you'll stand by Elvira's story?'

'I will.'

'And what about the folder? Can you put your hands on it?'

'Not at once. It's deposited, with a few other things, with my friend Pandelios in Heracleion.'

'How soon can you get it?'

'That depends,' said Balbo, and glanced at Jones.

'Could you give me a letter to this Pandelios, authorizing me to take the folder?'

Balbo hesitated.

'We want everything sewn up tight,' said Len, 'as soon as possible.'

'All right,' said Balbo reluctantly. 'I've got pen and paper in my room.' He rose, as did Jones. 'Damn. I've left the key in the dining-room.'

'Key's on the floor,' said Len, pretending to pick it up and passing it over. 'Must have fallen out of your pocket.'

'Thanks.'

'Jacquiz,' said Marigold, 'please get me my handbag. I left it in our bathroom, I think.'

Jacquiz looked troubled. Marigold smiled.

'Please,' she said.

Jacquiz rose and went.

Marigold brought her shining face very close to Len's spotty one. She put her hands on the insides of his thighs and scratched lightly with her finger nails.

'Nice Len, lovely Len,' she said. 'O lovely, beautiful Len . . .'


'What's in it for you?' said Syd Jones to Balbo. 'You write this letter, that chap Len collects your folder of notes from this Pandelios chap in Crete—'

'You met him, didn't you? Shall I send him your regards?'

'—And then on the strength of those, everyone starts screwing up Lord Constable, or rather, getting their way with him, which comes to the same thing. But what do you get?'

'I quite liked Ivor Winstanley,' said Balbo, 'and I quite liked Jacquiz Helmut. I don't want to see them fucked up. Come to that, I rather liked Constable too – he was quite generous to me when things were bad – but I don't mind seeing him put in his place for this once.'

Balbo finished writing the letter to Pandelios. He signed it, added a greeting from Sydney (' "Here's piss in yer socks from Syd, cobber" – an interesting example of the pseudo-Australian vernacular'), and put it in an hotel envelope.

'I'll tell you an interesting thing,' he said to Sydney. 'Those people – we don't know who they were, but they were probably Communists – those people to whom Constable leaked my notes . . . if they had tried out some of the lines which the results of the experiments suggested, then they could . . . they could, Sydney . . . have produced rats of this new strain that's occupying Canterbury Cathedral. Some of my experiments were to do with producing scavenger rats who would serve the purpose of cleaning up devastated areas by eating all animal corpses, if possible bones and all. This was when the back-room boys were working towards the atom bomb –

though of course I didn't realize that at the time – and they were envisaging huge areas of contamination and decay, bigger than had ever been known in history. Put the rats in, you see, and let them take at any rate the top off the mess before they themselves die on the job.'

'You'd still have had the rats to clear up.'

'They were going to be trained to incinerate themselves, only we never got that far with it. But you see what I'm getting at? If the Russkies or anyone else had the use of my notes, then an attempt to produce "bones and all" scavengers might well have produced a strain which liked very old corpses and *skeletons*. Which is what, it seems, you've got in Canterbury. Perhaps I'd better have a look at those notes myself before we go there.'

'We're not going there,' said Jones, S.

'You mean – they've dealt with the problem?'

'No. I mean you can't help them any more. Not at Canterbury. So the pressure's off. You're free to go where you like for as long as you like.'

'Good.'

'Not good. Why do you think I'm still here? Why do you think they're letting me stay with you and go on treating you?'

Balbo was silent.

'They want me to watch what happens, Balbo. You see, you've lost the Sign we spoke of. It's clean gone. They want to know what will happen next.'

'Nothing will happen next. I've never really believed in that Sign.'

'Take it from me: you had it and it's gone.'

'Even so, it's years, thirty years, since I worked with them; and only two or three years less since I finished my thesis about them. Since then I've had nothing to do with them. I can mean nothing at all to them.'

'Lets hope you're right.'

'From what I can see, my chance of finding out about the Rubies constitutes a far greater danger than any rats. Look what they've done to the Canon. It seems that the Curse can

357

affect anyone who ... comes in range, so to speak, with some sort of claim on them. Look how they killed Clovis. I've been looking for them; they might reckon that as a claim, they might reckon me as rightful an object of the Curse as they reckoned him.'

'Rubbish,' said Sydney. 'At the moment all you're doing is waiting, with the rest of us, while the Canon tries to discover to whom they really and truly belong. They can't hold that against you.'

But what Syd Jones was really thinking was this: if the tales we've been hearing should be true – and of course they can't be, it's all a load of crocodile crap – but *if* some small part of it all *should be* somehow true, then no one who gets near those Rubies, who even gets near just knowing where they are, is safe; and another thing: the Curse has a way of using the means that come easily and logically to hand – which in Balbo's case could be his quondam subjects and worshippers, the rats.

'... So it's because I want you so badly,' Marigold said to Len, 'because I long for the things you've done to me and could do again, that I am humbling myself to you, here in this hotel lounge, confessing my sheer lust for you and begging you not to take advantage of it. Begging you not to tempt me any more but to let me go.'

'Why don't you just let it rip? We could go to my room for a few minutes later on. No one would miss us, and it wouldn't much matter if they did.'

'Once it would not have mattered. Now it would. The journey I have just made ... am still making ... with my husband, a weird, exciting, happy journey, has made the difference. Because of it I am trying to love Jacquiz, and even if I cannot quite succeed, I cannot again hurt him. Please ... lovely, beautiful, adorable Len ... let me go.'

She shrank back into her chair and huddled there, looking at him with huge, watery eyes.

'Okay,' said Len, 'I'll not stretch a finger. On one condition: you tell me what's going on.'

'Nothing that concerns you.'

'Look, sweetheart. I've come here on business to Balbo Blakeney . . . who has some kind of agent with him that's been tagging him all across Europe. I also find my old boss from the Chamber of Manuscripts – whom, incidentally, I'm busy protecting in a roundabout way– and his randy wife. I find them all sitting in the same hotel, conspiring like a whole gang of Guy Fawkeses and sweating with excitement at the same dinner table. I also notice that Balbo Blakeney, my man of prime interest just now, once the lushiest lush who was ever tossed out of Lancaster College into the garbage bin, is at the table and not underneath it, drinking indeed, but only like any other moderate middle-aged gent. So miracles may happen, sweetheart, but don't tell me that nothing's going on or that it doesn't concern little Lenny.'

Jacquiz entered the lounge, carrying Marigold's handbag. Through another entrance came Balbo and Sydney, Balbo carrying the letter.

'I haven't time to tell you, Len.'

'You tell me, baby, or I'll turn you on like a geyser right under Jake's Jewish nose.'

'Follow us when we leave the hotel tonight. We're going to walk to a sort of graveyard place called the Alyscamps – just before midnight. There's a password – *Au bord des tombes*. Let us get clear, then say it at the gate, and you'll be let in. I can't explain any more; you'll just have to see for yourself.'

Len rose, took the proffered letter from Balbo, and said thank you very politely.

'All right if I go on to Heracleion at once?' he said. He glanced at the address on the envelope. 'You think he'll be at home?'

'If not, his wife will know where he is.'

'Okay, Balb. That's great,' said Len. Then to Jacquiz, 'I want you to know, Jake, that Ive and I will do our very best. You'll be back where you belong, in the Chamber of Manuscripts, you take it from me.' And to Jones, S., 'It's been swell meeting you, Syd. I wish you many runs and wickets in the Great Game which you're now playing.' And last, to the seated Marigold, 'Good-bye, Mrs Helmut.' He raised her hand to within an inch of his lips with an exquisite grace, then bowed elegantly to the gentlemen. 'Manners,' he grinned at the gaping company: 'I have them when I want them. Dear Ivor is giving me lessons.'


The Tracery Gate which guarded the entrance to the Alyscamps was locked. There was no sign of anyone who might have been waiting to open it, though a nearly full moon threw a clear light on all the approaches. A small chapel, which stood a few yards beyond the gate and had apparently been turned into a lodge, was unlit in any of its windows.

'Nobody around,' said Jones, S.

'Just say the password,' Marigold suggested, 'and see what happens.'

'*Au bord des tombes,*' said Jacquiz, in a low, firm voice.

There was a brief buzz, then a snap of metal. The gate idled open.

'Operated from a distance,' said Balbo, 'like the front doors of those houses which have been split into separate flats.'

'Only there,' said Marigold, 'you have to ring a bell first and talk into a machine, so that the person you want can hear you. How did anyone hear Jacquiz just now? And where's the switch that must have been pressed?'

'In there?' said Balbo, pointing at the lodge.

'Empty, by the look of it,' said Jacquiz. 'No point in asking unanswerable questions. Let's just press on to the Church.'

Two by two (Jacquiz with Jones and Balbo with Marigold) they walked down the avenue between the rows of sullen-lipped sarcophagi. The autumn trees muttered along their ranks, as if expressing surprise and suspicion that a party should be walking beneath them at such an hour as this; and the moon, briefly streaked by an occasional cloud, shone through the hollow, round-arched tower that capped the ruins of St Honorat's, transforming it into a lantern hung from on high to mark the pilgrims' goal.

From behind a tree which sprouted from the pavement near the gate into the Alyscamps, Len watched the quartet recede down the avenue. Why didn't they come by car, Jake's car? he wondered. Anonymity, I suppose: they think there may be dirty work afoot. Let 'em get well ahead ... After a while he stepped up to the gate, found it locked, and cooed at it:

'*Au bord des tombes.*'

Although nothing whatever happened, Len had a feeling, intense if inexplicable, that somebody, somewhere, was considering his application and what to do about it. Eventually there was a buzz and a click. As a distant clock called a light, dulcet twelve, Len passed into the Alyscamps; he did not close the gate, which, however, swung to of itself with a gentle clunk.

Len walked on the left of the avenue, between the tombs and the trees. Here he was in shadow, not to be searched out by the moon-rays of St Honorat's lantern. The party ahead disappeared through an arch. The last stroke of twelve rang and withdrew. Len quickened his pace, flitted along the line of stone coffins, slid through the arch sideways like a shade, and surveyed an area of sarcophagi, no longer ranked but scattered. He picked his way across till he came to a blank wall ahead of him (above which there appeared to be a crude pediment) and a second, a tumbled wall, which jutted out among the sarcophagi from the right-hand end of the first. A little to the left of the corner formed by the two walls was a narrow, jagged gap, through which, Len thought, those whom he pursued must surely have passed. Very slowly and carefully he pushed his head through and then slightly round to the left, and what he now saw, some fifteen yards away from him, was this:

Balbo, Marigold, Jacquiz and Sydney Jones, in that order and about a yard apart, were standing in a row that stretched away from him with a slight slant to the right. They were facing to the right, as observed by Len, towards an exceptionally large marble sarcophagus, the lid of which had a pronounced central ridge, with correspondingly steep sides, and corners elevated in the Greek fashion. The lid was very slightly out of true, with the result that there was a small triangular gap at the front corner of the coffin which was the nearer to Len.

Standing at the centre of the far side of the sarcophagus and facing towards Balbo and the rest was a tall, very upright figure in a black cassock; a white hood hung between its shoulder blades, while its head and its face, Len realized with a rather sick feeling at his stomach, were entirely encased by a shroud of white, in which were two holes for the figure's eyes. At the near end of the sarcophagus, just to the right of the corner with the gap, stood what was, to judge from the stance and figure as seen by Len from the rear, a youthful male; since his head was cowled and his face in any case invisible to Len, there could be no certainty, but line and poise suggested elegant virility. At the far end of the coffin, looking almost straight at Len but evidently seeing nothing (for the eyes were misted over in reverie or trance), was a young girl in black, cowled like the presumptive boy, but showing enough of her sweet and beguiling face (made somehow the more fascinating by an unequally cleft chin) to establish her sex beyond question; for here was the grave half-smile which had responded to the Announcement of the Angel or hovered above the Child in the Meadow.

The sarcophagus and the tableau round it were on a dais of stone about a yard high and were backed by an apsidal recess. The whole arrangement very much suggested a former sanctuary, in which an altar would have stood where the tomb now was. About twenty feet above the shrouded head of the central figure there was a window in the curving wall, unglazed and divided vertically by a thin central column some ten feet high; and down through this window shone the moon, by the unassisted light of which Len was able to see, very clearly, all that he had seen and all that he was now about to see.

At first, however, it was more a matter of listening. Some kind of exposition was in progress, which apparently (thought Len) had to do with some jewels with the fancy name of the Roses of Picardie. These, he gathered, were owned (wrongfully) by the figure in the shroud, who was now explaining, in round English but tones slightly muffled by his mask, just what he proposed to do with them, which was . . .

'. . . To restore them to the true heir, that the Curse may leave me. This must be an heir sprung from the loins of that old Jew of Antioch, from whom by violence certain serjeants had the Rubies at the sacking of the city, and from them by his command Count Bohemond, and from him by the theft the Lord Baldwin du Bourg, and from him by gift the Lord Clovis du Bourg, and from his descendants by wit and lechery the painter Van Hoek, and from him for love the Demoiselle Constance Fauvrelle who was to become Mistress Comminges, and from her, by witchcraft and murder, the family Comminges, whose sole remaining descendant am unhappy I. Therefore to the Jew of Antioch we must return, the last rightful owner that is known to us, and ask of him where and who his lawful descendants now may be.'

Followed a long chanted prayer in what Len failed to recognize as Hebrew. Then the figure in the shroud raised its arms on high, the boy and girl at either end of the tomb knelt down, and suddenly a cloud smothered the moon. All went dark except for a tiny light, a pinkish red light, playing over one elevated corner of the coffin lid, the Greek moulding of which it faintly illuminated. The light began to divide itself, into three, into six, into twelve small red glowing particles, suspended in the air.

'The ghost of the Rubies,' rumbled the voice of the figure in the shroud: 'this summons other ghosts.'

A lady in a long, crimson dress knelt by a chest and passed the red gems, now strung as a necklace, through her hands. She shuddered and ground them into her breast.

'The noble widow, Mirabelle, Countess de la Tour d'Abbéville, who is contracted to give the necklace to her lover, Master Van Hoek, if he succeed but once more in stirring and slaking her lust. She would kill or denounce him sooner than yield the Rubies, for all her given word; but for her was another fate in store. Yet here we may not linger; we must go our weary journey, back and back . . .'

A grave young man in long silver robes bent over a chemical retort and sniffed the contents. An elder man, wrapped in furs and with a deeply lined brow, shuffled anxiously about behind him. There was a slight stirring from where (as Len judged) the boy was kneeling at the near end of the casket; then, behind the elder man, a cowled youth appeared, stared from the depth of his cowl as it were through both other men and into the retort, then faded from the scene.

'The noble Count Clovis Philippe du Bourg de Maubeuge de la Tour d'Abbéville, with the alchemist who has mixed a potion to bring him happiness.'

The young Count lifted the retort and drank from it. The cowled boy appeared again, flashed his eyes and faded almost instantly.

'He drinks to gain eternal youth; but for him was another fate in store. Yet here we may not linger; we must go our weary journey, back and back . . .'

The Rubies, unseen since they had appeared as a necklace in the bosom of the Countess Mirabelle, now danced in the darkness again. For some minutes they danced. Then a hand scooped through the air and caught them. The hand lengthened itself into an arm which increased into a torso on which was discovered a skull-capped head with hooky nose and lank beard.

'Jew of Antioch, old Jew of Antioch, where are the heirs of your loins? You were the last true possessor of the Rubies.

Where are your heirs and by what name are they called, that we may find them and give them what is rightfully theirs?'

The Jew cackled and poured his handful of Rubies into a goblet on which he set a lid.

Clever, Len thought. Very clever illusions. But not all that difficult to manage, with that boy and girl to assist, no doubt, and a few *son et lumière* effects carefully put together beforehand. But what one asks oneself is, why is this creature so keen to impress Balbo and Co., and where, in any case, are the real jewels, which he said just now he was so keen to get rid of? Hang about a bit, Lenny boy, and you may get a few interesting answers.

'Jew of Antioch, old Jew of Antioch, soon Count Bohemond's serjeants will come to quarter you and take the jewels, and earn your dying Curse. Tell us where are your heirs, that restitution may be made and my poor body and soul delivered at last from your invocation.'

The Jew rattled the Rubies in the goblet and cackled. No, not quite cackled, Len thought. He was saying something, something that sounded like Skandroo or Eskandroo with another word (piediker? paedica?) after it. Was this the name the conjurer wanted (or was pretending to want in order to further whatever plans he had for Balbo and his chums)? And if so, what was he going to do about it? Tell them that the real owner of the Rubies was a descendant of this Jew called Eskandroo Paedica, or something of the kind and that they must hunt round all Jewry and all the diaspora to find him? Why on earth should they bother? What sort of con was it all intended to lead up to?

The Jew began to fade from the air; his voice cackled lower and lower, always the same sounds, then ceased completely. As the Jew disappeared the Rubies rose out of the goblet, danced in the dark, then poured themselves away into nothing, or rather poured themselves, so Len could have sworn, into the gap at the corner of the sarcophagus. But it was too dark to tell. Too dark? Here was the moon again; too late. The moon? A bird called and was answered. The red sun flared through an empty doorway in a wall beyond Syd Jones. Have we all slept? thought Len. The birds called again: the sun, the sun. Balbo blinked and stirred. Marigold stood pale and shivering. Jacquiz looked puzzled and rather annoyed. Jones, S., strode towards the sarcophagus. The black cassock sprawled over the high ridge of the lid and the white shroud, stained with red marks, hung over the side of the tomb which faced towards the approaching Sydney. The white hood had somehow become detached from the rest of the ensemble and had looped itself over one of the corner mouldings.

'Where are those bleeding children?' Sydney was saying. 'We'll need them to help with him if he's ill, or worse.'

But the boy (if boy he was) and the girl (as she certainly was) had both vanished. Syd reached the tomb, bent forward, and commenced a wary and gentle examination.

'Fuck me,' he said. 'The old bastard's gone as well. This here is just his clobber.'

# X

## De Profundis

Glendower: I can call spirits from the vasty deep.
Hotspur: Why so can I, or so can any man;
But will they come when you do call for them?

Shakespeare: *Henry IV*, I, III, i

What now? thought Len, as he adjusted his position behind the wall so that he might see through the gap yet not himself be seen in the new daylight. What will they do now? They're no wiser, except for that 'Eeskandrou Peediker' bit, *if* they got it, and even if they got it, how on earth should they interpret it and to what should they apply it? It could be the name of the rightful owner of those jewels, if one is prepared to believe that this Jew of Antioch had really risen from the dead to reveal the name of his descendant; but since none of them knows where to find either him or the loot, so what? The only person who might be able to help them is that man, that creature in the speckled shroud, and he's done a bunk, leaving the shroud and taking those two pretty kids. Or did *they* take *him*? Either way, he's gone – and with him any hope of pursuing the matter any further. Profitable it might have been, intriguing it certainly is – but it's all washed up for lack of more info. I'd better bugger off to London p.d.q., to drop my little parcel into Jermyn Street and collect the balance of my fee. I can then fly straight on to Crete via Athens (or perhaps direct) and use Balbo's letter to extract those documents from this Kyrios Pandelios, thus enabling us to shut Provost Constable's big gob for ever and a day, and be assured of what we need, Ive and me, to lead the good life as each of us sees it. Fucking amen.

And indeed Len would have left St Honorat's church and started looking for a way out of the Alyscamps (were the gates open yet?) without one second's further delay, had not Sydney Jones now said:

'There's something funny about this here stone box. There's no side here at the back. Yer can look straight in under the lid.'

'And what can yer see?' said Marigold.

Syd, who was now standing where the Canon had stood to officiate as Master of Ceremonies the previous night, stooped down and shoved his head under the coffin-lid.

'There's a lot of stuff,' boomed Syd's voice out of the hollow stone. 'The bag of tricks they was using last night. All those robes and things. Little lights, red 'uns, on a string. Fancy masks. Fake beads. Torches.'

'Somehow,' said Jacquiz, 'it all seemed too authentic to have been got up with fake beads and torches.'

'Well, that's what's in here, matey. And a lot more beside. There must have been enough room for a whole family of stiffs in this thing. Piles of damp books' – Sydney's voice gurgled – 'with rude pictures of the devil doing it to ladies up their bottoms. Talk about a prick of steel, it looks more like ice to me. I'm glad I'm not on the end of that thing. And now here's a ruddy great sack full of something.' There was a long silence. Then Jones's face, looking rather bemused, rose above the lid. 'A ruddy great sack,' he said, 'full of his nibs, the Canon. Stone dead, stark nude, and covered in sores the size of saucers, some of 'em. Eating right down to the bone. His head . . .' Jones grimaced ruefully. 'Those red patches on his hood – they must have been the only places on his face where he still had a little flesh left. Raw, bloody flesh. All the rest – it's a skull. Two thirds of the nose gone. He had no business to be alive.'

'How do you know . . . that it's the Canon? We've never seen him without his hood.'

'There's a bracelet on the left wrist with his name engraved on it. There's also a cross slung round his neck, a Maltese cross, with the name engraved again. Bernard Comminges.'

Again he disappeared below the lid.

'What shall we do?' said Marigold. 'If someone comes along and finds us, just standing about with this body, we're going to look exceedingly silly.'

'Police?' said Balbo. 'It must have been those children. But how? Why?'

'Crikey,' said Jones, appearing once more, 'it's under my bloody nose.'

'What is?'

'What we're all looking for.'

'*The necklace?*'

'No, I told you, only red lights on a string. But there's a map, for Christ's sake. A map . . . you're not going to believe this . . . which is formed by the navel and the ulcers on his stomach. There are names tattooed near them. By the navel it says "Rosae" – Roses even in my Latin – and just to the right of the navel, running up and down, there's a whole string of protruding lesions – most of them eat inwards but these are *protruding* – marked . . . "T" . . . "A". . . . "Y" . . . I've got it, "Taygetus".'

Georgics III, line 44, thought Len. 'Taygetique canes' – 'the hounds of Taygetus'. He had been attracted, while leafing through the Wandrille MS of the Georgics, by the illumination of the capital 'T', an affair of sportive satyrs and responsive nymphs. The name had stuck in his mind; and Ivor, when inquired of, had explained that Taygetus was a mountain range which descended through the heart of the Peloponnese and into a peninsula now called the Mani. By Len's reckoning, this meant that the Canon's navel must represent some place just under the Western slopes of the range, either on the coast of the Mani or on the Eastern edge of an area which Ivor had called the Messenian Plain: which of these it was would depend on how far it lay to the North.

By now Balbo and Jacquiz had joined Syd Jones behind the sarcophagus.

'What's that just about it? What's that name on the edge of that mauve patch of skin?'

'Itylus,' said Balbo peering.

'Itylus. A small town North of Cape Taenarus. Very old. It sent some ships to Troy. *Ships*. It's on the *sea*. Mauve for sea – Homer's wine-dark sea. But what scale was he using?'

'You're mad,' said Marigold.

'No, no, can't you understand? All sick people play this sort of game. When I had measles as a child, I used to look at my spots and think of them as people in a crowd or stars in the sky or *places on a map*. My places were imaginary, but there's no reason why *his* shouldn't have been real. We *know* they're real because somebody – himself or perhaps those children – somebody had tattooed real names beside them. He beguiled his illness by making a map of his diseased skin. What more appropriate than a chart to show the location of the jewels which had caused – or so he believed – the disease?'

'But to expect an exact scale, sweetheart . . .'

'What's this?' said Jones. 'In tiny figures underneath "Rosae"? Three . . . six . . . five . . . three.'

Ivor had even, Len remembered, got out a classical atlas, rather to Len's annoyance as he was already bored with hearing about Taygetus. But now, crouching behind the wall of ruined St Honorat's, he blessed the hour and the minute at which Ivor had opened Murray for his edification. 'Here we are,' Ivor had said: 'the range begins about as far North as Sparta – just above the 37th parallel – *there* – and runs South to Cape Taenarus, where there is believed to be an entrance to Hades.' '37th parallel,' Len thought now: parallel 37. If Taygetus starts just above the 37th parallel North, it must end, if I remember that map at all right, roughly half way between the 37th and 36th parallels . . . in which case 36.53 could be – must be – the exact latitude of the Roses at the old man's navel, obligingly tattooed into place by the Canon, to while away the weary time and take his mind off his torture. *They* won't know that, not yet, he thought: *they* haven't had the benefit of Ivor's geography lesson; and even educated men seldom know their own latitude or longitude at any particular time, let alone that of anything or anybody else.

So just you slip away quietly, Lenny boy: use your start.


'But why?' wailed Marigold. 'Why has he been killed? Why did he get us all here? Why the conjuring exhibition? What did he want us to know and why couldn't he just tell it to us straight out? After all, if that old Yid wasn't a ghost but just a trick got up with masks and so on, the Canon must have known what he was going to say, so why the hell didn't he just tell us himself?'

'What *did* the old Yid say?' said Jones, S. 'I couldn't make it out.'

'*Iskandrou Paidika*,' said Jacquiz: 'meaning Iskander's minion or male darling. Iskander, I should explain, is a corrupt form of Alexander, which would appear in some of the Greek dialects spoken in certain regions of the Middle East, after Alexander had conquered them.'

'Mister Know All,' said Marigold with some admiration. 'Can you be sure of that?'

'Yes,' said Jacquiz. 'Among the stuff in this tomb is a sheet of notes – obviously a synopsis or breakdown of last night's performance.' He held up a sheet of paper. 'The last item, added in a different hand but quite clear, is written down as *Juif: Iskandrou Paidika*. Greek letters, incidentally.'

'All right,' said Marigold, disdaining a look at the proffered paper, 'but how much further on does that get us? It doesn't answer any of my questions. Least of all does it explain how we were tricked after that last item happened. You know, pitch dark one minute, bright dawn the next. There must have been an interval which was kind of … missed out … at any rate by me. It must have been then that the old man was done in. How was he killed by the way?'

'No marks, other than those of his disease. He *could* have died of natural causes,' said Syd Jones. 'Heart attack brought on by stress, I dare say. Now, please, Mrs Helmut—'

'—Marigold, sweetie—'

'—Marigold,' said Sydney, looking happy, 'please, Marigold, what a nice name, please, Marigold, can we have no more questions just now? What we have to do is tidy up and go before anyone rumbles us.'

'Hear that, boys?' said Marigold to Jacquiz and Balbo, who were in earnest discussion. 'No standing about like you was two yakking old dons in the Fellows' Garden. Action and off.'

'What action?' said Balbo. 'Call the police?'

'No,' said Syd Jones; 'we should spend the next ten weeks of our lives in the gendarmerie in Arles. We clear this mess up and we go after the jewels. What else? Has anyone got anything different which he or she wants to do?'

'Good for you, sweetie,' Marigold said. 'So you give the orders.'

'Marigold, make an exact copy of that map on the Canon's belly. Use this.' He thrust a notebook at her. 'Balbo, Doctor Helmut, come with me.'

He led the way through the gap by which, until a few minutes before, Len had been spying on them, and into the area of scattered sarcophagi. He went through the arch at the far end of the area and turned right, through a file of tombs, through a line of trees. In front of him was a high wall. He looked left, he looked right.

'No way out,' he said to Jacquiz and Balbo who now joined him, 'except over that.'

'What about the other side of the avenue?'

They crossed to the other side. An even higher wall, even less accommodating to amateur climbers.

'Clearly the Canon had some sort of right or privilege here,' Jacquiz said. 'He was allowed to come in late at night and bring his friends. Perhaps it was bribery, perhaps it was intimidation, perhaps it was something to do with his ecclesiastical position; but whatever it was, someone must know he's in here and will be inquisitive when he doesn't come out. Now we have no tickets, remember; therefore no official entrée here. Should we be seen to leave before he does, even if we are not immediately obstructed, after a time his failure to emerge will be connected with us, there will be a search along here – and then a police alert with instructions to apprehend four very obvious-looking Britons, three men and a girl. Problem: how to get out unseen? There may or may not be someone in the lodge by the gate—'

'—No one last night—'

'—But in any case the gate will be locked this early.'

'How did those children get out?'

'Presumably they know about that device which unlocks the gate from a distance. One of them would have pressed the switch, the other held the gate open. Still dark then, I suppose.'

'Nothing for it,' said Balbo. 'We'll have to give up and tell the police. We'll never get out without being noticed or causing a shindy.'

'We *must*, Balbo,' said Jones, S. 'Whatever the logic of all this turns out to be, whatever the answer to Marigold's questions, we've got a map and we're in the hunt. We cannot afford to be delayed and questioned now. Almost certainly that boy and that girl have gone for the jewels, and we want to be there first.'

'But it isn't a map. It's just a rough sketch.'

'We know the place we want is on the coast of the Mani and South of Itylus,' Jacquiz said. 'Enough to give us a chance, if far too little to give us a good one. But in any case at all, we must hide the body and get out of France – before anyone else can find it or connect us with it.'

'Too right, sport,' said Jones, S.

'But we're entirely innocent,' said Balbo.

'That will take time to establish,' said Jacquiz, 'and time we have not got.'

'Too right, sport,' said Jones again. 'So here is what we do . . .'


Len solved the problem of egress from the Alyscamps by hiding behind the trees, until the keeper arrived to open the gate at nine, and then slipping out unseen while the man was busy fetching from inside the lodge all the rubbish which he hoped to sell to tourists. Such an escape, as Len rightly reckoned, was very easy for his inconspicuous party of one, but would not be possible, so early in the day, for four more unauthorized and ticketless visitors, together or separately, with or without a dead and naked Monsignor. With any luck, they should all be arrested for trespass, if not for something a great deal more serious, and considerably impeded. However, thought Len, he could not afford to presume on this and would do well to be speedy. It occurred to him, as it had to Syd Jones and the others, that the boy and the girl, whoever they might be, had very probably gone after the jewels already (likely enough with more accurate information than anyone else's, as they appeared to be connected with the old man in some way) and therefore that if he, Len, was to have any hope in the hunt, he must put on his racing skates. At the same time, he must not neglect the interests of Jermyn Street, for there were long-term possibilities in this region that must be looked upon with respect. Nor, of course, must he neglect the *affaire* Constable, with its substantial bearing on his own future and Ivor's.

Taking this with that and one thing with another, Len decided his most satisfactory plan was to fly straight back to London from Montpellier; to deliver his package in Jermyn Street; to telephone to Ivor that Balbo was cooperative and had told him where he could collect the notes in their stained folder; to fly to Crete and collect them; and then to try to pick up some form of air passage from Crete to Kalamata, whence, having hired a car, he might run down the Mani to where the latitude 36.53 (if latitude indeed it was), as tattooed on the corpse and read out by Syd, intersected the line of the coast. There or thereabouts must be the place, represented by the Canon's navel, in which the Rosae or Rubies were to be located; though precisely where the jewels were hidden was of course another matter. He might well, thought Len, arrive too late to take his chance there, which would be a pity; but then from what he had heard the previous night it seemed that the Rubies might not be a very desirable acquisition (that curse had certainly done the old man a power of no good whatever), whereas the good will of Jermyn Street and the containing of Constable were both, so to speak, bankable assets. All of which things being so, his plan decided and his heart high, Len put his best foot forward from the Alyscamps and within thirty minutes of leaving them was driving, very fast but very carefully, along the autoroute to Montpellier.

At about the same time as Len drove across the river and out of Arles, Jacquiz Helmut, acting under the plan devised by Sydney Jones, strode out of the Alyscamps, dressed (over his own clothes) in the cassock, hood and head-shroud of the late Monsignor Comminges, the whole topped by a biretta which had been found near the sarcophagus. 'You're the nearest in height to him,' Sydney had said, 'and you don't carry yourself much different from what he did. Whoever's in charge of the gate will say, "There goes the old bastard", and if things round here are like we think they are, no one'll interfere with you.'

Nor did anyone interfere with him. The only notice taken of Jacquiz' departure was a servile nod, or rather bow from the shoulders, with which the man behind the ticket and tourist muck table (now established at the door of the lodge) greeted him as he passed.

'Then push on like the devil and all his works back to the old bugger's place in that Cloister,' Syd had instructed him. 'The more people that see you, the better. We want the world to know that Canon Comminges is alive and back home. When you get there see if you can spot the boy or the girl. They've probably scarpered by now, but if they are still around, see if you can get anything out of 'em or, better still, line 'em up on our side. But don't hang about. If there's no sign of 'em, drop the clobber at once, get back to the hotel, pay the bill for all of us (refunds later). Nah then: is there room in yer Rolls for those two children, as well as for all of us — if you should find them and bring 'em round?'

'Just about,' Jacquiz had said.

'*Delicious*: sardines,' Marigold had contributed.

'Then tell the hotel to ring Avis and have them pick up the heap they hired to me. Keys on my dressing-table. It was done on Diners', so no cash problems either way. From now on I reckon it's safer, and more friendly, with everyone together.'

'Hear, hear,' from Marigold.

'So whether we're carrying those kids or not, that's how we'll do it. All in the Rolls, okay?'

'Okay. But how will the rest of you get out of here without being spotted?'

'Like this,' Syd had said, and told them.

All pretty well cut and dried, thought Jacquiz now, as he crossed the canal by a road bridge: a sensible plan in all the circumstances; though I'm sorry, very sorry, it involves my wearing this mask. Marigold had turned it inside out and repeatedly doused it in a very strong eau de cologne from a bottle in her handbag, thus eliminating any risk of infection; but this still left, as Jacquiz pointed out, the possibility that something – something, well, impalpable – might be transferred to him along with the linen.

'Rubbish,' Marigold had said. 'Skin complaints may be contagious, but not Curses.'

Jacquiz wasn't any too sure of that. A month ago, he reflected, he would have pooh-poohed the entire notion of the Curse (allowing it to exist only as a foolish legend), while Marigold would have shuddered at the thought of it. Now their attitudes had been reversed. Jacquiz, though not converted to any very substantial belief in the powers of darkness, was uneasily aware that more seemed to have been going on around them than met one full in the eye. Marigold, on the other hand, though by no means entirely sceptical, had developed a cheerful determination to face down any obtrusion of the apparently supernatural. It was she, for example, who insisted that the death of Constance could be and should be treated as a rationally explicable occurrence (if not exactly of an everyday character), whereas Jacquiz had caught a whiff (to put it no stronger) of greed and malignance revenant. By much the same token, she now made light of his assuming the Canon's persona, whereas he himself had an uncomfortable feeling that the pose, if not the garments used for it, might well bring some kind of re-tribution.

However, it was his clear duty to help his friends if he could, so he had made no more fuss but briskly put on his disguise and marched off. In any case, he now admonished himself as he crossed the main road into the public gardens, provoking many looks of distasteful recognition (that would please Sydney) – in any case, there is surely a far more weighty objection, far more firmly grounded than any super-stition of mine about this mask, to this course of action now in train: it is, incontrovertibly, a very grave offence to be present at the scene of a murder (and murder this well could be) without reporting it to the proper authorities. True, none of them had been in the least aware of the Canon's death or what had caused it: even so, to find the corpse and say nothing about it, nay more, to mislead the citizenry by ren-dering an impersonation of the dead man, and then to rush off about one's own business, surely amounted to criminal collusion with the murderer or murderers.

'We'll hide him away good and tight in this here masonry,' Syd Jones had said before Jacquiz departed. 'There's not much left to stink, and by the time it does, and if anybody smells it, we'll be half way to the Mani. Maybe no one will come near him and he won't be found for months.'

Sydney had then gone on to point out that even when the corpse was discovered, and even if it could be identified, there could be nothing, given the scheme he had worked out for the evacuation of the Alyscamps, to connect any of them with Comminges' death. All of which had been all very plausible, thought Jacquiz as he turned off the street towards the entrance to the Cloister, but he, Jacquiz, was a man who had a lot to lose and therefore looked to live within the law. As far as he was concerned, stone walls very definitely did a prison make and iron bars a cage if Marigold (with her newfound love for him, or so it seemed to be) and the Rolls-Royce were outside them. However, he had, in the end, allowed himself to be convinced by Jones, he had

379

consented to obey his immediate orders and follow his overall plan, because when all was said, he was confident that Sydney was thoroughly experienced in these sort of areas of behaviour and knew very well what he was doing. Jacquiz had a high regard for people who knew what they were doing and liked to watch them doing it. Something in Sydney Jones's tone and bearing told him that the man was competent to bring them through all this; and it was also to be remembered that Sydney, being in the trade, so to speak, might be allowed special licence by other (French) practitioners of it if there should, at any stage, be trouble.

In any case at all, thought Jacquiz, we are now committed. He tried the low door out of the courtyard, found it unlocked, and started up the stairs to the balcony over the Cloister.


Sydney Jones and Balbo Blakeney gave a combined heave: the still pliant corpse of Monsignor Comminges slid slowly down through the neck of a funerary urn.

'Pity they lost the stopper of this thing,' said Syd, rapping the urn; 'it'd look much tidier. But this slab should do the trick.'

The urn was six feet tall. With some difficulty, Sydney and Balbo between them managed to lift a loose flagstone, about a yard square and two inches thick, to the height of their heads and then to shove it over the mouth of the urn.

'That should keep him from advertising himself,' said Syd. 'Not that anyone much will be coming down here, I'd imagine.'

'We'd better be leaving,' said Marigold, 'before my torch conks out.'

She led the way up the winding stair out of the crypt of St Honorat's. After the thirtieth step she rounded a bend into the dim light of the ruined but still partially roofed North transept, extinguished the torch which she had prudently brought along for the outing, and returned it to her handbag.

'Right,' she said, looking at her watch: 'Jacquiz has now been gone thirty minutes. How much longer do we give him?'

'If he doesn't meet either of those mysterious kids,' said Sydney, 'and it's my bet that he won't because they'll be hightailing it into the Mani by now, then par for the course is one hour flat. We'll start discreetly down the avenue in fifteen minutes.'

'They need some explaining, those kids,' Marigold said. 'In some lights they look nearly twenty, in others about twelve. The boy seems to have been, well, keeping an eye on me and Jacquiz for some days now. And from what you say, the girl's been doing the same with you two. But how did they – or the old man – get wind that we were all on the trail?'

'He must have known that the Roses have received a lot of publicity,' Balbo said, 'because of Clovis's death. He may have guessed that someone would start looking. So perhaps he stationed the two children at key points on the two possible routes: the route back into the past which I was taking, starting with Stavros Kommingi in Nicopolis, and the route leading *out of the past* which was the one you took via Constance.'

They had already had some discussion of their respective journeys. It was as though both parties had been marching in opposite directions along the same historical line, Jones and Balbo out of twentieth-century Greece towards the past, Jacquiz and Marigold forward out of eleventh century Antioch towards the future; and now they had met in what was, in respect of their search, late seventeenth-century Arles. For their true meeting place was not so much the Canon's chamber, where they had physically encountered one another, as the 'fair, tall house by the Priory of the Knights of Malta', the house into which 'Poppa' Comminges and his second wife had removed from St Bertrand.

When both parties pooled information, Jacquiz and Marigold had been able to tell Balbo and Sydney how they had picked their way towards Arles through Montreuil, Jumièges and Pau, while Balbo and Sydney had been able to tell Jacquiz and Marigold how they had tracked down Andrea Commingi, the pirate from Provence, and had followed him back (aided by colossal luck) to the region of his origins.

Just as Balbo and Jones had known nothing of Poppa Comminges, so Marigold and Jacquiz had of course known nothing of Andrea; but now, as it seemed to both parties, the probability must be that Andrea Commingi and Poppa Comminges were two leads which locked together to join the historical line in the fair, tall house by the Priory; for surely Andrea (André) Commingi (Comminges) could have been, must have been, a son of Poppa Comminges and the fertile slut he had married, a son born after the deaths (recorded in the Abbé's scrapbook) of the 'two fine men-children' and in the year 1669 (why not?), thus growing to be thirty years old in the year 1699, when his portrait by Giocale *At Thirty Years Old* was dated and by which time he had already become Andrea Commingi, the privateering shipmaster of the Tyrrhene sea, and was well on the way to becoming Andreas Kömmingi (᾽Ανδρέας Κομμίγγι), the prosperous merchant of Corfu, nearly but not quite ennobled, who subsequently took off with all his riches for Lycia.

It did not matter now that they had not identified, and might never identify, the 'fair, tall house' itself. Very possibly it no longer existed. It was the point in time that was vital, and the fact that at this point the two strands of investigation met together: the strand which ended in Poppa Comminges (the last man known actually to have had the Roses in his keeping) and the strand that had led Jones and Balbo to Andrea Commingi, who was now almost certainly revealed as 'Poppa's' son. For although this had yet to be absolutely proved, it was felt to be a sound working hypothesis. Once it was assumed that Poppa Comminges had sired Andrea, then clearly André/Andrea/Andreas Comminges/Commingi/Kommingi (Κομμίγγι) was as likely a fellow as any to have had the Roses from his father, whether by fraud, theft or inheritance. If so, however, where had he taken them, what had he done with them? A very broad question, granted – but one which, it now seemed, was to be answered by the map on the dead Canon's abdomen. As Marigold pointed out (while decking up Jacquiz in his hood, shroud and biretta), somewhere on the coast of the Mani would have been a perfectly probable and sensible place for an adventurer in Greek waters to have dumped the Roses, whether before or after he left Corfu for Lycia.

Yes, indeed; but now came difficulties. Why should Andrea have wanted to dump them? And how had knowledge of their whereabouts come to the Canon centuries later? Presumably it had been passed down to him through a line of Comminges which must have inhabited Arles (so the goitrous cashier at the Musée Arlaten had indicated) since 'Poppa' had acquired his 'fair, tall house' there. But exactly what line of the family was that? Had Andreas or one of his children (if any) eventually returned to Arles to settle? If so, why had he left the Roses in the Mani? Or had Poppa fathered still more males, from one of whom the Cannon was descended? If so, the other question yet remained: how had they or their successors, and through them the Canon, come by their knowledge of the Roses' hiding place, far away on the Maniot shore of the rude Sicilian Sea?

All these questions were in Marigold's mind now, as she, Balbo and Sydney waited in St Honorat's until it should be time to leave the Alyscamps. Associated with them were rather similar questions about the amount of knowledge accorded (when and how) to the two children, the boy and the girl.

'We might accept that theory,' she said after Balbo had tendered his explanation of how the children had come to be watching them on their various journeys through France and Italy. 'Let's agree for now that the Canon posted them on the routes which treasure-seekers might come along – and indeed did: us. But there's a lot more inquiring to be done. How long have they known where the Rubies are stashed? Sydney here says he reckons they've gone after them now. But why *now*? Why not before, if they fancied them?'

'Because they didn't know where to go,' said Syd Jones.

'So you think they killed the old man last night in order to get a look at that chart on his tum-tum?'

'Something like that.'

'So how did they know it was there? And if they *did* know it was there, don't tell me they couldn't have managed a good look at it without having to kill him. And if for some reason they did have to kill him, why last night?'

'A good opportunity to land the corpse on someone else? On us.'

'Perhaps they were hoping it wouldn't be necessary to be so extreme,' Balbo said; 'until finally he held out on them so long that they got desperate.'

'Who the hell are they, anyhow? Where are they from? For Christ's sake,' said Marigold, 'where do they fit in?'

'A nuisance the old bazza's dead,' said Jones. 'He'd promised to tell us all the answers . . . in his own good time.'

'Now we depend on the children themselves to tell us – if we can ever find them – and I don't like the smell of them.'

'They're both beautiful,' Balbo remarked.

'Sure they are. The thought of that boy makes me wringing wet in the panties. But that's no reason to trust him.'

'The girl at least looks innocent.'

'You ever read a poem called *Lamia*?' said Marigold. 'Keats. There's this beautiful maiden who looks as if butter won't melt in her armpits. She turns out to be a snake. It's a way they have.'

'Time to go,' said Syd Jones. 'Remember, none of us is to be seen more than necessary, and we are not to be seen at all until Doctor Helmut arrives and starts doing his stuff. Until then we stay behind cover. There's plenty of that right along to the gate. What with the tombs and the trees you could take a bleeding circus down and no one the wiser. It's getting past that lodge – *that*'s the big ball-ache.'

'Lucky for me I don't have balls,' said Marigold.

Sydney Jones had been wrong in thinking that Jacquiz would meet neither of the children. In fact they were both in the Canon's chamber when Jacquiz arrived, the girl dressed in nun's black, the boy in a fawn ski-ing suit of expensive material and very close cut. Both looked about fifteen years of age, unsmiling and determined. When Jacquiz entered, they came forward as if they had been expecting him and at once helped him to remove the hood, shroud and cassock that he had been wearing in impersonation of their late 'uncle'. Neither of them spoke a word. The girl's touch, Jacquiz noticed, was marvellously soothing, though she did no more than accidentally twitch his hair, once or twice, with her fingertips and brush the back of one hand against his arm. The boy did not soothe; he excited: every time he touched Jacquiz, who had never before known the faintest physical desire for a member of his own sex, Jacquiz felt a swift *frisson* as of an intense but highly pleasurable electric shock, a feeling (no matter in which part of the body it occurred) comparable to the sensation which one had in the tip of one's penis at the height of orgasm.

However, it was clear there was to be no dalliance in any sense of the word. As soon as Jacquiz had been disrobed down to his own brown check suit, the girl went to a small statue of Eros dicing, lifted the head like a lid, put her arm down into the trunk, dredged up a sheaf of papers, and thrust them into Jacquiz' hand. She and the boy then nodded to each other and made for the door.

'Don't go,' called Jacquiz foolishly; 'stay and talk. There are lots of things I want to ask you. Who are you?'

The boy turned. 'I am David,' he said; 'this is my sister, Rebecca.'

'Well then ... David and Rebecca ... what happened last night?'

'You were there,' said David; 'you saw for yourself.'

'We shall go now,' said Rebecca.

'No, stay, there's so much—'

'—We shall go.'

They both turned their backs on Jacquiz and continued, hand in hand, with fingers linked, towards the door.

'*Where*, for Christ's sake?' called Jacquiz.

Neither answered. A horrible laughter, half way between hooting and cackling, came from the pair as they approached the door, grew louder as the boy opened it, rose to gibbering climax as he held it open for his sister, and ceased instantly and altogether the moment he closed it behind him.


As Balbo watched the gate of the Alyscamps from behind a tree some fifty yards inside, he saw Jacquiz' Rolls drive up and park on the other side of the road, and a pale and twitchy Jacquiz emerge from it.

He doesn't look at all himself, Balbo thought: I hope he remembers the plan.

He need not have worried. Although Jacquiz was certainly not feeling his best and his brightest after his encounter with the twins (for such he had decided, on no evidence, they must be), he was not a man to bungle a simple assignment. He approached the lodge, went to the ticket table, purchased his ticket and came away, after a polite '*Merci bien, M'sieur*' to the keeper. Then he sauntered up the avenue of tombs to St Honorat's, spent five minutes examining it in the manner of a casual tourist, came back down the avenue, and went to the ticket table again. There he started buying postcards, leaflets, maps, guide books, large volumes of coloured plates and finally a plastic model of St Honorat's, thus flustering and exciting the concierge to such a pitch that he did not observe the demure exit of three people whom he would at once have spotted, had he seen them, to be interlopers who had not purchased tickets. Nor was he watching, so busy was he collecting and counting Jacquiz' money, while these three people got into the Rolls-Royce, in which the M'sieur Anglais had arrived, and hid themselves below the level of the windows. After he had parcelled the merchandise, the M'sieur courteously accepted his offer to help him carry it across the road, then considerately declined it when two charabancs drew up by the gate. By the time the concierge had attended to the guides in charge of the charabancs, the M'sieur Anglais, his parcels and his Rolls-Royce, were gone; so that all he could have told anyone who might ever come to inquire about that day's traffic was that after the priest had gone that morning an obviously rich Englishman arrived, alone, and had shown mild interest in the avenue and the ruins of St Honorat's. He would not have added that the Englishman bought an eccentric, indeed lunatic, quantity of literature from the lodge, because no prudent Frenchman would disclose a cash transaction in which he had contrived to defraud his employers, in this case the Municipality of Arles, of eighty per cent of the profit due to them.

'So,' said Syd Jones as the Rolls drove towards Cannes, the coast and the Italian border, 'the Right Reverend Monsignor is stowed away safe in that urn but generally believed to have returned home to his Cloister. No one will look for him for a very considerable time. Should they ever find him, they will be at a total loss to account for his death and they will be able to put their hand on nobody who might have been present at it.'

'Unless,' said Jacquiz, 'that concierge at the gate was responsible for letting us all in last night and got a sight of us then.'

'I think not,' said Syd. 'All the indications are that the lodge is left empty at night and that the concierge or keeper, for whatever reasons, tacitly abandons control of the precinct to the Canon. Or rather, used to.'

'Certainly, he gave me a pretty fair grovel when I walked out,' said Jacquiz.

'That he will report – if anyone ever asks him. "The Monsignor went out of the gate that morning," he will say, "and did not come back while I was on duty." Therefore they will conclude that the Canon could not have returned to St

Honorat's and his death until tonight. Which lets us out,' said Syd, 'as by then we shall be well into Italy.'

'Those ... those children,' said Marigold: 'what about them?'

'Difficult to say. They were obviously expecting someone back at the Cloister,' said Jacquiz, who had already told his story once. 'I got the impression that they were waiting to hand over those documents I was given. In the glove compartment, if you want to take a look.'

Marigold leaned forward and got out the sheaf of papers which the girl, Rebecca, had presented to Jacquiz in the Canon's chamber.

'Just as well you didn't get around to inviting them to ride with us,' she said to Jacquiz as she sorted the papers. 'With that rubbish you bought just now, and Balbo's stuff and Sydney's, there wouldn't have been much room for their luggage.'

'I don't think they're the kind that have luggage.'

'What can you mean?'

'I mean that they seemed to be setting off without any.'

'They might not have been leaving.'

'They were leaving; they had that ... that aspect. They were off, and eager to be off, and they didn't want any more truck with me.'

He did not, however, tell them about the children's hideous laughter.

'Well, what's in those papers?' said Balbo to Marigold.

'All wrapping, except two things.'

Marigold held up something which looked like a folded map; then she opened it.

'A genealogical table,' she said at last; 'the Comminges family, starting with the first Vidames of Comminges. What with one thing and another, one tends to forget they were once nobility. The early bit checks with everything which Jacquiz and I found out about them in Saint Bertrand.' She turned to Balbo behind her. 'And now ... I think we're going to find out for certain about this Andrea number whom you and Jonesy tracked down. Yes ... "Poppa" Comminges, as

Jacquiz and I called him, was Louis' father, as we told you. Louis is marked here as having married Constance Fauvrelle – and there they stop, with a couple of crosses and R.I.P. written in. *That* hasn't been done for anyone else, so presumably whoever drew this thing up knew the tale about the dead Louis coming to Constance, and is expressing the hope – R.I.P. – that there will be no more of *that* kind of behaviour.

'Now then. Poppa's second wife seems to have borne him two sons in quick succession, the first of them in 1655, very soon after they came to Arles. That fits, as she was heavily pregnant when she left Saint Bertrand. The two boys apparently died – *mortui sunt*, that's died, isn't it? – on the same day. It doesn't say what of, but they must have been the two who were killed playing in the Roman Theatre – according to the Abbé's scrapbook.'

Marigold paused. They had climbed a little and were now coming to a heath of rock and scrub. A watery sun diffused a surprising amount of heat through the windows of the Rolls. A peasant sitting by the side of the road looked up and gave a modest salute, in honour, Balbo supposed, of their splendid equipage. Or had he been making the sign of the evil eye? Or the sign for protection against the evil eye? What with this and that, Balbo thought, we might be getting quite a bit of an aura about us.

'Then she laid off for a longish time – until, yes, 1669, when she had a son called André. He married, in 1693, a woman called Lucina, no surname supplied—'

'—Lucina? Obviously he was already in Italy—'

'—By whom he had two sons and two daughters. One son and both daughters died, it doesn't say when, just *Rosis Picardianis rupti et occisi*. Jacquiz?'

' "Broken and murdered by the Roses of Picardie",' Jacquiz said. 'Interesting, the use of the masculine plural, when there are two girls and only one boy.'

'Male chauvinism. Even more interesting,' said Marigold, 'that whoever made out this chart reckoned that the Roses were responsible for the deaths.'

389

'Which confirms,' said Jones, S., 'that André or Andrea had them, however he got them, and explains why he dumped them.'

'Poppa Comminges died in 1690,' Marigold now said, 'so I expect André just inherited them. It doesn't say when Poppa's second wife died, or the first for that matter. More male chauvinism.'

'What happened to André's fourth child – his other son?'

'Some more Latin happened to him. Rather a lot this time.' She passed the chart back to Balbo.

'He was seduced by a dancer in Ephesus,' said Balbo after a while, 'and went off with a troupe of actors, never to be heard of again. This misfortune too is attributed to the Roses. He could have been the ancestor of my man at Nicopolis. Ah, I see the death of André/Andrea/Andreas has only a rough date – *circa 1740, Xanthis dicunt.* "They say at Xanthe." Obviously he'd been getting rather out of touch. Not so much out of touch, though, but what he let someone know where he'd put the Roses. *Locum Rosarum ante adelpho nutiarat.* This Latin gets worse and worse. "He had announced the place of the Roses to his brother" – bastard Greek form – "beforehand." *What* brother? Yes, I see. Poppa Comminges' next and final effort after young André was François, two years later. So,' said Balbo, 'it looks pretty plain that André-cum-Andrea went off, taking the Roses as his legacy, when his father died in 1690; that he became a privateer, married and had children, probably about the time that he went to Corfu; and that all the children came to bad ends. André blames the Roses for this—'

'—But how does he *know*,' interrupted Marigold, 'that they're called the Roses? How does he know they have a curse on them? No one ever told Poppa any of this. Constance never spoke of the jewels to him. Just before she died she told *someone* – the dead but revenant Louis, as she thought, but really Poppa Comminges impersonating Louis, or so *we* hope – "where her treasure was hidden"; but even then, you notice, she used the general word "treasure". She can't possibly have had the time to go into details. So how does André come to know so much about them?'

'Louis would know it all,' said Jacquiz reluctantly.

'But Louis didn't tell. He never mentioned the Roses *as such* in his letter home, for reasons of security we think, and he died too soon to tell his family about them in person.'

'Unless he . . . did . . . get up . . . and come to Saint Bertrand. He could then have told his father everything about the Roses . . . before he went back to his grave in Pau . . . if that's where he did go,' said Jacquiz bleakly.

There was a silence in the car. Marigold looked both annoyed and rather anxious.

'I can answer that one,' said Jones, S., the cricketer, 'without any need of the dead walking. Those Roses had been famous all over Europe. If Poppa Comminges was keeping his ears open, he'd have heard, sooner or later, in an important centre like Arles, all about the Roses, their curse and their disappearance up at – where was it?—'

'—Montreuil, where the painter got them off the randy Countess,' Marigold said.

'—He'd have heard all about it, and he'd have had a good look and done a few sums, and he'd have realized what his dead daughter-in-law had left with the family. And no doubt told André when he was old enough to understand.'

'So André blamed the Roses for the death or departure of his children,' Balbo took it up again, 'and hid them on the Maniot coast. Then, before he dies, he lets his brother François know where they are. And from François' – he consulted the chart – 'the knowledge descends through . . . eight generations—'

'—To the Canon's grandfather,' said Jacquiz, 'the one who snooted up that nincompoop, Mistral, and so at last to the Canon, our Canon . . .'

'. . . Who recorded the information by making a chart of the sores and lesions on his stomach,' said Marigold, 'observing their relation to one another and then naming them . . . in such a way that the hiding place of the Rubies was represented by his own navel.' She produced from her handbag her transcript of the Monsignor's chart. 'Well below Itylus,' she said, 'and on the coast of the Mani. Quite a wide area to investigate.'

'Even if there's no competition from those kids.'

'How will they get there?'

'That's their biz. How shall *we* get there?'

'Through Italy,' said Jacquiz. 'Autostrada to Arezzo. Over the hills to Ancona, car ferry from there to Patras. Down the Peloponnese to Kalamata . . . and into the Mani.'

'Not worth flying? To get there quicker?'

'Anyone can fly that wants to,' Jacquiz said. 'I don't care for aeroplanes, especially not when there are curses in the air. I'm going there in this car.'

No one took issue with him.

'Well,' said Balbo, tapping Marigold on the shoulder after a long silence: 'what's the other thing you said was there in the wrappings?'

Marigold held up a red school exercise book.

'Title in Greek this time,' she said.

Balbo took it from her.

'*Iskandrou paidika*,' he read out.

'The Jew of Antioch's phrase at the end of that fake séance,' said Jacquiz.

'Also entered as last item on the aide memoire we found in the sarcophagus,' said Balbo. 'In a different hand from the rest.'

Nobody seemed to have any comment to make about this.

Balbo turned the cover of the exercise book.

'Apart from the title,' he said, 'it's written in French; a translation, apparently from the first-century historian and gossip, Hermogenes of Alexandria.'

'Can you read in a car?'

'In a Rolls,' said Balbo, 'yes.'

'Then read.'

'Right you are. *Istoria ton tou Iskandrou Paidikon*,' Balbo began: ' "The Story of Iskander's Catamite." '

Len reached London from Montpellier in time for an early luncheon, which he decided not to have since he was too busy running around and making arrangements.

First of all, he rang up Ivor Winstanley from the airport, to tell him that Balbo was prepared to support Elvira's accusation and had authorized him, Len, to take possession of the incriminating folder; this was now in Crete, whither, said Len, he would go instanter. To this Ivor replied that Constable had declared a state of armed truce pending the production of further evidence, but had indicated readiness to do a deal should such evidence be forthcoming. Since it now clearly was forthcoming, Ivor told Len, he would start hammering out exact terms with Constable while Len pursued his mission to Heracleion.

Len now took a taxi from the airport to Jermyn Street, where he delivered his parcel to Theta in person, and asked if he might be considered for similar employment in the future, as messenger, scavenger or whatever. Theta thanked him for his efficient service and remarked that the blood-stained Elastoplast was a most happy discovery. He did not, however, commit himself to employing Len in any role thereafter; he merely promised to bear him in mind, and added that if Len should ever come across any information in any area which he thought might be of interest to the department, the department would take very kindly to his sharing it.

It instantly occurred to Len that the department might take very kindly indeed to being warned that a party, which included one of their own agents and an ex-scientist with whom they appeared to be intimately concerned, was now either helping the police with their inquiries into a murder in Arles, or (presumably) in full cry after a fabulous cache of Rubies supposedly hidden in Southern Greece. But it was very clear to Len that since he was probably the only person who knew the exact latitude and therefore the exact point, more or less, at which the Rubies were hidden, he would do far better to hold his tongue on that topic and to operate, as far as the Roses were concerned, in a strictly private capacity.

It also occurred to Len that Jermyn Street might be grateful to know that Lord Constable, the Provost of Lancaster College, Cambridge, stood accused by his wife of having appropriated Blakeney's notes, years ago, and of having communicated their substance to the enemies of King George VI; but this might be to destroy Lord Constable, the very last thing which Len or Ivor wanted: they wanted Constable to remain secure of his throne and sceptre, providing only that he was prepared to wield the latter in their protection and advancement; and this, at the moment, was almost certain to be the case.

However, it seemed to Len that he could be of immediate and ingratiating service to Theta in at any rate one particular. Theta, as Len now reminded him, had expressed interest in seeing the notes for which Len was searching. Since these had now been traced to Greece, Len said, he would be happy to let Theta peruse them at leisure as soon as he himself had secured them and returned from Heracleion.

This consideration induced Theta to offer Len his expenses (gratefully accepted) for his new journey, and to order Q to procure him an instant flight direct to Crete. Q accordingly rang up an airline which was operating a charter flight for late holidaymakers that very afternoon. On being told the flight was fully booked, to say nothing of thirty passengers on the waiting list, Q reminded the manager that his concession was very shortly due for official renewal by the Government which Q had the honour to serve. A fifty-year-old nursing sister, who had scraped to pay for her fortnight in Crete for the last nine months and had dreamed of nothing else for the last six, was therefore thrown off the flight and Len was thrust into her seat.

This suited him excellently. Things were proceeding in the precise order he had planned. With any luck he could be through with the Kyrios Pandelios that very evening and off to Kalamata the next morning. It was a pity Theta would be expecting him back with the notes almost at once; but he could excuse any delay of up to (say) a week by pretending that Pandelios had not been at home in Heracleion, having gone away on business and having (for good measure) lied about his destination to his wife. And so, well equipped with a fresh overnight bag from Jermyn Street and his letter of credit from Balbo to Pandelios, Len lifted blithely off into the empyrean and followed his fortune to Crete.


'So,' said Q to Theta: 'one pair of Blakeney's used socks, one slightly blooded piece of Elastoplast, and some ten strands of hair from his comb. What now?'

Theta shrugged blandly.

'These items could make up a message,' said Lambda, 'to the – er – denizens of the tombs. "This king has lost his Godhead. Here is your evidence. Go to him." '

'They will require to know *which* King – there must be several scattered over the earth – and where he is.'

'They will trust others to find out for them. They themselves, I hazard, will be concerned only with one thing: getting out to join the hunt, so that each may have a share, however small, of the sacred victim.'

'Still sacred although now deprived of his numen?'

'Residually sacred, one might say. As to that, I am quite confident. These creatures have always, when possible, devoured their God-Kings when the Sign left them. This, I admit, was only discovered recently, but it now has all the force of a law.'

'Providing this new strain behaves like the old ones.'

'We shall have to assume that it will,' said Lambda, 'or simply admit defeat.'

'Very well,' said Theta. 'How shall we proceed?'

'These relics of Blakeney's,' said Lambda, 'are losing whatever virtue they have with every hour that passes. We must bring forward Operation Falx; it must happen no later than the beginning of next week.'

'But how,' said Q, 'will this new way work?'

'At the beginning of the operation, instead of producing

Blakeney himself to urge them out, we deliver this message. We place it in an obvious place where it will be easy for them to find and read it. In the Crypt.'

'You mean,' said Theta, 'we just leave these socks and the rest on the floor of the Crypt . . . for them to sniff at?'

'Just that. Near one of the tombs they are infesting. The Dean has been warned that the Crypt and the South-West Transept must be cleared for Falx, I think?'

'Yes. The South-West Transept will be needed as a communications centre and the Crypt will be closed . . . for obvious reasons. But we do not want to cause popular curiosity or resentment by closing the whole Cathedral at the same time as we are closing Dover Castle. Since it is not thought that . . . er . . . they . . . will make their exit through the main body of the Cathedral, we propose to admit the public as usual.'

'Very good. Simply warn the Dean that the date has been changed. Ditto the Brigade Commander.'

'*He* won't like it.'

'He'll have to. We have the necessary priority. So we post the troops as previously planned, and deliver our message. If our theory is correct,' Lambda said, with (Theta thought) a somewhat brittle confidence, 'they will be so eager to devour their God and King that they will at once leave the Cathedral – by the known routes, the routes by which we have now learned that they came in – and perish in the attempt.'

'And if they don't all perish?' said Theta.

'Then presumably they will pursue their original intention,' said Lambda. 'Since Blakeney is with Jones in Arles—'

'En route, now, for Italy,' said Q. 'He telephoned in at lunch time—'

'—In any case a very long way off, I don't think we need worry about him.'

'In any event,' said Q, 'we have no choice. If left to their devices, those creatures will undermine the foundations and reduce the Cathedral to a rubble inside months. The only possible way of getting them out is to use this bait unwittingly produced by Blakeney, and you tell us' – he turned to Lambda – 'that is it losing its efficacy every minute.'

'That at least is beyond doubt.'

'Then the thing is quite clear,' Theta pronounced. 'We must warn the Dean and alert the Brigadier: Operation Falx is brought forward to the day after tomorrow at dawn.'

' "... And so it came about",' Balbo Blakeney translated from the red exercise book, ' "that Alexander, or Iskander as he was known in the tongue of that region, took to his heart and his bed the Egyptian boy Arphisses, son of Maeris, of Egyptian Thebes. And for all the boy was of noble birth, his parents thought that Iskander did them honour, to pick a companion from their family, the more so as the boy (being then thirteen years of age) was designated a Page of the Household.

' "It is difficult to trace, with precision, the events which passed in the two years during which Arphisses remained with his Imperial Lover. We can affirm, however, and this on the boy's own showing later, that the years were happy for him. Be this as it may, the time arrived when Alexander, about to undertake a campaign, more arduous than any yet, into India, decided that Arphisses was too delicate in health to accompany him. He bade him farewell in friendship and in honour; and as a gift of parting, gave him a present of twelve fine Rubies, which he had had out of the Great King's treasure when he overthrew him. (The King's treasure had told him that the Rubies came from a land beyond India where the soil of the river beds yielded them abundantly, and Iskander had determined that one day he would venture to this land; yet death undid him before.)

' "To escort Arphisses home across the deserts to Thebes in Egypt, Iskander appointed a mounted bodyguard of ten men. But of these five fell into a fatal fever from drinking foul water in the stews of Babylon, and soon after the other five were over-run by bandits on the King's Road (in caring for which Iskander, with his eyes turned to the East, had lately been somewhat neglectful). The boy Arphisses, being now fifteen years of age and of a rare and tender loveliness, was eventually sold to Noah, a Jew of Joppa, who had been riding home with his caravan from Byzantium and had chanced in Ephesus on the day Arphisses was put up for sale there. This Noah was much moved by the boy's beauty, and was most amorous of him; yet would not fondle or possess him until his foreskin had been cut in the Jewish fashion, holding him to be unclean until this item of flesh were shorn away." '

'Really, you Jews,' said Marigold to Jacquiz. 'What a fuss about nothing.'

'I do believe,' said Jacquiz, ignoring this, 'that they have at last finished the stretch of autoroute above Nice.' He peered through the windscreen. 'No,' he said sadly, 'we're being sent off by the usual turning. It's the same every time. One thinks they *must* have completed the autoroute to by-pass Nice, it's the only section for hundreds of miles either way that wasn't finished years ago ... and there it still is, all cranes and piles of concrete, and a traffic jam waiting in the Promenade des Anglais.'

'It's the Jews who are queering the thing,' said Marigold contentiously. 'All those Jews in Nice who want the tourists to come through the town and be skinned there.'

'I didn't know there were many Jews in Nice.'

'Russian ones,' said Balbo.

'Let's hear more about this old bastard in Joppa,' Sydney Jones said.

' "When Noah's caravan reached Joppa," ' Balbo read on, ' "Noah engaged a Rabbi to come and cut Arphisses his fore-skin, but he was then beset by the pleas of his twin children, David and Rebecca, who were of an age with Arphisses and also of a Hellenized fashion of mind (as were many of the young in the Israel of that time). They represented to their father that circumcision would spoil the lad's beauty, and they begged Noah to spare Arphisses, whom already they loved as a brother." '

'Now this *is* interesting,' said Jacquiz. 'We know that young Jews of the Hellenistic period infuriated the Rabbis by exercising naked in the Greek manner and some of them even wore artificial foreskins to complete their illusion of being Greek. And of course for aesthetic reasons, which would seem to have been the twins' attitude here.'

'I *do* see,' said Marigold. 'Can you imagine a Greek statue with a circumcised cock?'

'Arphisses was Egyptian, so perhaps he didn't mind.'

'He minded like hell, at any rate at first,' said Balbo. ' "For a time Arphisses and the twins, who cherished him more each day, persuaded Noah to put off the Rabbi's visit. But then Noah said that he must fondle the boy or die, and fondle him he could not while he carried his impure appendage; and he again summoned the Rabbi. And Arphisses, who was beholden to Noah for much kindness, and for receiving him into his household as his birth did warrant, sadly yielded and consented to the surgery.

' "Now this Rabbi, guessing Noah's intention with the boy and holding such courses of pleasure to be against the Jewish Law, did deliberately cut Arphisses savagely and with an unclean knife, wishing thereby to mar and infect him and render his manly parts an object of disgust to Noah, that he might no longer lust for them.

' "But the Rabbi wrought more than he had designed. Not only did he raise a putrid sore where he had cut the boy, but he poisoned all his blood, so that Arphisses sickened to death. And as he lay dying, he bade David and Rebecca, the children of Noah, search through his hair, where they would find knotted into tufts and pleats the twelve fine Rubies which he had had from Iskander and had hidden in this wise, before ever he left Iskander's Court, for safety's sake. So David and Rebecca disentangled them from his hair; and when the twelve red, glistering jewels lay before him on the cover of his couch, Arphisses said:

' " "My master, Iskander, would have it that stones of Ruby bring wealth and happiness; yet these have brought but little to me. And so I call you to witness my last will in these matters, ye that have loved me and whom I have loved, for the brief time that Fate and Necessity have given me to be with you: from henceforth, whosoever shall possess these stones, let him have joy from them, for the two years of joy which I had with their giver and for the love with which Iskander gave them; but let him have pain and grief from them too, for the pain and grief I suffer now. And may this grief and pain be greatest when the stones come into the hands of Jews, for it is by the hand of a Jew that I am so sorely stricken now. And should my will and my words be disdained and forgotten, let the Rubies turn to baubles of coloured glass.'

' "The twins bore witness to their friend's prayer, of which they told their father after Arphisses was dead, urging him to sell the jewels or even give them away, rather than keep them, with Arphisses his Curse, within the family. But Noah did not heed them and for a time he flourished. But after the moon had waxed and waned some seven times, Rebecca said to her brother David, 'Our father has had joy from these Rubies, as Arphisses wished all that owned them should have; but our father has yet to feel the pain and grief which Arphisses wished in his Curse, and most urgently against the Jews. You and I must ensure that our friend's will be done. Were we not called to witness? Are we not thereby bound to Arphisses his service?' And David agreed they were so bound, and moreover that their father deserved to be most mightily chastised for that he had caused Arphisses to be maimed in the furtherance of his own lust.

' "So they poisoned their father slowly, day by day, with noxious herbs ground into his potage, thus giving him grievous agony; and they sold the jewels to a certain merchant; and being now orphans, they left their father's house, subsisting on the money they had for the Rubies, and evermore went about the world enforcing the Curse made by their friend Arphisses on those that should possess the stones. They inflicted great sorrow on the merchant to whom they themselves had sold them (by causing his son to be tainted with leprosy, by clothing him, when he was drunk, in a leper's garment); they brought lameness and mutilation on to the nephew of the merchant, to whom in time the stones did pass, and barrenness upon his wife, and the falling sickness upon her maid-servant, who stole them and fled away with them. And so, wherever the jewels went, went good fortune and then evil, both being inflicted, in some sort, by the Guardian Twins of the Rubies, who reward and punish, as seemeth to them meet, for the love they bore to Arphisses, wielding the Curse most cruelly against the Jews (albeit they were born Jews themselves); for they were ever mindful of the wanton crime of the Jew their father, and the vile bigotry and treachery of the Rabbi that wounded their friend.''

'There follows,' said Balbo, 'a long note.' He flipped over the pages. 'It is signed Bernard Comminges, who purports to have written it after he had made his translation of the above from the original Greek of Hermogenes. Shall I read it?'

'Exhausting, all this being read to,' said Marigold faintly.

'Treasure-hunting,' said Jacquiz, 'is an exhausting business. And worse, perhaps.'

'Read it,' said Jones, S.

' ''It is the work of the Guardian Twins which we read of down the ages. They it was who, by whispering rumours in the ears of the soldiery, brought about the butchery of the Jew of Antioch, whose own curse means nothing because it was made some 1300 years after the first and true Curse of Arphisses the Egyptian Catamite. They, the Guardian Twins, intrigued to enrich and then undo the first Marquis de Maubeuge, and the Comtes de la Tour d'Abbéville who came after him; they gave Constance Fauvrelle her escape from the plague in Montreuil, but at the price of marriage to a base man from whom she had no refuge even after his death; they made André Comminges a prosperous privateer but killed or crazed his children; they made the Comminges rich in Arles but also inflicted disease and misery upon them, as they have upon me up to this day; and they tore to pieces Clovis du Touquet, when I wished to pass the Roses on to him.

' "All this I know because the Twins, David and Rebecca, who live in my house and pass as my nephew and niece, have given me a full account, far fuller than I render here. Such of it as I have written here, I swear to be the truth. (Signed) Bernard Comminges, Canon Resident of the Cathedral of St Trophîme." '

For a long time there was absolute silence. An Italian face came through Jacquiz' window and asked for their passports. Without a word they all passed theirs over, and without a word received them back.

'Certainly,' said Jacquiz at last, as they entered the first tunnel on the Italian side of the border, 'those two did say to me this morning that they were called David and Rebecca.'

'People do not live over two thousand years,' said Marigold crossly. 'And another thing. There is gross inconsistency here. The Canon told us yesterday morning, and more or less repeated at that séance thing, that he was trying to rid himself of the curse of the Jew of Antioch by finding out his true heirs in order to give them the Roses. And now here he is, telling a completely different tale. A totally different curse, and two officious adolescents, who apparently stopped growing when Alexander was invading India, to enforce it. If we are to believe any of that, what possible meaning could last night's performance have had?'

'The thing is,' said Syd Jones, 'that His Reverence told the one story, and though this new one was apparently written by him, it's the *children* who want us to know it, because it's the *children* who gave the exercise book, along with the family tree, to Jacquiz here ... and were waiting in the Cloister, it seems, for just that very purpose.'

'So,' said Marigold, 'we deduce that the Canon had one plan for us, while the children, though pretending to go along with him, in fact had another. And when the time was ripe they bumped the old fellow off somehow and left us to cope with the cadaver ... presumably knowing that we were bound to spot that chart on his tummy. It looks as though they're trying to give us the come-on – to guide us. for whatever reason, to where the jewels are hidden. And at the same time they politely provide this rather unnerving account, translated from the Greek and then transcribed by the Canon, *on oath*, from their own utterance, of the very peculiar creatures whom they claim to be . . . an account,' said Marigold, 'which has to be rubbish. Anyhow, those two don't look Jewy, not in the least.'

'Not all Jews look Jewy,' Jacquiz said. 'I had a cousin who kept wicket for Oxford. You'd never have rumbled him.'

'Of course,' said Marigold, going off on another tack, 'there is one connection between last night's conjuring show and today's hot story. We did have the Jew of Antioch, last night, squealing away about "Iskandrou Paidika", presumably meaning that boy we've just been hearing of. So I suppose the Jew of Antioch was trying to tell us it wasn't his fault, it was this Arphisses to blame. But why did anyone go to the trouble of faking up that scene? The Canon wanted us to believe that the curse came from the Jew of Antioch, and the twins were planning to let us know about the Catamite by giving us that exercise book later. So who brought the Jew on to spill the beans, and why?'

'Two things are plain to me,' Jacquiz said: 'first, whoever or whatever those children are, they are resourceful and dangerous. And secondly: they have some purpose for us. Even now we are fulfilling it, by going towards that necklace.'

'Perhaps they just want somebody new to torment,' Marigold said.

'Perhaps. In which case we should do well to turn round and go home.'

'Too late to turn round. You know that,' Marigold said.

'In any case,' said Balbo, 'if they do have some purpose for us, we are probably safer fulfilling it than trying to escape.'

'Depends what the purpose is, cobber,' said Sydney Jones.

They drove into another of the countless tunnels of the Autostrada del Sol. Jacquiz switched on his headlights. Fifty yards ahead, side by side and hand in hand, facing into the headlights holding up their free hands to halt the Rolls, were David and Rebecca.

'Okay,' said the Kyrios Pandelios, 'okay, Kyrie Len. My friend Balbo, 'e says to give you the folder, so I give 'im.' He put a fawn folder, badly stained, into Len's lap, then went to the window and gazed lovingly out at the Venetian well-head in the little square.

Len checked the folder. The notes he could not begin to understand, but the tea stain on the folder itself (and on some of the notes), as well as the penned inscription, confirmed it as the one which figured in Lady Constable's delation.

' 'Ow is that old son of a w'ore?' Pandelios turned and asked, as soon as Len had concluded his examination. 'Still sucking up the juice?'

'No,' said Len. 'He seems much healthier than I remember him and far more restrained.'

'What 'it 'im? Some sort of vision at Damascus?'

'He has found a new friend,' said Len. 'I know how he feels. Rather the same kind of thing has recently happened to me.'

' 'E must feel fucking grand to lay off the juice.'

'I dare say . . . Well, Kyrios Pandelios, with many thanks for your kindness, I ought to be off.'

Off to Kalamata in the morning, reflected Len as he crossed the little square. Early plane. Decent dinner – if they have such a thing in Heracleion (poor Len, they hadn't) – and then bed. 'Whoops, sorry.' He had nearly blundered into a man in some kind of uniform. The man smiled and said something crisp. He went this way. Len went his.

Telegram, thought Pandelios, as he watched the man in the uniform walk across the square; for me, by the look of it. High priority it must be, probably foreign, or they wouldn't deliver it at this time of the evening. There was a colossal bang on his front door. Fuck you, thought Pandelios, crapping up my poxy paint and doubtless expecting a sod-arse tip. Down the bloody stairs he bumbled, like a fart out of a tube to get a gander at his telegram. It wasn't every day, by jiminy, that some cunt sent him one.


'And so, Provost,' said Ivor Winstanley to Lord Constable of Reculver Castle, at about the same time as Len was walking away from the Kyrios Pandelios's house, hoping for a nice dinner which he wasn't going to get, 'Blakeney supports Lady Constable's story and has agreed to let us have the folder and the notes inside them. The Under-Collator rang me up to tell me earlier today, as soon as he arrived back in England from seeing Blakeney in Arles.'

'Blakeney seems to be getting about a bit these days. What's he doing in Arles?'

'I don't know, Provost.'

'But you do know that the Secret Service is interested in him?'

'Oh yes.'

'Then doesn't it occur to you that he may be rather a dangerous ally? People in whom the Secret Service is interested are apt to come croppers. Or worse, Ivor.'

'Blakeney knows what he knows – and he is letting us have the folder. The Under-Collator has gone away to get it.'

'Where from, Ivor?'

'From Crete, Provost.'

'Yes, I must admit that sounds very plausible. He'd have left his gear in Heracleion, I dare say, which is where he is based . . . in so far as such a fellow ever is based. I fear lest you are getting the better of me, Ivor.'

'Then would you like to agree terms, Provost? The later you leave it, the stiffer they will be. Any number of little extras may crop up.'

'No, no, I'll bide a while yet. I have yet to be positively confronted with Blakeney or the folder. As I said at the end of our last little chat, Ivor, I'll settle at this stage for an armed but static truce. Just let's let the thing go on: one never knows what may or may not be in the cards.'

'A gambling metaphor from *you*, Provost,' said Ivor, who was genuinely shocked.

'Oh yes, Ivor. I don't think you realize – many people don't – what a highly moral business gambling is. It destroys the greedy but sometimes exalts the humble. It occasionally rewards the daring but always crushes the headstrong. To him that hath it tends to give and from him that hath not it taketh away even that which he has – a proceeding for which it can claim the highest warranty. It is, on the whole, not unkind to the genuinely diffident but stern, very stern, with sycophants and time-servers. Oh yes, Ivor, gambling is a great school of virtue: why should I be ashamed to use, for once, its idiom?'

There was no flight direct to Kalamata. Len had to go via Athens. As he was just about to board the aeroplane at Heracleion airport for the first leg of his journey, he saw the Kyrios Pandelios join the queue.

'Ah, Kyrie Len,' said Pandelios. 'Buggering off back to London, are you?'

'Yes, Kyrios Pandelios. Where are you buggering off to?'

'Only to Athens. I have some business appointments and I shall hope to get in a little low copulation.'

'Then the best of luck, Kyrios Pandelios.'

'And to you, Kyrie Len.'

'So that's it,' said Theta to Q and Lambda, as he put down the telephone receiver. 'Dean and Chapter of Canterbury warned, Brigadier at Dover Castle well briefed, blessing from on high accorded. Troops will take post at 0630 hours tomorrow, and at precisely 0645 hours the Blakeney relics, *i.e.* two worn socks, one piece of Elastoplast and a few hairs of his head, will be reverently deposited near one of the holiest tombs in the Crypt, that of His Grace the Archbishop Morton.'

Len was lucky, in thát there was an aeroplane leaving for Kalamata that morning only minutes after he had flown into Athens. Somewhat to his annoyance, however, he found Pandelios beside him in the queue.

'You said you had business and low copulation in Athens, Kyrios Pandelios. They do not appear to have engaged you long.'

'You said you were buggering off back to London, Kyrie Len. You appear to 'ave missed your way.'

Both grinned, in a foolish and not unfriendly fashion.

'I 'ad a telegram from the Kyrios Blakeney,' Pandelios said. 'It came from Arezzo in Italy, and it tells me he may be nearing the end of a mission which he is making for me.'

'I, too, know something of this mission,' said Len.

'You are 'is friend, you brought 'is letter to me, so I trust you – up to a fucking point,' Pandelios said. 'The Kyrios Blakeney and 'is friends embark at Ancona this noon time. They will be in Patras by noon time tomorrow.'

Right, thought Len: that gives me good time to slip down the coast by car this afternoon, work out exactly where the latitude 36.53 intersects it, and have a good sniff round the place while Jake and his group are still on the briny. Only thing is, what to do with chummy Pandelios here? We don't want him latching on.

'I 'ave had very sure instructions,' Pandelios went on. 'I am to stop in Kalamata till they come through tomorrow afternoon and meanwhile I am to procure and have ready for them one bucket, of wood or steel and of the largest size I can find, one strong cable of at least thirty yards long, and one pulley.'

'Sounds as if you're all going pot-holing,' said Len.

'Pot-holing?'

Len explained as they boarded the aircraft.

'Then there is another thing,' said Pandelios. 'I am to buy one live sheep. Kyrie Len . . . do they propose to 'ave a pic-neek?'

'You've got me there.'

'Shall you too stay in Kalamata? We might 'ave dinner. The food in Kalamata is beyond words disgusting, unless one 'as feesh by the beach. We could go there.'

'Sorry,' said Len, feeling (to do him justice) rather awful. 'I'd planned to hire a car and do a trip to Mistra and Monemvasia. I've got some research to do. Both places, you see, have been often used as subjects of illuminations in Greek manuscript prayer books.' Rather a good improvisation, he thought; thank God he knew about Mistra and Monemvasia from having once planned a tour of the area with Ivor, when they were thinking of treats which they might enjoy after everything at Lancaster had been comfortably settled and Len himself had duly vanished from the scene by easy stages. 'I'm sorry you can't come too,' he said, in one sense meaning it.

'So am I sorry, Kyrie Len,' Pandelios said, also partly meaning it and knowing that Len partly meant it. 'But what with bloody buckets and torches and fornicating sheeps . . .'

'Perhaps I shall see you later.'

'Ah. Do the Kyrios Blakeney and his friends expect you?'

'Not exactly,' said Len, 'but they won't be surprised, I think – or at least one of them won't – to see me.' *If* they see me, he added to himself, *if* little Lenny hasn't pocketed the prize and scarpered long before they get there. Because I know something which they don't: what 36.53 means. But it rather looks, he told himself reluctantly, as if they know something which I don't. What's all this with buckets and pulleys and sheep?

'Right,' said Jacquiz as the car ferry stood out from Ancona at ten minutes past noon: 'Who wants a cabin for tonight? I'll have to fix them with the Purser!'

Marigold, Balbo and Sydney nodded gratefully; David and Rebecca shook their heads with contempt.

'We shall sleep under the sky,' said Rebecca; 'we are long since used to it.'

Very tiresome, thought Marigold, this pose of superiority. Those two are too self-righteous by half. And yet, she thought, their halting of the Rolls in the tunnel the previous day had been a masterly performance. The boy had walked calmly some fifty yards to the rear of the car and had begun to divert the traffic round it and to its left. (Whooosh . . . WHOOOOSH: any minute now one of them will see him too late, Marigold thought, or just won't believe it and panic. Cars simple *don't* stop in tunnels.) The girl had come and spoken to Jacquiz through the driver's window.

'You have read what I gave you?' she said.

'Yes. Can we please get out of this tunnel?'

'So now you understand?'

'Yes. No. I don't know. If we stay here there will be an accident. Why stop us here?'

'To show you what manner of people we are. We shall stay here, all of us, until you promise to obey.'

Despite the boy's activities in the rear of the Rolls, other cars were swirling by within inches and hooting hysterically.

'Obey?' said Marigold.

'Obey my brother and me in everything we ask. You will see.'

'What's in it for us?' said Jones from the back.

'Getting out of this bloody tunnel before we're all killed,' said Marigold. 'Promise,' she urged Jacquiz.

Jacquiz nodded. 'We promise,' he said. 'Get in. Room for one in the front and one in the back.'

The girl whipped round into the back, next to Balbo.

'Now drive,' she said.

'What about your friend?'

'My brother. He has other business now. We pick him up where I shall tell you later.'

And an hour later she had said: 'Stop at this garage.'

When they stopped, the boy came out of the bar, bowed

to Marigold through the car window, opened the door, and settled gracefully on the cross-bench beside her.

'How did you get here so quickly?' Marigold said.

'There are cars, madame, even faster than your Rolls-Royce. Drive on, sir, please. You will of course have calculated that our journey is easily made from Ancona – or Bari, if the ship at Ancona is full. We shall go there, as you have doubtless decided already, by Arezzo. There will be no stopping until we reach Arezzo.'

'A little food would be nice. We had a snack on the auto-route near Cannes, but—'

'—No stopping until Arezzo. You may eat there what you wish,' the boy had said coldly. 'Now you tell *him*,' he said to the girl in the back, indicating Balbo.

'You have a friend in Crete?' she said.

'How would you know?'

'His is connected by marriage with the Kommingi – what is left of them – so it is our affair to know. We keep watch on the Kommingi, we keep watch on his wife, who was a Kommingi before she married him, and so we hear that you are coming.'

'How do you keep watch on them?'

'By paying money, Monsignor's money,' said the girl patiently, 'to someone in Heracleion who will see for us without being seen. And so in Nicopolis. Thus we watch and we know of them, although they know nothing of us. The Monsignor was a skilled genealogist. He was able to follow all the windings of his family, forward and back, forward to Greece, where they have almost forgotten who they are, back to before Andrea departed over the sea from Arles. And so, whoever comes and by whichever way, the approaches are guarded.'

'Rather what we thought,' Balco said.

'Then no more of this now. Pandelios. He is a man to trust, he is your friend. He will come without fail if you call on him?'

'Yes.'

'Then you will send him a telegram as soon as we reach

Arezzo. You will tell him to wait for us at Kalamata, the next day after tomorrow, and have ready for us the following things . . .'

That night they had spent at Arezzo, the adults in an hotel, the boy and the girl none save themselves knew where. And now, here they all were, en route for Patras, standing on the deck of the good ship *Petrarch* and being rejoined by Jacquiz, who handed over cabin tickets to Balbo and Sydney, told Marigold the number of the one she would be sharing with himself, and then courteously invited everybody to luncheon.

'Isn't he a love, when he's being nice?' said Marigold.

But David and Rebecca shook their heads at the invitation.

'Look here,' said Marigold, 'I'm sick of this rubbish. Don't you have to eat?'

The two children (for such they suddenly appeared) looked at her quietly, then turned, linked hands (fingers interlocking), and walked away along the deck. A very faint echo of the chilling laughter, which he had last heard in the Canon's chamber, darted back to Jacquiz. No one else appeared to hear anything.

'Those two are beginning to bug me,' Marigold said.


'By My Lord Archbishop's side?' said Theta. 'Or do you think that the floor would be more effective?'

'Scientifically it makes no difference,' Lambda said. 'Do what you think most appropriate.'

Theta bent over the tomb and distributed the Blakeney relics on to the heads of the six little canons who were praying, three on either side, over His Grace's recumbent effigy.

'Now let it work,' said Theta.

As Theta and Lambda left the Crypt, there were myriad cheeps and scutterings. Once safe up the steps and into the South-West Transept, they turned with relief to watch two soldiers block the passage with thick close-hedge barbed-wire.




While Pandelios waited in Kalamata for Balbo and his party to arrive, Len had pushed on down into the Mani. Since it had taken longer than he expected to hire a car, and longer still to find a reasonably large-scale map of the area, he had not left Kalamata until late in the afternoon; and after an hour of winding through steep shadows and deserted villages he had prudently decided not to undertake his investigation along latitude 36.53 until the next morning.

By the time he had spiralled down from the coastal hills past Itylus to Limini and spiralled up again to Areopolis, it was nearly dark; so he drove swiftly across the neck of the peninsula to the seaside resort of Gytheion, where he had spent a night of modest comfort in one of the still mercifully open hotels.

And now, shortly after dawn, he was driving back from Gytheion to Areopolis, where he must turn South through the region of broken towers and crooked sea-chapels to the latitude he sought. Preliminary calculations had apprised him that this passed somewhere just South of the little port of Gerolimin. He would, therefore, motor through Gerolimin, and then explore, in detail, the strip of coast below it.




'Sir,' said a Signaller in the South-West Transept of Canterbury Cathedral, 'the RT's swamped.'

'Swamped?' the Brigadier said.

'Can't get a thing out of it. Like a mass of static but worse; just a continuous high-pitched bleep.'

'Let me try . . .'

A dispatch rider came through the side door into the Transept. He saluted, then made urgently for the Brigadier.

'Well?' said the Brigadier, abandoning the RT set with a worried shrug.

'Heavy interference with RT, sir. Colonel de Courcy says we can't get on to your HQ by wireless any more, nor can we get through the other way, down to our sub-units. So he's sent me round with the news.'

'And what is the news?'

'The news is, sir, that not a single one of the – er – enemy has attempted to break through.'

'I see.'

The Brigadier crossed to where Theta and Lambda were admiring the triple tomb of Lady Margaret Holland and her two husbands.

'Rather daring,' Lambda was saying; 'troilism in the grave, so to speak.'

'I've just had a third report,' the Brigadier said; 'same as the first two: not a mouse stirring.'

'They were stirring all right when we left the Crypt.'

'Not now – or not according to these three reports. We shan't get any more for a bit. Radio's jammed.'

Lambda considered this.

'Buzzing?' he inquired.

'No. A piercing squeal.'

'With a slight variation in pitch on a regular rhythm?'

'Come and hear for yourself.'

Lambda went and heard for himself.

'Mutants,' he said at last. 'We knew they were a new strain. I should have expected something of the kind.'

'What kind?' said Theta and the Brigadier together.

'I'm afraid they're much too clever to fall for this dodge. They like it where they are. *But* they've got the message from those samples we laid out – and they're passing it on to their mates outside. Their ... neural means of transmission ... is what's interfering with your RT sets, Brigadier. Hence this abominable noise. Anyway, they're not going to budge, not in my view at least.'

'But surely,' Theta said, 'the whole point is that these creatures will want to share in the feast of Blakeney's flesh in order to absorb some of his wisdom and spirit. They won't just want to give others the tip and not get a share themselves?'

'I think we got that wrong too. I think we'll find the whole point is this: that the *race* wants to absorb the wisdom and numen of its defunct God-King, and this can be done quite easily by a few representatives on behalf of the entire species. No need for each individual to fight for a crumb. All that's necessary is enough of them to make a clean job and ensure that nothing is wasted. The virtue that lay with Blakeney, though absorbed by only a few, would go to strengthen what you might call the *corporate soul* of all. It's the corporate soul, incidentally, more fully understood and exploited by this new strain, that has enabled them to get up transmissions through the ether between themselves and separate groups or individuals a long way off. Before long the rest will learn the trick – if they haven't already.'

'So they are passing this message,' said Theta slowly, 'to their ... friends and relations. Over how wide an area can they broadcast? England? The British Isles? France? Eastern Europe?'

'What I've told you is little more than speculation. I can say nothing as to their precise capacities.'

'Well, we'd better hope,' said Theta, 'that their carrying power falls short of the Peloponnese. That, Sydney tells me, is where he and Blakeney are heading now. Meanwhile, Brigadier, we had better leave your men at their posts for the time being. Here is another lesson that there is no such thing as an exact science,' he said with a bland look at Lambda, 'and there may be more surprises yet.'


The Kyrios Pandelios was waiting, as he had been instructed by his telegram from Balbo, at the Messenia Airport just out-side Kalamata. Though encumbered with a coil of cable, a huge cement-bucket, a pulley, and a live sheep, he had in-sisted on his democratic right to use the airport lounge, even though neither he nor the people he was meeting were flying by the airline but were simply using its ample and prominent premises as a convenient rendezvous. How, Pandelios wondered, were his interesting items of equipment to be transported where they were going? He had been definitively ordered in the lengthy telegram not to 'bring or hire own vehicle'. No doubt the good Kyrios Blakeney knew best, but there would surely be a problem here.

It was very soon solved for him. As he was watching through the window for Balbo's arrival, he saw the most beautiful yet brutal car he had ever seen, with a bonnet like the port-cullis of a Byzantine castle, sweep into the car park, followed by a large Range Rover. Driving the car was a man with an imperial face, hooky nose, and powerful black and grey hair; next to him was a strongly set yet somehow dainty girl, ginger hair in page boy cut, quivering snub nose, and firm lemon-shaped breasts. Behind them sat beloved Kyrios Balbo; on one side of him was a fair boy with a face like a satyr's but without the grin or the leer; on the other side of Balbo was a girl with a sweet, rather lop-sided face surmounted by a cowl. Driving the Range Rover was a robust, slightly tubby little man with a wide, coarse mouth and merry eyes; him Pandelios recognized as the cricketing man who had come to see him in Crete to ask news of Balbo some weeks back.

Pandelios went out into the car park.

'Where's the gear, sport?' said the cricketing man.

Pandelios gestured into the lounge. The cricketing man, the imperial man, the fair boy and Balbo all tumbled out of their respective seats and rushed in the direction which Pandelios had indicated.

'Bear a hand, sport,' said the cricketing man as he raced past, 'then hop into the Rover with me. No time to lose. All hands to the pump, as the bishop said to the choirboy, and explanations later.'

Just South of Gerolimin, at the bottom of a hill, a rough track led to the right and towards the sea.

Worth a try down here, thought Len.

He parked his hired car by the side of the road and started down the track, along which swampy grass alternated with chunky rocks.

A good thing I decided to walk, thought Len.

There was a wind blowing. This had not been evident before, as Len had been in the car and the car (until it reached Gerolimin) had been separated from the coast by low, scrubby hills; but now that Len was in the open, walking towards a little bay (which he could see about 200 yards ahead of him), he was aware that the wind was both very rough and very keen. He remembered Ivor's telling him, when they had been discussing their possible trip, that the wind down here blew for 300 days of the 365.

'They have gardens walled off in squares by cypress trees,' Ivor had said.

There were two of these side by side on Len's right. On his left was a slope strewn with ruined stone houses of indeterminate date; the slope ascended quite steeply past the houses and ended sharply in a cliff. There was another cliff over to the right as well (beyond the gardens and the cypress trees), and in its face, about 300 yards along the beach, the high, triangular entrance of a cave. The cliffs delineated the jaws of the bay; they dipped in the centre, at its throat, to allow a tiny stream to piddle over the beach and into the salt water. On either side of the stream the ground was flat for about 100 yards. Len's path was about 70 yards to the left of the stream, as it ran to the sea, and parallel with it; he was therefore well over to one side of a wide, flat corridor which ran between road and beach, almost under the slopes with the ruins. The cypress gardens to his right were about 150 yards from the sea and half way between himself and the stream.

This path is as near as the devil on the right latitude, thought Len; this is as good a place as any to hide tainted jewels. He shivered from the wind and wished he'd had his lunch before coming there. That cave, thought Len. Too obvious. Those ruined houses to my left? But which?

The cypresses swayed in the wind, urging Len to them, inviting him to come into their shelter. Why not in a garden, Len thought, a garden among the trees? Oh the bitter wind; warm trees. There was fir and umbrella pine as well as cypress (odd, thought Len vaguely, I didn't think they grew down here), and Aleppo pine and ilex, lime tree and quercus robur, aeschylus and yew, all these inside the cypresses and forming a second wall against the wind, a wall so thick that there was hardly any space for the garden, which indeed consisted only of clumps of dear iris and long-necked sage of Jerusalem. Towards these Len walked as the trees swayed and soothed and enticed him, through these he blundered, to find at his feet a circle of low stones, over one of which he tripped, then fell, down and down into the darkness, until he landed heavily in water, sank a few inches, and settled (how cosily, thought Len before he thought no more, oh, how cosily) into thick, warm mud.

As Jacquiz drove the Rolls through Kalamata and then on to the road on which they would wind down the Mani, the twins, David and Rebecca, spoke of what had been and what was yet to come.

'When it was known to us,' said David, 'that you, Doctor Helmut, were coming from the West and that you, Mr Blakeney, were coming from the East, Monsignor Comminges made a plan for you all, and so did we.'

'But ours was different from that of Monsignor Comminges.' Rebecca said.

'Monsignor Comminges' plan was that you should be assisted to Arles if you faltered on the way, but that on the whole you should be left to guide yourselves, as a test of your worthiness. So we watched, my sister and I, we listened and followed and we occasionally put a clue, which otherwise you might have missed, in your way. The cheap copies of the Tarasque Medallion at Paestum, Mr Blakeney; the scrapbook in Saint Bertrand, Doctor Helmut. And as time went on you were found worthy.'

'Found worthy by the Monsignor for what he wished of you; found worthy by us for what we wished of you,' Rebecca said.

'So that's why everything was so ... so devious,' said Marigold: 'we were being tested. In the Musée Arlaten, for instance: that picture of Mistral and the Monsignor's grandfather – a test of observation, I suppose.'

'No,' said David. 'That was accidental.'

'It brought us to the Cloister at just the right time.'

'That would have been done in any case, by my sister or me, if you had not found out the Cloister by yourselves.'

'Then what *was* that Museum bit?'

'Accidental, as I say. There was no intention that you should follow me. I was going to the Arlaten to collect certain properties for the performance which we were later to put on at Saint Honorat's church. The Director of the Museum would, I knew, look kindly on my requests as I appeared before him dressed like a schoolboy in the days of his own adolescence. It seems that he has memories.'

'Were you required to share them with him?'

'No. Merely to wear the clothes and be deferential.'

'The man who sells tickets was afraid of you.'

'The man who sells the tickets is, as you would say, of the dregs of mankind.'

'But you must admit,' said Balbo, 'that there is something disturbing about you both. I mean ... you appear and disappear at the drop of a hat, you turn up in the most extraordinary places, wearing the most astonishing kit ... and on top of it all you make sure that we get hold of that exercise book of the Canon's and read all that stuff about Alexander's boyfriend and Noah of Joppa, thus more or less inviting us to identify you with the Guardian Twins in the legend who administer the Curse of the Roses.'

'It is no legend, Mr Blakeney. The Canon's researches have been very accurate.'

'But nobody can believe that tale about the twins.'

'Can they not? It is at least some sort of explanation,' the boy said. 'Two people who conspire to bring happiness and misery as they see fit, by their own agency and exertion. This is more credible than some vague kind of magical influence, some spell cast by the jewels themselves.'

'But it can't have been the same two people for the last two and a half thousand years,' Marigold said.

A small, square fort loomed (almost like a geometrical figure) above the hairpin bend round which the Rolls was now turning.

'Frankish?' said Balbo.

'Byzantine,' said Jacquiz; 'not enough vertical aspiration for the Franks. People often forget how skyward minded they were. Thank God for power steering,' he said as they moved smoothly out of the bend. 'I suppose' – he looked briefly across Marigold at the boy, David – 'I suppose there might be an inherited commitment, passed down from the original twins through generation after generation, to watch over and reward and punish the owners of the Rubies. I imagine that your function, if it is your function, is hereditary?'

'It is our function,' Rebecca said. And then, after a pause, 'You have yet to hear the plans that were made for you, ours and the Monsignor's.'

'His plan,' said the boy, 'was to employ you, as people proved intelligent and fitting, to take the Rubies from where they were hidden, and thus disembarrass him of the so-called Curse, and of my sister and myself who implement it. Once you had the Roses, he thought, we would leave him for you. He could not tell you the true story of the Curse – how it was made by Arphisses of Thebes and its enactment was entrusted to myself and Rebecca—'

'—To your ancestors—'

'—Is at any rate our sworn duty – he could not tell you that story, lest you should realize that the Curse would indeed come to you along with the Rubies. So he told you the false but often accepted story, that the Jew of Antioch first made the Curse, and assured you that if the Rubies were returned to his descendants the Curse would cease to operate. He then conducted his séance at Saint Honorat's. Had things gone as he wished, a rightful owner would have been fraudulently named, and you would then have agreed to fetch the jewels from the secret place and carry them to this owner – who did not, of course, exist. Thus you would have acquired Curse and Roses together, and would not easily have made yourselves free of them. As for him, he would at last have been released.'

'But things did *not* go as he wished.'

'No,' said the girl. 'We had another plan.'

'Another plan,' said the boy, 'to which there must be a preface.' He rested his hand very lightly on Marigold's knee, as if to reassure her. She gave a sharp gasp of pleasure, whereupon, but without haste, he removed it. 'Has it ever occurred to you,' he said, 'to wonder why the Curse – that is, We – operated so swiftly and finally at the expense of Clovis du Touquet? We cut him to pieces in Aix-en-Provence within hours of his being told by the Canon how he might possess the Roses. We did this because if ever a possessor, or near-possessor, deserved such a fate, it was this Clovis.'

'Oh, I say,' said Balbo, 'he wasn't as bad as all that. Don't tell me you two fixed the tables in the Casino for that incredible run of his just before he died.'

'Oh yes. He had left the Canon in Arles and was on his way to find the jewels. We met him, suggested he should spend a night in Aix-en-Provence, and should go to the Gaming Rooms (once a favourite amusement of his), where we would arrange that he won heavily – providing that he promised he would cease to gamble when we gave him the sign (no more diamonds in his hand of cards) and also promised to grant one special request which we would proffer to him later. He duly promised, and so we procured a ticket for him (by theft), as both his identity card and his passport had long since been endorsed against admission to such places, and escorted him during his triumphant progress. In the event he kept his first promise—'

'—But how had you rigged the tables?'

'Not the tables, The cards he received. We are skilful conjurors, as you should know by now. He was standing back from the card table. We could easily substitute, in his hand, the cards he needed for the cards he had been given. He hardly knew it himself.'

'But the roulette wins which started him off? And helped him later with funds for the baccarat game?'

'Pure luck. Gamblers sometimes win. These gains simply saved us the trouble of putting him in funds for the card tables by stealing plaques from the Caisse – or picking clients' pockets.'

'I see. So he went on playing until you issued him with cards which no longer had diamonds among them?'

'Yes. A crude symbolism. Red diamonds to stand for red rubies, which playing cards do not carry. As soon as the red jewels were withdrawn, he was to desist.'

'And desist he did, as he had promised?'

'But he did not keep his other promise. When we accosted him outside the Casino, he heard our request and then refused it: he would not grant it, he said, until we had made for him *une vraie fortune* – a hundred times what we had won for him that night.'

'But did he really deserve to be butchered like that – like a pig in a shambles?'

'He had, at any rate, refused our request.'

'And what *was* this request?'

'Rebecca and I are weary of our task. But we may only abandon it if the possessor of the Rubies sets us free. We have him in our Guardianship, along with the necklace, but he has us in his, because we may only be released from our oath as Guardians if the possessor consents to this.'

'Why should he possibly object?'

'Because the Curse of Arphisses states, you remember, that on the day the Curse ceases to operate, on that day the Rubies will turn to coloured glass. For fear of this, many succeeding owners have refused to release us. So did Clovis du Touquet, when we approached him after he left the Casino.'

'But for God's sake, why have they refused to release you? By releasing you from your oath – from your distant ancestors' oath – they release themselves from you and from the Curse. Surely the Canon would have jumped at it. He didn't need to make elaborate plans to shift the ownership: all he had to do was release you.'

'He would not do this, out of greed and out of pride. It had been the same with all of them before him. To know that there were such rare and ancient jewels, and they were his—'

'—But he was plotting to get rid of them—'

'—Yes. That he would do. He could endure that *his* stones went to another, but *not* that they should cease to exist. They had been his and his family's for so long: he might dispose of them, but in his pride, some might say in his honour, he would not destroy them.'

'And neither would Clovis?' Balbo asked.

'No. For greed was on him and arrogance of birth. His House, he thought, had a most just and ancient claim that went back through many centuries of time. So in his haughtiness and folly we destroyed him. And then, when we discovered that *you* were all coming, we made *our* plan. We too found you worthy, as the Canon did but for different reasons. Not only were you brave and clever enough to venture into the abominable place where the Roses are hidden, you were also honourable enough and kind enough to give me and my sister our quittance. You will . . . Mr Blakeney, Doctor Helmut, Mrs Helmut . . . you will set us free?'

'From your hereditary oath,' said Marigold carefully. 'Have we the power?'

'If you have the Rubies, you may, if you will, free us from the oath that has been binding for so long. That is what we have prayed, Rebecca and I. We changed the form of the séance, to give you the first hint of the true story of Iskander's catamite (a sad name for the friend whom we loved), of Iskandrou Paidika. I played the Jew, with properties from

422

the Arlaten Museum to assist me. We killed the old man by suffocation first, and as the séance ended we hypnotized you by using the little red lights that were meant for the Rubies, into brief unconsciousness on your feet while we escaped. (Yes, we Guardians have learned many such tricks in our generations.) Then came the last test of all. Would you read the Canon's body, then dispose of it and escape from the Alyscamps? Or would you raise the cry against us with the police? If the former, you were of the calibre we needed. If the latter, you had failed us both in courage and in love.'

'You hadn't done all that much to make us love you,' Marigold remarked.

'Are we not beautiful, my brother and I?'

'In any case,' said David, 'you passed the final test. Doctor Helmut came to the Cloister, as we hoped that he or another of you would, and we gave him the two documents which would make all plain to you. And then we waited by the way for you and extracted a promise. You promised to obey, and so you have; but we know we cannot compel your obedience to the extent of freeing us and thus destroying the Roses: that is a great matter and must be of your own will.'

There was a long silence. Eventually Balbo said:

'Speaking for myself, and, I think I can safely say, for Sydney and Pandelios, I am of opinion that the only decent thing, whatever the real truth behind all this, is to do what we are asked. Our two friends here say that it is what they wish, and I think we should respect that wish, never mind what may happen to the jewels. If people pray to be released, whoever they may be and whatever, precisely, they may mean, then one must help them as best one can. Otherwise, you know, one finds it difficult to look in the mirror.'

Rebecca put her hand on Balbo's thigh; he felt a sudden piercing spurt of lust, lust of such quality that it was enough simply to have experienced it; it was so weird and thrilling that it was its own satisfaction.

'Agreed,' Marigold said.

David pressed his thigh against Marigold's. She writhed in her seat and nearly moaned aloud.

'Yes,' said Jacquiz, 'but it would be nice to see the Rubies, as they are, first.'

'You will see them first.'

Both David and Rebecca reached to stroke Jacquiz' hair with their fingertips. He whistled softly.

'You could have got round us all at once just by . . . just by touching us.'

'But we could not prove your good will just by touching you. You had to show that of yourselves, without being enticed. Now you have done this, and we are going to the place where the Rubies are hidden. Before you can release us, you must see them and hold them; there is also a ceremony to be performed. Now it is night: soon we shall stop for you to dine, as you must, and for the two gentlemen in the vehicle behind to be told all and acquainted with your decisions. Then we shall go on through the darkness and come to a certain place. There we shall seek out the Rubies, the Roses of Picardie, and do all else that must be done.'


'Ah, Ivor,' intoned Lord Constable as he swept across the lawn of the Great Court of Lancaster. 'Ah, Ivor,' he grated, as he halted and gathered his multifarious gown about him. 'Ah, Ivor,' he snarled, as he lifted his mortar board in courteous greeting, 'have we any news of your Under-Collator?'

'I can't say we have, Provost.'

'Due back yesterday, wasn't he?'

'Or today, Provost. Aeroplanes don't always run at our exact convenience.'

'Today is nearly over, Ivor. Today is now this evening.' He loomed imperious in the dusk, cassock and bands and full-length gown. He was still holding his mortar board above his head, but now replaced it, dead central but tilting slightly downwards, so that one corner pointed straight at Ivor's throat. Like a Provost in an eighteenth-century print, thought Ivor, but life size: a figure comprising the entire English academic tradition, comprising Bentley, Arnold, Jowett, Cornford, Robert Birley and Whipping Keat.

'Indeed, Provost, the day is far spent, and the night is at hand. But truth will out,' said Ivor sententiously, 'even in the darkness.'

'Will it, Ivor? We shall see. Just remember this: that poor fool, Elvira, is a bungler. Even when she doesn't bungle, anything she takes up has a way of going wrong. How is she, by the way?'

' "Well, I thank your Lordship; well, well." '

'Gentlemen in converse,' said Lord Constable, 'confine themselves to occasional and strictly relevant quotations. Yours, Ivor, are profuse and dispensable. It is, they say, a sign either of bad nerves or premature senile decay.'

The Provost raised his mortar board to Ivor Winstanley and stalked off into the fenny mist.


Jacquiz, instructed by the twins, stopped the Rolls just South of Gerolimin. The Range Rover stopped behind. All disembarked from both vehicles and gathered in a group between the two, lit by the headlights of the Range Rover.

'There is a car parked just ahead of us,' Jacquiz said.

'Ah,' said Pandelios.

He went to examine the car and returned,

As I thought,' he said. 'I have seen lately a young man from Cambridge, the Kyrios Under-Collator Len of Lancaster College. He seems to know something of this matter.'

'Does he, by God?' said Jacquiz.

'How?' said Balbo.

'In any case,' said Pandelios, 'that car is the one he hired in Kalamata. I saw him driving past in it, with these own eyes, as I came out of the shop with the damn bucket.'

'There was another present,' said the boy, David, 'on the night of the séance in Saint Honorat's. I was at the end of the electric speaker when he applied for permission with the password. Something, I do not know what, something in my head told me that he had a part to play in what was doing, so I pressed the switch and let him in. This will be he.'

'Delectable Len,' said Marigold lubriciously. 'But there isn't any sign of him.'

'Never mind Len,' said Jacquiz; 'let's get on with what we came for.'

The boy and the girl, with torches, led the way slowly down the track, which Len too had taken, towards the sea. The sheep followed behind them like a dog. At their command, Jacquiz and Syd Jones carried the coil of cable between them, Marigold and Pandelios carried the pulley, and Balbo the bucket, which was all but too large for him. The wind had ceased altogether since Len passed that way in the morning, and the squares of cypress ahead of them stood absolutely straight in the light of a three-quarter moon.

'There are two gates to the place where we are going,' the boy's voice floated back to those behind. 'Only one may be opened from outside, and it is very dangerous. My sister and I shall gain entrance that way, then we shall open the other gate from inside to admit all of you.'

'Where are we?' asked Jacquiz.

'A forgotten port of the Roman Empire of the East. You may see some ruined houses on your left. It was called Ventilitus, the shore of the wind, by the Romans, though some say it was used before by the Phoenicians and had a name in a tongue even older than Greek. Where we are going was once the Roman Governor's garden.'

David and Rebecca led the party over the wall of cypress on the right. They went through the cypresses, through the other trees inside them, into an open space with bushes and tall dead flowers, which spiked jaggedly into the torchlight. They came to a circle of stones.

David handed his torch to Rebecca, who applied them both while her brother set up the pulley, attached the bucket to the cable, passed the bucket through the circle made by the stones and into the cylindrical shaft which ran down from them into the earth. Rebecca handed one torch to Jacquiz, then slipped neatly down and stood in the bucket, the rim of which cut into the base of her buttocks; her brother got down and stood belly to belly with her.

'Lower the bucket,' said the boy to Jacquiz and Jones, 'until I call out. Then stop; secure the cable, so that the bucket will stay steady at the depth it has reached; and then go to the shore, where the stream runs into the sea. Just before the stream reaches the beach there is a small stone house, with two rooms and no roof. Once a Customs' House, they say. Wait in the room to the right of the door but keep well clear of the seaward wall. Bring the sheep.'

'Wouldn't it be better if one of you stayed to show us the way?'

'You have the moon and one torch. It is better that Rebecca and I make this entrance together. Sometimes, in the past, it has been necessary, when there was no help, that I should go first and then admit her by the other gate, after she had lowered me. But this they do not like. Of late they have been changing very much, and I do not wish to risk giving them offence.'

'Giving whom offence? The Rubies?'

'Lower, please.'

Very carefully, Jacquiz and Sydney played out the cable through the pulley. The torsos and heads of the children disappeared. The sheep nuzzled Marigold and Pandelios.

'I wonder what's in store for you, girl,' Marigold said.

After some minutes of heavy breathing from Jacquiz and Sydney, a call came from the depths.

'That is enough. Secure the cable and go.'

Sydney locked the pulley and further secured the unused length of cable by winding it round a tree and knotting it.

'Bonza job,' he said.

Jacquiz then led them, with the torch, back through the close-packed ranks of trees and out on to the track. The rest of them followed him (the sheep now in close attendance upon Marigold) down to the beach and then to the right and along it. After seventy yards or so they came to a small, whispering stream. As the boy had said, there was a little

427

stone house beside it, just where bush and thorn gave place to pebbly sand.

They waited in the right-hand room for a long time.

'What a peaceful night,' Marigold said.

The sea pattered on to the shore and the moon flashed in the sea. The sheep made a pile of droppings and a small noise as of apology.

'Granted, I'm sure,' Marigold said to it.

A stone flag in the floor, very close to the seaward wall, slowly rose.

'One cannot lift this from outside,' the boy's voice said to them softly. 'It would not do to have an entrance which could be opened from outside and in such an obvious place as this. The other entrance, as you will have deduced, is three-quarters of the way down that well.'

'Where is delectable Len?' said Marigold, à propos of nothing.

'You shall see,' said the boy. He climbed up into the room. 'There are steps.' He pointed at the raised flag. 'You will go first, Doctor Helmut, with the torch; then Mr Jones, then the Kyrios Pandelios; then Mrs Helmut—'

'—Marigold—'

'—Then Mrs Helmut. I shall come last, to make sure that this stone is properly down, and I shall bring the sheep.'

One by one they climbed through the square hole and started down narrow, winding steps.

'The way down to the Governor's store rooms and dungeons,' came the boy's voice behind them. 'A Governor of even so small a port as Ventilitus reckoned to make his fortune out of excise.'

The sheep, who was finding the going difficult, made a sharp bleat of disapproval. Jacquiz reached the bottom of the steps and started along a broad, high corridor. Damp streamed down the walls and warm, heavy drops fell on to his head from the ceiling. When he trained his torch up on to it, he saw that it was barrel vaulted with thickly cracked stone.

'I have always heard,' said Pandelios's voice in answer to

his thought, 'that there is many hot springs and underground streams in bloody Taygetus. They are pissing down my neck now.'

'Kindly be silent, Kyrie,' the boy said. 'We are nearly there.'

The corridor took a bend to the left. The boy came up and joined Jacquiz.

'Raise your torch, Doctor Helmut.'

A strong arch with elegantly carved Roman letters.

'The Governor's Treasury,' said the boy: 'appropriate.'

He preceded Jacquiz through the arch. The sheep loitered with Marigold and turned its face into her thighs, but the boy reached back to seize it by the hind legs, whereupon it gave a hideous, pitiful, long-drawn baah—

'—I knew that sheep was not going to have a nice time, poor darling—'

—and was flung violently forward by the boy.

'An offering,' he said. 'Stand clear and watch.'

Peering through the arch, Jacquiz saw a tall, dim chamber, lit by a burning brand of wood which was held aloft by Rebecca. Round her feet scurried a torrent of little furry creatures, squeaking and scrabbling.

'The rats guard the necklace for the Guardians,' said the boy, 'and have done for many centuries since Andreas Kommingi first hid it here. When we come, we bring them a sheep on which to feast. So they know us, and admit us, as they would none else. They do not like it when we come separately, for they seem to know that our trust is for both of us together.'

'But is Len in here?' said Marigold. 'And is he all right? You did say we'd be seeing him.'

For a moment the boy looked irritated, the first time his face had ever expressed anything so petty, Marigold thought, and he did not answer. Meanwhile the rats scurried on over the floor towards the sheep which was trying in vain (on the slippery stone floor) to struggle to its legs. But as the rats came up to it, the little creatures stopped. They seemed to be looking beyond the sheep at the visitors under the arch. Thousands of little gold eyes stared steadily ahead of them. No squeaks, no scrabbling now; total silence.

'I think,' said Balbo, 'that they have recognized me for what I am, or what I was. They were bound to, I suppose. They must know that I once had grace with them and have now lost it,' he said, low but clear, 'either from what they scent in myself, or even' – he came forward and craned, as if listening – 'because they have somehow been told that such a one as I might come.' He paused. 'Yes, that is it. Word has spread across the whole continent,' he said in equable tones, 'that one such as I has been traced to this region. So they are not altogether surprised to see me, and now, with the greatest respect, they will . . . do what they must with me. They will not, I think, this time,' he said to the boy, 'be much interested in your offering of a sheep.'

The front rank of the rats began to edge forward round the sheep. Behind were squadrons more, regiments, whole armies.

'Do something,' said Jacquiz to the boy.

But the boy shrugged.

'I know nothing of this,' he said.

'Jesus Christ, won't some bugger get rid of these bastards,' shouted Syd Jones. He stepped forward and began to kick at the rats. They leaped nimbly over his shoes, evading but otherwise ignoring him.

'This cannot be,' said Pandelios faintly.

The girl held the torch higher. Len, naked, stepped out of the shadows.

The rats hesitated then turned; a swirling mass of cheeping fur.

'He was here when we came,' the boy said. 'I do not understand this. I only know what I have always known. Us, my sister and me, they recognize and admit here. But this is different.'

The rats were crowding back past the sheep and on to where Len stood, poised like a classical Greek statue, left hip above right, right leg slightly bent at the knee joint. There was another flurry.

'They're lying down,' said Marigold.

'They're offering their throats,' said Balbo. 'That means that they surrender themselves, they obey, they adore, they worship. They offered them to me once . . .'

'. . . And now,' said Jacquiz, 'they're offering them to Len.'

'He has the Sign,' said Sydney. 'I was told how to recognize it. For one thing, look at his forehead.'

Jacquiz took a step forward and flashed his torch on to Len's face. Len's forehead was smooth, unlined.

'It wasn't like that, not when 'e flew across with me yesterday,' Pandelios proclaimed.

'The Sign appears,' said Jones, 'in response to their desire that it should appear – if, and only if, a man is worthy.'

'Do you mind, Jake,' said Len. 'That torch is rather bright. Thank you. I think . . . they somehow called me. I went into a daze and wandered into those trees – and the next thing I knew I'd fallen into that well. They came and got me out, and brought me here. They took off my wet clothes, and dried me, and put me into a sort of bed. And then, when I came to again, I realized.'

He surveyed the carpet of supine rats. Others were scampering from all directions, laying themselves down on top of their fellows, till in places they were two or three deep.

'They have already done this once,' said Len. 'Then it was in welcome and in acclamation. Now it is in courtesy. They are asking my permission to go ahead and perform their customary sacrament. With Balbo.'

'You must forbid them,' said Jones, S.

Len turned his head, then tilted it as if listening.

'I'm not sure that I can. You see they're asking me only as a courtesy, as a formality.'

'Try.' Sydney turned to the boy. 'The Roses? Where are they?'

'They will be handed to those who now possess them while they perform the rite of releasing my sister and myself.'

'But which of us is to release you? Which of us counts as possessing the jewels?'

'Any or all of you that have come here to get them.'

A wild idea crossed Sydney's mind.

'Let it be Mr Blakeney.' And to Len: 'Ask those creatures to wait.'

Len looked uneasy.

'They're not liking it,' he said. 'They say – that is, their collective soul says – that it is their custom and duty to consume, in all piety, the man that has been their God but is no longer.'

'Ask them to wait just while he himself performs another rite, a rite which will increase his value as their victim.'

Len closed his eyes and passed his hands up and down his body. The rats cheeped louder; then their noise diminished, slowly and reluctantly, into a low twittering of provisional consent.

'It is best,' said the boy, 'that there be another as well as Mr Blakeney. My sister and I . . . before we are released . . . we must offer ourselves. And be taken. It is easier, I think, for two people to take us than for one. My sister can offer herself to Mr Blakeney; by whom shall I be taken?'

'By me. For Christ's sake, by me,' said Marigold, remembering how the boy had touched her with hand and later with thigh while next to her in the car.

She smiled at Jacquiz.

'All right?' she said. 'You know it makes no difference to what we have now. What we've begun to have since we started on this search.'

'It may not,' said Jacquiz, 'be quite what you think it will be. With this boy, I mean. But if you're prepared to risk it . . .'

'A boy's a boy. And what a boy.'

'Agreed.'

'You can hold them?' said Sydney to Len.

'For a little. Can it help?'

'I'm playing a long shot.'

More rats from the shadows joined those already massed round Len. There was a renewed cheeping, possibly of the newcomers. Once again, this diminished into a low, general twitter.

'These rats, I cannot bear the fucking bastards any longer, mother of God,' Pandelios said. He slumped to the ground.

Balbo went to Pandelios.

'No, Mr Blakeney. Come here to me,' the girl said.

Balbo, remembering the caress she had given him when he spoke up for the twins in the car, turned eagerly to her, forgetting for the time his good friend from Heracleion.

'Mrs Helmut,' the boy said.

Balbo and Marigold came forward. The boy went briefly into the shadows and came back with a carved wooden box. The girl handed the burning brand which she was holding to Jacquiz, the torch bearer. The boy placed the box on the floor, at the feet of Balbo and Marigold. He opened it. There was a quick flash of red and gold in the light of Jacquiz' brand. The boy and the girl knelt down, the boy before Marigold, the girl before Balbo. Then both rose, advanced on to Balbo and Marigold, and began to undress them and themselves, the girl assisting the boy with Marigold (and occasionally caressing her intimately), the boy assisting the girl with Balbo (stroking his thighs and buttocks), the girl turning for a moment to strip down her brother's tights and reveal a perfect (if circumcised) crescent. This she briefly stroked, murmuring to herself, while he, also murmuring, passed his fingers along her cleft.

'Who are you both?' said Marigold, trembling. 'Where will you go when we release you?'

'I give the Roses of Picardie into your keeping,' said the boy. Gently and neatly he eased himself into Marigold, who splayed where she stood to receive him.

'I give the Roses of Picardie into your keeping,' said the girl. She put her hands on Balbo's shoulders, coaxed him on to the ground, and lowered herself, cleverly straddling and fingering back her lips, upon him.

'Jesus Christ,' howled Marigold, 'he's as cold as ice. *Ice.* Let me go, let me go.' But the boy held her closely to him and pumped steadily with his buttocks.

Balbo yelled out in pain and tried to throw the girl off him. But she had him trapped and continued to ride him.

'I can't hold them any longer,' called Len. 'I can't concentrate any more.'

He began to masturbate savagely, gazing at Marigold as she jerked and wriggled on the boy's phallus. Already the rats had turned from him. With a sudden hysteria of squeals and yelps they raced across the floor.


Theta and Lambda stood and watched as the last of the Army's RT equipment was carried out of the South-West Transept of Canterbury Cathedral.

'No good,' said Lambda. 'Not one of them's stirred in twenty-four hours. Except to examine the bait in the Crypt.'

'No one will hold you to blame,' said Theta. 'I promise you that.'

Theta turned to look at the triple tomb of the Lady Margaret Holland. As he looked a small crevice opened just below the coronet of her second husband and ran slowly and jerkily down to the floor. There was a kind of muffled crunch, and the whole tomb tilted three inches to the right.

So soon, thought Theta: I thought it would take longer. He put his hand in Lambda's arm and led him thoughtfully away.


'So they came on with this tremendous rush, millions of them, squealing like banshees. Then suddenly they stopped, cobber, absolutely dead,' said Sydney Jones to Pandelios (who was being told what had happened after he fainted), 'and two of the bigger ones came out of the ruck and seemed to kind of detail off a company of about a hundred of the bastards all told. Then the bigger of the two big buggers looked at Len, who was busy beating his meat and gawping at the fornication scene, and Len gave a hopeless shrug, and the company of a hundred ran straight to Balbo, where he was lying on the floor being rogered by this gorgeous girl but yowling with the pain of it. "Cold, so cold," he kept moaning, just like Marigold. But just as you could have sworn they were about to dismember Balbo under our own eyes, the company split into two. Half of 'em leapt up at the girl without even touching Balbo – and that did move her. She was off his cock in a trice, rolling round on the floor with the rats all over her, on her thighs, on her belly, in her hair, at her ears. And the other half of the squad, bazza, had gone for the boy – who was out of Marigold in no time and rolling on the ground like his sister. And as they struggled, they both – well, they both kind of cackled . . . a sort of dreadful, tortured laugh they made, as if they were laughing on the other side of their faces at what was happening to themselves. Then at last the boy, with ten of them at his throat, raised his hand to his sister, who raised hers back, as if they was sort of saluting each other, and called out:

' "This way too we are released. My duty is done."

' "And mine," she called back.

'A few seconds later the rats had split their wind-pipes and that was that for them, but not for the chosen rats, who started in to gorge themselves on the bodies. Len, who had finished abusing himself, watched in a kind of trance. Inside ten minutes those rats had stripped both of 'em clean, bellies and all, after which they rejoined the ranks and were crowded round, as if they were being congratulated and asked what it tasted like. Then all of them, the whole lot, suddenly dribbled away into the darkness and were gone. At this stage, Len came to, and said:

' "There was something for them in this feast which they would not have had from Balbo. The wisdom of centuries. They understood that just in time." '

Syd Jones permitted himself a brief smirk of self-congratulation.

' "The inherited wisdom of centuries," Jacquiz kept insisting.

' "But even so," said Len, "they would have had Balbo too

– had not the essence of his virtue passed into the girl at their joining. As it is, having absorbed him through her, they will not worry Balbo any more." '

'What about the Rubies?' Pandelios said.

'Come and look.'

Balbo led Pandelios out of his hotel bedroom and along a corridor.

'Where are we?' said Pandelios.

'Sparta. We knew there was a comfortable Xenia here, so we drove up this morning. You were asleep. You hardly knew it even when we put you to bed.'

Syd knocked on a door.

'Come in,' called Jacquiz' voice.

Jacquiz was standing by a window, looking out on to a little clump of fir trees. Balbo and Marigold were sitting on the bed. Between them was the wooden box which the boy had produced the previous night. On the sides, Pandelios saw, were carved little semi-circular ships, which sailed through curly billows. The lid was up. Pandelios could not see what was on the outside of the lid, but on its inside were more ships, caiques, sailing from an island on the shore of which tiny figures shook fists and brandished swords. Below this scene, in the box itself, lay a bright yellow chain to which were attached, by crystal pendants, several stones of sullen red.

'The gold is gold and the Rubies are rubies still,' Jacquiz said from the window. 'Perhaps the boy's assumption, that his release and that of his sister would mean an end of the Curse, was unfounded. It needs that the Curse should die, you remember, before the Rubies turn to glass. Perhaps, despite their death, the Curse remains.'

'Look here,' said Jones, S. 'That boy was very clear that the Curse was associated with him and his sister. They, and their ancestors, have administered the Curse since it began: how can it survive without them?'

'Because they will have issue,' said Marigold. 'That boy . . . discharged himself into me just before the rats came. "My duty is done," he said, just before he died. And it had been

436

done. I felt an icy flood where before there had been an icy dagger, thrusting. There will be twins: David and Rebecca; Jewish twins for me to rear with my Jewish husband, who is not, who cannot be, their father.'

Jacquiz, by the window, nodded, accepting her entire statement.

'They were weary,' said Balbo, 'but they had sworn an oath—'

'—Their ancestors had sworn an oath,' insisted Jacquiz.

'—And they knew it must be kept,' said Marigold. 'So they tricked us with this tale of release to them and an end of the Rubies. They, perhaps, are indeed released, at any rate for a time; but they have left the Rubies to Balbo and me, their paramours, and they have left the Curse, which lies dormant, but only for a while, in my womb.'

'How can you know this?' Pandelios said.

'We know it,' said Balbo. 'When you have coupled with the living dead, as we have, you understand their will. Marigold will be mother to the new twins; Jacquiz, appropriately a Jew, will be in name their father; and I, having been joined with the girl, Rebecca, will be their godfather. Godfather? Father in Satan. For the girl too has done her duty, as she claimed. For all the pain of it, I left my seed in her, and so there is a bond, a bond between me and whatever Marigold may bring forth.'

'I don't get it,' said Syd. 'You mean ... almost as if your seed has passed through her to him and into Marigold.'

'Succubus and incubus?' said Jacquiz from the window.

'Something of the kind; morally if not physically.'

Pandelios and Sydney, assuming all this to be a temporary disorder brought on by the events of the night, did not attempt to argue any more. Jacquiz brooded by the window. Eventually Pandelios said:

'Where's that Len?'

'He drove back to Kalamata to fly home,' said Jacquiz. 'He has business in Cambridge with those notes of Balbo's. At least he should be able to bring Constable to heel.'

'Apart from all that,' said Syd Jones, 'what was actually in those notes?'

'I told you in Arles,' said Balbo. 'Information and suggestions which might have enabled anyone who followed them up to produce just such a strain of rats as are now, it seems, infesting Canterbury. A durable strain which could eat through old bones ... which could eat through a stone fabric that carried, after many centuries, the savour of death.'

'Surely,' said Jones, 'now that Len is enjoying their favour, he could get them out of Canterbury?'

'Perhaps. That is no longer my concern. My concern lies here.' Balbo touched Marigold's belly.

'What shall you do with the Roses?' said Sydney. 'To whom do they rightly belong?'

'God knows,' said Jacquiz. 'We shall place them for keeping with the FitzWilliam Museum in Cambridge. The matter will be made known and claimants may come forward if they wish.'

'There will be no claimants,' said Marigold. 'The Roses belong to Balbo and me. But since it will please Jacquiz, and since I have come to bear great charity towards him, I have said, and Balbo has agreed, that he may present them to the FitzWilliam Museum as his gift, on condition that Mr Pandelios, who has been so kind to Balbo and put him in funds for the search, is named as co-donor.'

'I shall be most heartily honoured,' said Pandelios, flushing with pleasure.

'You too, Sydney,' said Balbo: 'you can be a co-donor.'

'Good on you, sport. But that wouldn't go down at all smooth in Jermyn Street,' said Syd Jones. 'I shall go to Cambridge and look at 'em often, Balbo; look at 'em and remember.'

'They may as well be there as anywhere else,' Marigold said. She stroked her stomach. 'Though what *these* may think remains to be seen.'

'Very well,' said Constable to Ivor and Len. 'I yield. I give you the terms you ask for. Ivor to be re-elected a fellow; Jacquiz Helmut to remain in the College, when he returns at the end of his sabbatical, on his present footing; Balbo Blakeney to be in some way re-instated – perhaps as Fellows' Steward; and you, Mr Under-Collator, to be free to depart with your monetary gains and The Wandrille Georgics at the end of the academic year.'

'Very civil of you, Provost,' said Ivor.

'And now everything is so agreeably settled,' said Len, 'there is one question I long to ask. When you had copied Balbo's notes, all those years ago, to whom did you in fact send them?'

'Although I have outraged all canons of academic and social decency,' said Lord Constable, 'although I did indeed pirate Balbo's notes, I am not a traitor. I sent those notes where conscience and duty bade me – to the appropriate department of the British Labour Government of the day, where Balbo, black reactionary as he was, would never have placed them.'

'Did you ever hear what use was made of them?'

'For obvious reasons, I sent them anonymously. But much later on, inquiring in a roundabout way, I did hear that my contribution had been considered indecipherable by all the scientists to whom it was shown and had been used, in that lean period, to light an Under-Secretary's fire. I dare say,' said Constable, 'that I was an incompetent copyist. It is one more lesson to us all not to interfere in matters which we do not understand.'


Theta was speaking to somebody very superior indeed on the security telephone.

'And so, sir,' Theta was saying, 'it appears that there is now another forlorn hope. We positively know of another man who has been granted the kind of Grace or Godhead with which Blakeney was formerly endowed . . . A graduate student, sir, of Lancaster College, Cambridge, and Under-Collator of the Manuscripts there. One of my own agents, junior but highly trustworthy, was present, on a singular occasion in Greece, when the said Under-Collator received the obeisance and at least partial obedience of a huge number of rats in the cellar of a ruined house on the coast of the Mani ... Yes, sir. I can vouch for the total integrity of my agent, and I *believe* the story he has told me. The question now must be, do we give the Under-Collator a trial at Canterbury? Do we invite him, as we would have invited Blakeney, to try to exert his authority over those creatures in order to expel them from the Cathedral? ... That, sir, I cannot answer. He definitely had some control, if not total, over the rodents of the Mani; whether he would have the same influence over the rodents in Canterbury is, I agree, another matter.'

Theta now listened for some minutes. At the end of them he said, 'Yes, sir, I understand.' Then he put down the receiver and looked steadily at Jones, Q, Lambda and Len, who were sitting in a semi-circle in front of him.

'Change of policy,' he said. 'Quite logical in all the circumstances, I suppose. Economic and probably effective.'

There was silence along the semi-circle.

'Since it is plain,' said Theta, 'that no one can guarantee to remove those creatures from the Cathedral in order that they may be destroyed by the troops outside it, and since they *must* be destroyed before they reproduce themselves to an uncontainable number, it is clear that they must be destroyed where they are. *In situ.*'

'But,' began Lambda, 'there is no known poison that will—'

'Precisely,' said Theta bleakly. 'So there are only two things for it. Explosion or combustion. Since explosions are too haphazard, the rats must be burnt out, by troops with flame-throwers both within and without, burnt out inch by inch, down through the Crypt and into the tombs, beneath the tombs and into the earth far below.'

'Even so,' said Lambda, 'some might escape.'

'Not very many. A controllable number, wherever they go next.'

'But this operation is impossible,' said Q, 'without destroying the foundations of the whole Cathedral ... and therefore the building itself.'

Theta nodded. There was a light, bright gleam of a tear in Syd Jones's eye.

'When you played on the County ground in Canterbury,' he said, 'you always knew it was there. You couldn't quite see it from the ground, but you knew it was there. It won't be the same, playing at Canterbury without it.'

'You won't be playing at Canterbury,' said Len, not unkindly. 'Not any more.'

'I s'pose not.'

'They might have given me a chance,' said Len. 'I might have got them out without destroying the Cathedral.'

'After our last failure,' said Theta, 'they are in no mind to fiddle about. Orders have already been given. Irreversible orders. It is now necessary, you see, on every possible count, to act very swiftly indeed ... before there is some serious public accident, or before the rats leave of their own accord, *not* to be slaughtered while they escape, as they would have been during Falx, but at liberty to infest more and more churches and cathedrals, more and more (as they breed) of the country at large.'

'So that's it,' Len said.

'As far as we public servants are concerned. Not quite, Mr Under-Collator, as far as you are concerned. Although my correspondent on the telephone was sceptical about your – er – qualifications, he is inclined to concede that your position *vis à vis* the rodents is in some way privileged or special. He therefore thinks it important to procure your ... let us say, discreet good will. He is prepared to reward you quite handsomely for ... how shall I put it? ... simply and entirely ceasing to interest yourself in the matter. I dare say you will find the terms acceptable.'

'I can quite easily,' said Len, 'find a lot of other interests. But I think I should warn you: those rats out in Greece – I

441

reckon they're beginning to go the same way, I got a feel of something very worrying in their minds – their corporate mind, rather – when they made . . . the choice which they did make. Old bones,' he said aside to Jones, S., who nodded. 'And once it starts spreading on the continent,' Len mused, 'it may not be easy to stop.'

'We'll have stopped it here at any rate,' said Lambda. 'As for Europe,' he said, laughing raucously, 'let those damned foreigners take care of their own bloody rats.'


Extract from *Peterborough Daily Telegraph*, 2 January 1975:

What a pleasure to see at least one well earned honour in the New Year's List: Doctor Jacquiz Helmut to be a Knight Bachelor for his services to antiquarian research. It will be remembered that it was Doctor Helmut (together with his ebullient associate from Crete, Mr Pandelios) who brought back to England last November the fabulous Rubies, the Roses of Picardie, and presented them to the FitzWilliam Museum in Cambridge. I'm told the French take rather a jaundiced view of this treasure's departure to perfidious Albion, but since they themselves had succeeded in mislaying it for the last three centuries, and since it was not in any case discovered on French soil, there is very little they can say or do about it.


'Pity about St Peter's,' said Ivor to Len about a month after Jacquiz had been knighted; 'so soon after Canterbury and Milan.'

'Horrible. Still, there's lots of other things left. Let's take a trip round all the Cathedrals in the Midi, as soon as term's done.'

'Oh, my dear, I've had rather a bad time on the share market lately. Nothing really disastrous, you understand, but no treats for a little.'

'I'll stand treat, Ive. I'm all right at the moment, very much all right. Besides, I shan't be seeing so much of you after I sugar off next summer, so let's make the most of our time now. And another thing; Balbo Blakeney might like to come along, now he's back with us. He seems a bit pre-occupied about Marigold's baby, but she's not due for months and months. He'd probably come with us if we also asked that old cricketing number from Jermyn Street.'

'Jones, S., once of Glamorgan. I like Jones. Balbo says he's due down again next weekend.'

'Right,' said Len. 'All ways round, things are pretty good, Ive. So let's have good times quickly, while they stay that way.'


Well, thought Lord Constable, now Helmut's been knighted he's really rather a credit to the place. That Ruby business was quite a *coup*: good publicity for the College, at all levels. Perhaps it's just as well we've still got the blighter after all.

As for Balbo Blakeney, he seems a new man. Half a bottle of red burgundy every evening and the occasional brandy. One really can't complain. An efficient Fellows' Steward too – and there's no doubt, it does keep them all quiet if their meals are to their liking. Food and drink never interested me; but if they keep all my Fellows calm and docile, I've nothing to say against them.


EXTRACT from *The Times*, 30 July 1975.

BIRTHS ...
HELMUT To Sir Jacquiz and Lady Helmut, a boy and girl: David and Rebecca.


*Deal ... Corfu ... Venice ... Cannes ... Athens ... Rome ... Monte Carlo ... Dieppe.*
1976 to 1979

## THE WORLD'S GREATEST NOVELISTS
## NOW AVAILABLE IN GRANADA PAPERBACKS

**John O'Hara**

| | |
|---|---|
| Ourselves to Know | £1.50 ☐ |
| Ten North Frederick | £1.50 ☐ |
| A Rage to Live | £1.50 ☐ |
| From The Terrace | £2.50 ☐ |
| BUtterfield 8 | 95p ☐ |
| Appointment in Samarra | 95p ☐ |

**Norman Mailer**

| | |
|---|---|
| The Fight (non-fiction) | 75p ☐ |
| The Presidential Papers | 95p ☐ |
| Barbary Shore | 40p ☐ |
| Advertisements for Myself | 95p ☐ |
| An American Dream | £1.25 ☐ |
| The Naked and The Dead | £1.50 ☐ |
| The Deer Park | £1.75 ☐ |

**Kingsley Amis**

| | |
|---|---|
| Ending Up | 60p ☐ |
| The Riverside Villas Murder | 95p ☐ |
| I Like It Here | 50p ☐ |
| That Uncertain Feeling | 50p ☐ |
| Girl 20 | 40p ☐ |
| I Want It Now | 60p ☐ |
| The Green Man | 95p ☐ |
| The Alteration | 95p ☐ |

## THE WORLD'S GREATEST NOVELISTS
## NOW AVAILABLE IN GRANADA PAPERBACKS

**Alberto Moravia**

| | |
|---|---|
| Bitter Honeymoon | 75p ☐ |
| Mother Love | 60p ☐ |
| The Wayward Wife | 60p ☐ |
| Conjugal Love | 50p ☐ |
| The Fetish | 75p ☐ |
| Roman Tales | 50p ☐ |
| Time of Indifference | 60p ☐ |
| The Two of Us | 50p ☐ |
| The Lie | 75p ☐ |
| The Empty Canvas | £1.50 ☐ |

**Gore Vidal**

| | |
|---|---|
| Washington D.C. | 95p ☐ |
| Burr | £1.95 ☐ |
| 1876 | £1.00 ☐ |
| A Thirsty Evil | 75p ☐ |
| The Judgment of Paris | 95p ☐ |
| The City and the Pillar | 80p ☐ |
| Julian | 95p ☐ |
| Two Sisters | 75p ☐ |
| Myron | 60p ☐ |
| Myra Breckinridge | 75p ☐ |
| Messiah | 75p ☐ |
| Williwaw | 60p ☐ |
| On Our Own Now (Collected Essays 1952–1972) | £1.50 ☐ |
| Kalki | £1.25 ☐ |